W9-BSH-871

STATE OF
EMERGENCY

STATE OF
EMERGENCY

MARC
CAMERON

PINNACLE BOOKS
Kensington Publishing Corp.
www.kensingtonbooks.com

PINNACLE BOOKS are published by

Kensington Publishing Corp.
119 West 40th Street
New York, NY 10018

Copyright © 2013 Marc Cameron

All rights reserved. No part of this book may be reproduced in any form or by any means without the prior written consent of the publisher, excepting brief quotes used in reviews.

If you purchased this book without a cover, you should be aware that this book is stolen property. It was reported as "unsold and destroyed" to the publisher, and neither the author nor the publisher has received any payment for this "stripped book."

All Kensington titles, imprints, and distributed lines are available at special quantity discounts for bulk purchases for sales promotions, premiums, fund-raising, educational, or institutional use.

Special book excerpts or customized printings can also be created to fit specific needs. For details, write or phone the office of the Kensington special sales manager: Kensington Publishing Corp., 119 West 40th Street, New York, NY 10018, attn: Special Sales Department; phone 1-800-221-2647.

This book is a work of fiction. Names, characters, businesses, organizations, places, events, and incidents either are the product of the author's imagination or are used fictitiously. Any resemblance to actual persons, living or dead, events, or locales is entirely coincidental.

PINNACLE BOOKS and the Pinnacle logo are Reg. U.S. Pat. & TM Off.

ISBN-13: 978-0-7860-3180-1
ISBN-10: 0-7860-3180-8

First printing: May 2013

10 9 8 7 6 5 4 3 2 1

Printed in the United States of America

First electronic edition: May 2013

ISBN-13: 978-0-7860-3181-8
ISBN-10: 0-7860-3181-6

For Daniel—
A man of genuine good

Ne puero gladium

(Don't give a sword to a boy.)

PROLOGUE

December 9
11:30 PM
Near Karakul, Uzbekistan

Riley Cooper inhaled slowly, ignoring the metallic odor of violent death. He lay on his chest, watching, flat against a long wooden table four feet off the stone floor of the kill house. Once a fortified rest stop for man and beast on the ancient Silk Road, the dilapidated caravanserai was now a patched stone structure of cell like rooms. Sagging sheep pens ran along the west side, forlorn and empty in the purple darkness. A toothed wind, heavy with the smell of wool, swept through the open window from the northern desert. S-shaped metal carcass hooks clanged like blood-rusted wind chimes above his head.

Cooper pressed an eye to the night-vision monocular and wished it was attached to a rifle. Coming into Uzbekistan unofficially was dangerous enough for a man in his position. Possession of a sniper rifle could cause an international incident. Still, he wasn't the type to be completely unprepared. Just after he'd arrived, he had haggled with a small-time gun dealer in Tashkent for a Russian GSh-18 nine-millimeter pistol. The handgun, along with eighteen armor-piercing rounds, had cost him his five-thousand-dollar Rolex Submariner. He loved the watch, but such things were often the coin of the realm and the price was well worth the comfort the pistol brought resting on his hip under the navyblue hooded sweatshirt.

Cooper was slender, a shade under six feet tall. His narrow waist and powerful, ostrich-like legs had shouted Olympic sprinter when he was in high school, but, on the advice of a family friend, he'd decided to go another route. That route had put him here in a freezing Uzbek desert with a night-vision scope to his eye.

A ring of curly blond hair bristled from the edge of the black watch cap pulled tight over his head. His skin was on the pale side—making him particularly visible in the darkness. Before climbing into position in his hide, he'd taken the time to smear black paint over the high spots of his nose and cheekbones, breaking up the form of his face in the moonlight to anyone who might glance his direction.

Nestling down against the chill of the night wind, Cooper peered through the green reticle of his nightvision scope to study the Russian less than thirty feet away. They had met two years before in a bar outside Manas Air Base in Kyrgyzstan. Mikhail Ivanovich Polzin had honest eyes and a no-nonsense manner. Cooper liked him as much as a man in his position could like a communist agent. They'd shared many bottles of Aksai Kyrgyz vodka and stories of home. Some of them were probably even true. Still, meets like this were touchy and had the Russian known he was being secretly watched from the slaughterhouse, he might very well have put a bullet in Cooper's head on principle alone.

Polzin stood along a ribbon of moonlit dirt track, facing the feeble twin headlights of an approaching truck, emerging from the frowning black mouth of the desert. A chilly wind wracked his body with a violent shiver and Cooper watched him snug the fleece collar of his greatcoat up around his ears. The American found it ironic that Polzin wore a coat and hat made of Astrakhan, the finely curled pelts of day-old Karakul lambs. Tens of thousands of the tiny things were slaughtered here at this very kill house and places like it every spring. The slaughter had to take place only hours after the lambs were born, before their pelts, valued for centuries because they were smooth as wet silk, lost their curl. Within a few days of birth the Golden Fleece became nothing but coarse wool.

Cooper tried to push the stench of old death out of his mind. His thoughts drifted for a quick moment to his fiancée, Jill, back in Richmond. He couldn't help but chuckle. As much of a meat eater as she was, had Jill seen this Russian wearing the fleece of a half dozen day-old lambs, she would have clawed his eyes out.

Rattling in from the darkness, the rusted green hulk of a UAZ flatbed truck squeaked to a stop beside Mikhail Polzin. A plume of fine dust blossomed around the truck as the driver's door creaked open. A stooped and bony man who looked to be in his sixties—which in the hardscrabble life of this part of the world could mean late forties—climbed from the rounded, egg-like cab. He approached the Russian agent, right hand over his heart in traditional Muslim greeting.

A big-busted woman with a body shaped like a fuel

drum sauntered around from the passenger side, rocking back and forth in a waddling walk as if she had a bad hip. The grimy belly and frayed knees of her smock and trousers suggested she was used to a life lived close to the dirt. A black headscarf pulled her jowly face into a permanent scowl. She took no time with the niceties of introduction and began to wave gnarled fingers at two boxes in the bed of their truck. One was the size of a military footlocker, the other, made of the same olive drab material, the size of a large suitcase. She ranted in a shrill mix of Uzbek and Russian, her words pulled tight as an overly wound clock. A gust of wind ripped away the bulk of her animated lecture, but the part Cooper heard caused him to lean forward, straining to hear more.

Their small peasant farm had been cursed with sick livestock and bad water. She spit disdainfully on the ground and threw her hands into the air, clutching at her headscarf with both hands for effect. Rheumy eyes glowed through the green pixilated image of the night-vision scope.

Cooper understood some of the words all too well. Gritting his teeth, he rolled slightly to remove the pistol from his waistband and place it on the table within quick reach. He slid the satellite phone from the cargo pocket of his pants. His position was several feet back from the window, making it impossible to get a signal, but he punched in a number anyway, entering a coded text before pressing send. The phone was programmed to continue its search and send the message in an instantaneous burst as soon as it located a satellite, even if it was turned off and on again.

Outside, the Russian took an envelope from the

breast pocket of his wool coat and handed it to the old man. The Uzbek passed it to his wife, who promptly opened it and began to count the thick stack of what looked like American bills.

Polzin followed the old man to the bed of the truck, took something from his pocket, and played it back and forth across the boxes, nodding.

"Many thanks, my friend," Cooper heard the Russian say. "There will be another payment, double the one in your wife's hands, as soon as I get these items back in safekeeping."

"What good is money if our sheep are dead?" The old woman took the time to stuff the envelope inside her smock before throwing up her hands again. "Take our truck, we will walk ba—"

The desert suddenly erupted with a swarm of blinding lights as four all-terrain vehicles roared in to surround Polzin and the Uzbeks. Clouds of dust cast crossed shadows from the headlights as they all came skidding to a stop. A tall, slender man in a puffy, lime-green ski parka and designer blue jeans dismounted his four-wheeler with a theatrical flourish. Even in the darkness, Cooper could make out the black line of a thin mustache. Striding purposefully to the ranting Uzbek woman, the newcomer raised a pistol and shot her in the face.

The man spun, giving an exaggerated shrug. "What? Isn't anyone going to thank me for shutting her up?" He spoke in accented Russian, slurring heavily as if he had marbles in his mouth. "I should think you of all people would be grateful," he said, addressing the old man. "No? Well, you may as well join her then." He pressed the muzzle of his pistol to the trembling

Uzbek's chest and pulled the trigger. He stepped back to let the old man sag, then pitch headlong into the dust beside his dead wife.

A short female in a matching lime parka and dark green tam dismounted her own all-terrain vehicle.

She shook her head. "Aren't we in a mood tonight." She laughed, indifferent to the cold-blooded murders. The tam slouched forward over her eyes and kept Cooper from getting a good look at her face. Skintight black pants hugged broad hips. White running shoes seemed to glow in the headlights. "This bores me. I go for a walk." A moment later she had disappeared behind the dead Uzbeks' truck.

A third man, dark, more slightly built and jumpy, took the shooting as an indication he should get off his ATV to climb onto the bed of the truck. His face glistened with perspiration even in the cold night air. It was difficult to tell in the darkness, but he wore heavy gloves and he looked to have some sort of protective vest under his open coat.

He spoke English, but from his accent, Cooper guessed him to be Pakistani. "Ahhh!" he said after examining the contents of both boxes with gloved hands. "Just as you suspected."

"You are certain?" The man with the thin mustache giggled, wide-eyed.

"Quite," the Pakistani answered. "No doubt."

"Oh, this is most excellent news!" The man in the lime-green ski parka clapped his hands, one still holding the pistol. His eyes fell on the Russian. "How rude of me," he said. "I am Valentine Zamora."

He pronounced it Valenteen.

The fourth rider, a thick-necked brute with a dark

tangle of curly hair and a broad nose squashed above his bearded face, took up a position to Zamora's left, two paces behind him. He was obviously the muscle.

"Polzin," the Russian said. He'd raised both hands to shoulder level without being asked.

Good, Cooper thought. *Do this on your terms, Misha. This is big. . . . Keep ahead of the curve.*

"Mikhail Ivanovich." The fingers of Polzin's left hand fiddled with something as if he was nervous. The ring, Cooper thought. It was the first thing he'd noticed about the Russian agent when they'd met, a gold two-headed eagle ring that symbolized Mother Russia. It was an odd thing for a spy to be so brazen about his affiliations.

"Oh," Zamora said, almost yelping as he rubbed his hairless chin. He bounced on his feet as he spoke, brimming with energy. "I am well aware of who you are. People in my line of work tell frightful stories of people in your line of work. The secret group deep inside the Federal Security Service. . . ."

"So . . ." The Russian hunched his shoulders slightly as if stricken with a chill. "What is next?"

Zamora gave him a slow up and down, appraising, saying nothing. He suddenly spun on his heels, moving with an agitated flourish very close to dancing. He swung his arms back and forth for a time, as if walking in place, before beginning to speak. Facing away, much of what he said was impossible for Cooper to hear.

". . . must be smart . . . Vympel unit . . . selective. I assume . . . also a scientist?"

Polzin shrugged, his hands dropping little by little as he spoke, fingers still toying with the ring. "I am no scientist, merely a civil servant. She is very old, you know, well past her useful life span. And there are the codes to consider. My own government does not even know what they are. You may as well let me take her home." He nodded toward the boxes in the back of the truck.

"Take it home?" Zamora spun. His bouncing grew more pronounced. "Oh, no, no, Mikhail Ivanovich, that is not necessary. I myself will provide her a fantastic home. She may very well be old, but Dr. Sarpara is extremely talented. He assures me he will be able to make her viable as ever. You know, there are those who would have me use such a thing against your country." He leaned in as if with a secret. "But you should know I have other plans that involve something more . . . red, white, and blu—"

The Russian's hand flashed to his coat pocket. He rolled, snatching up a hidden pistol to fire through the cloth. At least one of his rounds hit the Pakistani man on the truck.

Cooper reached for his own pistol, cursing the darkness. The night-vision monocular was useless for aiming and the headlights didn't offer enough light to engage two armed opponents at that range.

Polzin got three shots off before Zamora and his thug mowed him down.

It was over in the span of a breath.

The Pakistani doctor clutched at his neck. He teetered for a moment on the back of the truck before falling headlong, arm draped over the wooden rail.

Zamora spun, running to the wounded Pakistani. Checking the man's wrist for a pulse, he turned again, one hand clasped over his mouth, the other brandishing the pistol. He launched into a string of Spanish curses, pacing back and forth in the eerie pool of red light cast by the UAZ's dusty tail lamps.

"Monagas." He turned, nodding to his thick-necked companion. "Comrade Polzin has caused me a great anxiety."

Unleashed, the man called Monagas smiled a crooked smile, then strode to a writhing Polzin and put two bullets through the back of his head.

Cooper's mind raced in the relative safety of his hiding place. He concentrated to slow his breathing. Knuckles white around the butt of his own pistol, he flinched at each shot the man put into his friend.

Zamora's hand still hung over his mouth, as if keeping it there helped him think. His gun hand hung loosely at his side.

"Perhaps one of your contacts in Iran," Monagas offered.

"No." Zamora waved him away. "The Americans hover over them like hawks. I have to think. . . ." He leaned over, hands on both knees. For a moment, it looked as if he was going to be sick; then just as quickly he bolted upright. "There is someone, but . . ." He tapped his forehead with the slide of his pistol as he paced back and forth, stopping every so often to kick the dead Russian and curse him in breathless Spanish. Dust from his feet puffed up in the headlights.

At length he stopped, staring into the blackness of the Uzbek desert.

"I need to think," he said, muttering something Cooper couldn't make out as he walked through the curtain of darkness.

His boss gone, Monagas stooped in the dust to lift the dead Russian's hand. The eagle ring, Cooper thought. This pig-eyed son of a bitch took trophies.

Cooper lowered his handgun and grabbed the satellite phone. Intelligence was about information, not revenge. If the back of the Russian truck held what he thought it did, Cooper knew he'd eventually have to make a stand to keep this insane SOB outside from ending up with it. Until then, he had to make certain the information got back to higher—at all cost. Caught up in the drama unfolding outside his window, he'd neglected to send more texts as information became available. Such a rookie mistake.

Thumb-typing with both hands as fast as he could, he didn't hear the hissing scrape of shoes on concrete until it was too late.

He froze, straining his ears in the darkness. The sound was behind him—and close.

Too close.

Cooper's hand shot toward the pistol before he even understood the context of the sound. At the same instant a peculiar whoosh, like fluttering wings, came from above. Something heavy struck the side of his neck, the force of it rolling it half up on his side. A wave of nauseating pain sank down his spine. His right arm fell, slamming against the table, limp and useless. His fingers were still inches from the pistol. He gagged as some unknown force yanked his head back and forth like a frenzied dog. Unable to move on his own, the cold realization that he was paralyzed washed over Riley Cooper.

A flaccid cheek pressing helplessly against the table, he could see the heavy hips of a female figure wearing tight spandex pants. The woman. He should never have let himself lose track of her. She clicked on a flashlight and tapped the toe of a white running shoe on the concrete as if annoyed that he was taking so long to die.

Cooper found it impossible to breathe. Straining his eyes, he found the problem. An S-shaped carcass hook stuck from his neck, just below the jaw. It was a miracle that he was still conscious.

A small hand with manicured black nails grabbed the rusted hook and gave it an impatient twist. Metal scraped bone and Cooper groaned reflexively, choking on his own blood. His eyes fluttered as he watched the woman stuff the satellite phone in the pocket of her jacket.

That's right, he thought. *Take the phone outside with you. . . .*

He wracked his foggy brain, trying to remember how much of the text he'd completed. He'd hit send the moment he'd heard the noise, just before the woman hit him. He hoped it was enough.

The beam of a second flashlight played across the stone floor. A set of black boots clicked into view.

"I have it, my darling," Valentine Zamora said, broken, distant in Cooper's ears, as if coming through a long pipe. "Can you believe it? It is actually mine."

"It means you are rich?" The woman's voice was whiskeyed and raw, as if she'd been screaming for three hours at a rock concert.

"I am already rich." Zamora giggled, a high-pitched, almost feminine sound. "No, no, no. This will show the world that your precious Valentine is not a person to shove about like a little child."

Cooper strained to hear more. Through the gathering fog, and unable to turn his head, he could only see the murderous couple from the waist down. They stood together, arm in arm as if watching a sunset, waiting for him to die.

"It is amazing!" Zamora stomped his foot. "Baba Yaga is mine."

Baba Yaga.

The words struck Cooper as cruelly as the rusty hook. He'd feared as much, even alluded to it in his text, but the reality of hearing it spoken filled him with overwhelming dread. He fought to stay conscious, suddenly cold beyond anything he'd ever experienced. Years of training barked inside his head, screaming at him to get to his feet and do something.

Baba Yaga was an intelligence black hole, a poisonous soup of Cold War theory and whispered stories of gray-haired Soviet spies.

No longer able to focus, Cooper's mind drifted back and forth from his mission to thoughts of his family in Virginia. By slow degree the bone-numbing chill melted into waves of enveloping warmth. His breaths grew shallow and further apart. There was nothing he could do, no matter how great the threat. His eyes gave up a single tear as they fluttered shut for the last time.

A crimson ribbon seeped from the wound in the young American's neck and dripped to the broken stone below, mingling with the blood of countless slaughtered lambs.

Turkmenbasy, Turkmenistan
The Caspian Sea

Two grubby boys in thigh-length wool coats and tattered ski hats carried the wooden crates along the weathered planks and onto the deck of the cargo ship. A stubby vessel, the *Pravda* was not quite seventy feet long. It was hardly big enough to be called a ship, but Zamora preferred not to think of his precious cargo heading out to the world's largest inland body of water in a mere boat.

Monagas stood with his thick arms behind his back, shouting savage threats to keep the lazy boys motivated.

Zamora sat at the stern next to the thick-hipped woman on boxes marked as tins of sturgeon caviar. He held a phone to his ear. A sly smile crossed his face, twitching the corners of his pencil-thin mustache. The woman leaned back on both hands, eyes closed, face to the sun.

"Hello, Mike," Zamora said, speaking louder than usual, as was his habit when he was talking to someone halfway around the world. He kept his voice sickeningly sweet. "How are you?"

"Mr. Valentine," Mike Olson answered. His breathy Texas drawl was almost giddy. "I'm fine, sir. How are you?" He pronounced Zamora's name like the lover's holiday. It was a convenient and easy-to-remember alias.

"Just fine, Mike, just fine," Zamora said. His English was accented but flowed easily due to his time at American universities. "Listen, I talked about a donation to your program, but I've come into a sort of a windfall. I'd like to do something . . . I don't know . . . more significant in nature."

"Deanne and I are so grateful to you, sir," Olson answered. "You've already been so generous." The sound of a children's choir singing to the soft notes of a piano purred in the background. "And the kids appreciate the support. To date, we've heard from over three hundred. They're flying in from all over the U.S. for the event— from all denominations and cultures. Christians, Jews, Muslims, Hindus, a group of Baha'i children from Illinois. Imagine, so many ethnicities and religions, uniting their voices for peace, right here in the Bible belt."

Baha'i, Zamora thought. His Iranian mother would have a fit at that. "Very nice," he said, running his fingers like a spider up the woman's thigh beside him. "I have something very special in mind. One of my colleagues will be in touch shortly."

"Thank you so much, Mr. Valentine," Olson gushed. "We could make a real difference here."

"Yes," Zamora said, "I do believe we will." He ended the call.

Giggling loudly, he tromped his feet against the deck of the ship as if he was running in place before finally leaning back beside the thick-hipped woman.

"What is it?" She opened her eyes, blinking against the bright sun. He could just make out the tiny dark hairs that ran along her upper lip. Sometimes he thought she could grow a better mustache than him if she'd wanted to.

"Nothing, really." The corners of his pencil-thin mustache twitched. "I was just thinking of how I will get our Yemeni friends to blow the buckle off the Bible belt."

"You're tickling me, my darling." The woman put her hand over his, pressing it hard against the inside of her thigh. "You know I'd rather be slapped than tickled."

"As you wish." Zamora gave the soft flesh inside her thigh a rough squeeze.

The woman yawned. "In any case, before you can blow up anyone, we have to get your precious cargo past the authorities and all their radiation detectors."

"We will put Baba Yaga in the normal pipeline, hide her in plain sight, so to speak. As long as the containers aren't specifically interrogated by sensors we will be fine." He grinned, pounding a fist repeatedly against his knee as if he couldn't contain himself. "While we go south, Monagas will continue on to Finland with the loose material. Do you know what they call it?"

She shook her head, causing her black bangs to shimmer in the chilly breeze. "What, my love?"

"MUFP." He giggled again, putting a hand to his mouth. "Isn't that a funny word? It reminds me of the sound you make when you are . . . you know . . ."

"MUFP?"

He winked a dark eye. "Missing Unaccounted-For Plutonium."

December 15
Harborview Hospital
Seattle

Trauma doctor Eileen Clayton was standing beside Birdie, the charge nurse, leaning over the other woman's desk to show off photos of her new grandbaby, when a heartrending wail curled in from the waiting room. Birdie shivered at the sound, searching for her Crocs under the desk with the toe of her stockinged foot.

"What the hell was that?"

Clayton took off tortoiseshell reading glasses and shoved them in the pocket of her scrubs. She was a tall, African American woman, and her extremely short hair accentuated high cheekbones and the length of her neck. Like Birdie, she wore pink scrubs. Her natural smile fled as another wailing moan rose from the waiting room.

At fifty-one, Clayton had been a doctor for long enough to hear her fair share of pained cries for help, but this one chilled her to the bone. She leaned around the wall that separated the office from the waiting room. An attractive young woman in a stylish brown leather jacket clutched her stomach just outside the registration window. Grisly black mascara blotched both eyes, making her look like a maniacal raccoon, and ran in long lines down a round face the color of bleached bone.

"Get this out of me!" Her voice was a ragged hiss, the torn cry of a damned soul.

Dr. Clayton ran from the reception office to the lobby, followed by Birdie. They caught the girl just before she collapsed.

"Have you taken any drugs, sweetheart?" Birdie.

The girl looked up, squinting as if trying to figure out where she was. "I don't . . . I mean . . ." She vomited, missing Birdie by inches. "Ooohhh, please let me die. . . ." She threw her head back and howled in pain, voiding the contents of her bowels. She let loose a string of vehement curses, shrieking as if she'd drunk a bottle of acid.

Birdie helped steer the dizzy girl around the mess on the floor, guiding her toward the nearest trauma room. She shot a glance at Clayton. "If her head starts spinning around, I'm leaving her to you."

With all the screaming, the ER instantly became a buzzing hive of activity. Clayton and Birdie got the girl out of her soiled clothing.

"Note the navel jewelry. We'll need that out if we do an MRI," the doc said, touching the gaudy stainless-steel butterfly hovering over the girl's belly button. "Looks like it may be difficult to remove."

A male lab tech with a receding hairline struggled to start an IV while a heavyset nurse checked vitals.

Her eyes narrowed in concern. "106.4," she said, popping the plastic thermometer cover into the trashcan.

"Let's see if we can get your temp down," Clayton said before patting the girl's cheek with a gloved hand. "What's your name, dear?"

"Taylor Bancroft," she whispered through cracked lips. Wracked with another spasm, she grabbed the front of Clayton's scrubs with surprising speed and strength. "It was just supposed to be this once—" Too exhausted to even turn her head, she vomited on her chest. Grimacing, she collapsed back on the bed.

Birdie stripped off the dirty gown and tossed it in a tray for testing.

"What was just once?" Clayton asked, helping the nurse put a damp sheet across Taylor's chest. The poor thing was burning up.

She motioned for the nurses to go ahead with the IV.

"It was all . . . in condoms," the girl whimpered between ragged breaths. Tears streamed down her face. "Two thousand bucks to swallow, fly into the country, and poop them out." Bloodshot eyes begged for understanding.

"Easy money . . ." Clayton sighed.

"I know, right?" The girl nodded, misunderstanding Clayton's comment as approval. Her body tightened as another wave of pain washed over her. "I turned it all over to the guy . . . but one must have leaked."

Clayton bit her lip. This girl wasn't much younger than her own daughter. Her clothes were new and of the latest style. She was probably from a well-to-do family. "Do you know what kind of drug you swallowed, sweetheart?"

"I guessed it was coke, but he didn't tell me." She stared up at the ceiling, sniffling between frantic gasps. She beat dimpled fists on the mattress. "I can't believe it leaked! It was double bagged, one condom inside another. I went straight from the airport to the address like the guy told me to."

"This guy," Dr. Clayton said. "Can you call him and see what kind of drug it was?"

Bancroft wiggled her jaw back and forth, looking hollow as if she was going to be sick. "No, I mean . . . I just met him at a club in Helsinki." She licked her lips as the nausea passed. "He's Spanish, I think. . . . There was something wrong with his lip he tried to hide with a beard."

"Where did you go from the airport?" Clayton prodded, more to keep the girl talking than to gather any information. A blood test would show what drug she'd ingested well before they could contact the smuggler who had put her up to this.

Bancroft swallowed hard, squinting at the pain in her head. "Some warehouse down by the pier. It was a place where they stored a bunch of bank machines— you know, like ATMs." Her body began to shake with sobs. "He told me it was safe. I mean, I just wanted to get a little extra—"

The girl's eyes sagged in midsentence and the heart monitor went flat.

ER staff swarmed in with the crash cart, pushing medication and attempting to shock her heart back into rhythm. Nothing worked.

"Note time of death at 6:05 p.m." Dr. Clayton sighed. Less than fifteen minutes after she'd entered the hospital, Taylor Bancroft was dead. In twenty-six years of practicing medicine, she'd never seen anyone without a gaping wound go from ambulatory to flatline that fast.

"Poor kid," the charge nurse said, pursing her lips. "Wonder what she was doing in Helsinki?"

"Who knows?" Clayton moved to cover the girl's face with the sheet, and was startled to find wads of blond hair that had fallen out on the pillow.

The charge nurse leaned over the body helping, her hospital ID dangling from her pink scrub top. A series of black dots traveled up the badge next to it.

"Everyone move away now!" Clayton snapped, snatching the dosimeter badge from her own lab coat.

"Shit!" She took another step back without thinking. This was no reaction to drugs leaking from a swallowed condom. In the short minutes she'd been around Taylor Bancroft, four of the small circles were now darker than their corresponding backgrounds, indicating over twenty-five rads of exposure.

Clayton rushed to the door of the trauma room, eyes frantically scanning the waiting area, where a college-age orderly worked on the mess Taylor Bancroft had made on the floor.

"Jeremy," she snapped. "Leave it alone!"

The orderly looked up, mop in hand. He wore protective gloves, slippers, and a face mask—unlikely to protect him from the real danger. A blank look crossed his face.

"Leave it be!" Clayton said again, terror edging into her normally calm voice.

An elderly couple and a haggard mother with her small sleeping toddler sat along the far wall of the waiting room. Two fishermen types in wool sweaters and rubber boots occupied the center seats, staring up at the wall-mounted flat screen above the child's head.

"Everyone outside," Clayton yelled, summoning all the bravado she could muster. "The ER is closed."

Taylor Bancroft's insides had been cooked from radiation poisoning—and every drop of fluid that had escaped her body had turned the ER into a hot zone. If the deadly stuff wasn't still inside her, then it was floating around somewhere out there—in the hands of someone sick enough to smuggle it into the U.S. inside a college student's gut.

DIRTY

In the absence of orders, go find something and kill it.

—Erwin Rommel

CHAPTER 1

December 16
1110 Hours
Arlington, Virginia

Jericho Quinn twisted the throttle on his gunmetal-gray BMW R 1200 GS Adventure, feeling the extra horses he needed to keep up with the frenetic thump of D.C. traffic. Six cars ahead, the man he wanted to kill activated his turn signal, then moved a forest green Ford Taurus into the left lane.

The big Beemer was a leggy bike, aggressive like a mechanical predator from a science-fiction movie. Tall enough to be eye level with passing cars, it flicked easily for what some considered the two-story building of motorcycles.

Even locked-on to his target, Quinn was watchful. Riding on two wheels required constant awareness—as his father constantly chided: *Ride like everyone else is on crack and trying to kill you.* In truth, though he'd been riding since he was a small boy in Alaska, each time he hit the street awakened an intense hyperawareness, like the first time he'd tracked a wounded brown bear, worked outside the wire in Iraq, or kissed a girl.

Following the Taurus in the heavy afternoon traffic took concentration, but every on-ramp and intersection, every car around him, presented a possible assault. The Brits called them SMIDSY accidents—*Sorry, mate, I didn't see you*. There was hardly a summer growing up that Quinn or his brother, Bo, hadn't been consigned to some sort of cast due to such encounters with absent-minded drivers.

And still they rode, because it was worth the risk. When they were younger, he and his kid brother had come to the conclusion that miles spent on the back of a motorcycle were like dog years—somehow worth more than a regular mile.

Now Quinn tracked the little Ford like a missile, taking the left off 395 at the Pentagon/Crystal City exit, then the ramp to the Jeff Davis Highway. He stayed well back, leaving three vehicles as a cushion between him and his target, accelerating then tapping his brake in a sort of fluid Slinky dance. The Taurus moved into the right lane. Quinn glanced over his shoulder, then, with a slight lean of this body, took the right lane as well.

He wore a black Transit riding jacket of heavy, micro-perforated leather and matching pants against the humid chill of a Washington December. The Aerostich suit was waterproof with removable crash armor to guard against any asphalt assaults. Quinn's boss had seen to it that the Shop, a subunit of DARPA—the Defense Advanced Research Projects Agency—added level IIIA body armor for traditional ballistic protection along with a few other modifications like a wafer-thin cooling and heating system to bolster the suit's amazing versatility. His Kimber ten-millimeter pistol, a small Beretta .22 with a XCaliber suppressor, and a thirteenth-century Japanese killing dagger, affectionately called Yawaraka-Te—or Gentle Hand—were all tucked neatly out of sight beneath the black jacket. A gray Arai helmet hid Quinn's copper complexion and two-day growth of dark beard.

They'd come from downtown, outside the Capitol on Constitution Avenue, under the Third Street Tunnel and onto 395. Though it was lunchtime, rush hour in D.C. seemed only to ebb slightly during the business day and the low winter sun glinted off a river of traffic. The Taurus looked remarkably like eighty percent of the other sedans on the road and Quinn had to concentrate as he moved from lane to lane to keep from losing track amid the flow.

Knowing who was in the car made the hair bristle on Quinn's neck. After a year of doing little but sitting back on his haunches and watching, he itched for the opportunity to make a move. Now it looked as though Hartman Drake had given him that chance. People accustomed to a diet of Kobe beef and champagne didn't suddenly trade it all in for hamburger and tap water. The Speaker of the House of Representatives was certainly used to traveling in more style than the plain vanilla sedan. He had chosen the innocuous Taurus for a reason.

Agents of the Air Force Office of Special Investigations were well known in law enforcement circles as experts at handling confidential sources. Vehicle surveillance went hand in hand with that particular expertise. As an OSI agent and a veteran of multiple deployments to the "sandy-stans" of the world, Quinn had ample training in both disciplines. Now, as an other governmental agent, or OGA, working directly for the president's national security advisor, he had plenty of opportunity to put these skills, and others more unique to his personality, to frequent use.

He reached up and opened the face shield on his gray Arai a crack to let in a whiff of crisp winter air. An airbrush of crossed war axes, dripping candy-apple blood, detailed the sides of the helmet. Along with the black leathers and aggressively beaked BMW 1200 GS, it brought to mind Frank Frazetta's brooding horseback warrior, *The Death Dealer*. Quinn didn't mind the comparison. His ex-wife would say he even worked at it.

The neatly spaced trees scattered among the hotels, apartment buildings, and holly bushes of Crystal City had long since given up their leaves. A stiff wind blew from the northeast, shoving Quinn's bike like an unseen fist and threatening much colder weather. Thankfully, there was no snow.

"What are you up to, Drake?" Quinn whispered to himself, throwing a puff of vapor against the visor of his helmet. He had to suppress the urge to ride up beside the Taurus to shoot the driver in the face. The Speaker had ducked out on his security detail for a reason, and from what Quinn knew of him that meant he was up to something deadly.

Half a block ahead, the green Taurus bore right where the Jeff Davis Highway split to become North Patrick and Henry Streets with Henry continuing south. Quinn fell back two more cars, to merge in front of a black Mercedes coupe, easing into the slower rhythm of the narrow one-way street leading into historic Old Town Alexandria.

The American people might believe Hartman Drake still mourned the death of his devoted wife the year before, but Quinn knew better. He lacked the proof to accuse such a powerful man, but Quinn was certain the Speaker had been responsible for the poor woman's death. Losing a spouse had gained him sympathy and given him an excuse not to attend the event that should have killed both the president and the vice president— leaving Drake, as House Speaker, the next in line of succession.

Ahead, the Taurus stopped at the intersection on a green light, waiting for a gaggle of well-dressed lobbyist types walking to Hank's Oyster Bar for a Friday lunch. Quinn brought the bike to a stop, planting his left foot and feeling the familiar horizontal torque of the engine while the group crossed the street as if it belonged to them. Once they cleared the crosswalk, the Taurus turned east on King. Quinn fell in behind, three cars back now, biding his time.

Restaurants, tourist shops, ice cream parlors, and attorneys' offices occupied the multicolored brick and stone buildings crammed in on either side of the shady street. Many were older than the United States itself.

Hartman Drake took a quick right on the last street before the Potomac River, then whipped into a fenced parking lot beyond a hedgerow and a line of leafless trees. Seldom seen without his trademark French cuffs and colorful bowtie, the speaker wore faded blue jeans and a brown leather bomber jacket. A baseball cap and aviator sunglasses rounded out his disguise. It was common knowledge around Capitol Hill that Drake prided himself on a trim physique and powerful chest. In his mid-forties, he worked out religiously every day in the House gym.

He paused for a moment at the car window to adjust the ball cap and sunglasses. For a moment Quinn thought he was looking for a tail, but soon realized the narcissistic peacock was merely checking out his own stunning reflection. His self-admiration complete, the Speaker retrieved an aluminum briefcase from the backseat before trotting across a park-like lawn, still green from the unseasonably mild winter.

Quinn bit his bottom lip. Drake was heading for the river.

Letting Drake make it ahead for a five-count, Quinn motored his GS into the same parking lot, across the street from the old torpedo factory turned art mall.

He dismounted, peeling off his helmet and kangaroo-hide riding gloves in time to watch Drake pass behind a hedgerow, then through a gap in a wooden privacy fence. Quinn's cell phone began to vibrate in the inner pocket of his Transit jacket. He unzipped the jacket to give him quicker access to his weapons, but ignored the call, tapping the butt of the Kimber over his kidney, just to make certain it was there. The suppressed Beretta 21A hung in an elastic holster under his left arm. Yawaraka-Te rested upside down along his spine.

Gripping the helmet by the chin guard in his left hand, Quinn strode quickly across the lot, skirting a line of sports cars belonging to the boat owners at the marina beyond the wooden fence. So far, he had the entire parking lot to himself, but a rustle behind the shrubs told him that wouldn't be the case for very long.

Though Quinn had loved a good scrap for as long as

he could remember, he'd learned early on that there was a serious difference between squaring off with someone in a contest and the dynamic, kill-or-be-killed world of close-quarters battle. In simplest terms, combat was nothing more than brutal assault, with one party trying to crush the other.

A certain amount of posturing might precede the actual conflict, but when violence came, it came lightning fast on fist or blade or bullet. If the attacker knew what he was doing, it came from every direction and all at once. Fairness, rules, and linear time flew out the window.

When Quinn was still ten meters from the gap in the hedge where Drake had disappeared, an Asian man in his late teens stepped into view. His shaven eyebrows and short, Chia Pet–style punch perms identified him as a *bosozoku*—literally *violent running tribe*—the youthful street gangs who often acted as acolytes to the Japanese mafia. Along with a sullen sneer, he wore baggy red slacks and a white *tokko-fuku,* the knee-length *Special Attack* jacket worn by kamikaze pilots of World War II. Boldly embroidered Japanese kanji covered the coat and proclaimed ridiculous statements like: *Mother, I have to Die!* and *Speed and Death are my Life*!

The *bosozoku* planted his feet firmly in the center of the path, blocking the gap, and folded his arms across a thick chest. A six-inch knife blade glistened in his right fist.

Japanese youth gangs were relatively rare in the U.S., and Quinn was surprised to see one in northern Virginia.

Quinn slowed his advance slightly but did not stop, preferring to press the advantage of momentum and psychological force. Knowing Tokko-fuku couldn't be alone, he whispered his familiar mantra to himself as he walked. "See one, think two."

As if on cue, two more *bosozoku* filed through the gap behind their apparent leader. Each of the newcomers carried a wooden baseball bat and wore jeans and white T-shirts as if they hadn't quite earned the right to wear a Special Attack coat. The last one in line stepped tentatively to Quinn's right. The boy's eyes flitted back and forth, shifting just enough to show he wasn't fully committed to the attack.

Quinn would start with him.

CHAPTER 2

Katya Orlov was in love enough to let herself be dragged through uneven drifts of grimy snow along Zagorodny Prospekt. Her boyfriend, Wasyl, had suggested she borrow her mother's Sberbank card. It wouldn't be stealing, he'd assured her, merely a loan they would pay back after he got work aboard the fishing boat.

The columned entries of Vitebsk Station loomed before her, bathed in brightness against the dark night. Slush soaked through her tattered leather boots. She wore thin cotton socks and her American straight-leg jeans did little to protect slender legs from the cold. She'd thought of packing a few things, but Wasyl had said it wouldn't matter. They could buy what they needed—and they would need little, for they were soul mates.

Rafts of evening commuters, recently disgorged from an outbound city train, flowed in a gray woolen sea.

New snow hung heavy on the night air. The greasy smell of sausages and boiled potatoes drifted from the green kiosks up on the platforms inside the station. As a girl, Katya had thought Vitebsk's stone breastwork and clock tower made it look like a palace. It was a fantastic place with interesting people—but she'd never met anyone as interesting as Wasyl.

Of course, her mother hated him. It was not because he was nineteen and handsome and three years Katya's senior—but because he was Ukrainian and often spoke of taking her to Odessa. He was a man with dreams and a real plan to get her out of their drafty flat in Pushkin— where she would surely have to live with her mother forever unless she found someone to marry her. Wasyl promised they would travel by train, rent a berth where they could sleep in each other's arms and eat eggs and fresh green salads. Once in Odessa they could stay in his rich uncle's beautiful dacha on the Black Sea. Wasyl had a friend with a fishing boat who'd promised him a job.

It was perfect. All they needed was train fare—and perhaps a little sum more to tide them over.

"There," Wasyl said, flipping a thick swath of black hair out of his face once they jostled their way through the doors and into the echoing marble main hall of the station. He pointed to a row of ATMs—*bankomats* in Russian—along the sidewall below a Soviet-era mural of dedicated factory workers and a sweeping Art Nouveau staircase. "We can get the money there."

The damp heat of so many people hit Katya full in the face. A woman with two toddlers on a dog-leash tether fell in beside them, the little ones in tiny wool coats chattering between themselves. A bent and wrinkled *babushka* shuffled along beside them, pushing a creaky metal cart and working her way through the crowd toward the same bankomats.

A businessman in a sable hat and long black coat stood at the nearest machine and Wasyl crowded in front of the woman and her jabbering children to make sure he got to the next one first. He flipped his hair again and held out his hand for the Sberbank card.

Katya reached in the hip pocket of her jeans and handed it to him.

"The PIN?" Wasyl demanded, sliding the card in the slot.

"My birthday," Katya said, the heavy weight of guilt suddenly pressing against her shoulders.

Wasyl sighed. "And exactly when is that again?"

Katya shook her head in disbelief. Surely a true love would remember such a thing.

"Tomorrow," she whispered, heartbroken.

Wasyl did the math in his head and punched the buttons. The machine gave a faint pop.

Katya thought she heard a child's worried cry. At the same instant a molten ball of flame erupted from the bankomat, cutting Wasyl, then Katya, in half.

Ninety seconds later
Embarcadero BART Station
San Francisco

Jordan Winters leaned against the train window and shut his eyes against the stark interior lighting. He felt the swaying rumble through exhausted bones. Night shift sucked. By the time he got home his kids had already caught the bus and his wife was headed out to her shift at the hospital. But jobs were as scarce as politicians with backbone and he was lucky to have work at all. To make matters worse, the Pontiac had lost a U-joint the week before, so he'd been forced to take the train and then the bus to and from work. That meant another half hour on each end of his trip if he made the connections just right. At this rate, he got to see his wife fifteen minutes a day and on weekends—if they were lucky and she didn't have to cover for another nurse.

They made up for it by talking on the phone every day during his commute as soon as he got phone reception. Tuned to the timing of it all, his eyes flicked open the moment he felt the train shudder and began to slow.

"Good morning, bright eyes," he said, glancing at the older man next to him who gave a rolling eye. Jerks blabbed in public on their phones all the time about much less important things. Trains going outbound from the city weren't nearly as crowed as those packed with commuters heading in at this time of day, but they were still full enough you could read the paper of the guy sitting next to you, so Winters kept his voice at a respectful level.

"Hey, Jordy," his wife said. She sounded hoarse. Her cold was getting worse. "How's my man?"

"I'm fine," Winters said. He gathered his jacket and moved toward the doors as they hissed open. "You're sick. Why don't you call in today?"

"I do feel like crap, baby," she said. "But you know I can't call in. I don't qualify for OT if I take a sick day this pay period and heaven knows we need the money, honey."

Jordan pushed his way along the packed platform,

ducking and dodging the endless tide of morning commuters. He could smell the relatively fresh air of Market Street rolling down the stairway above as he passed the ATMs in the ticketing lobby.

"We don't need the money that bad," he lied. "I can pull an extra shift this weekend if I have to."

He worked his way toward the escalator and what his buddies on the night shift called the "world of the day-worker."

"I'd better not. . . ." Her voice wavered.

After fourteen years of marriage, Jordan knew that slight hesitation meant he had her. "It'll be worth it to spend the day with you."

"That would be nice," she said, sniffling.

He sweetened the deal. "I'll stop by that Czech bakery you like before I catch the bus and get you a couple of kolache. That'll put meat on your bones."

She giggled. He loved it when she giggled.

"It's settled then. I . . ." He paused, one foot on the escalator, cursing under his breath. He'd loaned his last ten bucks to Cal at work.

Jordan pushed back from the escalator and through the crowd, past the guy playing his saxophone in front of an open case, toward the bank of three ATMs along the white tile wall. Most people were coming to catch the train so it was easier now that he'd turned around and wasn't a salmon swimming upstream.

"Oh, Jordan . . . you really think I should?"

"No question about it." He felt the thrill of getting to spend a few precious moments with his wife—even if it meant feeding her soup and fruit kolache.

With a new spring in his step, he made his way to the ATM just as the headlight from the next city inbound beamed out of the tunnel. Brakes squealed above the din of frenzied commuters, desperate to catch this particular train as if it were the last one on earth. Hundreds of people shoved and jostled their way from the stairs and escalators, flinging themselves into the bowels of the packed station.

Jordan chatted happily with his wife as he put his card into the slot, thankful to be going home.

"You just get better." He began to punch in his PIN. "I'll be there—"

A blinding flash of heat and light shoved the words back down his throat.

The initial blast all but vaporized Jordan Winters and everyone else within five meters. Commuters were blown from their expensive loafers and high heels. Their bodies, some intact, some in mangled bits and pieces, hurtled across the tracks in front of the oncoming train.

Above, at ground level, passersby felt Market Street rumble under their feet. A blossom of inky smoke belched from the dark stairwell, carrying with it the screams of the dying and the smell of the dead.

CHAPTER 3

Virginia

Jericho Quinn had been steeped in conflict for most of his life. He'd made a conscious effort to excel at boxing, jujitsu, blade work, and the all-out brawl. The most accomplished fighters would call him an expert—and still, three against one was something he took seriously.

No matter what Internet self-defense gurus taught, a violent encounter against multiple attackers was no simple application of a few snazzy techniques. The slightest mistake could nick a tendon or slice a nerve—and end his career. A larger error could end his life.

"Sticks?" Quinn walked forward, speaking Japanese in derisive tones, as a medieval samurai might speak to a dog. He gestured to the bats with his helmet. "You think to stop me with sticks?"

The apparent leader, wearing the *tokko-fuku,* brandished the knife but kept his feet rooted, not fully realizing the posturing phase was over.

Still ten feet away, Quinn suddenly changed direction, picking up speed before the uneasy kid to the right realized he was the intended target. The startled *bosozoku* had thought he was working as backup and hardly had time to raise the bat before Quinn bashed the helmet into his face and sent him staggering backwards in a tangle of feet and misgivings.

Quinn spun immediately, crouching to keep his center low and fluid. Tokko-fuku and the second helper moved in a simultaneous attack, slashing wildly with blade and bat. Quinn stepped under a crashing blow from the bat, swinging his helmet in a wide arc as he moved, connecting with Tokko-fuku's jaw then the second man's knee. The leader growled, caught only with a glancing blow. The second was driven to his knees.

Tokko-fuku wasted no time pressing his attack, slashing out with the knife in a flurry of blows. At least two landed with sickening scrapes against the crash armor of Quinn's thick Transit jacket. A wild swing caught Quinn under the eye, slicing flesh but missing anything vital. In the heat of battle, it felt more like a punch than a cut.

Quinn advanced, pushing Tokko-fuku back with the swinging helmet. He didn't have time for this. Drake was getting away.

To his right, the kid with the bum knee stumbled to his feet, yanking a pistol from his waistband.

Not wanting to alert Drake, Quinn snatched the suppressed .22 from the holster under his arm and put two rounds straight up under the kid's chin as he stumbled past. The wide-eyed *bosozoku* clutched at his neck, full of the horrible knowledge that he was already dead.

"Fool!" Tokko-fuku attacked again before his partner hit the pavement. Blood and saliva covered his teeth, dripping from a pink sheen on his chin. He screamed at his surviving partner, who cowered on the ground. "Get in the fight!"

Amazingly, the frightened boy sprang to his feet. Brandishing the bat, he rushed at Quinn with a stifled yell. Quinn got off three quick shots with the Beretta. Perfect for quick, silent work, the diminutive .22 had little effect on a deranged boy trying to redeem himself in front of his peer. The *bosozoku* crashed in, knocking the little pistol from Quinn's grasp and driving him backward. Quinn moved laterally, ducking a flurry of strikes with the bat. He kept the scared kid between him and Tokko-fuku long enough to draw Yawaraka-Te from the scabbard along his spine. Horrified at the sight of the Japanese killing dirk, the kid dropped his weapon.

There was no time for mercy in an uneven fight. Quinn extended the blade as he spun, drawing it across the kid's throat in a wide arc on the way around to face Tokko-fuku.

Wasting no time, the *bosozoku* leader feinted with the blade, edge upward, intent on delivering ripping blows for maximum effect. Narrow eyes searched for an opening.

Quinn gave him one.

Dropping his left shoulder a hair, he dragged his foot as if he was about to stumble. Tokko-fuku fell for it, lunging forward with his arm outstretched. Quinn stepped deftly to the right, avoiding the blade and letting Yawaraka-Te windmill in front of him. Three of the *bosozoku*'s fingers came off in the process. His knife clattered to the pavement roughly twenty seconds after the fight began.

For the first time, Quinn stood his ground, letting

Yawaraka-Te's point float inches from the bleeding Tokko-fuku's heaving chest.

"Who sent you?" Quinn whispered. He had no time for a lengthy interrogation. Every second put Drake farther away. "I will ask you only once more. Who sent you?"

Tokko-fuku's lips pulled back over bloodstained teeth in a maniacal grin. Shaved eyebrows and a false widow's peak gave him a ghoulish, Kabuki-like appearance. Instead of speaking, he released a long, rattling breath. Rushing forward, he impaled himself on the gleaming blade, then, glaring hard at Quinn, twisted sideways as if wanting to inflict the most damage.

Quinn felt a sickening scrape as the dagger known as Gentle Hand grated on bone, then snapped. He stepped back immediately, withdrawing the blade to find three inches of steel remained inside the grinning youth. Gasping, Tokko-fuku stepped forward. The mangled remnants of his bloody hand clawed at the air as he fell.

Beyond the hedgerow a boat motor burbled to life. Quinn's phone began to buzz again, more urgently this time, it seemed. He ignored it.

Quinn stood rooted in place, his broken dagger dripping blood. The entire event had lasted less than half a minute. He scanned the three dead attackers before turning his back on them. As the Chinese said, dead tigers kill the most hunters.

He made it through the hedge in time to catch the glimpse of Drake's bomber jacket as he stepped into the cabin of a powerboat fifty meters away. An Asian woman with black hair piled up in a loose bun held the door, then followed him inside. Quinn didn't get a good look at her face, but judging from the height of the cabin door, she was as tall as Drake. She was older, maybe in her late fifties. She'd surely been the one to station the young goons to watch Drake's back trail, which meant she was likely also Japanese.

Focused on a rapidly departing boat, Quinn grabbed his BlackBerry. He had to find someone who could get eyes-on while he worked out how to follow. The phone began to buzz with an incoming call before he could punch in a number.

"Quinn," he snapped without looking at the caller ID.

Fifty meters away, the boat backed out of her slip and onto the Potomac, headed south toward points unknown.

"I need you to come in." The president's national security advisor charged ahead as soon as Quinn picked up. In the mind of Winfield Palmer, if you answered, you were available on his terms. If you didn't answer, he simply called over and over until you did. It was no consequence to him that you might be holding a bloody weapon or standing over a dead body. When he wanted to talk, the boss expected you to listen.

"Sir, Drake is on the move," Quinn said, exasperated. "We need to get with the Coast Guard and have them track the ves—"

"No time, Jericho," Palmer cut him off. "There's been a bombing."

Quinn stopped. "A bombing?"

"Listen, I'm attending a funeral," Palmer plowed on. "Can you meet me at the Tomb of the Unknowns in half an hour?"

"I'll be there," Quinn said. He glanced down at the dead *bosozoku*s at his feet. A knot of puzzled onlookers already gathered across King Street, staring at the broken killing dagger in his fist. "But I might need your help with Alexandria Police."

Quinn ended the call, then used his phone to snap a photo of each dead man. He felt sure the Asian woman on the boat with Drake had hired them—making it a good guess that she was Yakuza. Maybe there was another way to find out who she was. Before heading back to the bike, he stooped to pick up Tokko-fuku's severed fingers. Rolling them in a blue bandana, he shoved them in the pocket of his leather jacket.

Back on the BMW he turned on the FM radio, letting the horrific news of panic and death surrounding the dirty bomb flood the speaker in his helmet. Hartman Drake, terrorist mole, murderer, and Speaker of the House, would have to wait.

CHAPTER 4

Aleksandra Kanatova slumped against the wheel of her black Lada sedan and wiped the tears from her eyes with the heel of her hand. She was smartly dressed in a white down ski jacket, gray cowl-neck wool cardigan, and jeans snug enough to show off the round hips of her gymnast's body. A stylish blue fox *ushanka* sat low over her ears against the cold. The splash of freckles across her tawny complexion made wearing makeup an afterthought.

At first glance one would say she was the icon of a young Russian professional. But something was not quite right. The clothes she wore were crisp and fashionable—but her fingernails were chewed down to sorry nubs. Golden green eyes that should have sparkled in the glow of streetlights held the damaged, sidelong stare of a young woman with a deep bruise on her soul.

Aleksandra's grandmother was one of the few in generations of Soviets who had consistently read the Bible despite the atheist views of her government. She called Aleksandra a pretty whited tomb with dead men's bones inside, ever chiding her for some unatoned sin. Babushkas were known more for their unbridled candor than their tact.

Aleksandra was well aware that she carried a heavy load of unresolved sins, but these were not the cause of her darkness. Her eyes had once shone as they should have, before Mikhail was dead. There was nothing she could do to bring him back, but such deep and abiding sadness was not a thing she could peel off like a dirty cloak and exchange for a new one. Death was final, and now, so it seemed, was despair.

The coffin-like cold inside the musty car and the heaviness in her heart pressed against Aleksandra's chest and threatened to rob her of all auspices of control. She pounded on the steering wheel with both hands and screamed at the top of her lungs for a full minute. Then, drying her eyes, she squared her shoulders and cursed herself for such weakness.

The Lada's fan had a difficult time keeping the windscreen free of encroaching frost. Aleksandra had to lean forward with her eyes just above the top of the steering wheel, to peer through the tiny oval of clear glass as she drove. With such a small view of the world, it was difficult to make sense of everything amid the flashing lights and glowing ice fog outside. It was chilly enough in the car to make her blue fox hat a necessity to keep her ears from freezing while she drove. Some men in her unit insisted that the sedan was in perfect order and it was she who frosted up the windows with her frigid heart.

Traffic on Zagorodny Prospekt had snarled to a standstill with gawkers and arriving *politsia* vehicles.

A heavy snow poured from the blackness above the city as if from a sieve, choking arterial roads and slowing emergency vehicles. Mournful wails of the wounded—and Russian women were masters at wailing—mingled with the hi-lo sirens of arriving ambulances.

In well-practiced Soviet bureaucratic fashion, a roadblock had been erected even before rescue efforts had begun, as if it was a foregone conclusion that there was something to hide at the blast site. Two bleary-eyed *politsia* sentries in navy-blue waist-length parkas with curly gray Astrakhan collars and hats stood in the swirling snow. The shorter of the two, an Asian-looking woman with almond eyes and huge metal hoop earrings, held back while her male partner, a young man with the piercing look of a Cossack, stepped officiously in the middle of the street and flagged down Kanatova's black Lada. His Astrakhan hat was thrown back on his head at a cocky angle. Both officers were more bone than muscle, and looked as if they wore the uniforms as a costume instead of a badge of authority.

Kanatova rolled down her window and extended the credential card identifying her as an agent of *Federal'-naya Sluzhba Bezopasnosti,* the Federal Security Service. The modern progeny of the heavy-handed Soviet KGB, FSB agents still commanded fear if not actual respect from local politsia.

Presidents Putin, Medvedev, and then Putin again had vowed to clean up corruption among the nation's police forces. Judging from the two standing outside Kanatova's sedan, their proposed housecleaning hadn't made it as far as the St. Petersburg suburb of Pushkin.

"I was not aware the FSB employed beautiful actresses," the young man said, in a foolish attempt at flirting. The smell of alcohol clung to his wool coat like an extra layer of clothing.

Aleksandra ignored him and pressed the accelerator, forcing his bejeweled partner to scamper out of her path.

With her petite figure and pouting lips, Kanatova felt she looked more like someone's baby sister than a beautiful actress. Uncommonly rich mahogany red hair stood out in stark contrast to the golden green of her eyes. Evidently, many men preferred the baby-sister look. She heard it all the time from her male counterparts when they were trying to get her into bed.

It was no accident that Aleksandra found herself in St. Petersburg. Mikhail's last report had mentioned the possibility of loose plutonium hitting the black market. Old Soviet ordnance popped up with great regularity now, and it was the job of her unit to track it down. More often than not, the weapons were rifles, or dilapidated shoulder-fired antitank missiles that were more likely to blow up the shooter than the intended target.

Mikhail's find had been different. If he had been correct, the weapons that had gotten him killed were far worse than a few rusted RPGs.

When she was a child, Aleksandra's uncle had told her frightening stories of Baba Yaga. Sometimes called the Bone Mother, this Slavic folk villainess was a wicked old hag who lived deep in the forest. Her house moved through the woods on gnarled chicken feet and was surrounded by human skulls. The Bone Mother was attended by a set of bodiless hands and her best friend and lover was Koshchey the Deathless, a bearded old sorcerer who rode naked on an enchanted horse calling down whirlwinds and stealing little girls. Sometimes the Bone Mother gave secret advice to children who were on quests—but more often, she simply ate them with sharpened iron teeth.

As frightening as the stories were, the Baba Yaga Mikhail Polzin proposed was far more dangerous.

Aleksandra slowed to allow an ambulance to pass. She glanced at the pile of folders on the passenger seat. Her willingness to use her looks along with her persuasive demeanor had netted her a sizable stable of informants from St. Petersburg to Vladivostok.

Information from this source said Rustam Daudov, a Chechen resistance leader, had been in Uzbekistan at the same time Mikhail was killed. Stories of Baba Yaga were rife among Chechen terrorists who considered such a thing the holy grail of weapons caches. And they were right to. Rustam Daudov would do anything to get his filthy hands on such a find. Aleksandra had put out feelers with every contact she could think of, offering twenty thousand American dollars for information regarding the terrorist's present whereabouts. It was too big a coincidence that a killer of his prominence had been in the same city as Mikhail on the day he was murdered.

Days went by with nothing.

Then a college student had fallen dead of radiation poisoning at St. Petersburg Clinical Hospital No. 15. Local agents said he'd died of massive exposure, but there was no material found. Kanatova's superiors had sent her to check the local pulse and see what she could learn. Reports had pointed first to the Petersburg Nuclear Physics Institute in Gatchina. A lonely widowed scientist there who seemed overly interested in Aleksandra's freckled nose assured her the institute was missing no plutonium. He did, however, remember that a Chechen resembling Daudov's description had been asking questions. The last he knew, this Chechen had rented a flat in the suburb of Pushkin, five blocks from Vitebsk Station.

Pitiful official estimates initially put the Vitebsk death toll at eleven. Accounting for traditional Russian understatement when it came to catastrophe, Aleksandra assumed the count would nudge upward exponentially in unreleased reports. It was only a matter of time before the media began to hazard all sorts of guesses and accusations. Unlike the past sensibilities of Pravda and the glory days of the USSR, Russia's modern media had grown into a ravenous beast that had to be fed. The first releases to go out on the Internet said a train had derailed. A ruptured gas line had been the next blogosphere theory.

Five minutes after detonation, reports of a bombing in an American train station had ticked across the bottom of the television in Aleksandra's hotel room. A moment after that, *politsia* radios buzzed with word of a bomb in Vitebsk.

Rescue workers in yellow reflective vests swarmed the area like ants. Some carried stretchers laden with mangled bodies out of the smoldering building. Vents of steam hissed here and there as fire crews worked to control secondary blazes. Aleksandra drove past a green commuter bus that lay knocked on its side like a wounded dinosaur, blown over by the initial blast that had torn the heavy wooden doors off the station. She shook her head at a pair of stockinged female legs protruding into the snow under the street side of the bus, their owner crushed like the witch from *The Wizard of Oz*.

Past the overturned bus, Aleksandra maneuvered around a queue of three ambulances and nosed the Lada up against a sooty, three-foot snowbank in front of an idling blue and white police truck. A stout man wearing a digital camouflage parka bearing the three stars of a senior *politsia* lieutenant waved his arms and shouted for her to keep moving. She turned the key to kill the engine as he stomped up to the car door.

Lieutenant Sergey Tarasov stopped short and his graying mustache curled into a full grimace when he recognized Kanatova. She was well aware of the *krysha* protection rackets he set up for the pimps and their prostitutes in St. Petersburg. *Krysha* meant "roof" in Russian, and the lieutenant provided such a shelter from government meddling as long as he was well compensated.

Russia was a land of workarounds where the shortest distance between two points often meant leveraging dangerous liaisons. Aleksandra's knowledge of Tarasov's criminal activities made him a possible threat— but it also allowed her a certain degree of control as long as she didn't stretch him to the breaking point. And this she found vastly more important than the Russian mob paying a "police tax" to be left alone with their whoring ventures.

Kanatova adjusted the blue fox ushanka on her head and dropped her car keys in the pocket of her down parka. Deep snow crunched under her boots as she surveyed the riot of activity. A flick of her wrist signaled the snarling Lieutenant Tarasov to follow. He was a pig, a slob, and most certainly a rapist, but his rank might come in handy tonight. Aleksandra gave her head a shake as if she'd sneezed, annoyed at the very stench of the man. Hers was such a nasty business.

The five doors under the double-columned windows at the near end of the station were gone. Dark fans of soot and debris had spewed across the snow from each gaping hole as if some angry giant had taken a broom to the inside of the great hall and swept everything out into the street. A tangle of gray hair and blood-sodden wool was wrapped around a yellow traffic bollard beyond the doors, flung there by the blast. Closer inspection revealed pieces of charred limb embedded in the snow.

White goose down flakes sifted around flashing emergency lights. Heavy snow dampened the cries of the wounded—and gave the feeling of a garish snow globe of carnage. Aleksandra paused twenty meters from the demolished doors beside a woman's high-heel boot. It was expensive, probably American, and made of black leather. A five-inch shard of shattered bone stuck from the boot top.

"Ah, yes," the pig Tarasov said, sneering as he misjudged her reason for stopping. "This is most certainly close enough for your investigation. It is well and good to stop outside the real horror. The destruction inside the station is much more gruesome. It could be quite traumatic to one not accustomed to—"

Aleksandra pushed back the thick fur of her fox hat so she could glare up at the stupid man. He could have no idea of the blood and sorrow her eyes had seen. She said nothing, but reached instead to the pocket of her parka for a metal box the size of a cigarette pack. She stooped to hold the device over the mangled boot, playing it over the burned leather. A thin needle jumped across the illuminated face. Kanatova stood quickly, taking a half step back in spite of herself. Her heart pounded inside her chest. The cold air suddenly took on a bitter taste.

"You will get used to it, my dear," Lieutenant Tarasov said, his false compassion congealing in the cold like sour milk. "If you think this poor piece of bone is bad, the interior would certainly be too much for your stomach." Tarasov puffed up like a self-important toad. "I myself found a victim's tongue stuck to a tile—"

"You have been inside the station?" Aleksandra's head snapped up.

The lieutenant seemed to take her question as a sign of admiration. He shrugged. "Good citizens are in danger—"

"It is a simple enough question, Tarasov." She held the metal box against his camouflaged parka. The black needle pegged to the right. "But I have my answer."

"Someone had to oversee the rescue, my sweet." He smoothed the corners of his mustache.

"Stop touching your mouth."

"You are easily excited," Tarasov chuckled. "I can appreciate that." He took a step closer, putting a hand on Aleksandra's shoulder, then letting his hand slide down to her breast. "May I call you Aleks? Do your friends call you Aleks or Sasha?"

Aleksandra closed the gap between them in a flash, bringing her hand from the pocket of her parka to shove it between his legs. "You will call me Agent Kanatova!" she hissed.

"Ahhh." Tarasov raised a wicked brow. " 'Though she be but little, she is fierce.' "

"I would not quote dead Englishmen if I were in your shoes." Aleksandra gave a little tug, letting the lieutenant feel the hooked blade she had at his groin.

"You would threaten me?"

"I do not threaten." Aleksandra shook her head. "You are already cut. Give your leg a shake. If you do not hear a little thud, perhaps I have not yet removed anything important."

Snow continued to sift down around them. She sniffed from the cold.

"What do you want?" Tarasov's shaggy mustache appeared to wilt as a dawning reality chased away his bravado.

"I want you to shut your mouth and listen to me," she said. "You must be decontaminated before you leave this site—you and everyone else who has gone inside."

Aleksandra stepped away slowly, withdrawing the cruel-looking knife. Shaped like a talon, there was indeed fresh blood on the curved blade. She kept an eye on the pallid Tarasov as she took a cell phone from her pocket and punched in the number with her thumb. She'd given him too much to think about for him to try and hurt her anytime soon.

"This is Kanatova," she said when the other party had picked up. "Polzin's information was correct. Radiation is confirmed. Someone should tell the Americans." She shoved the phone back in her parka.

"Wha . . . what are you saying?" Senior Lieutenant Tarasov attempted an angry stomp of his foot, but Aleksandra could see there was no commitment in it. He seemed scared to look down and see how much damage her knife had done. "Radiation? Do you think this is connected to the dead boy at the hospital?"

Of course it was connected, Aleksandra thought, gritting her teeth. What sort of idiot could possibly think a dirty bomb and a college student dead of radiation poisoning could be in any way unrelated? The problem was figuring out how. Instead of voicing her opinion, she nodded slowly, surveying the scene of mangled bodies and destruction. "There is much worse to come, I assure you," she said, almost to herself.

"Worse than this?" Tarasov's eyes flew wider under wild gray brows. "Worse than you cutting my . . . worse than radioactive?"

Aleksandra bit her bottom lip fighting the urge to chew on her already horrid fingernails. The chilly air suddenly grew more bitter and metallic. The smell of cooked flesh made her stomach turn flips. "Vitebsk Station still stands. Life muddles on for kilometers in every direction." She looked directly at the lieutenant. "Oh yes, there are things much worse than this. . . ."

Tarasov tugged at the collar of his uniform. "You spoke of decontamination?"

"The teams are on their way," Aleksandra said, taking out her phone again.

"What do you intend to do?

"Now?"

"Yes, now." Tarasov's hand trembled at the end of his powerful arm, an arm he would have been all too happy to strike her with two minutes before.

"I'm but a lowly civil servant," she said. "I will call in for orders."

Kanatova took shallow breaths. Falling snow helped

to scrub the chilly air to be sure, but there could still be dangerous levels of radiation floating around her in the darkness. She'd made her next decision before she pressed the buttons on her phone. She knew Mikhail Polzin better than his own wife. She would naturally be the one to pick up this investigation. Her bones ached with dread at the daunting thought. The layers of Russian bureaucracy surrounding his death, stolen Soviet-era weapons, and the detonation of a dirty bomb would be like trying to walk a tightrope in the dark. It could be done, but one would have to be extremely careful—and extremely lucky. She had no time for such things. By the time she got the approvals she needed, it would be too late.

Growing up Russian had instilled in Aleksandra the value of the workaround. If something was against the rules, one found a way around that particular rule. If the bureaucracy of the Russian government would hinder her investigation, she'd simply go to America. They'd surely be neck deep in their own investigation by the time she arrived. Following their discoveries wouldn't be difficult at all—the silly Americans paraded their best information on the television. CNN would indeed be her source.

CHAPTER 5

Arlington Cemetery

The angry grumble of a motorcycle engine, taken from the open road and confined to an enclosed parking lot, blatted off the walls of the concrete structure. Jacques Thibodaux rolled into the space beside Quinn with his red and black BMW GS Adventure. Jericho stood at the back of his own bike stowing armored kangaroo-leather gloves in a boxy Touratech aluminum side case.

Corps to the core, Marine Gunnery Sergeant Thibodaux was tall and broad as a mountain. The big Cajun was an accomplished mixed martial artist who fought under the name Daux Boy. His square jaw, combined with the black Aerostich Transit jacket, brought the image of Arnold Schwarzenegger in *The Terminator* to Quinn's mind. He wore a high and tight flattop, trimmed so precisely that the barber must surely have used a level to get it right.

A veteran of countless deployments, he'd still found time to father seven sons, the youngest of whom was just a few months old. Like Quinn, Thibodaux had been handpicked by Winfield Palmer as a blunt instrument on one of the Hammer Teams. A Marine to his very soul, he was now assigned to Air Force OSI, a branch of the service he and his fellow leathernecks generally considered bus drivers.

Neither Quinn nor the gunny wanted to keep the boss waiting, and three minutes later saw them trudging up the cordoned asphalt road between the Arlington Cemetery Visitors Center and the amphitheater overlooking the Tomb of the Unknowns. Row after row of some three hundred thousand white markers lay in ghostly perfect lines among the leafless trees on either side of the road.

"I gotta tell you, Chair Force," the big Cajun muttered as he walked beside Quinn, his shadow all but blocking out the sun. "This place always gives me a case of the jumps."

"It's hallowed ground," Quinn mused, thinking of the friends he knew who rested here. He often wondered if they might not be the lucky ones. "Sacred."

"I reckon that's it, *l'ami*," Thibodaux said. "I get the same feelin' when Camille drags me to church. Makes me feel all . . . I don't know . . . mortal and shit. I hate it." He shot a glance at Quinn. "So, you were followin' numb-nuts again, weren't you?"

Jericho nodded. He hadn't mentioned the fight to anyone but Palmer, but the scabbed cut under his eye and slashed leather on his jacket were evidence enough.

"He's the damned Speaker of the House," Thibodaux said, ignoring the damage as if he expected Quinn to show up looking like he'd been dragged behind a truck. "Half the country holds him up as a hero for savin' us from sleeper spies."

"I know." Quinn walked on without looking up.

"I guess the old man still says no to just killin' the SOB." Thibodaux's wife was a devout Catholic and allotted him only five non-Bible curse words a month. For a Marine gunnery sergeant, his language bordered on crystalline.

"Not without more information."

"How about he's an orphan like the rest of the moles, with a history that's a blank slate before he was fifteen years old?"

"That's not the point." Quinn shrugged. "Palmer agrees that Drake's dirty. He assures steps have been taken to isolate him from anything that could compromise national security. He just wants to know what Drake's up to—who's controlling him—before we take any . . . permanent action. He'd like to take him down politically if possible."

"Roger that." Thibodaux nodded in agreement. "But this rat bastard is Teflon. We'd have to find him in bed with a dead woman or a live boy. . . ."

Ahead, Winfield Palmer looked down from near the top of the hill, at the base of the white amphitheater. Special Agent Arnie Vasquez of the Secret Service stood under the shadow of the marble colonnade, back a few feet from his boss but within arm's reach. Quinn marveled at the way the former Marine made executive protection look easy. He knew from experience it was anything but.

As the president's national security advisor, Win Palmer rated a small but full-time protective detail. As the president's longtime friend and confidant from their days as cadets at West Point, he got the pick of the litter from the U.S. Secret Service—and he'd chosen Vasquez for his discretion as much as his skill at arms.

"Uurrah," Thibodaux grunted as they approached.

Vasquez returned the greeting, giving a conspiratorial wink to his fellow Marine. He greeted Quinn with a polite nod. He was, after all, merely Air Force—a wing waxer.

"Thank you for coming on such short notice," Palmer said. His face turned down in a ruddy frown. He wore a dark suit with a conservative black and yellow striped silk tie. Slightly balding, with close-cropped sandy gray hair and arms folded across his chest, he could have been someone's father, angry over some house rule infraction.

"The bombings are all over the news," Quinn offered. "Hitting the U.S. and Russia simultaneously . . . makes things interesting."

"Interesting is a hell of an understatement," Palmer said. "The markets have taken a nosedive and banks all over the country have reported long lines of people wanting to withdraw their cash. People don't feel safe— over a hundred thousand travelers have canceled airline tickets in the last hour alone. Congress is already talking about demanding X-ray body scanners at every port of entry."

"How do you *talk* about demanding?" Thibodaux scratched his head. "My experience, you either demand or you don't."

"We're talking about Congress," Palmer said.

"Do we know where the material came from?" Quinn asked, eyes locked on the precise movements of the "Old Guard" 3rd Infantry soldier marching, machinelike, thirty yards away. Behind the ramrod-straight young man, carved on the front of the white marble tomb was the inscription: *Here rests in honored glory, an American soldier, known but to God.*

Palmer took a deep breath. "Maybe," he said. He handed his smartphone to Quinn. "The Bureau got this from the security cameras in Helsinki. It's dated yesterday."

Quinn and Thibodaux crowded around the phone to watch a young woman move from the long queue of travelers and step through the metal detector. There was no sound with the video, but from the security screener's reaction it was clear the machine had alarmed. The video blinked to show a change of cameras. In this view, the girl could be seen lifting her shirt and pointing to a piece of jewelry in her navel. The female security officer administering the secondary screening passed a hand wand over the young woman's belly, then sent her on her way.

The video complete, Palmer resumed his explanation. "Preliminary reports say the bombs in both California and St. Petersburg were conventional Semtex salted with plutonium. Analysis points to material manufactured by the Soviets. The girl in the video came in from Helsinki yesterday. She died within hours after hitting American soil. According to the story she gave medical staff, she swallowed the material in condoms, believing it was cocaine."

Quinn rubbed his face, feeling a sudden weariness creep into his bones. "I was in Helsinki earlier this year," he said. "They have state-of-the-art radiation detectors. I'm surprised she didn't set off the alarms."

"Alpha and beta radiation would have been stopped

inside her," Palmer said. "Gamma would have been detected, but if she swallowed the material immediately before passing through customs . . . theoretically she could have made it into the U.S. before she became 'hot' enough."

"Now hang on one damned minute." Thibodaux grimaced as if he'd just eaten a bitter pill. "You mean to tell me this girl ate plutonium?"

Palmer nodded. "Sources inside the Kremlin tell us a college student in St. Petersburg died of the same sort of radiation poisoning. So far the media hasn't gotten wind of it, but an art dealer in Manhattan was found dead in her apartment this morning. FBI confirms it was radiation and that she'd been to Helsinki."

"I'm guessing she had a belly button ring," Thibodaux said.

"That means more material out there for another dirty bomb," Quinn said. "Odd. It's as if they want the mules to be found—otherwise they could have just killed them when they off-loaded the merchandise."

"Uncertainty spreads terror almost as well as violence," Palmer said. "But that's not the worst of it."

Thibodaux gazed across the field of crosses, shaking his head. "There's something worse than people eatin' plutonium?"

"One week ago we received two encrypted texts from an agent in Uzbekistan. The first was five words long: '*Contact made. Suspect Yaderni Renit.*' "

Thibodaux's head snapped around. "A portable nuke?"

Palmer raised a sandy eyebrow. "I had no idea you spoke Russian, Jacques."

"As a point of fact, I do not, sir." Thibodaux shook

his head. "But I do speak *threat*. I can understand 'Kill the Amercanski' and 'Let's cut his ass' in fifteen languages. Nuclear bombs fall into that category."

"You said there were two texts?" Quinn prodded. He knew Palmer liked being prompted to ensure people were engaged in the conversation.

Palmer gave a deep sigh. "Looks like he was cut off mid-message. '*Martel theory appears corre . . .*' "

"Martel?" Quinn mused. "Like Charles Martel—the Hammer that stopped the Muslim invasion into Western Europe at Poitiers?"

"That's the one. Charlemagne's granddad," the national security advisor said. "Code name for Russian agent Mikhail Ivanovich Polzin. Polzin was known for his belief in the existence of a powerful, man-portable nuke from the Cold War days. If he was correct as the text suggests, Baba Yaga has been found."

"Baba Yaga?" Thibodaux tilted his head as if trying to call back pertinent memory. "Sounds familiar . . ."

"An evil witch from a Russian fairy tale," Palmer said. "Intelligence sources back in the seventies picked up chatter about a Soviet nuclear device code-named Baba Yaga. Small and portable enough to be moved by a single man, it was thought to be double the power of similar known devices. Langley believes it to be as much as five kilotons."

"You said we're dealing with dirty bombs," Quinn mused. "A man-portable nuke is another thing altogether. Does your agent in Uzbekistan have any more information?"

"Damned little, I'm afraid." Palmer tipped his head toward a freshly covered grave in the distance. "I just presented a flag to his mother."

Thibodaux released a captive breath.

They'd all lost far too many brothers and sisters at arms over the last decade.

"Cooper was a good man," Palmer whispered. "Worldly-wise and innocent at the same time. His father's a Virginia state trooper."

"Wait," Quinn said. "Are we talking about Riley Cooper? OSI, stationed at Manas?"

"He was one of mine." Palmer nodded. "We used to hunt birds together when Riley was a boy. . . ."

Quinn gave a low whistle. "I thought I knew Riley Cooper pretty well. He was two years behind me at the Academy, but he beat me to OSI because I did Combat Rescue first. He graduated from FLETC in the OSI Basic ahead of me but came back to visit when we got our B's and C's."

FLETC was the Federal Law Enforcement Training Center near Brunswick, Georgia. B's and C's were badges and credentials, presented at graduation from OSI Basic.

"I wish I'd known," Quinn said, put out that Palmer hadn't seen fit to mention the death of a fellow agent until now. "I could have attended."

"The family requested a private ceremony," Palmer said, sensing Jericho's concern. "OSI will release a story this afternoon about him being killed by a roadside bomb."

"Riley Cooper . . ." Quinn shook his head, processing it all. Of course there were others like him. Palmer had made it clear early on that he had a special arrangement with OSI. It stood to reason that other agents Quinn knew would be part of his unit.

"He wasn't aware of you either," Palmer said. "If that makes you feel any better." He motioned for them to follow him up the steps and into the amphitheater proper, taking a seat on one of the long marble benches. A small crowd had formed outside, waiting for the changing of the guard that would happen every half hour, but they were alone inside the amphitheater.

Palmer glanced up from black, spit-shined shoes.

"At any given moment, at least a dozen credible threats against the United States fall across our radar. The Bureau and the CIA investigate the bulk of them with military Special Ops mopping up the pieces overseas. Our alphabet-soup agencies do a damn fine job of mounting a wall of defensive offense. But, as you know, some cases need less bureaucracy. Riley Cooper did jobs for me all over Central Asia. His father is my friend. I watched him grow up, so I knew I could trust him." Palmer stared back down at his feet, rocking slightly on the cool stone bench. "He wanted to be an Olympic sprinter when he was a kid. Did he ever tell you that?"

"No, sir." Quinn shook his head. Thibodaux sat completely still.

"He was so very talented," Palmer went on. "When he talked about going to Virginia Tech, I was the one who convinced him to attend the Air Force Academy. I told him he could make a difference there." He glanced up at Quinn, eyes brimming with the pain of a leader who sent young men into battle. " 'If they question why we died, tell them because our fathers lied. . . .' "

Quinn was all too familiar with the Kipling verse, written in the writer's grief of losing his only son in

World War I. "I knew Riley Cooper, sir. He was not only where he needed to be, he was where he wanted to be."

"I told him he was cut out for something big," Palmer said. "Saving the free world and all that."

"Who knows, sir?" Quinn looked out at the distant crosses. "Maybe he has."

"Maybe," Palmer said, his voice tinny and unconvinced. "But one day, in the not too distant future, I owe his parents an apology."

Thibodaux shuffled in his seat, uncomfortable seeing a superior showing so much emotion. "What was his business in Uzbekistan?"

Palmer nodded as if he realized it was time to move on. "Following a Russian agent when he was killed."

"Martel?" Quinn asked. "Is he good for the murder?"

"Martel." Palmer's normally expressive face had fallen placid from sadness and fatigue. "His body and Cooper's were discovered only a few yards apart. We have a little intel on him, but not much. Mikhail Ivanovich Polzin. Forty-one years old. Attended university in Moscow and joined the military shortly after graduation. Served as an army Spetsnaz troop and was eventually recruited for the Federal Security Service. We believe he worked *Spetsgruppa* V."

"Vympel," Jacques said, obviously impressed. "That's my old man's KGB."

"We know he saw service in Chechnya," Palmer said. "Other than that, he's been off our radar for the last several years."

"Until?" Jericho prompted.

"Until Cooper ran into him eighteen months ago in a Bishkek bazaar favored by black-market arms dealers. Some of our intel boys and girls think the Soviet Union lost track of as many as eighty Special Atomic Demolition Munitions—portable nukes—in the aftermath of its collapse. Hell, even Putin admits he can only confirm the security of their nuclear devices from the time he came into power. We believe Vympel is the unit within FSB charged with finding and retrieving these lost items."

Thibodaux leaned forward to rest massive forearms on his knees. His Transit Leather jacket hung open to reveal a black AC/DC T-shirt. "So whoever killed Cooper and Comrade Polzin got their hands on a Soviet nuke?"

"We have to assume so."

"What about the dirty bombs?" Quinn said. "Maybe it was nuclear material they found and not an intact device."

"We considered that." Palmer rubbed his eyes with a thumb and forefinger. "Cooper knew the difference between material for a dirty bomb and a portable nuke. Intelligence files regarding Baba Yaga during the Cold War noted a significant amount of plutonium was stored with her. Sources inside the Kremlin called it a package deal—Baba Yaga and her children."

Quinn looked out across the field of crosses and sighed to himself. There were those who thought al-Qaeda already possessed a nuclear device. He was no such believer, knowing from firsthand experience that though jihadi operatives clamored for a nuclear weapon at every turn, if they had a bomb, they would have already used it. The hate they carried for the West was too great to hold off and posture. The posturing would come later, on the heels of their attack.

"I'm assuming you have some sort of lead," he said, studying Palmer. "You've never been one to use your blunt instruments as investigative personnel. . . ."

"We have several in fact," the national security advisor said. "But one in particular seems tailor made for you two."

CHAPTER 6

Palmer leaned back, stretching as if he'd not slept in days. "Sources put a Venezuelan arms dealer named Valentine Zamora in Uzbekistan eleven days ago," Palmer said. "That's less than a week before Cooper sent the texts. Look up 'sick bastard' in the dictionary and you'll find this guy's photo."

"Why don't we just pick him up?" Quinn asked the obvious.

"We're playing a little waiting game. Special Purpose Islamic Regiment of Chechnya has claimed responsibility for the St. Petersburg bombing. So far, no one is taking credit for San Francisco."

Quinn nodded. More than a few jihadi groups would jump at the chance to work in concert with the Chechens toward a common goal. SPIR had no qualms about killing dozens of Russian schoolchildren if it furthered their purposes. It was well within reason to think they would move to dirty bombs if given the opportunity. If they couldn't get their hands on a weapon of mass destruction, a weapon of mass distraction would do.

"First reports are saying the bombs in both California and Russia detonated near or in ATMs. They went off within minutes of each other, presumably loaded with the nuclear material smuggled in by the dead college students."

"SPIR and al-Qaeda have plenty of ties to each other." Thibodaux shrugged.

"They do," Palmer said, "but the methods here suggest a high level of sophistication we've not seen from these organizations. We're talking about groups who both hate us but can't agree among themselves over their own brand of dogma. Someone with a certain amount of control over both is running the show here."

"And you believe that person is Zamora?" Quinn mused, half to himself. Palmer wasn't the type to blame organizations for bad behavior. He believed all terrorist acts could generally be traced back to a single despot pulling the strings. So far, he'd been proven correct.

"The Bureau suits have their eyes on a couple of Hezbollah possibles their agents followed out of Bishkek the day after Cooper was killed. One is an Iranian student named Naseer al-Karradi. His uncle is a nuclear scientist for the regime. Langley likes a Saudi merchant they tagged in Tashkent shortly after Cooper's murder. They link him to a plan to get a Soviet man-portable antiaircraft missile into Manhattan."

"They still got eyes on their suspects?" Quinn asked.

"Both Karradi and the Saudi are in the wind," Palmer said. "Every asset in Asia and Europe is looking for these guys. We don't know who's allied with who or, more importantly, who has the bomb."

"Why doesn't the Bureau like Zamora as the coordinator?" Quinn asked.

"Profilers at Quantico believe he's too unstable to

carry out this kind of orchestrated action." Palmer leaned back, looking skyward to stretch his neck. "To be honest, it's hard to disagree. Everyone who's met him says he bounces all over the place—erratic and flighty like a BB in a boxcar. But he was in Uzbekistan and he's a killer. I don't care what the Feebs say, this is too important to rule him out just yet."

"Let's go get him then," Thibodaux said.

"I'd like nothing more than to have you jerk a knot in this guy's ass, Jacques," Palmer said. "But that wouldn't get us very far. Interrogation won't do us any good at all if the bomb is moved. If he does have it, chances are his people would move it the moment we pick him up. NSA is up on all the phones we know about, but he's got access to some pretty sophisticated technology so who knows what we're missing. We need to watch for a few days, see what we can learn. The FBI can look for their boy from Bishkek. Langley can follow theirs. I want you two to check out Zamora."

Palmer reached into his jacket pocket to produce a folded piece of computer paper.

"I'll send an encrypted file with what we have to each of your phones. But the small screen won't do justice to the twisted sort of man we're dealing with. Zamora supplies heavy weapons to the Zetas Cartel in Mexico, among others." He handed the document to Quinn, who held it so Thibodaux could look as well.

Palmer looked away, apparently having seen enough.

"The dead girl was a student from the University of Matamoros. She wrote a thesis indicting the cartel's cruelty toward regular citizens, so they kidnapped her and made a gift of her to Zamora." He nodded at the photograph. "Informants in the cartel say he did this for no particular reason but to impress a sadistic girl-friend."

In another venue the girl in the picture would have been pretty. The stark whiteness of naked flesh under the flash of the crime scene photo made even Quinn, who had seen more than his share of carnage, flinch in disgust. She was stripped of her clothing and bound to a wooden bedframe on a blood-soaked mattress. Some-one had traced a sloppy outline of her body with gun-fire, stitching the bed with a dotted line of bullet holes. Zamora hadn't been any too careful with his aim, tak-ing bits of flesh and shards of bone every few shots. One of the poor girl's elbows was completely gone. Her left ear, the opposite knee, and right shoulder suf-fered the same grisly fate. A single gunshot to the center of her chest had finally ended her agony—presumably when Zamora and his girlfriend had grown bored with their game.

Quinn's gut turned. The sight of any woman in pain made him associate the victim with his own daughter or ex-wife, so much so that he had to check himself when he was around them or become maniacally over-protective.

"I think I might throw up," the big Cajun groaned. "I'm really gonna enjoy gettin' my hands on this shit-head."

"Good to hear," Palmer said, "because I want you in Florida in three days. Zamora likes to present himself as the globetrotting playboy—extravagant parties drip-ping with women and booze, expensive cars, ski get-aways to the Alps on a whim. He hosts a track day in Homestead twice a year." Palmer looked at Quinn. "Fan-cies himself quite the motorcycle racer, so this should be right up your alley. I'd like you both to try and get close to him. See if you catch anything that would indicate he's got the bomb. If you don't get anywhere, then we'll pick him up as a last resort and . . . talk to him."

Thibodaux bounced on his feet. Even his flattop seemed to stand a little taller. "Hang on now, sir," he said. "You mean I actually get to follow Chair Force on a mission?"

During the last two major operations, the mountainous Cajun had been forced to stay behind while Quinn traveled overseas. He made no secret of the fact that as a Marine used to being the tip of the spear, he'd been more than chapped over such an arrangement.

Palmer chuckled. "Mrs. Miyagi says it's about time you earned your keep."

The Cajun darkened. "She would say something like that."

Since they'd been recruited to work for Palmer, Emiko Miyagi had become the men's official trainer and quartermaster. A more enigmatic woman Quinn had never met. Perhaps it was because Japanese was one of the five languages he spoke, but she'd seemed to have an instant affection for him. For whatever reason, Thibodaux brought little more than a resigned sigh of barely hidden disdain.

"Chin up, Jacques," Quinn said. "She'll eventually warm to you."

Palmer rose from the marble bench to brush off the front of his suit.

"One thing," Quinn said, standing along with him. He reached in the pocket of his leather jacket and took out a crumpled blue bandana. "Regarding that little roadblock I was telling you about in Old Town. If you could have these identified it might lead us to who the Speaker is working with."

Palmer looked inside the bandana. "I certainly pick the right sort of man for these jobs." He smirked. "But this is the last time you're allowed to give me the finger." He rolled up the bandana and slipped it inside the pocket of his suit coat, apparently unbothered that it contained severed human body parts. "Mrs. Miyagi will set you up with a race bike to help you cozy up to Zamora. I think you could use a little female help down there."

Thibodaux's head snapped around. "You mean to tell me she's coming with us? Oh, this should be rich—"

"You misunderstand me, Jacques." Palmer winked. "Not Mrs. Miyagi. I have someone else in mind. This one's a killer, though—make no mistake about that."

Quinn groaned. He knew full well who the boss would send. His gut tightened at the thought. Sadistic, gunrunning terrorists notwithstanding, it was this woman who was likely to get him killed.

CHAPTER 7

Valentine Zamora blotted his lips with a folded handkerchief and smiled sweetly.

"I'm sure we can reach some form of agreement that is . . . mutually beneficial," he said.

His Portuguese was better than his Russian, which was the main reason he liked to do business in this particular backwater republic. Beyond the language, the added benefit of working in one of the poorest countries in the world was that officials were more easily bought. Mafia states, they called them. U.S. pundits ranked Zamora's own Venezuela among such mafia states where the criminal enterprises were not only condoned, but intermingled with the business of government. From what he knew of his father's drug empire, Valentine could hardly disagree.

Outside, a pleasant ocean breeze rustled feathery albizia trees, carrying their faintly sweet odor of tobacco, but the interior of the metal airplane hangar was stifling. The smell of jet fuel and burned engine oil hung heavy on the humid air. Monagas stood back a few steps beside a rusted single-engine Piper Cherokee that, amazingly enough, had flown in a few minutes before with General Alberto Kabbah and his aide, both of the Bissau-Guinean military. The men wore freshly pressed olive-green uniforms and sat on metal chairs behind a long folding table in the center of the hangar, as if holding court. The general wore a dress hat complete with gold scrambled eggs on the brim to befit his high rank and status. His chest held more varied medals than Idi Amin.

"Negotiations are a fluid thing," General Kabbah said, taking a drink from a bottle of Aquafina. He had an annoying way of smacking his lips that made Zamora want to cut them off.

"Yes, they are indeed," Zamora said, working to keep his voice low and even. "But need I remind you, General, that I have been doing business with your military for almost a decade? Your predecessor grew quite rich from our dealings before his . . . untimely death."

Kabbah smiled, showing what looked like more than his fair share of teeth. Everyone in the country knew he had murdered his former boss to take the post of general for himself.

"Our arrangement is a win-win for you," Zamora continued. "You are paid handsomely to look the other way when drug shipments arrive from South America. Then we pay you to look the other way a few moments longer while we put my merchandise on the same plane for the return flight. You are, in effect, getting paid double for an extra two hours of doing nothing."

The drug flights coming to West Africa were from Venezuela and organized by Zamora's father. The elder

Zamora knew nothing of the return loads of illicit weapons or the extra risk involved, but the general did not need to be bothered with such trivial details.

General Kabbah replaced the lid on his Aquafina bottle, gave the annoying pop of his lips, then set the water on the table in a show of finality. He leaned back to fold his hands across a round belly. "Still—" He smacked his lips, giving a long sigh. "The risks are greater than they used to be. The World Customs Organization and Interpol snoop around more and more each year. I would hope that larger risk would bring a more substantial reward."

"How much more substantial?" Zamora rubbed his chin, expecting this.

"Double," the general said. "But you would have my personal guarantee the price would not go up during my lifetime."

"I see," Zamora said.

Kabbah nodded his jowly head. "And I would need certain assurances that I won't end up in prison."

"You may rest assured," Zamora said. "I won't let that happen."

"Very well," General Kabbah said. "If we are in agreement. You may resume shipments on return flights as soon as the first payment arrives in my account." He gestured to his aide. "Major Bundu will see to the particulars."

"*After* the money arrives in your account?" Zamora ground his teeth. He gave the slightest flick of his wrist.

Monagas stepped forward with an aluminum briefcase. Instead of setting it on the table, he made a motion of giving it to the general, then smashed it edgewise into the man's face. Before Kabbah could react, Monagas drew a pistol from behind his back and shot him twice in the forehead. He pitched forward, slamming against the table, arms dangling at his sides.

A plume of blue smoke curled from the muzzle of Monagas's pistol.

Major Bundu sat with his mouth agape, mesmerized at the pool of blood that blossomed from under the bill of the general's fancy green hat on the white Formica tabletop.

"Now, Major . . . pardon me, *General* Bundu," Zamora said. "You see how I keep my promises? Kabbah will never end up in prison."

Bundu gulped but said nothing.

"Where I come from we have a saying." Zamora stepped forward to push the aluminum case across the table. He gestured for the newly promoted general to open it. "*Plata o plomo.* It does not translate quite so poetically into Portuguese." His eyes narrowed. "But I believe you understand the message. *Silver or lead,* the choice is yours."

Bundu patted the unopened case with a trembling hand. "I am satisfied that whatever arrangement you had with General Kabbah's predecessor will be quite acceptable to me."

"So." Zamora clapped his hands together and brought them to his face, top teeth against his knuckle. "I may assume you and your men will resume their noninterference immediately when it comes to my shipments."

"You may indeed," Bundu said.

"Very well." Zamora smiled. "I'll send a man in a few days' time to see to the next load of merchandise—

and I must warn you, I have a strict time line that must be observed."

"I und . . . erstand . . . perfec . . . tly." Bundu appeared to be having a difficult time swallowing.

"Very well," Zamora said. "You will most certainly find something extra for you if things go well." He watched as Monagas dug around on the dead general's uniform until he found a medal he liked for his collection.

Bundu looked on in morbid fascination. He forced his mouth into a tight smile. "I can assure you, the price will never go up during my lifetime."

Zamora had no sooner stepped from the stuffy confines of the metal hangar than his cell phone began to ring. All the joy from standing in the wind immediately bled from him when he heard the voice on the other end.

"Why have you not returned my calls?" The voice spoke in English but with the clipped intonation of the Yemeni Yazid Nazif.

"I have been extremely busy," Zamora said. If not for the fact that Nazif held the key to his plan, not to mention the purse strings to three hundred and fifty million dollars, Zamora would have ended the call on the spot. Instead, he worked to gently explain. "There is still some work to be done on our prize to make it functional. But I have things well in hand. Did not the first step work out as I suggested?"

"It did," the voice said. "Why did you not tell us of the Chechens?"

"I merely allowed them to take the credit." Zamora shrugged. "It was the only way to get the timing correct."

"Did you not consider the fact that they themselves would want the device?"

Zamora ran a hand through his hair. "Of course I did," he said. He neglected to mention the fact that the Chechens had paid him handsomely to choose the target for the St. Petersburg bomb action. Now they were, in fact, clamoring for more of the same. If they knew about Baba Yaga, they would stop at nothing to get their hands on her.

Nazif's voice was breathy, snakelike. "Need I remind you of our timetable?"

"No, you do not," Zamora said, rolling his eyes at Monagas as he stepped out the door, wiping blood off his hands. "If you will recall, it was I who suggested such a ripe venue in the first place."

"We have paid a great sum of money for this thing," Nazif said. "And with such a large sum come certain expectations. Do you understand?"

"Of course," Zamora said. "But things happen—"

"We have no interest in excuses," Nazif said, and ended the call.

Bundu stepped out of the hangar just in time to see Zamora fling his phone into the weeds, cursing vehemently in Spanish. The Venezuelan stood there for a full minute, panting and glaring toward the sea. At length his breathing slowed and he looked at the newly promoted general.

"Well, don't just stand there," he said. "Go bring back my phone."

CHAPTER 8

Austin, Texas

Since the days after 9/11, Pastor Mike Olson and his wife Deanne, had nurtured a dream. Death and fear and hate had no place in the world, particularly when it came to religion. An open-minded couple, they allowed all men the right to worship according to their own conscience while adhering strictly to their own beliefs. Deanne was an accomplished musician who ran the youth ministry at the Sacred Peace Interfaith Church. It had been she who'd first voiced the dream a Peace Choir made up entirely of children of all ethnicities and faiths. What had taken over a decade to fully form was now just weeks from becoming a reality. Through a televised extravaganza they would show the world that children—and everyone—could come together through music, no matter their views about what God looked like or what He liked to be called.

Mike wiped a tear from his eye and sniffed. Deanne sat beside him and patted the back of his hand. They read the letter on the desk together for the third time.

"I just can't believe it, hon," the pastor said. He pushed a lock of blond bangs out of his eyes. "He's paying the entire bill."

Graying around the temples, Olson hadn't changed his John Denver hairstyle since he'd graduated from the University of Texas in 1989. He'd gone on to get his master's in divinity at UT as well and it was then that he'd met Deanne, the daughter of a local Presbyterian minister. She shared his goals in the ministry, and like him, wanted nothing more than a family. Though the good Lord hadn't seen fit to bless them with children of their own, He had provided them with an outstanding youth group—and now this saint of a man, Mr. Valentine.

"The Erwin Center . . ." Deanne squeezed his hand. "Can you believe what we talked about all those years ago is actually happening? A choir of four hundred children from all over the world and now seating for over fifteen thousand. Oh, Mike, this could make a real difference. Mr. Valentine is truly an instrument in the Lord's hands."

CHAPTER 9

December 19
Mt. Vernon, Virginia

Emiko Miyagi reached across the seat of the fire-engine-red bike to hand Quinn the end of a ratchet strap so he could tighten it down to the wooden pallet for transport. Presumably in her early forties—though she could have been considerably younger—the enigmatic woman had her black hair pulled back in a stubby ponytail, exposing the nape of her neck. She moved easily, each action with a specific purpose but without apparent forethought. Hers was an egoless air. She wore formfitting jeans and a red three-button polo, open enough at the neck to show the hint of the mysterious tattoo above her breast.

Neither Quinn nor Thibodaux could figure out what it was. They caught no more than a glimpse of the thing during her beloved yoga sessions or defensive tactics when she was kicking the stuffing out of both of them, often at the same time. Neither was brave enough to stare at her chest long enough to ascertain the true nature of the tattoo.

She patted the small seat on the angular red bike. "Zamora rides a Yamaha R1," she said absent any trace of a Japanese accent, though English was her second language. "It should help you get close to him if you ride the same motorcycle. I've done a bit of work on this one to coax out a little more horsepower, so watch yourself around the corners."

She leaned across the bike to pull in the clutch and pressed the starter, bringing the R1 to life. The throaty roar sounded more like a pair of motorcycles running together than a single race bike. "It is not the fastest motorcycle available, but with your riding skill, you could beat him if you wish."

"I should probably avoid that," Quinn said.

Miyagi killed the engine, showing the hint of a smile from her normally placid face. The guttural howl of the uneven firing sequence from under the seat was enough to put a grin on a marble statue.

"Palmer-san believes Agent Trainee Garcia will provide the bait you need to draw this man in close enough to see if he has the device."

"Yes," Quinn mused, picturing Ronnie Garcia's long legs and broad smile. "She's definitely good bait."

He hooked the strap to an eyebolt on the pallet and worked it tight before tying off the trailing end. Satisfied the Yamaha was secure, he looked up at Miyagi. Apart from her assignment to keep Quinn and Thibodaux trained and outfitted, she was also a defensive tactics instructor at the CIA training facility outside Williamsburg known as The Farm.

Garcia had been in training there for almost two months now, and she and Quinn had not parted on the best of terms.

"How's she doing?" he asked.

"She works harder than most," Miyagi said. "Though she does not need to. I suspect she is trying to impress someone. Her shooting has improved dramatically—and it was not too bad to begin with."

Quinn gave a slow nod, thinking about the times she'd saved his life. He started to say as much when the BlackBerry on his belt began to buzz.

Mrs. Miyagi motioned for him to take it and excused herself.

"Daddy?" It was Mattie, his seven-year-old daughter.

Quinn melted inside each time he heard her voice. She had his dark hair and copper complexion, but Kim's accusing blue eyes.

"Three more days!" she squealed.

"You're funny, sweet pea," he said. "Christmas is still over a week away."

"I know that, silly," she said, sounding more and more like her mother used to, all those years ago when they were young and happy together. "I know when Christmas is. I mean when you're coming home. I have a big purple circle around December twentieth on my calendar."

"Yeah," Quinn sighed. He had to be in Miami on the twentieth. "About that . . . how would you feel if I celebrated Christmas with you a little later this year?"

There was silence, the rustle of paper, and a sniff.

"You okay, sweet pea?"

Fortunately, Mattie had not inherited Kim's unforgiving nature. "I'm sad," she said. "But you tell me what day and I'll put a circle around it."

"Let's make it January twenty-fifth. One month. If I can be there earlier I will."

"Okay," Mattie sighed. "Will you be sure and be here?"

"Count on it," Quinn said, hoping he wasn't telling his daughter yet another lie. "Can you put Mom on the line?"

Mattie giggled. "She's been on for the whole time," she said. "You're my bestie, Dad."

Quinn heard a faint click on the line.

"You still there, sweetie?"

"She hung up." It was Kim's voice, quiet, brooding like a glowing ember in a steady breeze.

Unable to stand the nights of sleepless worry, she'd told him to hit the road not long after he returned from his first deployment with OSI. She still loved him, she'd said, still wanted to keep in touch, but as long as he carried a gun and put himself in harm's way for a living, she couldn't be married to him. As much as he loved her, as much as he wanted to quit and work as a greengrocer or a postman, Quinn knew he'd die if he did anything else.

When he'd given the broken thirteenth-century Japanese dagger Yawaraka-Te back to Miyagi, she'd simply said: "It broke doing what it was made to do—and so it is with you Quinn-san. *The blade must cut, even at its own peril.*"

Quinn waited for Kim to say something else, anything. She didn't.

"How are you doing?" he said, craving a few more words in spite of himself.

"We're fine," she said. "My mom's retiring this year so that will help out with carting Mattie around to orchestra practice and indoor soccer and everything else."

"I don't remember being that busy when I was seven," Quinn said, a weak attempt at conversation.

"You were never seven," Kim said. "Your dad once told me you popped out already grown up and ready to pick a fight with the doctor for putting your mom in such an unladylike position."

Quinn sighed. "Guess you heard I can't be there till later," he said, sounding more sheepish than he would have liked. It didn't suit him.

"I heard," Kim said.

"I'm really sorry," Quinn went on. The conversation was beginning to make his head hurt. "If it wasn't extremely important, I'd blow it off."

"I know where we rank, Jericho," Kim said, her voice quieter now, but just as acid.

"That's not what I meant."

"I know," she said. "But I gotta tell you, I don't deserve to worry myself to death all the time and Mattie doesn't deserve to grow up with a part-time father."

"Okay," Quinn said. "I am sorry, though. Someday I'll be able to explain."

Kim sniffed. "Seriously, Jer," she said. "Don't worry about it. To tell you the truth, I stopped putting circles around important dates on my calendar long before we ever got divorced."

CHAPTER 10

Moscow, Idaho

Professor Matthew Pollard leaned against the lectern with both hands and tried to identify the new couple sitting at the back of the amphitheater classroom. At six-four he was too tall for the lectern, causing him to stoop.

Given his own way, he would have been wearing an unbleached hemp shirt and a pair of surf shorts, but his wife—not to mention the dean of the College of Philosophy—insisted he dress like a professor. Wavy black hair was pulled back in a short stub of a ponytail. His neatly trimmed beard would have made him look "bad" if not for his easy grin and the slightly too-large academic corduroy jacket complete with suede elbow patches.

He flipped through a notebook, pretending to look at it while he glanced up at the two strangers.

They weren't his students. Pollard knew each of the fifty-three moldable freshman minds in his ethics class by face if not by name. The man was in his mid-twenties, blond and shaggy. He was likely a local, wearing blue

jeans and a faded Carhartt denim jacket—typical dress
for winter in northern Idaho. The woman wore tight
jeans and a fashionable black turtleneck, leaning forward, plump and partridge-like, on the back row of the
small auditorium. She held a green jacket across her
lap and looked toward Pollard from beneath a set of
heavy black bangs. Her head tilted as if she wanted to
give the impression of paying attention, but the con-
tours of her bronze face were slack with boredom. She
reminded him of someone he'd known long ago, someone from a time that he did his best to forget.

This particular class—he called it Who Are the
Monsters?—was known for its heated, gloves-off de-
bate. But the strangers didn't seem the least bit interested in the subject matter of his class. They appeared
to be focused solely on him, studying him like an in-
sect under a magnifying glass. He tried to calm his racing heart. He was an ethics teacher now, nothing more.

A restless buzz ran through the students and he
pushed the thoughts away.

". . . going to give us our final today, Professor Pollard?" A tall girl slouching on the front row of seats
rescued him. Dressed in a black knee-length canvas
jacket festooned with lengths of bicycle chain, she
asked the question the rest of the class was dying to
have answered.

Her name was Katherine, but she preferred the
name Crash. Of the students who showed up regularly,
only this one seemed to grasp even a tiny shred of his
message. Three-inch platform boots with gaudy chrome
buckles, and a mop of coal-colored bangs that gave her
the appearance of a baby face Hitler, belied her true intelligence. Pollard thought she might be a pretty girl if

not for the fact she was running from any and all aspects of life she thought could be considered normal. A pierced tongue and the tattoo of a fishhook at the corner of her heavily rouged lips told the world she flowed an entirely different direction than the mainstream.

"As a matter of fact I am." Pollard nodded, trying not to focus on the strangers in the back. "Remember our very first assignment?"

"Sure." Crash shrugged, but sat up straighter as she always did once they started a discussion. "You had us define evil."

"Okay, then," Pollard said, beginning to pace back and forth on the raised platform behind the lectern. "We've read, discussed, debated, written papers . . . and read some more. Some of you believe you can now define evil. So now, a semester later, let's drill down."

He looked directly at Crash's eyes. Despite her counterculture costume, they sparkled with inquisitive brightness. "Is it ever right to do something evil in order to achieve an end state that is good?"

Crash rolled her big eyes and tossed her pen on the desk. "Governments use that excuse all the—"

"Save it." Pollard raised an open palm to shush her. "That's your final. Give me between fifteen hundred and two thousand words on whether or not evil actions can be used for good purpose. Quote three sources from your reading this semester." He smiled. "Only one of them can be me and you may not use Chuck Norris as a source."

A boy with a buzz cut leaning against the side wall raised his hand. "Professor, how many pages does it have to be?"

Pollard sighed. "Go for word count, Royce. If you

give me something that's twenty pages long and huge font, I'll move you into my own personal 'evil' category. Same goes for you overachievers who use those tiny, unreadable fonts so you can cram more in to a few pages. That, my friends is the pure epitome of evil. E-mail your papers to me by next Wednesday."

The woman in the back stood and motioned for the man in the Carhartt jacket to do the same. There was no doubt that it was she who was in charge. She flicked her bangs, and made momentary eye contact with Pollard, as if she wanted him to remember her, then walked out with her apparent lackey close on her heels.

"Okay." Pollard rubbed his beard, trying to get the image of the dark woman out of his head. "I'm expecting great things here. . . ."

He watched Crash as she gathered her books and shoved them in a backpack with a gaudy red anarchy symbol painted on the back. For all her posturing against "the man," for all her outward trappings of rebellion, Pollard could see the goodness and intensity in her eyes. She'd grow out of her funk and become a doctor or a lawyer or some other high-powered professional. She was that smart and that good.

He, on the other hand, was an entirely different story. Oh, he might put on a good show, but no matter what sort of academic haircut and tweed jacket they stuffed him into, he would never be able to shake his past.

Matt Pollard knew all too well how to define evil. Something deep down in his gut told him the two visitors to his class had come to remind him of that fact.

*   *   *

By the time Pollard made it from his office to the parking lot, he'd managed to convince himself that the visitors were just curiosity-seeking locals. He'd grown to be an expert at rationalizing things away. He tossed his unbleached canvas book bag in the backseat of his silver-blue Prius and climbed in behind the wheel. He'd ditched the tweed for a fleece jacket made from recycled soda bottles and wore a Nepalese wool beanie against the overcast winter day. He was tall and fit, and apart from the rumpled clothing, he carried himself with a military bearing. He looked a decade younger than his thirty-seven years and could have passed for a student rather than a professor.

His cell phone rang before he made it out of the lot.

"Pick up," Pollard said, activating the hands-free mike. He grinned when he heard Marie's voice.

"How's that sexy wife of mine?" Pollard pushed through a stale yellow traffic light and was surprised to see a white Ford Explorer shoot the red light behind him.

"I have Ellie lined up to babysit." Marie's honeyed voice purred from the dash speaker.

"That's good. . . ." Pollard watched in the rearview mirror as the white Explorer fell into the flow of traffic two cars back. "Really good," he mumbled.

"You don't even know what I'm talking about, do you?"

Marie's teasing yanked him pack to reality.

"Sorry, honey," he confessed, an eye still watching the Explorer. "I really don't."

"Wow," Marie laughed. She had to be used to him after thirteen years. "For a genius professor you'd forget your shoes if you didn't stub your toes all the time."

Marie's family sprang from Bremerton, Washington, and her easygoing Pacific Northwest demeanor came through even when she was miffed. "You know you have to guess now, right?"

Pollard tapped the wheel, thinking. The white SUV stayed glued to his bumper as he another corner.

"Listen," he said, biting his bottom lip. "You're going to think I'm crazy, but someone might be following me."

"Oh no, you don't, Mr. Matthew," his wife chided. "You're not getting off that easy—"

"Seriously," Pollard said, fighting to keep calm.

He took another right.

The Explorer followed.

"You're a bona fide genius," Marie said. "Lose them and get your butt home. Simon is getting on my last nerve and we have tickets—"

"I'm serious, sweetheart." The white SUV maneuvered around the only remaining car on the road and moved up just inches behind the Prius.

"Maybe they just happen to be going the same direction." Marie's voice held a frightened edge.

"Maybe," Pollard said, but his churning gut told him otherwise. His past was hunting him down. "I'm not far away, but I'll make a block before I come home and see what happens. If I can't lose them I'm going to call the police."

Sweat beaded on his upper lip, hidden by his dark beard. He turned right again, a block before his street.

The SUV stayed on his tail, unwavering. He could make out the faces of the two earlier visitors to his classroom. The blond man wore a ball cap and sunglasses and leaned forward from the backseat. The woman sat in the passenger seat; her eyes still sneered with boredom. The driver was a smallish Hispanic man with a craggy face he'd never seen before.

Pollard swallowed hard. "Take Simon to the bedroom," he said, feeling sick. "Lock the door and get my shotgun out of the closet—"

Nothing but dead air crackled over the speakers.

"Marie," Pollard shouted at the silence. "Marie! Are you still—"

"Matthew? You sound absolutely flummoxed." The voice was cold and soulless. "You have a beautiful wife, such an innocent child. Come home so you can formally introduce us."

Pollard's retched, his throat seared with acid dread.

He shoved the gas pedal to the floor and whipped the wheel sharply left, spinning the little Prius in the narrow residential street. Metal shrieked and groaned as the front fender careened off the tailgating SUV's driver's door, then slid down the side. He caught the glint of a cruel grin on the woman's face as he sped past toward his wife and son.

CHAPTER 11

Pollard burst through the front door.

"Marie!"

A male voice answered him from the around the corner in the parlor where Marie kept her piano. "We're all here, my friend," it said. "Please, come join us."

Pollard froze at the doorway when he saw the dark man with a thin mustache lounging on the love seat. His legs were crossed and a glowing cigar hung from his fingers. Marie sat in a matching chair to his right. She was tall and slender with short caramel-blond hair pulled back with a red polka-dot band. Her normally wide smile had fallen away and her lips parted in shock. Her chest shook with uncontrolled sobs as she clutched their squirming baby in her arms as if he was a life buoy.

A thuggish man with a crooked nose and broad shoulders crowded in between the back of the chair and the wall, towering over her, arms folded across a chest. A sparse beard did little to hide the burn scars on his lips and chin. The glint in his eye said brute intimidation was a favorite pastime.

The front door slammed as the man and woman

from the SUV came in behind Pollard. He shot a glance over his shoulder and saw that a third man, the Hispanic driver, limped badly. His heart sank. Five to one were impossible odds.

"Matt . . ." Marie looked up when he came in the room. "Who are these people?"

Simon, just under a year old and teething, sucked on a peeled carrot. He was just beginning to take a few steps and stood on Marie's knee, holding the edge of her chair.

Pollard's face twitched with rage. "What are you doing in my house?"

The man on the love seat looked back and forth from Matthew to Marie. At length, he turned his body to face Marie, leaning forward with his elbows on his knees.

She coughed as the cloud of smoke from his cigar enveloped her.

"You must forgive me, my dear. I've been hopping from Africa to New York then Spokane. . . . I must confess the last several hours have been a blur." The man yawned, blinking as if he was about to fall asleep. He shot a glance up at Pollard, batting his eyelashes. "I am shocked your husband has not mentioned me. We were . . . Matthew, would you have called us friends?"

"Hardly."

"Pity." The man gave an exhausted sigh. "I would have called us friends. My name is Valentine Zamora. The man behind you is my associate, Julian Monagas. We had the good fortune to work with your husband some years ago."

"You know these people?" Marie turned toward Pollard, eyes pleading to understand.

Zamora stood, reaching for the baby.

Marie screamed, but Monagas yanked her back by her hair.

Pollard roared, bolting to protect his family no matter the odds. Something heavy caught him across the back of the head, driving him to his knees. He pushed himself up with one arm, holding his head with the other, waiting for the waves of nausea to pass.

Zamora stood beside the love seat, an anxious Simon pressed to his chest. His actions were soft and gentle, but his face and words made it clear he had dispensed with all other niceties.

"I find myself in need of your expertise, Matthew," he said, looking up at Marie. "Did you know your dear husband is a nuclear genius?"

Tears streamed down her face, but she didn't move.

"It doesn't matter." Zamora shrugged. "There is often much we do not know about our loved ones. Pack a bag. You are coming with us."

"My family?"

Zamora cocked his head to one side. "Do as I say and they will be fine."

"I'm not leaving them."

Zamora flicked his fingers, and Pollard heard the men behind him step away.

"There's only one reason you'd need me, Valentine," Pollard said. "I'm not going to help you blow anything up."

"Oh, Matthew," Zamora said, giving a weary sigh. "Let me see. . . . How shall I explain myself?" He bounced Simon to keep him calm, but looked down at Marie with a leering eye. "Some men prefer to see their women in a flimsy negligee, the delicate lace of underthings hiding just enough to enhance the mystery of the feminine form." He glanced up at the dark woman who stood in the doorway behind Pollard. "Lourdes, darling, how do I like my women?"

"Naked." She chuckled.

"Precisely," Zamora said. "I despise mystery. I want to have all the goods exposed and on the table, so to speak." He craned forward with narrowed eyes, staring at Marie but speaking to Pollard. "So let me be plain. You will help me do anything I ask or I will quite literally rip this lovely boy into tiny pieces."

Marie choked on a sob.

"I know you, Valentine." Pollard set his quivering jaw. Inside, his bowels churned. "My family has seen your face. No matter what I do, they're as good as dead once we leave."

"Tsk, tsk," Zamora said, stroking Simon's sandy curls. "You have serious trust issues, my friend."

Pollard wracked his brain, searching for any alternative to what he was about to say. Tears poured in earnest from his eyes as he looked back and forth from his precious little boy to a baffled Marie. He ground his teeth until he thought they might shatter.

"Bullshit!" he sniffed, his voice harsh and cold. "You hate loose ends the way you hate mystery. You're forgetting, I've seen what you do with witnesses."

The Venezuelan's lips turned white under his pencil-thin mustache. He rocked the baby back and forth. "You can't be certain. It's not worth—"

Pollard rose to his full height, fists clenched at his side. His shoulders shook with rage.

"Kill us all now!" Pollard demanded through clenched teeth. "We are all already dead, and I know it."

Zamora's flat-nosed thug, Monagas, gave a startled jerk, yanking Marie's head back by her hair. Marie's eyes bulged like they would pop out of her head.

Pollard could feel the three from the SUV loom closer behind him, but he didn't care.

Zamora took a measured breath, clutching the baby close to smell his hair. At length, he dropped the burning cigar on the carpet and drew a black pistol from under his jacket. Finger on the trigger, he pressed it gently to Simon's cheek, and then looked at Marie with a sickening smile.

"You see? No mystery here, my darling. You should speak to your husband. His attitude is about to make your child very dead." The words dripped from his mouth like poison. "He seems to have lost his way."

Marie's lips moved, but she was too terrified to speak. Unable to turn her head because Monagas still had a fist around her hair, her eyes shot frantically between her husband and her little boy. She blinked bloodshot eyes at a heartbroken Pollard.

"Matt?" she pleaded.

He met her gaze, begging for her trust as he struggled to quiet his quaking legs. Marie's was a world of playgroups and Pampered Chef parties. She knew little of his past and could not fathom such brutality. A brutality he thought he'd left behind, dead and buried.

He locked eyes with Zamora. His words spilled out in ragged, panting breaths.

"You're an intelligent man, Valentine. Do you believe killing my son would force me to comply? You have me cornered. That makes me more dangerous than you could ever imagine."

Someone attempted to grab his arm from behind—

and got an elbow to the nose for his trouble. Pollard heard the snick of a pistol cocking near his head, but he didn't bother to turn around.

Simon batted at the barrel of Zamora's pistol with chubby hands, cooing, oblivious to the danger.

"Move the gun away from my son or shoot me now," Pollard whispered, surprised at the sudden calm that washed over him. "Otherwise, I'm going to beat you to death."

The room seemed to freeze as Zamora considered the situation. Grinning like a madman, he pointed the pistol at Pollard, his chest heaving with the first signs of real emotion.

Pollard met his stare with stony resolve. "It was a grave mistake to take away my hope."

Zamora's face twitched and then erupted into laughter. He shoved the pistol behind his back and pushed the baby toward Pollard.

"Take him," he said, suddenly sounding fatigued. "I must admit, I forgot how well you play this game. I will leave some people to keep your wife company. You may speak to her daily via the Internet." He raised a dark brow and flicked his hand toward the front door. "Provided you do your part and cooperate. Forget packing a bag. We'll purchase what you need en route."

Pollard's shoulders slumped. He gave an almost imperceptible nod.

"Matt! You're not actually going with him?" Marie gasped. "What is happening?"

Zamora nodded toward Monagas, who instantly released her hair.

Pollard handed her the baby and took them both in his arms.

"*Apurate*!" Zamora snapped his fingers. "As lovely as this scene is, my dear Matthew, you have a plane to catch. Say your quaint good-byes and let us be on our way."

Marie's shoulders quaked as Pollard held her to him, breathing in the smell of her and his child.

"You can't help him hurt anyone," she whispered, her voice soft against his neck.

"I won't let it come to that," Pollard lied. There was nothing he would not do to save his family.

"I mean it, Matt," she hissed, regaining the iron will that had drawn him to her in the first place. "No matter what happens to us."

Pollard kissed her long and hard, their tears mixing against moist cheeks. He held her shoulders firmly as he pulled away, looking directly into her eyes. He knew he'd probably never see her again.

"Trust me. Like you said, I'm a genius."

Every word stuck in his throat. He'd brought this misery on his family. Valentine Zamora was evil, the exemplification of what he wanted his students to write about—but Pollard knew he had no one to blame but himself.

CHAPTER 12

Valentine Zamora stood on the Pollards' front porch beside a pouting Lourdes. A wind chime made of colorful shards of pottery clanged softly over their heads. Together, they watched Monagas load the professor into the backseat of the white SUV. There was no need to tie him. He was restrained enough by his emotions. The fool would do exactly what he was asked now that his beloved family was in jeopardy. Love complicated things that way.

Jorge's leg had been injured when Pollard had hit the SUV with his Prius, and he iced it while he waited inside with an inconsolable Marie and her baby.

Lourdes stomped her foot. She had a certain smell about her when she was angry. Though not unpleasant, it reminded Zamora of burning sugar. "You grow tired of me?" she snapped. "That is why you toss me to the side like a piece of garbage!"

He gave her shoulders a squeeze and looked down into the black depths of her gaze. When he was a young boy, Valentine's Iranian-born mother would often warn him of *Cheshm-Zakhm*—the evil eye. The phrase literally meant to strike a blow with one's eye.

Two years before, when Zamora had first met Lourdes Lopez, his mother's warning was the first thing that
had come to his mind.

He'd been at a bar near Bullhead City, Nevada, to
discuss the need for certain firearms and explosives
with a group of methamphetamine dealers looking to
expand their territory. The bar—located well outside
town—was a confusing rabbit warren of separate
rooms and gaudy stages where all sorts of illicit behavior, labeled "special events" by the establishment, took
place. Raucous laughter, cheers, and even screams sometimes wafted into the main barroom at each opened
door. Assorted pieces of underwear, apparently do-
nated by patrons in moments of abandon, had been
nailed to every inch of the clapboard walls. The entire
place stunk of sweat and stale urine. Zamora found it
exhilarating.

While waiting for his contact, a series of muffled
cheers drew Zamora toward a side room through the
shadows behind the main bar. The whistling and applause grew louder as he approached. A deadly glare
combined with a folded fifty-dollar bill got him past
the fat baldy with a flashlight guarding the door.

The intense beam of a spotlight hit him full in the
face as soon as the fat guy pulled open the door. As
Zamora's eyes adjusted from the darkness of the outer
barroom, the stark image of a woman filled his vision.
She faced him dead-on, wearing only faded blue jeans
and a pushup bra of white lace that contrasted beauti-
fully with the rich bronze and pink of her flushed skin.
The muscles of her face twitched as he joined the
chanting crowd in the packed room. Blue-black hair
was cut short in a Cleopatra style with bangs straight

across severely painted brows and eyes as sharp as straight razors. She trapped his gaze the moment he looked at her as surely as if her stare had been made up of steel jaws. Full lips, tinted with metallic green makeup, clenched tight in intense concentration. Her entire body quivered; her face ran with beads of sweat.

Straining less than ten feet from the door, she leaned forward, groping the air for him with long, tan arms. The tendons in her neck were drawn into tight cords.

"Take me," she hissed through clenched teeth. Blood-red nails beckoned him closer. "Grab my hands, quickly!"

Entranced, Zamora had stepped to her. The strength in her hands still haunted him. She'd grabbed the lapels of his shirt, digging her nails into his chest. There was a smell . . . no, a taste of burnt sugar as she leaned in, straining to try and kiss him with trembling lips.

A frenzied cheer erupted from the mob of onlookers ringing the edges of the room.

It was only then, startled from his trance by all the yelling, that Zamora had even noticed the other woman. A blonde, she was similarly dressed in jeans and a bra but facing the opposite direction. Two shining steel hooks pierced floral tattoos over her shoulder blades, pulling the skin away from a gaunt body. Lines of blood ran from each set of wounds and down the naked flesh of her back. A length of sturdy chain connected her to an identical set of hooks piercing the back of the dark woman, the woman who now clutched his hands.

"Be still!" the dark woman gasped.

Helpless to do anything but obey, Zamora had frozen in place. Inch by agonizing inch, the dark woman had pulled herself toward him, using his weight as an anchor to pull the blonde toward a red line drawn in the middle of the tile floor.

The tattooed woman screamed as one of the hooks ripped through her flesh. She pedaled backward to keep the other hook from tearing, crossing the line and thereby conceding the contest.

And thus, with two stainless-steel hooks and a length of chain hanging from the smooth flesh of her back, Lourdes Lopez had fallen into Valentine's arms. He had good enough looks—and, more important, enough money—that he was accustomed to taller, more refined women with the look of swimsuit models, but this creature with smallish breasts, powerful thighs, and a heavy brow had left the bar with him that night and followed him faithfully everywhere. Every day when he'd looked at her over the ensuing years, he had been struck by the darkness of her eyes.

Cheshm-Zakhm indeed.

Others might find her deep brow and the willingness to bite the heads off baby chicks frightening. To Valentine Zamora, such a multifaceted woman was intriguing—or at least she had been.

Now, on Pollard's porch, he reached to stroke the back of her head. "I am in dire need of someone I can trust at this moment," he said.

She shrugged him away. "Maybe this is only a convenient time to scrape me off your boots?" She shot a glance at the SUV. "My love, I beg you to let Julian stay here with the pitiful woman and her filthy whelp."

Zamora put a finger to her cheek and turned her face toward him. "My darling," he said. "Where I am going, I need Monagas with me."

"I should be with you."

"I know," he said, but not feeling it himself. She was right. It was time for a much-needed break. "I need you here."

Always one to respond to his needs above her own, she gave him a sullen nod. She sighed, staring out at the SUV and Pollard.

"You trust this weakling?"

"Don't let him fool you," Zamora said. "We have his wife and baby so we can control him, but he's a brilliant man with two doctorates. His expertise in the U.S. Navy was in nuclear devices. He can and will do what I need him to do."

"I hate babies," Lourdes muttered under her breath, uninterested in any more specifics.

"Chin up, my darling," Zamora said. "This should be great fun for you." He waved at a despondent Pollard, who slumped in the SUV, leaning his head against a window, beaten. "When our professor is finished with what we need him to do, you may kill the woman and her child in whatever manner pleases you. I only ask that you keep them alive until that time."

"Must I keep them comfortable?" Lourdes asked, pouting.

Zamora dipped his head toward the SUV. "Enough to speak to him online each day."

"So I can have a little fun?" the dark woman brightened.

"Just don't kill them." Zamora chuckled, afraid to guess what she had in mind.

"Yet," she reminded him, a quiet grin crossing her long face.

"See." He gave her a pinch on the backside, hard

enough to make her flinch. Anything else, she would have ignored. "I told you you'd enjoy it. Now, Monagas and I need to hurry. We have another surprise for the authorities to keep them guessing while we get Professor Pollard set. I think this might amuse you as well."

CHAPTER 13

A misshapen sun squatted smugly on the horizon over Biscayne Bay, its December warmth pushing moist fingers of ground fog across the racetrack, streaked black from thousands of spinning tires.

Quinn leaned into the fifteenth and final corner of his fourth lap. It was shallow and relatively easy, but he felt the bike wobble when he caught a glimpse of Veronica Garcia standing beside Thibodaux along the fence. As in life, the bike generally went the direction the eyes were pointed.

He poured on the gas, putting the sight of the beautiful woman behind him to begin another lap. Cranking his head as far to the left as it would go, he pushed the purring Yamaha R1 hard over as he took the third turn, tickling his inside knee against the pavement. Emerging from number three, his head snapped quickly right, then left, as he slalomed through four and five before standing up to gain speed on the relatively long straight-away toward the next turn.

Riding in general and racing in particular were good metaphors for living. Quinn looked in the direction he wanted his bike to go, all the while focusing on the moment he was in. And the uneasy tension at seeing Ronnie Garcia translated directly from hand to handlebar to wheel.

The throaty brap of the R1's cross-plane engine and the humming vibration of spinning tires against the track mere inches below his boots kept Quinn glued to the "now" of his ride. A healthy respect for Homestead's hairpin corners forced him to think and look well ahead. The speed and turns he could handle. Veronica Garcia, however, might just get him killed.

Jacques Thibodaux leaned across the low rail, biceps bulging from the arms of a gray T-shirt, his back flared in a massive V. His eyes were glued to Jericho as he took a red and white Yamaha R1 around the eighth turn, a hairpin corner on the far side of the roughly U-shaped course.

Without turning his head, the big Cajun spoke to the buxom Latina woman leaning against the rail beside him.

"You ready for this, cher?"

The daughter of a Cuban mother and Russian father, Veronica "Ronnie" Garcia was fluent in the languages of both parents. Nearly thirty, she was tall with strong legs and the broad shoulders of collegiate softball player. A white tank top and matching terry-cloth short shorts displayed the delicious curves of her rich café latte skin. Black hair pulled back in a thick ponytail that matched her round Hollywood-starlet sunglasses.

The breeze toyed with her hair. "You trying to psych me up for battle, Jacques?"

"Hell yes, I am," he said, putting on his best gunnery sergeant bark. "Take a stance and give me a loud, vicious, tigerlike growl. . . ."

She turned up her nose. "Seriously?"

"No," he chuckled. "It's somethin' my drill sergeant used to yell at us. I reckon it don't really fit what we're doing. In my experience, lovin' ought to be scream-your-head-off loud—killin's best done quietly."

The woman smiled, turning back to watch Quinn make another lap around the track. "How could a girl disagree with that?"

Garcia had worked with Jericho before in Western China and the mountains of Afghanistan—a mission that had almost gotten her killed. Her behavior and bravery—along with a helpful recommendation from the president—had earned her an appointment as an operations officer candidate in the CIA. Palmer had pulled her out of her training at Camp Peary for this mission, hoping she would be the type to catch Valentine Zamora's eye.

Thibodaux watched as Quinn took another sharp turn at speed, dragging a knee. He swooped the bike through the gentle curve at the ninth turn, then popped it back upright on the long straightaway until the next set of corners. Even as a motorcyclist himself, the big Cajun found watching his friend hurtle around the concrete track at speeds well over a hundred miles an hour made his teeth hurt.

The throaty moan of Quinn's Yamaha grew louder as he approached, then quickly faded as he sped away toward the first set of turns on his next lap.

"I wish our dirtbag would get his ass out here," Thibodaux said, leaning his chest against the fence and rattling the chain link.

Garcia looked up with a sly wink. "You're not the one with your boobs and butt cheeks hanging out of your clothes to bait him in. I should be the one whining."

"You watch yourself, cher." Thibodaux wagged a finger at her. "Valentine Zamora is a bad dude. You get a chance to read the file?"

Ronnie glanced up, leaning forward, both elbows propped against the fence. The muscles in her long legs showed almost orange in the early light. "I read enough. Sleazebag gunrunning playboy with ties to Hezbollah, FARC, and AQAP. Daddy is some muckity in the Venezuelan government who'd just as soon disown him. Mommy is an Iranian diplomat's daughter and spoils him rotten. By eighteen, junior got himself kicked out of University of Texas for a couple of rapes. . . . One girl disappeared so he's most likely a murderer too. Mommy convinced Daddy to pull some political strings and got charges dropped and him admitted to U of Oregon, where he promptly started his guns and bombs business supplying hairy, unwashed environmental terrorists on the West Coast."

Finished, Garcia turned up her nose. "I shouldn't complain about showing a little skin on such a beautiful morning. I'd take my shirt off just to catch this son of a bitch."

"I got the best job in the world," Jacques said to no one in particular.

"Anyway—" Garcia ignored him. "It doesn't hurt my feelings to get away from The Farm for a few hours." Her voice grew softer as she gazed across the infield at Quinn. "It's not too bad seeing Jericho either. He and I never could seem to get our schedules to work out after he got back from visiting his daughter—so I've had nothing to do but hit the books."

Thibodaux turned his head to study her. "Our buddy Mr. Quinn is a mighty private soul," he said. "Just so you know, he's never said a word about what happened between you two."

Garcia shrugged, sighing heavily as Quinn roared past again in a red and white blur. "I'm pretty sure his ex-wife happened. He was on the phone with her earlier and it had to be, what? Two in the morning in Alaska?"

"Never can seem to make a choice between her and any other woman," Thibodaux said. "Can he?"

"Yeah, well." Garcia gazed out at the track. "That in itself is a choice."

"Mmm." Thibodaux gave an understanding nod. The way Quinn clung to the idea that he'd someday get back with his ex-wife bordered on insanity. "I never met the woman," he said, "but he made a damn poor trade if you ask me."

"Thanks, Jacques, but I—"

A high whistle came from the race bays behind them, underneath the stands. Thibodaux's wrist brushed the butt of the baby Glock under the loose tail of his shirt as he turned. He carried a Colt Detective Special on his ankle in case things really went rodeo. In his experience, the fastest reload was another gun.

"Why are you so early?" A dark man with a tightly curly black hair and a scarred upper lip called from the shadow of the pits under the stands. He was thickly muscled with a bull neck and angry scowl. Strong arms swung stiffly from a loose, cream-colored guayabera shirt.

"My boss came out to run a few laps before they open," Thibodaux shouted back, facing the newcomer as he approached. It was his job to act as Quinn's bodyguard. With his towering height and his back as broad as a barn, it was an easy assumption for people to make. "Don't worry, amigo. There's still enough track left for everybody."

Garcia leaned farther over the fence, arching her back slightly, pointing her tight terry-cloth shorts toward the new arrival.

The bull-necked man paused as if Jacques had just challenged him to a duel. "I am not your amigo," he yelled back, picking up his stride.

A second man walked a few steps behind the first, wearing a bright green and yellow racing suit. The tight leather suit was built for sitting, not walking, and that, along with the protective hump on his back, made him appear to waddle. He raised a gloved hand to silence his companion when they were still fifty feet away.

"It is fine, Monagas," he said. "This man is correct. There is plenty of track for all of us." He was tall and slender, with a pencil-thin mustache and a heavy brow. His black hair was slicked back to reveal a prominent widow's peak. His eyes were transfixed on Garcia.

"You can go home if you want to, Jacques," Ronnie whispered, throwing a quick glance over her shoulder. "I think I can handle this one."

"Smartass," Thibodaux hissed under his breath. "This guy is a stone killer."

She winked at him again. "Smart's got little to do with what he's looking at."

Zamora strode purposefully up to Thibodaux. An entire entourage had followed him out of the tunnel, complete with two young men wearing green mechanic's shirts pushing a Yamaha R1 identical to Quinn's but for the fact that it was black. There were no fewer than fourteen women in the group, including a set of gap-toothed blond twins that Thibodaux suspected were from some British modeling agency. All of them but the mechanics dragged along as if they'd been pulled away at this early hour from an all-night party. Most wore shades. One, a short brunette wearing red spandex shorts and a yellow tube top, sported a fresh black eye. A redhead in a gaudy green halter-top carried a char-treuse motorcycle helmet that matched Zamora's suit.

When the little procession was within earshot, Ronnie Garcia bounced on her toes and looked up at Thibodaux.

"One-twenty-six and change," she said as Quinn brapped by in a red blur. "That's his best lap yet."

"He can do better." Thibodaux leaned against the fence watching the parade of newcomers. "I've seen him."

Zamora stood completely still, his eyes flitting back and forth from Garcia's body to Quinn ripping around the track. "Very nice," he said at length. "Very nice indeed." He tilted his head, leaning toward the shorter

man, who Thibodaux could now see had the flattened
nose of a brawler and a deformed cauliflower ear to go
with his thuggish scowl. "Monagas, what time is it?"

Monagas consulted a heavy Seiko dive watch on his
wrist. "Seven-fifty-five, *patrón*. Do you wish me to
show them out?"

Zamora raised a gloved hand, pursing his lips as if in
thought.

The throaty rumble unique to the R1's exhaust grew
louder as Quinn came around again. Instead of slowing, he seemed to dig in, wringing a louder smoker's
howl from the Yamaha's pipes as bike and rider shot
past like a bullet aimed at the first turn.

Quinn took another easy lap, then pulled into the pit
area, coming to a rolling stop beside Garcia. He stayed
on the bike as he peeled off red and white Phantom
gloves and red helmet that matched the red, white, and
black panels of his leather race suit. Fingers of ground
fog swirled around his boots in the long morning shadows. Quinn tipped his head toward Zamora, giving him
a polite two-finger salute.

"I heard somebody rented the track for the entire
day," he said. "Thought I'd get a few laps in before you
started. Warm it up for you, so to speak."

He'd not shaved in two days and already the dark
stubble of his beard combined with the rich bronze
skin tone of his Apache grandmother made it hard to
tell his origin. The fact that he was fluent in Arabic—
and three other languages besides his native English—
added to his ability to blend in in a multicultural place
like south Florida. Still, with all his years in this line of

work, he wondered if the contempt he held for a man like the one standing before him shone through in his eyes. He forced what he hoped looked like an easy smile and swung a leg over the bike to extend his hand.

"Impressive." Zamora raised a skeptical eyebrow. "Your attractive lady friend said you ran a one-twenty-six lap."

"I've been riding a while." Quinn shrugged, grinning as if full of false modesty.

"I am Valentine," Zamora said, stepping forward to shake hands.

"Quinn," he said, taking the offered hand. "You know, it's really all about the bike."

"Twenty percent bike, eighty percent rider, some say." Zamora nodded toward his flat black R1, then let his eyes play over Ronnie Garcia. She leaned backward against the fence, elbows on the top rail, her back arched, eyes closed to the sun. The corners of Zamora's mouth turned up in a sly smile. "You have excellent taste, Mr. Quinn," he said.

"Well, then." Quinn saluted again. "You paid to have the track for you and your guests. We'll leave it to you."

"Good," Zamora said, letting him walk past.

The blond twins stood along the chain-link fence at the head of the entourage, eyeing Quinn like he was a piece of meat. Garcia drew a jealous, gap-toothed smirk as she walked beside him while Thibodaux pushed the bike.

"One-twenty-six is a scant two seconds off the track record," Zamora called out. "How would you feel about a little wager? If you're a sporting man . . ."

Quinn turned, grinning. "Mister, I'll be happy to take your money if—"

The mousy brunette's cell phone chirped, bringing a crippling glare from Zamora. She cringed, rushing to silence the thing before it earned her another black eye. Another phone began to ring among the group, then another and another. Garcia shot a glance at Quinn as her phone began to ring as well.

She picked up.

"Well, go on," Zamora said, flicking a hand at his entourage. "It's obviously something important."

The brunette's hand shot to her mouth a moment after she put the phone to her ear.

Garcia's lips parted in genuine surprise. She did her best to remain in character. "Some kind of explosion near JFK airport in New York," she said.

"You think it was a bomb like the one in California?" one of the blond twins asked.

"Maybe a plane crash," the other twin said, her voice breathy and shallow.

"Relax, my darlings. New York is a very long way away." Zamora waved his hand as if brushing away a fly.

The brunette spoke through clasped fingers. "My auntie lives in New York."

She drew another glare from Zamora, but this time she didn't notice.

"Monagas will turn the radio to the news," he said. "So we can find out exactly what is going on."

Agreeable nods and nervous chuckles ran up and down the fence line.

"I'd still enjoy making that wager with you, Señor Quinn." Zamora leaned against the seat of his bike, hands clasped across his lap. "But I'm afraid I won't have much of a ride today. I have business ventures in New York I should see to."

"That's okay," Quinn said, not wanting to appear too eager. "I'll take your money some other time."

Monagas stepped up with a cell phone. Zamora took it, putting a hand over the receiver. A sickeningly sweet smile crept across his face. His eyes flitted to Ronnie Garcia, lingered there, then moved back to Quinn. "I host an after-party at a villa near Miami." He tossed a glance over his shoulder. "Monagas, please give our new acquaintance the address and details." He turned back to Quinn. "You and your friends, please be my guests this evening."

"I do not trust that one," Julian Monagas said, watching the Americas leave. "You have important meetings tonight, *patrón*."

"Duly noted," Zamora said, swinging a long leg over his motorcycle. "And while I appreciate your advice, if I only invited people I trust, it would be a very small party indeed." He bent forward, draping his arms over the handlebars, gushing with enthusiasm. "Did you see their faces when they heard of another bombing in the States? It was priceless, my friend, just priceless. Do you not see the brilliance of it all? While the Americans look one direction, our friends will hit them in another."

CHAPTER 14

Texas

The air was cool and crisp when the baby-faced man with a curly head of black hair peeked out of the earthen tunnel to find himself inside a dust-filled barn five hundred yards inside the U.S. border, not far from the Mexican city of Miguel Alemán.

His coyote, the Mexican who'd helped him come across, called him the "Quiet One" because he tended to talk in a hoarse whisper—when he spoke at all.

The coyote had climbed up the ladder first, followed by a young couple and their two small daughters. Eleven other men, ranging from their late teens to well past fifty, rounded out the troupe. Each had paid two thousand U.S. dollars for the privilege of using the tunnel. All had agreed to be blindfolded before they went out to meet the waiting truck so as not to be able to inform on the tunnel's location if detained.

Coyotes—also known as *polleros* or chicken herders—took a great many risks, but the return was good. Sixteen "chickens" through the tunnel brought thirty-two thousand dollars for two hours' work. False documents, transportation within the United States, safe houses—those all cost extra.

"How long?" the mother of the little girls asked, spreading a cloth over a dusty bale of straw so her children could sit down and share an orange and some water.

"We just wait." The coyote shrugged. "The truck will get here when he gets here." He was a skinny, sunken-chested man, nervous and bouncy as if his neck were set on a spring. Going by the name of El Flaco, he was said to have a connection with the notorious Zetas Cartel—former paramilitaries from the Mexican Special Forces who'd decided protection rackets and narcotics trafficking were preferable to military discipline. Like the Sinaloa and other cartels, Zetas used tunnels to move drugs into Texas and guns back to Mexico. These same tunnels came in handy for smuggling illegal immigrants.

The Quiet One sat on the ground, leaning against a large wooden crate that lay on its side. A sliver of metal stuck out of the lid, so he slouched to keep it from poking him in the back. Still, he didn't know how long they'd be there and it was preferable to leaning against nothing.

One of the little girls offered him a piece of her orange.

He took it with a smile. She couldn't have been over six.

"What is your name?" she asked with the audacity peculiar to small children.

"Pablo," the Quiet One said. "What is your name?"

"Beatrice," the little girl said. "You talk funny. Where are you from?"

"Beatrice!" The girl's father clapped his hands. "Stop bothering him." He smiled apologetically. "I'm sorry, my friend."

Pablo waved him away. "It is fine. I'm sure I do sound odd to her. I went to school in Italy."

"That explains the accent," the man's wife said, nodding to her husband as she peeled another orange. "I told you so."

Pablo smiled and closed his eyes. Inside, his stomach churned. Was his accent really so noticeable that he could be undone by a small child and a witless woman? The squeal of a truck grinding to a halt outside roused him from his worries. So far, the journey had been dull and he hoped it stayed that way.

El Flaco climbed to his feet with a groan at the sound of the truck doors. He motioned for everyone else to stay put until he went outside to talk to his contact.

Before he took a step the barn door swung open and a man in a dark green uniform stepped inside pointing his pistol.

"Mierda!" Flaco turned to run but found a second Border Patrol officer waving at him from the back door. He hung his head in defeat.

Pablo was astounded to find that the arrest team consisted of only three Patrol agents—an older man with graying hair, a Hispanic man whose brand-new uniform screamed "rookie," and a thick-hipped woman with frizzy blond hair. Seventeen against three seemed like bad odds. If it had not been for the trainee, he suspected there would have only been two of them.

The senior agent and the woman provided cover while the rookie acted as contact officer and went from person to person applying plastic zip cuffs behind their backs, then giving each a quick pat-down for weapons. The rookie brightened when he found Flaco's pistol and passed it back to the female agent. The coyote's head bobbed back and forth, alternately praying and cursing under his breath. Once searched, each prisoner was made to sit back down.

Pablo kept his face passive, but his mind raced to find a way out. Too much depended on his freedom of movement. Going into custody was out of the question. Leaning back against his crate, he began to work his restraints against the sharp metal shard that had poked him in the back earlier.

The senior agent holstered his sidearm and took off his green ball cap to run his hand through his silver hair. He nodded at the rookie. "I'll call in for a bus. Cardenas, you and Stanton start getting names now. It'll speed up the processing back at sector."

The plastic flex cuffs broke, freeing Pablo's hands moments before the female agent worked her way around the barn to him. She stopped directly in front of him, peering down across a small spiral notebook. She tilted her frizzy head and blinked large eyes as if seeing him for the first time.

"What is your name?" she asked in excellent Spanish.

"Pablo Mendoza," he whispered, keeping his eyes wide and passive as he took note of her sidearm and the retaining strap on her holster. He'd watched her from the moment the rookie handed her Flaco's pistol and knew it was still stuck behind her back in the waistband of her trousers.

"Where were you born?"

"In a village near Bogotá." Pablo told the same plausible lie he gave everyone. Who in their right mind would admit to being from a country known for drug production and deadly cartels? Incriminating lies were so much easier to swallow.

"Colombia," she said to herself, making a note beside his name in spiral notebook. "OTM."

She was a tall woman, and her hips would provide her with a low center of gravity. Seated as he was, Pablo would need her off balance for his plan to work, even if his hands were free.

"Will they send me back to Bogotá?" he whispered, stuttering a bit as if he was frightened.

"Pardon?" She stooped, bending closer so she could hear him.

Pablo caught the woman's legs between his own, clamping down like a vise. Locking his ankles, he rolled sideways, throwing his full weight against the startled agent. Already off balance, she toppled easily, landing flat on her face in the dust with a sickening thud.

Pablo was on her in an instant, straddling her back as if she was a horse. He grabbed a fistful of frizzed blond hair with his left hand, brutally pounding her head against the ground. His right hand went for the H&K pistol in her holster. He'd reasoned that as a law enforcement officer her sidearm would be in better working order than Flaco's rusted thing. In this situation, he could not afford a single malfunction.

Stunned, the female agent put up little resistance and her H&K slid easily from her holster with a satisfying snick. He shot her once in the back of the head, not because she was an immediate threat but because he couldn't shoot accurately at the others with her bucking and thrashing beneath him. The rookie was closest so he got the next two rounds, one in the vest, then a follow-up to the neck. Pablo spun immediately, throwing rounds at the senior agent who'd already dropped his cell phone and drawn his weapon. The agent fired as he fell, but the rounds went high and wide. Pablo shot again, striking him high in the ribs. The round hit his vest, but blunt trauma caused him to drop his pistol. Now Pablo had time to take careful aim and finished him with a shot to the head.

Flaco bounced on the floor, jerking against his bonds. His face a twisted shout, his mouth moved, but no sounds came out. The rest of the group had fallen to the dirt at the first sign of shooting, becoming the smallest targets possible. Little Beatrice and her sister whimpered next to their parents.

The coyote found his voice as Pablo kicked the pistols away from the dead Border Patrol agents.

"What have you done, señor?" Flaco whispered. "The Americans will hunt us down like dogs."

Pablo raised a wary eyebrow. "Our contract was for you to get me into the United States safely with no law enforcement involvement." He retrieved Flaco's pistol, then rolled the dead woman before using it to shoot her once in the forehead.

Little Beatrice flinched at the shot and buried her face in her mother's lap.

Flaco's mouth hung open as Pablo's plan began to dawn on him.

"So," he said, nodding frantically. "You shoot them with my gun, then kill me with one of theirs to make it look like a gunfight."

Pablo grinned. "You are smarter than I first believed," he said.

"You should reconsider," the coyote said. "If you do this thing, my people will come looking for you. They are very cruel and powerful."

"Your people?" The Quiet One smirked. "You have no idea who I am."

Flaco's eyes jumped from person to person around the dark confines of the barn. "But what of all the witnesses, señor? Surely you would not kill them all. Even the little children?"

"Some things are too important for sentiment," the Quiet One said, inhaling quickly through his nose to steel his resolve. "It is best I begin at once." He retrieved the rookie agent's pistol and a second thirteen-round magazine from the dead man's belt. He had little time, but plenty of ammunition.

The idiots just sat there, trussed up like lambs for the slaughter, blinking stupidly.

Ibrahim Nazif, a Yemeni citizen educated from the age of fourteen at an al-Qaeda camp in Paraguay's lawless Triple Frontier, smiled. He thought of what the blond agent had noted about him in her book. "OTM," he chuckled to himself as he shot Flaco in the back of his bobbing neck and continued down the line, stopping only long enough to look each victim in the eye as he pulled the trigger.

OTM—other than Mexican indeed.

CHAPTER 15

Coral Gables, Florida
8:35 PM

Quinn shut the door of the black crew cab Silverado and tossed the keys to a Hispanic teenager beside the valet stand. The kid was so busy watching Garcia's long legs spill out of the backseat that he missed the keys completely. Quinn had to admit, she looked incredible in a white wraparound sundress. A simple gold chain fell across high collarbones to rest in the cleft of her breasts. She winked playfully at the boy and looped an arm through Quinn's, showing she belonged to him. Quinn caught his breath at the simple act.

Thibodaux shut the door and fell in behind the couple as they walked toward the sprawling Italian villa, shaking his head.

Quinn's mind reeled at the thought of Garcia walking beside him. Over the years, as Kim had grown more distant and Mattie had gotten older, thoughts of them and the difficulties of trying to hold the family together had threatened to knock him off task. He'd become a pro at compartmentalizing during missions, focusing on the problem at hand, then allowing himself a moment of melancholy only when the shooting stopped and he was in a safe place.

He shook off the worry and steeled himself to Garcia's touch as she snaked her arm around his waist, getting into character as his girl-toy. He could not dwell on the fact that he was standing next to one of the most amazing women he'd ever met. Dealing with a man as brutal as Valentine Zamora would require his full concentration.

Hanging torches lit a wide cobblestone walkway that led from behind the marble stand up a series of steps nearly thirty meters to the massive columns that comprised the front entrance to Valentine Zamora's rented villa. The whiteness of the limestone structure appeared to glow against the dark green of the surrounding gardens and deep purple of the night sky.

Both men wore light khaki slacks and polo shirts, Thibodaux's navy blue to Quinn's black. The colors made them less visible if it became necessary to work among the shadows—urban camo, Jacques called it. The Cajun, supposed by Zamora to be Quinn's bodyguard, carried his Kimber ten-millimeter in an inside-the-waistband holster over his right kidney, hidden by the tail of his polo shirt. The small Colt revolver still rested comfortably on the inside of his left ankle. Garcia carried no gun. Her weapons were more formidable than any bullet or blade. As the principal, Quinn went in clean. There would be plenty of killing tools available at such an event if he found one was needed.

"Twenty-nine dead in New York," Quinn said as they approached the front door. He wanted them all to remember what they were dealing with. "Three times that wounded."

"One-day missions suck," Ronnie whispered. "If I didn't have to get back to training tomorrow, I'd dearly love to help you nail this son of a bitch."

Quinn thought about her leaving and didn't know if he felt sadness or relief.

"*Laissez les bons temps rouler,*" Thibodaux said, clenching his square jaw as he reached for the brass doorknocker shaped like a lion's head. *Let the good times roll.*

The gap-toothed twins greeted them under a heavy wrought-iron chandelier. Honey-colored clay tile and thick wooden ceiling beams accented the whitewashed walls of the spacious foyer. The blond twins wore black one-piece swimsuits with necklines that plunged well past their belly buttons, exposing enough cleavage that Thibodaux, who constantly worried that his wife had her very own spy satellite, hunted for a place to cast his eyes. Zamora seemed to have invited a great many similarly dressed woman to the party. In fact, though the interior of the house was exquisitely decorated in finely carved wood and tapestries, it was impossible to notice much beyond the female décor.

"Looks like you're a bit overdressed," Quinn said as the gap-toothed twins jiggled and flounced their way through the double doors to let Zamora know Quinn, and more importantly Veronica Garcia, had arrived.

"You say that to all your girls," Ronnie said with the confident verbal equivalent of a shrug.

"How many guests you reckon are here?" Thibodaux grabbed a mojito from a passing waiter in khaki shorts and a white polo.

Quinn scanned the mass of people. "Maybe a hundred and fifty."

A crowded great room, adorned with waist-high Tuscan vases and an eighteenth-century Italian fresco, separated the entry from a long covered porch. People milled here and there in knots of four or five under the pool-length lanai and at small round tables set around the cabanas on the other side of a long, rectangular pool. A covey of tittering girls soaked in the steaming Jacuzzi. Underwater lights flashed and swirled as guests dove and swam in the blue-topaz water.

The air was heavy with the smell of chlorine, sunblock, and alcohol. Stubby palmettos and sculptured hedges of holly and long-leafed oleander beyond the cabanas gave the entire area a jungle-like feeling, affording small, isolated pockets where couples could get away for a few private moments.

Zamora stood with four other men, one of them the ever-present Monagas, who kept back a few steps behind but within arm's reach of his boss. Zamora wore a white linen sport coat with black slacks and matching shirt, open at the collar. The two men with him looked Hispanic. Shorter, stockier, and a decade older than Zamora, both spoke with the abrupt, animated gestures of men used to having things go their own way.

The Venezuelan's head snapped up the moment the twins got to him. He excused himself immediately from the conversation and all but ran to meet Quinn and Garcia at the veranda. Cathy, the mousy brunette from the track, padded up behind him. She'd been dangling her legs in the pool and little puddles formed on the concrete around her toes. Arms folded across her chest, she kept one leg slightly ahead of the other as if she would have rather been wearing anything but the scrap of a bikini.

Monagas stood beside her. A disgruntled curl hung beneath the scraggly beard on his uneven upper lip.

Quinn forced a smile as Zamora took Garcia's hand and pressed a kiss.

"I am overjoyed you decided to come, Mr. Quinn," the Venezuelan said, stifling a giggle. He kept Garcia's hand until Quinn threw an arm around her shoulder and tugged her away.

"This is a beautiful place, Mr. Zamora," Garcia said, full lips parted slightly. She was very good at what she was doing.

"Call me Valentine, I beg you." Zamora swept his arm around the grounds, narrowly missing Cathy standing behind him. He shot her a hateful glare, then smiled back at Garcia. "I have rented it every year of the past seven. It is modeled after a villa in Tuscany that I also rent during my trips to Italy."

"You know," Quinn said in spite of himself. "I'm in real estate. If you want, I could help you get into a place of your own so you don't have to rent all the time."

Zamora stared, his eyes narrowing to tiny slits. "I rent because I want to, Mr. Quinn. Not because I have to. It keeps me fluid."

"He knows that," Ronnie said, squeezing Quinn's arm. "You should have heard him talking about you and your big entourage back at the track. All the way here he was Valentine this and Valentine that. You'd think he was your groupie."

Zamora raised an eyebrow. Pleased. "Is that so?"

Quinn shrugged, wishing he could drag the guy behind one of his manicured hedges and beat him to death.

"I have to finish an important business matter," Zamora said. "Then you must let me show you around. Please enjoy the pool until then. Cathy, my darling," he spoke over his shoulder without taking his eyes off Ronnie. "Please find Ms. Garcia a bathing suit."

"It's okay," Ronnie said, opening her clenched fist to reveal the tiniest crumple of yellow cloth. "I brought my own."

The corners of Zamora's lips perked under his pencil-thin mustache as if he'd just spied his favorite entree on the menu.

"Most excellent," he said. "Cathy will show you the changing room."

Quinn gave her shoulders a squeeze. "Hurry back," he said.

"You are a very lucky man," Zamora said, watching the women walk away.

"Oh," Quinn said. "I don't know about that. I just have the one. You seem to have an entire harem."

Zamora swept his arm again. "Pick any one of them. I won't mind."

"What about their dates?" Quinn asked.

"The only man here with a date is you, Mr. Quinn." Zamora leaned in, confiding a secret. "And someone may try and steal her away if you are not very careful." He stood back and clapped his hands together, holding them to his lips as if in thought. "Now, you must excuse me while I attend to the drudgeries of my business."

Monagas remained a moment longer, giving them each a long up-and-down look. Scoffing to himself as if he couldn't be bothered with speaking, he turned to join his boss.

"I'm feelin' a need to whip that guy's ass," Thibodaux said as Zamora went to rejoin the men at the other end of the pool.

"Which one?" Quinn said. "Zamora or his thug?"

The Cajun shrugged, wagging his head. "I don't know, either . . . both."

"In time." Quinn nodded. He consciously kept himself from staring at the Venezuelan for fear that his own disgust would be too obvious.

"There are way too many women here," Thibodaux groaned.

Quinn frowned. "You're not tempted, are you?"

"Hell no," the big Cajun said. "Turn 'em upside down and they all look like sisters. My Camille is plenty enough for me."

"She gave you seven sons," Quinn chuckled. "I'd say that's apparent."

"What about you, *l'ami*?" Thibodaux looked down at him. "You can't tell me Ronnie don't tempt you a teensy bit. Aaiiee! I mean, she's wearin' that Bible dress and everything. . . ."

"Bible dress?" Quinn had worked with the good-hearted Marine for more than a year. Battle and blood had made them fast friends, but sometimes, he had a hard time understanding the man's euphemisms.

Thibodaux tipped his head toward the departing Ronnie, sighing. "You know, a Bible dress." He put his hands to his own chest as if holding up a particularly large bosom. "Lo and behold."

"There is that." It was Quinn's turn to groan. In truth, he'd been battling the notion of Veronica Garcia all day long. Seeing her had brought back a flood of conflicting emotions. "I owe it to my daughter to try and work things out with Kim."

"You mean the same Kim who bitched you out for saving her from a bunch of assassins?" Thibodaux shook his finger, scolding. "You know what you are, Chair Force? You are *uxorious*."

"I speak five languages and I have no idea what that means." Quinn scanned the crowd, arms folded across his chest.

"I accidentally made it when me and Camille were playing Words With Friends," Jacques said. "But that ain't the point. It means overly fixated on your wife."

"Says the man two sons shy of a baseball team," Quinn scoffed.

"Seriously, beb," Thibodaux said. "One dude to another—you gotta stop frettin' so much over the fair sex. It's gonna get one of us killed."

"I have an idea," Quinn said. "You think we could focus on this little nuclear bomb problem instead of who I ride into the sunset with?"

"It's your ride, brother." Thibodaux shrugged. "Just pointing out some things you might be too . . . close . . . to . . . see. . . ."

The noise around the pool seemed to hush when Ronnie stepped out of the nearest cabana. Quinn closed his eyes, hoping to escape the sight of her.

"Good lord," Thibodaux moaned. "You mean to tell me all that could be yours if you just said the word?"

"Shut up, Jacques," Quinn said. "It's not that simple."

"Chair Force, you listen to me. There's a lot of things in this life that's complicated, but this ain't one of 'em."

Quinn gave a long sigh as Garcia padded barefoot across the pool deck, smiling at him as if they were lovers. Jacques had no idea what he was talking about. This was the most complicated situation in the world—and the swimsuit didn't help matters at all.

Canary yellow, it stood out in warm contrast to her rich coffee-and-cream skin. On paper, Quinn was sure the thing had been designed as a modest one-piece with easily twice as much material as most of the suits around the pool. But the way Ronnie wore it made it anything but modest. The taut curves and swells of her body arced and dipped as if aching to escape the fabric. It covered everything—but hid absolutely nothing.

Ronnie did a pirouette to show off the suit when she got closer. It scooped low in the back, revealing a pale scar the size of a dime below her left shoulder blade, a reminder of another time when they'd depended on each other for their lives.

Zamora abandoned his poolside meeting as soon as he saw her, shoving aside anyone who dared get in his way.

"Come," he said, taking her by the hand. "I want to show you the garden, though I must say, not a single flower is more vibrant than you." He raised an eyebrow at Quinn. "With your permission, of course."

Jericho shrugged, fighting the urge to split the Venezuelan's skull. "Go for it," he said. "I have plenty here to keep me occupied."

"Remind me to pass you a slap if you let that get away," Thibodaux said, eyes glued to the sight of Garcia's swaying backside as she walked arm in arm with Zamora toward a garden of hanging flowers opposite the cabanas.

Quinn took a quick step back from the pool to avoid getting splashed by a team of piggyback couples wrestling for control of a volleyball. All six-packs and cleavage, these "beautiful people" were as much a part of the décor as the tapestries in the great room.

"Take a look over there if you can pry your eyes away for a minute." Quinn gave a discreet nod toward the other side of pool. "Isn't Farris bin Ushan supposed to be in jail?"

"You mean that kid that looks like a Yemeni *Leave It to Beaver*?" Thibodaux shrugged. "Sounds right."

"I think that's him hiding in the shadows over there ogling girls." He nodded to the string of cabanas. "What's the name of the Chechen bus driver from Grozny?"

"Are you serious?" Thibodaux said. "I have trouble remembering my own kids' names in a pinch."

"Come on. The Russians were looking at him for that most recent school bombing. . . ." Quinn pounded a fist into his palm, thinking. He wondered if it was the fog brought on by too much Ronnie Garcia or maybe too many years of boxing at the Air Force Academy—not to mention the countless other blows he'd taken to the head. In this business, the ability to remember names and faces was as crucial as knowing how to shoot.

"Beats me," Thibodaux said. "I know who you're talking about now—"

"Akhmad Umarov." Quinn snapped his fingers, recalling the name. He watched as the Chechen and another man he didn't recognize stood from a poolside table, leaving two cute blondes they'd been chatting up. The second was younger than Umarov by a decade. He wore tight, peg-legged jeans and a black, muscle-mapping T-shirt. Even from a distance, Quinn could see the kid moved with the gawky arrogance of someone thrust into a position of authority because of birth or association rather than talent. Passing the cabanas, Umarov and his companion walked quickly, as if they were late for an appointment.

Quinn watched as a compact woman broke from the game of water polo. She swam to the edge and did an easy hand press onto the deck. A forest-green bikini with a stylish white belt revealed powerful, if somewhat short, legs and the compact, muscular body of a gymnast. Intent on the departing Chechens, the woman took a quick moment to adjust the seat of her swimsuit and squeeze the water out of shoulder-length red hair before ducking down the path after them.

Quinn gave Thibodaux a jab with his elbow. "You enjoy your mojito and keep an eye on the Yemeni," he said. "I'm going to take a walk and see what Akhmad and his friend are up to out there in the dark."

"Watch yourself, *l'ami*." The Cajun snatched a stuffed mushroom off the tray of a passing waiter and stuffed it in his mouth. "That *jolie fille* goin' after him got a crazy look to her."

"Come on, Jacques," Quinn said. "You got that from watching her walk away?"

"I've done studies, *l'ami*. You can tell a lot about a woman from her ass." Thibodaux winked. "And this one's crazy."

CHAPTER 16

Quinn moved as fast as he could without actually running, but with the milling press of partygoers and roving waitstaff it took him nearly a full minute to make his way around the pool and past the corner of the limestone pool house. A carbon dioxide mosquito trap whirred in the darkness at the trunk of a stubby palmetto. With every step Quinn took, the din of playful cries and splashing water behind him gave way to an intense buzz of hushed voices.

Thankful for his dark shirt and the ability to blend in, he stepped into the shadows, ears straining to pinpoint the sounds coming from the path ahead. A half dozen steps brought him around a tall oleander hedge to a sudden clearing. The muffled sounds of a struggle filtered through the foliage in the humid darkness.

Quinn took a series of measured sidesteps in a movement known as "cutting the pie" to bring the clearing into view without exposing himself too quickly. Three steps in, he saw the shadowed form of the woman from the pool lying flat on her back. Akhmad Umarov knelt on top of her, a mop of thinning hair across his eyes. For a moment, Quinn thought he'd happened on a clandestine meeting of two lovers, but another half step in brought the younger Chechen into view. He stood watching, his back to Quinn, a pistol clutched in his hand.

In a fluid movement, the woman trapped the Chechen's hand and left arm against her chest. Hooking his left foot with hers, she bucked her hips with powerful legs. With nothing free to check his balance, the Chechen rolled away. It was a Brazilian jujitsu technique Quinn often used himself.

Covered in a layer of dirt and twigs, the woman delivered a series of kicks to the Chechen's face. He groaned but didn't cry out. Neither, it seemed, wanted to be discovered fighting.

The youngster with the pistol must not have wanted to get his hands dirty because he just stood there.

Quinn kept to the shadows. He was all about saving the girl when it was time, but stepping into the fray before he had all the players sorted out was a recipe for getting killed. Hundreds of police officers were hurt every year saving abused women when the enraged victim clobbered them with a frying pan for trying to take their man to jail.

In any case, this redhead knew how to handle herself.

Umarov rushed forward wildly through the kicks, throwing a straight punch. The woman easily sidestepped it, driving the plodding Chechen headfirst into the hedge. He spun quickly and was able to land a backhanded slap across the woman's face.

Momentarily stunned, she fell again, landing on the ground with a muffled cry. Something bright, like a piece of the jewelry, glinted on the ground beside her.

Umarov scooped it up with his free hand and put it in his pocket. Still on her back, the woman acted as if she wanted to scuttle away. The Chechen crawled after her with a whispered snarl and got a snoot full of her foot for his trouble.

The muscle-bound youngster with the pistol chuckled, and then grunted something Quinn didn't understand.

Rolling away, Umarov came up on all fours with a sinister growl. "*Haa-ha*, Bulat!" He held up the flat of his hand in the universal sign for no, wanting to finish this himself. Embarrassed, the husky Chechen pushed the mop of hair from his face and reached behind his back to yank a knife from his belt.

Quinn felt a surge of adrenaline rush down his arms. He slowed his breathing to counteract the buzz.

Now it was time.

Quinn's first reaction was to draw his pocketknife, but it was bad form to go around slitting throats at parties. Instead, he padded up behind the youngster with the handgun. Crouching slightly to lower his center, he gave a loud hiss. Bulat led with his head, bringing up the pistol too late to stop the underhand arc of Quinn's forearm. Rolling as he struck, Quinn let his arm "die" with a sickening thud against the base of the kid's neck, stunning the brachial plexus nerve and dropping him like a sack of sand.

Quinn kicked the kid's pistol into the hedge and made it to Umarov in two steps. Grabbing a handful of collar and belt, he drove a series of brutal knee strikes to the Chechen's ribs, smiling at the satisfying crunch as bone and cartilage cracked and separated. The knife flew from Umarov's hand as he rolled away like a bowling pin. Quinn kept coming and delivered a snap kick to the side of his head, sending him sprawling into the oleander hedge. Growling but beaten, the Chechen grabbed his staggering companion and stumbled away, both plunging headlong into the thick foliage.

Quinn exhaled through his nose, feeling the white heat of conflict subside in his belly. He reached for the woman's outstretched hand and helped her to her feet. She had a strong grip and was amazingly solid for such a small woman. What little light filtered through the tangle of leaves and palm fronds revealed a thin trickle of blood from her nose. Quinn pulled a blue bandana from his back pocket and moved to dab at the wound.

"*Chert poberi!*" She jerked away, slapping him hard across the left ear in the process. Before he could move, she delivered a savage snap kick to his groin.

Quinn exhaled fast, fighting nausea. He advanced immediately, giving the woman a straight jab to the nose. Evidently used to being punched, she let her head snap back to absorb the blow, then moved quickly to counter with a double palm strike to Quinn's ears.

"Hey!" Quinn warded off the blow and grabbed a wrist, chiding himself for allowing the woman to surprise him. He brought her hand up and over her head, spinning her like a dancer to cross her arms and pull her in snug against his chest. Her skin was slick and wet from the swimming pool. Holding on, he couldn't help but feel he'd grabbed a live electric wire. He had to lift her off the ground so she couldn't stomp his feet and arch his back to avoid a series of vicious head butts to his nose. Chlorinated water dripped from her hair and he could feel it soaking through the chest of his shirt with the warmth of her body. In all his years of fighting, he had little experience holding onto a wet, half-naked woman—at least one who seemed intent on clawing his eyes out.

"They might have killed you," Quinn groaned in her ear, still waiting for the nausea to pass.

"And you allowed him to escape." She squirmed against his grip. The edges of her bare feet raked against his shins. Whoever she was, this one knew a thing or two about scrapping.

Quinn stomped his foot to help relieve the pain in his groin and tightened his grip around the woman, trying to decide what to do with her. "Who are you?"

"None of your affair," she groaned. "Let me go. You are . . . breaking . . . my ribs. . . ."

Quinn let his grip relax a notch, expecting another attack for the favor.

"You fool," the woman spat. "I had him, and your interference allowed him to slip aw—"

A crunch of footfalls on the path behind him made Quinn release the woman and spin on his heels.

It was Valentine Zamora with Ronnie Garcia tucked in close to his side. The goon, Monagas, followed directly behind him. Crickets chirped in the bushes. A lizard scuttled along the branch of a tree directly overhead, rustling the leaves.

The Venezuelan grinned broadly, nodding at the debris-covered woman and the dampened front of Jericho's khaki slacks and polo shirt.

"I see you have made yourself quite at home, Mr. Quinn. Not the prize I would have chosen when compared to the lovely Miss Garcia, but a change is as good as a rest, as they say." He rubbed his chin in thought.

Ronnie's mouth fell open, her full lips pouting as

only they knew how. She drew back and slapped Quinn hard across the face. It was an honest slap, full of true emotion—as if it was something she'd been wanting to do for a very long time. She launched into a string of Cuban curses that caused Zamora to giggle, shooting a knowing glance at Monagas.

Quinn stood and took it, watching the redheaded Russian woman flee toward the safety of the pool and crowds.

Zamora held up his cell phone. "I can stop her with one call, my friend."

"That won't be necessary, Mr. Zamora." Quinn gave a dismissive shake of his head. "Just let her go."

Still deep in her staccato Cuban tirade, Garcia moved to slap him again. He caught her wrist in mid swing, pulling her close. He couldn't help but think he probably deserved the second slap as much as the first, but Garcia yielded immediately. She stood quietly beside him as the playthings of powerful men were supposed to do.

The Venezuelan put his arm around Quinn's shoulders, squeezing as if they were old friends. "Call me Valentine, I beg you. It seems we have common passions, my friend—fast motorcycles, beautiful women . . . getting exactly what we want." He stared openly at Garcia, his eyes playing lustfully across the tight fabric of her yellow swimsuit.

Thibodaux appeared from the direction of the pool, puffing out his chest at the sight of Quinn so close to their intended target. Ronnie took the opportunity to pull away. She ran past Jacques toward the pool.

Good girl, Quinn thought. She'd be trying to identify the redhead.

Thibodaux stepped forward, big hands open at his side, ready for trouble.

"You okay, boss?"

Monagas moved immediately to interdict him.

Both Zamora and Quinn raised their hands, halting their men.

The Venezuelan giggled maniacally. "And it seems we each have devoted protectors." He stepped back and tilted his head to let Monagas whisper something in his ear.

"He tells me you move like a boxer," Zamora said.

"I've spent some time in the ring," Quinn said. It was the truth. He'd won the Wing Open boxing tournament his senior year at the Air Force Academy and earned a broken nose for the effort.

Zamora sniffed, scanning up and down as if assessing him as a possible opponent. "I trust Julian above all others, you know. The Monagas family has served the Zamora household for generations, since Julian's great-great-great-grandfather Monaghan came to my country from Ireland. Monagas is very good at what he does. I think he'd like to see what you're capable of in the boxing ring."

"I would enjoy that very much," Quinn said honestly, giving the stocky Irish Venezuelan a dismissive glance. "But I don't think my bodyguard would let me fight your bodyguard. It only confuses matters."

"Not to mention the fact that you'd need a new bodyguard," Thibodaux scoffed.

"I have seen Julian shatter a man's cheekbone with a single punch." Zamora looked back at Monagas. "However, I must admit, in this case I'm not entirely sure who I would bet on." He sighed. "Such a shame. I wish we had time to get to know each other better. You are a very interesting man, Jericho Quinn."

"Maybe we can have that race you talked about this morning." Quinn kept his voice cavalier but felt his chance at a more substantial meeting slipping away. His gut told him this was the guy with the bomb, but a couple of Chechens and a Yemeni visiting an arms dealer hardly constituted proof.

"Another time." Zamora shrugged. "I leave for Mar del Plata in a few days' time."

Now it was Quinn's turn to smile. Maybe there was a chance after all. "Mar del Plata?"

"Pity." Zamora nodded. "Beating you would have been a pleasure."

"Well, my friend, Valentine." Quinn wagged his head as if he'd had one too many drinks. "As it happens, I am on my way to Mar del Plata as well."

"You can't be serious?" The ever-present giggle rose like a wave on his voice.

"Indeed," Quinn said, copying Zamora's inflection.

"That is most excellent." Zamora slapped him on the back. "What a pair we make, you and I." His eyes were wild and glassy with alcohol. "But now I have to piss. Meet me at the bar in five minutes and we can talk this over. I will find you another girl since yours ran away."

"I'll be fine with Veronica," he said.

"Suit yourself." Zamora grinned. "But let me know if she begins to bore you again. I keep Cathy on hand for just such eventualities. . . ."

* * *

Thibodaux stepped closer as soon as Zamora and his thug were out of earshot. "I want to staple that guy's lips shut every time he cackles like that." The big Cajun shivered. "Gives me the damn creeps. You ask me, he ain't sane enough to have the bomb."

Quinn rubbed his jaw. His ear still rang where the red-haired woman and then Garcia had smacked him. "What, only stable people can have nuclear weapons now?"

"Hell no," Jacques said. "That ain't what I mean and you know it. I mean to say it'd be a miracle if he was able to get his hands on such a thing without blowing his own ass off."

"Don't forget about the Yemenis and our Chechen friends. A man-portable nuke would be as good a reason as any for them all to be here."

"His daddy's with the Venezuelan government," Thibodaux said. "Everyone knows Iran and half the other bad actors in the world are allied with Venezuela. Maybe they're trying to get in good with Junior. He is a damned arms dealer after all. Maybe they're just some of his regular customers."

"Maybe," Quinn said. "Or maybe they're sniffing around for the bomb."

"Seems like Zamora's more interested in beatin' up women and ridin' fast bikes."

"And now that's exactly what he thinks of me," Quinn said.

"Lucky us," Jacques muttered. He stared into the thick tangle of foliage. "You find out who the freckled gal is?"

"A Russian," Quinn said, rubbing his jaw again. "And

she was *nyet* too happy with me for breaking up the fight with Umarov. Could be SVR tailing Chechen terrorists. Whoever she is, she knows how to scrap."

"Maybe so." The big Cajun raised a thick eyebrow. "So, you gonna tell me what you meant about Mar del Plata?"

Quinn turned toward the pool. "I told Zamora I happened to be entered in the same little motorcycle race he is."

"In South America?"

"Yep," Quinn said.

"When?" A look of dread crossed the Cajun's face.

"It's still a week out." Quinn kept walking.

"Whew." Thibodaux smirked. "A whole damned week. That's not so bad. I was afraid you were gettin' us in over our heads."

"There is one thing." Quinn stopped, turning to face his friend. "When my brother and I rode it in Africa it took us over a year to get ready. This particular race runs over five thousand miles through the deserts of Argentina, Chile, and Peru—"

"Hells, *l'ami*!" Thibodaux spat. "You're as crazy as Zamora."

"Maybe." Quinn shrugged.

"Seriously, a week?" Thibodaux said, the timing finally setting in. "Are you shittin' me? That's right after Christmas. Camille is gonna cut my cojones off with a butter knife."

"Come on, Gunny, this is the kind of race where you mark all your gear with your blood type—just our kind of thing." He stopped a moment, wiggling his jaw, then adjusting his belt. "You were right about that redhead's tail end, by the way."

"Crazy?" Thibodaux gave him a big grin, nodding.

"As a loon. How could you tell?"

"Well, *l'ami*—" The big Cajun looked around before leaning in closer. "Don't tell her I said this, but from the angle I saw, that redhead looked an awful lot like my Camille."

Quinn chuckled, moving again.

"Speaking of crazy," Thibodaux said, walking beside him toward the riotous sounds around the pool. "You think he has it?"

"I do," Quinn said. "But the question is where. I have an idea I want to run by you and Ronnie that might help us find out."

CHAPTER 17

December 21
2:15 AM

Valentine Zamora lazed in the deep end of the swimming pool listening to the young Chechen in the black T-shirt whimper like a stomped puppy. His slouchy friend Umarov had disappeared, leaving the poor man to take the full brunt of the Venezuelan's rage.

Cathy floated to his immediate right, a milky white thigh grazing his. Her makeup had washed off, revealing the dark purple bruise under her eye. Her pale body shook as if she was about to freeze to death—but Zamora knew better.

Bulat Daudov lay on his stomach to Zamora's left, close enough to reach out and slap. Tied belly-down to a heavy lounge chair with nylon ratchet straps, the Chechen's chin hung off the end of the seat facing the pool. His legs were bent at the knees, secured to the back so his bare feet faced upward, naked and exposed to the night sky. His eyes were rimmed in red. Snot hung in strings from his nose to the tile.

On the far side of the pool, the Yemeni, Farris bin

Ushan, stood fidgeting, sucking on his bottom lip. His face had gone pale.

Zamora leaned against the wall, arms stretched along the cool edge. He sighed, waving a fat cigar as he considered his big toe floating just above the surface. Blue shadows from the underwater lights danced across his angular face. Dear, devoted Monagas was at the head of the lounge chair, a three-foot length of bamboo cane in his fist.

The rest of the grounds were deserted. Zamora had announced the end of the festivities shortly after Veronica Garcia had gone, and his guests had departed obediently.

Zamora blew a cloud of smoke across the rippling surface of the pool. He sniffed, tapped a bit of ash into the pool, and then gave Monagas a nod.

An instant later the stiff cane whistled through the humid air. A ragged scream spilled from Daudov's throat a half second before the bamboo slapped the bare soles of his feet. Monagas delivered three more blows, sending the young man twisting and thrashing to escape the torment.

Bastinado, or foot whipping, was a favorite form of torture among many cultures. The multitude of nerve endings combined with the small bones and tendons in the bottom of the feet made for a perfect target with maximum torment. The Iranian secret police were particularly fond of such beatings because they left few outer signs of trauma.

Cathy tried to swim away, but Zamora grabbed her by the hair and yanked her back. He wagged his finger in front of her face, chiding, then turned to stare at the moaning Chechen.

Across the pool, the big-eared Yemeni gulped, but said nothing.

"Oh, my dear Bulat," Zamora sighed. "Monagas has not even broken a sweat. He relishes bastinado the way some love baseball. I do believe he could go on all night. Unfortunately the bones of your poor feet cannot."

Striking like a snake, he grabbed the Chechen by the forelock and lifted his face to look at him eye to eye. His voice was low and soft, almost sweet, belying the ferocity of his movement.

"Tell me, where is your friend Akhmad Umarov? I saw him here with you tonight."

Bulat coughed, gagging on his own words. "My . . . brother . . . will kill y—"

Zamora nodded again, bringing a whistling swat from the bamboo rod.

The Chechen screamed, jerking against his bonds.

"My brother," he said, panting. Blood dripped from his mouth where he'd bitten through his tongue. "We want what you have. . . ."

Zamora snorted. "I know that. You may proceed, Monagas—"

"Wait!" the Chechen panted, clenching his jaw in anticipation of the next blow.

Zamora raised his hand.

"Yes, my friend," he said. "You have something else to say?"

"I don't know where Umarov is," Bulat sniffed. "My . . . brother sent us. . . ." His words came in broken stops and starts. "I . . . I mean we . . . we were to find where you have it . . . then kill you."

Zamora snorted, chewing on his cigar. "And how is that working out for you, my friend?"

The Chechen seemed to know that he was as good as dead. His body deflated as the will drained out of him. He turned his head to face Zamora, cheek against the bar of the lounge chair.

"I tell you the truth," he whispered. "My brother will kill you—"

Zamora grabbed the Chechen and dragged him into the pool. The long chair planed in the water, hanging on the surface for a long moment, before shooting at an angle toward the bottom like a torpedo. A line of silver bubbles trailed in the flickering blue light.

"There now." Zamora puffed on his cigar, blowing a cloud of smoke into Cathy's horrified face. "My mother says one must periodically cut the head off a servant for the others to see. What do you think of that, my darling?"

He may as well have been swimming with a wet loaf of bread for all the excitement Cathy offered. Shaking like a naked fawn, her chin hovered just above the water. A lock of wet hair hung like a piece of dead seaweed across her face. She was too lazy or terrified even to brush it away. It took all his self-control to keep from shoving her head under and holding it there.

Instead, he turned to look at Farris bin Ushan. "Come join us," he said, flicking his hand to motion the Yemeni into the pool.

Ushan was in his mid twenties, with short, dark hair. His black suit pants and a white long-sleeved dress shirt were wrinkled, as if he'd slept in them.

"His face looks too sweet to be that of a ruthless terrorist." Zamora nudged the girl with his elbow. "Do you not agree, my darling?"

"I . . . I shouldn't be here." She tried to swim away again, but Zamora grabbed her ankle, tugging her back. He gave the inside of her thigh a cruel pinch between her knee and her groin. She cried out, but sadly, and went completely limp at his touch.

Zamora beckoned the young man closer with his cigar.

"I am sorry about her." He looked over at the quivering girl. "*As-salamu alaikum*, Farris. I hope your stay in Florida has been a pleasant one."

"*Wa alaikum as salam*." Ushan nodded, putting his right hand to his breast. His eyes were fixed on the body of the dead Chechen at the bottom of the pool. "Most enjoyable."

"Join us," Zamora said again.

"I do not swim." The Yemeni swallowed. His face twitched as his nervous smile grew larger.

Zamora's face darkened.

"Get in the pool!" A cloud of cigar smoke erupted with his snarl, enveloping his head.

Ushan complied, walking down the steps fully clothed. His white shirt clung to his skinny chest.

"See?" Zamora smiled sweetly again. "The water is really quite nice. Come and let us talk."

The pool grew deeper as the Yemeni sloshed his way toward them. Three feet away, only his head remained above the surface. He smiled, fanning his arms to keep his balance. Water sloshed at his absurdly large ears.

"I have no wire." He sputtered. "Your bodyguard already conducted a most embarrassing pat-down."

"Indulge me." Zamora gestured toward the body of

the dead Chechen at the bottom of the pool. "You no doubt understand that I would kill you very slowly if I suspected you were an informant." He took another puff of the cigar.

"I am no informant!" Ushan said, forgetting to raise his chin. He took in a mouthful of water.

"I believe you," Zamora said. "I could not help but notice you looking over some of the women here tonight."

The Yemeni shook his head. "Surely you are mistaken," he stammered.

"Perhaps so," Zamora said. "But I think not." He grabbed the tremulous Cathy by the arm and shoved her through the water toward Ushan. "You may consider this one a gift. Call her a consolation prize for not being able to pick up a better one at the party."

Cathy's mouth hung open. She blinked wide doe eyes. "Why?"

"Why not?" Zamora said.

The Yemeni licked his lips. "I may keep her for the entire night?"

"You misunderstand me." Zamora waved his hand. "I do not want her back."

Five minutes later saw Zamora standing naked in the middle of the great room, toweling himself dry. He saw no reason to go to his bedroom. All the members of his entourage had long since passed out in the cabanas. The entire villa was his suite.

He stepped into a pair of purple silk sleeping shorts, glancing up at Monagas.

"Make certain you tell the idiot to kill her when he is finished."

"Yes, *patrón*." Monagas lips turned up in a crooked smile. "Should I take care of him as well?"

Zamora fluffed the towel through his hair. "I am inclined to say yes, mainly due to his ears." He sniffed. "Do they not seem excessively large to you, Monagas?"

The boxer nodded, his crooked lip turned up in a slight smile, scarred hands folded in front of his waist. "Indeed."

"I do not trust him with those big ears. He hears too much and may decide to inform. And yet, it is his people who want the device . . . We had best wait on that," Zamora said. "The Chechens are angry that I did not sell Baba Yaga to them. I do believe the fool Bulat on that account. They will try to kill me for it. I would very much appreciate it if you would stop them from doing that."

Monagas smiled. "Of course."

"And you may go ahead and take care of Umarov. I doubt Rustam Daudov would trust that idiot with any details, but see what he knows before you kill him."

"As you wish," Monagas said. "May I ask a question, *patrón*?"

Zamora nodded.

"Do you still plan to go to Argentina, considering the work that must be done on the device and the problem with the Chechens?"

Zamora slumped in a plush, high-backed chair. "Absolutely," he said. "I have been planning my entry into the Dakar for many years. The professor has some work to do to make Baba Yaga viable again." He giggled, taking another cigar from a silver case. "I don't know about you, but I don't want to be anywhere near him in case he makes a mistake. What good is an investment if one does not live to spend the profits? Anyway, the race will be great fun, you will see. It will be like a carnival, especially if Mr. Jericho Quinn is there." Zamora bit the end off the cigar and spit it on the floor.

"I do not like him," Monagas grunted, stooping to pick it up.

"I haven't decided if I do or if I don't." Zamora smiled. "But he has pleasant taste in women, doesn't he? See what you can find out about him."

His thoughts drifted to Cathy for a moment and he gave a long sigh, overcome with melancholy. Not for the stupid brunette, but because he wished he'd not been so hasty to leave Lourdes Lopez in Idaho. He felt the overpowering urge to call the fiery woman. He glanced at his watch and cursed. It was nearly midnight there and she would surely be sleeping . . . or torturing Pollard's wife. In either case she would not want to be bothered.

CHAPTER 18

Marie Pollard sat in the corner on a lumpy mattress that had been thrown on the floor. It was clammy and damp and smelled of mildew. Simon slept next to her leg, rolled up in a striped beach towel—the cleanest thing she could find in the vacant farmhouse. A tamarack fire popped in the woodstove in the corner, helping the ancient boiler keep up against the chilly wind that rattled the windows and creaked at the walls. Marie had no idea what time it was. Ripped from everything she knew, she found it impossible to focus. Her eyes hurt when she breathed. She'd been crying so long her skull felt as if it were full of molten lava.

Lourdes straddled a kitchen chair that she'd turned backward. Resting her chin on bare arms over the backrest, she stared down with squinting black eyes at Simon. Marie tried to make small talk, to find some connection in their womanhood—but Lourdes only ignored her.

"Your baby is very ugly, Marie Pollard," she finally

said, using both her names as if they were one word. "You know that, don't you?" She spoke without lifting her chin from the back of the chair, making her sound bored.

Marie bit her lip to keep it from trembling.

Lourdes arched her back, looking up at the ceiling. "I have never understood what people see in babies," she said. "They are like insignificant worms at the bottom of a bottle of tequila. I drink them down without a second thought."

Mercifully, Lourdes's cell phone began to ring. Her eyes brightened when she looked at the number. The hint of a smile perked her lips. The frown came crashing back the moment she noticed Marie looking at her, but she couldn't hide the girlish lilt in her voice. Turning, she walked down the hallway.

Marie let her head fall back against the wall, happy for a moment's freedom from the woman's hateful stares. It gave her time to catch her breath and take stock of the situation.

Lourdes and her two cronies had loaded them up in the backseat of a cramped four-door pickup that reeked of stale fish sticks and tobacco. None of the neighbors on their quiet street noticed a sobbing Marie and her little boy being trundled off to who knew where. She'd taken a rape prevention course with her women's group at church the year before and the words of her instructor came back with the brilliant clarity of a bolt of liquid lighting. *If you are assaulted and find yourself being forced to go to a second location, fight with all you have because that second crime scene will almost always be a murder scene.*

Marie couldn't fight. She wasn't even sure where

they were. She remembered headlights playing off a dense pine forest and drifted snow when they turned off the blacktop of Highway 95 at some point after they left Moscow. But terrified with worry over Simon, her brain had lost all sense of time and distance.

The two men hardly spoke to her at all. The one they called Jorge walked with a bad limp and swore under his breath at every step. He was in his forties, and had a sizable belly, which made the limp worse. Though he was injured, the other two seemed content to let him do the lion's share of the work. He unloaded the truck. He brought in wood. Now, Marie could just make out his right shoulder around the corner of the far wall, where he hobbled around in the kitchen making pancakes.

A large television in the dining area flickered with the news. Marie didn't know if he even thought about it, but Jorge kept the volume down, allowing Simon to get a little more sleep. He got cranky without a nap and she was terrified of what Lourdes would do if he launched into one of his crying fits.

Pete, the second man, slouched in a sagging recliner and killed zombies on his smartphone. Not far into his twenties, he wore his Carhartt ball cap turned sideways like some sort of farm-boy rapper. A tiny blond soul patch bristled under his bottom lip.

Jorge leaned around the wall. He'd used the tail of his checkered flannel shirt as a towel and it was covered in flour. "You think the kid will eat some pancakes?"

"How'd I know?" Pete muttered, entranced in the gore of his iPhone. "I look like a baby to you?"

"A little bit." Jorge smirked.

Ignoring him, Pete leered at Marie, licking his lips. Before he could say anything Lourdes skulked in from the back room. Marie could feel the heaviness of her presence before she even rounded the corner.

"The worm will eat what we feed it or it will starve," she said. "It makes no difference to me." She carried a laptop computer with the screen half closed. Stooping down beside the mattress, she shoved it in front of Marie.

"Tell him you and the worm still live and breathe, Marie Pollard," she said, flipping up the screen.

Marie found it hard to breathe when she saw Matt's face. The image was jerky and pixilated from the connection, but it was Matt. He was pale and his beard already bristled like it needed trimming.

"Are you all right?" His eyes sagged with guilt.

"Yes." Marie nodded, blinking back tears.

"Simon," he said. "Can I see Simon?"

She turned the computer toward the baby. "He's sleeping."

"You're not hurt?"

"We're fine," she said, whispering in spite of herself. "I don't understand, Matt. Who are these people?"

"I'll explain everything when this is over," he said.

Lourdes grabbed the computer and slammed it shut. "That's enough," she said. "He knows you are alive."

It felt to Marie as if the evil woman had just torn away her heart. She pressed her head against the wall, eyes clenched tight as Lourdes leaned in close enough she could smell the odor of her heavy powder makeup.

"Do not get your hopes up, Marie Pollard. You will never understand. Before this is over, I will find out if your little worm tastes better boiled or fried. . . ."

On the mattress beside Marie's leg, Simon threw his head back and began to wail.

CHAPTER 19

"**S**o," Thibodaux said, craning his head to look at Garcia in the backseat. "They teachin' you about surveillance at CIA school?" He sat behind the wheel across from Jericho, who looked through a set of binoculars. Both stared at the door to the eastern-most room on the bottom floor of the Green Flamingo Motel. Just a few yards beyond the end of the building the parking lot melded into the dark pine forest. The only streetlight in the lot was burned out and what little light there was leaked from the tattered blinds of the rooms themselves, making the lot and the motel itself the perfect place for someone who wanted anonymity.

"They do indeed," Garcia said. Thankfully, she'd already wriggled into a pair of jeans and a dark T-shirt, but Quinn could still smell the faint jasmine odor of her skin wafting up behind him. "But role-playing is never like the real thing."

"My uncle was a deputy sheriff in Terrebonne Parish," Jacques said in the darkness. "He used to tell me stake-

outs were nothin' more than two people sittin' in a stinking car with the collective urge to pee. I think he was
right 'cause I'm feeling the need right now."

"Well, you better use your Dr Pepper bottle," Quinn
said, his voice muffled against the binoculars. "I got
movement at the room."

Quinn watched as the Yemeni man they knew as Farris Ushan stepped out of the gaudy green door at the
end of the rundown motel.

"What's he doing?" Garcia put both hands on the
back of Quinn's seat.

Quinn passed the binoculars back to Garcia, his
hand already on the door.

"He's dragging a girl out of the trunk."

Quinn was out of the truck and moving the moment
Ushan shut the door to his room. Thibodaux trotted
alongside him while Garcia held back a few steps act-
ing as a rear guard.

"We're in the U.S. of A now, Chair Force, and we got
no warrant," the big Cajun said, crouching as he ran.
"Just checkin', but are we gonna knock and announce?"

Quinn looked him in the eye. "What do you think?"

The beautiful thing about cheap motels was that most
of their doors were routinely subjected to the boots,
rams, or threshold spreaders of the local police. A sideways pull on the handle allowed Quinn to push this one
open with hardly more than a shove. A little gentle per-
suasion tore the flimsy privacy chain out of the wall.

The Yemeni stood at the far side of the bed, towering
over a bound Cathy with a leather belt in his hands. His
head snapped up at the intrusion.

"Wha—?"

Quinn never stopped as he shouldered his way past the chain and bounded up on the bed to step over the cowering girl. He caught Ushan across a big ear with a brutal slap. Snatching the belt, he looped it quickly around the Yemeni's neck and pulled it tight.

Garcia appeared at the open door, tiny Kahr pistol in her hand. Thibodaux, who scanned for other threats in the room, motioned for her to take the girl to the corner.

The Yemeni's eyes bulged. The veins on his neck swelled red under the leather belt as if they might burst. When his head lolled, Quinn shoved him face forward onto the bed, patting him down for weapons.

He moaned when Quinn flipped him over.

"Where is your friend?" In reality Quinn knew of no one else, but it didn't hurt to make the stunned Yemeni believe he did.

"Zamora gave me the girl." Ushan shook his head, blinking. "I wanted her for myself, so I came here alone."

"Where is the bomb?"

"Who are you?"

"The bomb, Farris." Quinn drew back as if to strike him with the belt.

"What bomb?" Ushan worked his jaw back and forth, obviously stunned by the cuff to his ear.

Quinn gambled, throwing more cards than he actually had on the table. "I know Zamora has Baba Yaga." He fell into easy Arabic. With his three-day growth of dark beard and copper skin, he could easily pass for someone from the Middle East.

Ushan's eyes narrowed, trying to make sense of things. "Who are you?"

Quinn shot a glance at Ronnie, who attempted to comfort a hysterical Cathy in the far corner of the room. He shuddered to think what would have happened to her if they hadn't decided to follow the Yemeni away from the party.

"I am the man who will cut out your worthless heart if you do not tell me what I want to know," Quinn whispered, not entirely bluffing.

"If you want to kill me," Ushan said, "you will have to get in line behind the Chechens."

"The Chechens don't have you here now," Quinn said. "I do." He acted disinterested, but took careful note of every word the Yemeni breathed.

"Yes." Ushan smiled. "But you do not know this particular Chechen. He would—"

A loud whack, like someone hitting a softball, turned their attention to the door as it flew open. Quinn looked up to see a shotgun barrel pointing through the gap.

Thibodaux reacted immediately, bringing his forearm up under the barrel an instant after the first booming shot split the air inside the cramped hotel room. The Yemeni's head burst, spilling onto the sheets. Grabbing the intruding shotgun's fore end with his free hand, the big Cajun gave a hard yank and pulled the shooter, a balding man with a dirty blond beard, into the room. He used the butt of the weapon to smash the man in the face on the backstroke.

His lips pouring blood, the shooter rolled across the carpet, trying to access a pistol on his belt. Thibodaux held the shotgun to the side and used his Kimber to give the guy a double tap to the chest.

Quinn dove to the floor as more gunfire shattered the glass and tore the mini-blinds off the windows.

Tires squealed in the parking lot. Car alarms began to honk and beep from the commotion.

Shotgun still in hand, Thibodaux did a quick peek out the open door. "Looks clear." He turned back to Quinn. "You okay, *l'ami*?"

Quinn stood up, looking at Garcia. She nodded. "We're okay," he said.

Thibodaux pulled back the dead man's shirt. He was bony and gaunt, and a crude eight-pointed star was tattooed on each skeletal shoulder, just above his collarbone. "Eastern Bloc mafia," the Cajun said. "Could be Chechen. Tats are older, probably made in some Russian prison with ash and piss."

"Not too much of a jump from Chechen Mafia to Chechen separatists," Quinn said. "Guess this guy was right about them wanting to kill him."

"Over the bomb?" Ronnie asked. "Do you think they saw us?" Ronnie stood up from where she'd used her own body to shield a hysterical Cathy.

Quinn set his mouth in a tight line.

"They sure enough saw him," Thibodaux said, looking at the mess of blood, brain matter, and ears that had been Farris bin Ushan.

CHAPTER 20

Quinn turned on his phone while the plane from Miami was still rolling down the taxiway. There was a missed call from Bo.

He punched in the number and was relieved to hear his kid brother's voice.

"Boaz Quinn," he said, giving him the older sibling's chiding tone. "I've been trying to get in touch with you for days."

"What can I say?" Bo laughed. "My life of crime takes me places cell phones don't work so well." Quinn could hear the sun-bleached surfer attitude in his brother's voice. Four years younger than Jericho, the unrepentant prodigal had left home after a not so stellar year at University of Alaska to start over in Texas. He'd landed on his feet, but square in the middle of a motorcycle club that dabbled in several lucrative, but not so legitimate, businesses. Not the academic that

Jericho was, Bo was bull strong and incredibly smart. A natural leader, he worked and fought his way up through the ranks of his new club and found himself in charge in a matter of years.

"Your passport still valid?" Quinn asked. "Or did you have to surrender it to your probation officer?"

"Very funny," Bo said. "As a matter of fact, I am clear to travel and free for the next few days."

Quinn smiled at the thought of seeing his kid brother again, even under the circumstances of tracking down a nuclear bomb. "Have I got a deal for you," he said. "I can't talk about it on the phone, but how do you feel about Argentina?"

"He is walking toward baggage claim now," a Japanese man wearing a tan golf jacket whispered. He stood in line at the Dunkin' Donuts holding a newspaper under his arm. His black hair was moussed and combed up in the earnest businessman style. He ordered a coffee from the tired-looking black woman behind the counter as Quinn walked past, almost close enough to touch.

"I am interested in what an American OSI agent would be doing with a Japanese killing dagger," a female voice answered over the earbud that was paired to the cell phone on his belt. "You know what to do."

"Of course," the Japanese man said. He tossed a five-dollar bill on the counter to pay for his coffee and fell in with the arriving passengers as they walked in small groups along the dimly lit hallway, past the ever-present construction that seemed to define Reagan Airport and down the escalator to baggage claim. For an international airport across the Potomac from the nation's capitol, Reagan saw little traffic at this time of morning.

The Japanese man loitered near the carousel as if he was waiting for his own baggage. Quinn stood with his back to one of the large support columns inside the rail that separated the baggage area from the front walkway. His eyes were constantly on the move, flitting from one person to the next, as if sizing them up as potential threats or, the Japanese man couldn't help but think, possible targets. There was no doubt in his mind that Quinn carried a weapon. As a government agent, he would have been allowed to fly with it—and men like this one did not walk around without weapons unless they were forced to do so. His black leather jacket was loose, so it was impossible to know if it was on his belt or under his arm, but he was definitely armed. Quinn's demeanor, the predatory way in which he carried himself, spoke louder than any outline of a pistol under his clothing.

Truly dangerous men, the Japanese man thought, recognized others of their kind.

Quinn grabbed a camel-colored ballistic nylon duffel and turned toward the escalator to long-term parking. Following, but not too close, the Japanese man didn't get on the escalator until Quinn neared the top. He'd already marked Quinn's vehicle in the lot, and parked his own car nearby. It would be easy enough to follow him from a distance.

The Japanese man was halfway up the escalator, trapped between a large Sikh in a black turban and a group of Georgetown coeds dressed in droopy sweats, when Quinn met him, coming down the escalator on the other side.

*   *   *

Quinn spotted the tail at the baggage carousel. A compact Japanese man with neatly trimmed hair to match a military bearing loitered as if he had bags of his own, then left moments after Quinn without retrieving anything. Perhaps it was his earlier encounter with the *bosozoku*, but Quinn had become hyperaware of Japanese men.

With no way to know if the man sought to do him harm or just to test him, Quinn took three steps off the escalator, then turned to take the ride back down, meeting his pursuer face-to-face.

Both of this man's hands were visible, one hanging loosely at his side, the other holding a Dunkin' Donuts cup. It was a calm person indeed who could hold a cup of coffee at the same moment he intended to do violence. Still, Quinn kept a hand in his jacket pocket, fingers wrapped around the Beretta. In his other hand, he held his BlackBerry.

The man's jaw hung open in mortified surprise when he saw Quinn, but his hands remained motionless.

"*Sayonara dake ga jinsei, sa*," Quinn said, snapping a photo with his cell phone as he passed by on his way back down. It was a line from an old movie, certain to make sentimental Japanese women cry—and the man looked as if he was close himself. *Life is nothing but good-bye*.

Quinn dropped the phone back in his jacket pocket and nodded at the man, whose face now burned at his error. At the bottom of the escalator Quinn walked briskly toward the exit door that would take him to the taxi stands. He'd come back for his car later with a bomb tech. For tonight, a random taxi seemed the more prudent way home.

CHAPTER 21

2:30 PM
Mt. Vernon, Virginia

A quick 5K run under the leafless oaks and syca-
mores of George Washington's old haunts raised
Jericho's spirits. Zamora's girl, Cathy, hadn't given
them anything useful except that her boyfriend was a
cold-blooded killer. They already knew that.

Garcia had returned to training, leaving Quinn feeling
empty and mixed up. He'd kept the pace to a brisk six-
minute mile in an effort to keep Thibodaux from broach-
ing the subject of relationships. It had worked. The big
Marine stayed right beside him through the entire run despite his massive bulk. He hadn't liked it, but he'd done it,
along with the hour of yoga led by their defensive tactics
trainer and quartermaster, Emiko Miyagi.

Now, the enigmatic Japanese woman sat ramrod-
straight at the edge of a high-backed wooden chair in
her study. Small hands rested neatly in the lap of her
faded jeans. The open collar of a robin's-egg-blue shirt
revealed the slightest corner of her hidden tattoo.

In point of fact, neither Quinn or Thibodaux knew

much about the mysterious woman except that Palmer trusted her implicitly both in ability and devotion. She could have been forty or fifty. Flawless skin and extreme athletic ability made it impossible to tell her age. If she was younger, she had crammed a great deal of knowledge and skill into a short life span. She went by Mrs. Miyagi, but wore no ring and Quinn had never heard anyone mention a Mr. Miyagi. It seemed impolite to ask.

A flood of morning light reflected off the highly polished bamboo flooring in the study. Though numerous books on kendo, yoga, and the philosophy of combat lined the back wall, the room was sparse, with only a small center table and four identical wooden chairs. Contemplation and comfort did not, in Miyagi's opinion, go hand in hand.

Sitting in the chair beside the woman, Quinn used a remote to scroll through a series of photographs that flickered across a flat-screen monitor in the center of the bookcase. Thibodaux stood, wearing a pair of Miyagi's required fluffy maroon house slippers with his 5.11 tactical khakis.

Winfield Palmer was connected by video link, his face appearing in the bottom right corner of the monitor. He was able to view the same files from his remote office near Crystal City, a stone's throw from the Pentagon.

"No word yet on the fingers you gave me," the national security advisor said from behind his huge mahogany desk. "Or the photo of the man at the airport. I have a friend in the Japanese government who's checking back channels, though, so I'm not giving up yet."

"I appreciate it, sir," Quinn said.

"As for your mystery woman at Zamora's party," Palmer continued, "NSA gave us everything they have on known female Eastern Bloc operatives. I had them prioritize from your description."

A series of new photos began to flash on the screen. Quinn found the woman he was looking for less than ninety seconds into the search.

"That's her there," he said, hovering the cursor arrow over the headshot of a pleasant-looking woman in her twenties. She had emerald eyes and a splash of freckles across a smallish nose. Her particulars appeared under the official visa photograph. "She looks less world-weary than when I saw her and her hair is longer now, but it's definitely the same person."

"Agent Aleksandra Kanatova of the *Federal'naya Sluzhba Bezopasnosti*," Thibodaux mused. "FSB. You were close, *l'ami*, when you guessed SVR."

According to official policy the FSB, or Federal Security Service, generally worked within the confines of the Russian border, much as the FBI or Homeland Security operated in the United States. Like the CIA, the Federal Intelligence Service, or SVR, was supposed to handle missions outside the Russian Federation. In reality, the lines often blurred. Each agency had authority to act on orders directly from the Russian president to carry out actions up to and including directed assassination—and agents from both worried little about borders when it came to the security and intelligence needs of Mother Russia.

Quinn scrolled through the sparse NSA file.

"She comes by her job naturally." Palmer's voice crackled over the video link as he perused the file on his own. "Her father was a colonel in the KGB and her mother was a gymnastics coach, so they traveled a great deal when she was young. Looks like she was an Olympic hopeful until she shattered her wrist at sixteen. . . . Studied international business at Moscow University. . . ."

"International business." Thibodaux smirked. "Another term for majoring in spy craft."

Miyagi glared at him.

"Just saying." He rolled his eyes.

"You're right, Jacques," Palmer said. A photograph of a much younger Kanatova appeared on the screen. She was standing on a rooftop restaurant somewhere in New York with the Empire State Building in the background. A rugged-looking man with a weathered face and wide grin stood beside her. He looked to be several years older than Kanatova. His broad arm draped around her shoulders.

"This photo is from eleven years ago. She speaks fluent English and German," Palmer said. "CIA shows her working in Manhattan as a translator for two years right after college. She was likely already set up with FSB by this time."

"Who's the guy with her?" Quinn asked.

"Mikhail Polzin," Palmer said.

"Hmm." Thibodaux gave an understanding nod. "The agent who was killed with Cooper in Uzbekistan."

"That's right," Palmer said. "We don't have any record of him coming to the U.S., so he must have been active then. Polzin was believed to be her handler."

"They seem pretty damned cozy," Thibodaux said. He kept his head turned so he wouldn't have to see Miyagi's glare.

Quinn used his remote to scroll through the attached pages on the screen. "Doesn't appear to be much else. She shows up in Chechnya for a short time as some sort of military liaison, then nothing."

"The fact that she and Polzin were acquainted means something," Palmer said. "On another matter, this race you've signed up for is causing me no small amount of heartburn. I may as well be buying a banana republic with the money we're paying to get you in at the last minute and on the QT. The cover is that you signed up months ago but your paperwork got lost."

"Thanks, boss," Quinn said. "It looked like the best way to stay close to Zamora for a while." He couldn't help but feel a sense of exhilaration just thinking about the sand and heat and speed of the Dakar Rally. The wildness of it made him breathe a little faster.

"Border Patrol popped a Syrian with ties to al-Qaeda coming across from Canada near Niagara Falls. Documents in his car tie him to a shipping container that delivered, among other things Chinese ATMs manufactured by Shenzhen KVSIO, the same company that made the ATMs used in the first two bombings."

"Is he talking?" Thibodaux asked.

"Won't shut up," Palmer said. "He swears someone is trying to frame him. The Bureau and Homeland are putting the squeeze on all the ports as we speak. . . ."

"But you think the evidence was planted?" Quinn nodded in agreement.

"It all seems a little too neat," Palmer said. "From your report, I'm not willing to write Zamora off just yet. The Russians think there's something going on or you wouldn't have run into Ms. Kanatova. I've got to tell you, though—doesn't it seem odd that he'd be off running a race like this if he was trying to move a weapon worth over a quarter billion dollars?"

"He's a flake," Thibodaux offered. "Bomb or no bomb, he's gotta have the three A's to be happy—adventure, approval, and . . ." He looked at a stoic Mrs. Miyagi before continuing. ". . . women."

Palmer leaned back in his chair as the phone began to ring on his desk. "Keep me informed," he said. "Emiko, I have to take this. If you don't mind filling them in on the rest."

Mrs. Miyagi bowed slightly in her seat.

"Of course."

Palmer disconnected.

Mrs. Miyagi stayed in her high-backed chair. "Due to the short lead time involved, Mr. Palmer has ordered the KTM 450 rally bike you require, along with your support truck, to be flown south to rendezvous in the South Atlantic with a cargo vessel already en route to Mar del Plata. It should arrive shortly before you do, giving you time to clear Argentine customs before the race." She handed Quinn a small device the size and shape of a dash-mounted GPS. "This will scan for gamma radiation. You can use it to interrogate Zamora's vehicle and equipment. If he has the bomb with him, it should leave a signature and we can take appropriate action. Now, I understand your brother is to accompany you?"

"Yes." Quinn took the handheld sensor and slid it in his jacket pocket. "He's a wild child, but he's also a competent mechanic. We'll need someone we can trust handling that side of things."

"Very well," she said. "A contact from State who cooperates with Mr. Palmer will provide an unregistered sidearm for each of you upon your arrival." She rose quickly, turned away as if to leave, then spun back with a sort of snap aggressiveness that reminded Quinn of a shark.

"I am to make you truly aware of what this device

will do," she said. Her dark eyes, multihued as mossy agates, flicked back and forth between the two men.

Though he'd seen plenty of devastation and heartache during his deployments to the Middle East, Quinn was not entirely sure he comprehended the magnitude of a nuclear detonation on American soil.

Miyagi saw it in his face and her eyes softened. In her mind, ignorance was better than swagger—so long as her students were willing to learn.

"It has become almost trite," she said with her oval face canted a little to the side as it often was when she explained things. From anyone else, it might have come across as condescending, but Emiko Miyagi looked as if she merely wanted more than just her words to be understood. "Do you remember where you were on September 11, 2001?"

Quinn nodded. Thibodaux looked at the tatami floor.

Miyagi continued. "Nineteen al-Qaeda terrorists murdered almost three thousand people that day. Over six thousand more were physically injured, but we will never know the true human cost. The U.S. stock market lost almost one and a half trillion dollars in value that week—and, of course, we went to war." She raised her hand as if to ward off a question. "I do not condemn the war. I am, as you have observed, perhaps as bellicose a woman as you will ever meet. I merely point it out as a consequence of September 11. The entire world changed that day.

"Those nineteen killed three thousand and changed so very much, but we have rebuilt and made ourselves, as Hemingway says, 'stronger at the broken places.' " She sighed, slowly nodding her head. "But gentlemen, my people know something of a nuclear bomb. Even a small device will bring more destruction than we as Americans can imagine. Our economy is a fragile egg, ready to be crushed underfoot at any moment by the next catastrophe. If intelligence reports are true, Baba Yaga is capable of delivering five kilotons of destructive power. That's a third the yield of the bomb dropped on Hiroshima that killed a hundred and forty thousand and forced the surrender of the Japanese government.

"Now, imagine how this will change the world: A five-kiloton explosion would produce a firestorm over two square miles. If such a device were to be detonated in Lower Manhattan it would not only destroy the major buildings of the Financial District, but virtually everything from Battery Park through Chinatown and Little Italy all the way to SoHo. Great volumes of superheated air would shoot into the sky. Hurricane-force winds would drive the flames through the rest of the city. Police and fire rescue would be completely overwhelmed. National Guard would mobilize, but by then thousands more are dead or dying from radiation exposure. If detonated in the right location, tens of thousands would be gone within the week.

"I have explained the effects of such a device on New York," Miyagi concluded. "Now think on this. A bomb such as Baba Yaga could be placed in Anchorage or New Orleans—in short, anywhere."

Thibodaux breathed in heavily through his nose, clenching the muscles in his massive jaw. "Well," he said. "I guess we'd better find the damned thing."

Miyagi raised a delicate black eyebrow. "Yes, Jacques, you'd better, for there is no surrender."

"That's fine," Quinn said. "Because I'm not the surrendering type."

"And I don't suggest you are." Miyagi's voice was strained, as if the weight of the world rested on her small shoulders. "But that does not matter. The people we fight now do not care if we surrender or not. They only want to see us dead."

Quinn's phone buzzed just as he threw a leg over his motorcycle. He tapped the Bluetooth device on the side of his helmet and answered.

"Daddy!" Mattie Quinn's voice filled his helmet and his heart.

"Hey, kiddo," he said, leaning forward to rest across the tank and handlebars.

"Do you have my Christmas present yet?"

"That's a surprise," he said. In truth, he had no idea what to buy a little girl. Kim proved little help, seeming to enjoy letting him twist in the wind with his decision. "Do you still want to be a doctor when you grow up?"

"Not anymore," she said. "Now I want to be a scientist or maybe a teacher . . . or a lawyer."

"A lawyer?"

"No." She giggled. "Mom told me I should say that to bug you. Really and truly, right this minute, I think I want to go into the Air Force."

"Did Mom tell you to say that?"

Mattie sucked in her breath. "Oh no." She giggled again. "But it bugs her when I do."

Jericho grinned while his little girl shared her dreams and goals and wishes for Christmas. She might look like her mother, but sadly for her, Mattie Quinn was an awful lot like him.

CHAPTER 22

Miami

The SinFull strip club hadn't changed décor since it was the Booby Trap in the late eighties. Aleks Kanatova sat in a corner booth and wondered if the carpet had ever been vacuumed. A black light hung on the wooden paneling made the tonic water in her gin glow an eerie blue. Cigarette smoke hung in swirling plumes and dance music vibrated the walls with a rhythmic bass thrum. The heady odor of desperation made it difficult to breathe.

Umarov had been sitting at the bar for nearly an hour, drinking vodka martinis and throwing lousy tips at a sullen pole dancer named Cinnamon—whose black G-string did a poor job of covering her C-section scar. The only other dancer, a roundish Latina in nothing but a flimsy open teddy and a pair of red stiletto heels, ate a Big Mac and fries at the end of the bar. There was a kitchen in the back, but Aleksandra made a mental note to stick with just her drink. It was a bad sign that the hired girls wouldn't eat from the menu.

It was midafternoon and there were less than a half

dozen patrons in the place. Cinnamon hung by one arm off the pole with all the charisma of someone waiting for a bus. In a city where titty bars were as plentiful as corner gas stations, the blue-collar customers seemed more interested in a European soccer game on the flat-screen television than in any of Cinnamon's labored gyrations. Despite the seedy atmosphere, the bartender smiled a lot and chatted easily about local politics with the Latina eating the Big Mac—as if she wasn't naked. From the bulk of his arms, Aleksandra guessed he doubled as the bouncer during the day shift.

Following the Chechen had been easy enough. During their struggle at Zamora's party, Aleksandra had dropped a gold money clip from a belt pouch on her swimsuit, making certain it fell right before his eyes. Umarov was known to like shiny things and Aleksandra had correctly assumed he would pick it up if given the opportunity. The clip itself was plated, but three gold ten-ruble coins bearing the head of Tsar Nicholas II were brazed along its length. Inside the hollow coins and body of the clip hid the circuitry of an electronic tracker. Even when she lost sight of him, Aleksandra could read the signal on her smartphone as long as she was within a mile of the coins.

"Finally," she mumbled to herself. The Chechen pushed away from the bar and staggered toward the long hallway leading to the restroom without giving her a second look. He smelled of alcohol and his lap was covered with dancer dust, the telltale body glitter that had surely gotten more than one husband in trouble after he'd stopped for "drinks" on the way home from work.

She counted to twenty after Umarov shut the bathroom door, then followed him down the hall. Between the soccer game and Cinnamon, no one gave her a second look.

Relatively sure no one else had gone in the men's room, Aleksandra waited outside for another ten count to listen just in case. Daring was good; calculated daring was more likely to keep her alive. She heard nothing but the sound of a fan through the door. Satisfied, she took a last look down the hallway behind her and, seeing no one, tried the handle. As she suspected, it was locked. Operatives like Akhmad Umarov didn't live so long by being careless while they relieved themselves.

Restroom locks were only meant to discourage accidental walk-ins and it took Aleksandra less than fifteen seconds to quietly slip the mechanism. Drawing an H&K P7 nine-millimeter from under the tail of her loose shirt, she pushed open the door.

Inside, she eased the flimsy wooden door shut behind her, twisting the lock again. The room was small and there was barely enough space for the single urinal squeezed in between the porcelain sink and two toilet stalls. The far door was slightly ajar, but the Chechen's feet were visible under the edge of the nearest stall, his pants pooling in a wrinkled heap around his ankles. Aleksandra had to force herself to keep from gagging at the noxious smell that hung like a biological weapon in the small room.

The Chechen coughed, the universal signal to let someone know the stall was occupied, as if his odor wasn't already indicator enough.

Pistol in hand, Aleksandra kicked open the stall door

and pointed it at the Chechen's face. There were few things worse than facing a determined woman with a gun while sitting on the toilet.

But it was Aleksandra who froze.

What she'd thought was a warning cough had been a death groan. Dark, arterial blood soaked Umarov's gray T-shirt—but she hardly noticed. From the pattern on the tile floor it looked as though he'd tried to put up a fight—but that made little difference to her.

Above the Chechen's left eye, on the greasy smooth skin of his forehead was the unmistakable imprint of a double-headed eagle.

Whoever hit him had been wearing Mikhail's ring.

Aleksandra's heart shivered in her chest. She'd seen no one else come or go from the restroom since Umarov had gone in and there were no windows—

She dropped instantly, spinning as she fell to shoot through the wall separating the two stalls. Working on a sudden dump of adrenaline, she heard no shots but watched bullet holes appear in the metal divider as someone—the man who'd killed her friend—returned her fire. He must have been perched on the toilet for her to have missed his feet when she first came in. She cursed herself for such stupidity. Instinctively, she grabbed the dead Chechen and yanked him down on top of her for cover, shooting around his flopping arm.

Her H&K carried nine rounds, including the one in the chamber—not enough to conduct the type of gunfight Americans called spray and pray. Aleksandra had already used six firing through the stall. She was an excellent shot but held little hope she hit anything vital shooting so blindly.

She was vaguely aware that the far stall slammed

open. She caught a shadowed glimpse of the other shooter as he lunged across the room and crashed out the flimsy wooden door.

"Idiot!" Aleksandra spat, as much to herself as the dead man in her lap. She collapsed back against the clammy wall, gun in hand, half expecting the shooter to come back and finish the job. She would never have left a witness alive.

Excited voices streamed in from the hallway.

Moving quickly, she tucked the pistol back in the holster over her kidney, then ripped the buttons of her shirt to expose her bra. She rubbed her hand across the Chechen's chest, then wiped a smear of his blood on her face and exposed shoulder.

Umarov was heavy and it took all of Aleksandra's strength to push his dead weight off her legs as the bartender peeked his head into the men's room.

He stood in open-mouthed shock as she crawled across the tile floor toward him, blood smeared across her face.

"He . . . he . . ." She said little, letting her appearance and the dead man with his pants around his ankles tell the story. Willing her body to shake, she conjured up buckets of sniffling tears and tugged at the collar of her torn shirt in a show of horrified modesty. She'd worn her green lace bra and knew the bartender would be hard pressed to recall much for a police artist. Right now he saw her only as a pair of heaving breasts covered in gore.

"You'll be okay," he whispered, helping her to her feet. He passed her back to a wan-looking Cinnamon, who looked sickly pale and out of place, wearing nothing but her G-string and body glitter in the stark light of the restroom.

While the bartender and others went in to investigate the dead man with his pants around his ankles, Aleksandra slipped down the dark hallway and out the front door before anyone figured out that she was a great deal more than an innocent victim.

She had reached her rental car two blocks away by the time she heard the sirens. She put on a fresh shirt from her bag in the backseat. The bloody one she stuffed in an old McDonald's sack before tossing it behind a palm tree. Less than six minutes from the time she'd exchanged gunfire with Mikhail's killer, she took the entrance ramp to I-95. The man who wore Mikhail's ring had surely murdered him—and was sure to be the one in possession of Baba Yaga. Whoever he was, that same man had just killed the Chechen she'd seen at Valentine Zamora's party. Aleksandra calmed herself with slow, rhythmic breaths. She used her thumb to punch numbers into the disposable cell phone as she drove.

Somehow, Valentine Zamora held the answers, and if he had the answers, it was very likely he had the bomb.

"It's me," she said. "I'm going to South America."

CHAPTER 23

"Your employer is very persuasive," General Bundu of the Bissau-Guinean Army said. He stood with his arms folded over his belly, which had grown considerably since his ascendance to top military leader. Legs spread wide apart like an oil derrick, he peered up at a cloudless West African sky.

"You have no idea," Matt Pollard mumbled from his spot in the dry grass beside the general. Above them, well out over the Atlantic, a slender Boeing 727 came out of a long downwind to bank slowly for a final approach. The runway was little more than five thousand feet of relatively obstacle-free hardpan with the trees and shrubs cleared from the parched salt grass on either side to give wing clearance to large aircraft. The ocean lapped at a breakwater of large black stones at the far end of the strip.

Behind Pollard and the general, two dozen riflemen, dressed in the woodland camouflage uniforms of the

Bissau-Guinean Army, stood guard over five palletized stacks of assorted boxes. The box Pollard was the most concerned with was packed in the center of the second pallet in line, hiding in plain sight. As far as he knew, no one at the airstrip but him was aware of the true contents of that particular case.

Off to the side, two rusted fuel trucks idled under the sparse shade of three lonely palms beside a tethered goat. Each truck contained about nine thousand gallons of jet fuel, more than enough to get the thirsty 727 refilled for her return flight as long as she was fitted with extra tanks.

Though Zamora hadn't explained the details of his operation, it hadn't been too difficult for Pollard to put it together. The U.S. war on drugs made it increasingly difficult to smuggle large quantities of product across the Mexican border. South American cartels had branched out to lucrative European markets. Large oceangoing trawlers were still a favorite method of transport, but with the glut of retired commuter aircraft on the market, cartels were able to purchase planes for pennies on the dollar. Large quantities of cocaine now moved via these DC-9s, 727s, and older Gulfstreams, primarily from Venezuela to West Africa. Sometimes it was cheaper to pay the pilots two or three hundred grand to fly over a load of dope, then once the delivery was made, torch the plane and fly home commercially.

But Zamora dealt in weapons, many of them coming from former Soviet Bloc countries. The return drug flights offered the perfect way of getting his guns and explosive ordnance back to South America.

Zamora had been clear on one thing. Pollard's job

was to escort the bomb back to Venezuela, where he could work on it away from prying eyes, perform what maintenance it needed, and get past the Permissive Action Link. In simple terms, the PAL was the arming code for the bomb, the encrypted signal that permitted someone to blow it up. The U.S. had been using them since the 1960s in one form or another to safeguard against the very scenario Pollard now faced. Later PALs were impossible to bypass. As nuclear physicist Peter Zimmerman put it—"Bypassing a PAL should be about as complex as performing a tonsillectomy while entering the patient from the wrong end."

Pollard wasn't entirely sure he'd be able to pull it off. He was, however, certain that if he didn't, Zamora and his insane girlfriend would murder Marie and Simon without a second's thought.

It was the perfect conundrum for his ethics class. Who is more important? The two people in the world you love the most, or fifteen thousand strangers? Should sheer numbers matter, or was the worth of one soul comparable to that of a thousand others? Pollard's skull ached from rehearsing the arguments over and over, then sobbing himself into an exhausted sleep.

Zamora was obviously sure enough Pollard would choose his family that he didn't even bother to put a guard with him. Perhaps Zamora knew him better than he knew himself.

General Bundu raised his hand and twirled it in a tight circle as the big jet made a breaking turn at the end of the runway amid a cloud of red dust and lumbered back toward them. His men sprang into action, jumping onto a gang of three ancient forklifts to be ready to unload as soon as the plane came to a stop.

More time on the ground meant more chance of interception.

"The goal is to exchange cargo by the time they have finished fueling," Bundu said, taking a square tin of snuff from the breast pocket of his uniform. "The pilots don't like to stay on the ground too long." His men moved with antlike precision, but the general's eyes flicked this way and that with each order he gave as if the entire operation was his first time.

One of the forklift operators rolled up to the front of the aircraft and raised an empty pallet up as the front door swung open. A slender man who was obviously the pilot stepped onto the pallet and grabbed the attached handrail. He wore sturdy boots, jeans, and a well-worn leather jacket. Silver-gray hair was mussed from wearing a headset for hours on end.

The forklift driver backed up a few feet and lowered the pallet smoothly to the ground. The pilot stepped off and strode over to where Pollard and Bundu stood.

Pollard started to shake hands, but realized maybe that wasn't the thing to do with these drug-running types.

"Change of plans," the pilot said, peering between bushy gray eyebrows and the top of his Ray-Bans.

Bundu tensed and Pollard held his breath.

"How so?" the general asked.

"We're offloading here as usual," the pilot said. "But the boss says we are not to take this cargo back to Caracas."

"The boss?" Pollard asked. "Zamora said not to take the load back?"

"That's right," the pilot said. "But we still need to get airborne again right away." He began to look longingly at the dilapidated hangar. "I gotta take a serious dump and I'd just as soon not cram myself in the head on board that box of bolts."

"I don't understand," Pollard said. "What am I supposed to do with the . . . items we have on hand?"

"I don't give a shit," the pilot said, turning for the hangar. "And neither does Rafael Zamora."

Pollard grabbed him by the shoulder.

"You mean Valentine Zamora," he said.

The pilot tore off his sunglasses and glared at Pollard. "Son," he hissed. "You'll want to let go of me now."

Pollard nodded and stepped back.

"Sorry," he said. "Rafael?"

The pilot turned to go. "Rafael is Valentine's daddy. Those are *his* drugs being off-loaded from *his* airplane."

"But we have to get this load back," Pollard said, his voice sounding more desperate than he would have liked. He left out the part about his wife and son being killed if he failed.

Pollard borrowed Bundu's phone and called the emergency number Zamora had given him.

The Venezuelan sputtered with anger at the news. "He said what? Never mind what he said. . . . The device must get to . . . Tell the pilot I will pay him double. . . . No, tell him I'll have him shot. . . . Wait, put him on and let me tell him myself. . . ."

Pollard took a deep breath and held it for a long moment, wracking his brain. It killed him to think up viable solutions for this man.

Before he could speak, Zamora began ranting again. "I'll call my father and find out what this is all about. Tell General Bundu to shoot the pilots if they try to leave before I call back."

The line went dead and Pollard relayed the message to a stunned Bundu.

"This job proves much more difficult than I imagined," the deflated general whispered. His round face drooped like a despondent schoolboy's. "If I shoot Rafael Zamora's pilots he will send men to murder me. If I don't shoot Rafael Zamora's pilots, Valentine Zamora will come to Africa and murder me himself."

Luckily for everyone involved, the pilot's business inside the hangar took long enough that Valentine was able to call back and ask to speak to him. The pilot stood chatting for a full minute. His head swiveled this way and that as if he expected a raid at any moment. At length he shrugged and said, "Okay, I'll keep our deal going. But if your father finds out, we're all dead."

He passed the phone back to Pollard.

"It seems my father believes our shipments bring unnecessary scrutiny on his high office," Zamora said. "The bastard has barred me from doing business in my own country, Matthew. Can you believe that? He said he'd have me arrested if I landed in Venezuela with a load of weapons."

Pollard swallowed. He didn't know what to say. He only wanted to see his wife and son again.

"In any case," Zamora went on. "Your priorities have not changed. Do as the pilot tells you. I will see you soon—and when I do, I hope for your family's sake everything is in working order." His voice grew giddy as if they were old friends. "Okay then, bye now. . . ."

Pollard switched off the phone and let his hand fall to his side. He looked at the pilot for directions.

"Load your shit," the pilot said. "Looks like I'm taking you to Bolivia—if the bastards don't shoot us out of the air."

CHAPTER 24

The spacious interior of the Gulfstream V gave Valentine Zamora room to stretch his legs as he reclined in one of two buttoned leather seats at the front of the cabin. Monagas sat in the other, and the gaptoothed twins lay in the settees along the cabin walls behind, each with her nose glued to a cell phone.

Zamora had a wet cloth over his eyes and his own phone pressed to his ear.

"I told you, we have nothing to worry about," he said. Discussions like this made him want to strangle something helpless. "The move to Bolivia is a mere hiccup."

"I understood our purchase included the use of your pipeline into the United States," the voice on the other end said. It clicked with a thick Arab accent "The American border is a very long way from Bolivia."

"I am aware of the geography." Zamora clenched his teeth. "All that is left is for you to transfer the balance of what I am owed to my Cayman account. Things are already set in motion to move the product north. I have planned for all eventualities, *Inshallah*." He threw out the Arabic as a statement of solidarity.

"Oh," the voice said, unimpressed. "Make no mistake. This is most definitely God's will. We are looking closely at the target you suggested. It seems worthy—"

Zamora rose up in his seat, ripping the wet cloth from his eyes. "Of course it is worthy!" He fought to keep from screaming. "What could possibly hurt the Americans more than this?" The call was scrambled, but he stopped short of actually naming the interfaith choir. One could never be certain of the American NSA.

"Is not the device ours once we purchase it?"

"Of course it is." Zamora stood to pace up and down the aisle as he spoke. One of the gap-toothed twins reached out to give his leg an affectionate touch and got the back of his hand in return. "But things are already set in motion."

"Relax," the voice said. "We are merely exploring other avenues. My brother is looking at your route as well as your target."

Zamora ran a hand through his hair, wracking his brain. "Do you not trust me, my friend?"

"Of course," the voice said. "I trust—but tie my camels tightly. Before there can be a target, I need your assurance that you can actually move the device up from Bolivia."

"You have my word," Zamora said. "There is nothing to worry about."

Zamora ended the call and turned to watch the clouds outside the G Five's oval window. Of course there was nothing to worry about. Nothing but thousands of miles of jungle, poorly maintained aircraft, guerrilla armies, and the governments of most of the free world that wanted to see him killed—and that didn't even take into account his father.

But before any of that mattered, Matthew Pollard had to make the damned thing work.

CHAPTER 25

Virginia

His bags packed, Quinn switched on the standing lamp beside his leather sofa and plopped down with the two-foot cardboard box he'd picked up from the post office. Flicking open his ZT folder from his pocket, he broke his own rule about using a "people-killing" knife to cut cardboard.

Quinn knew what was inside before he opened it. Smiling, he lifted the fourteen-inch curved blade.

He picked up his phone with the other hand.

"Ray," he said when the other party answered. "You are the man!"

"You got it?" Ray Thibault's smiling voice came across the line. He and his son, Ryan, ran Northern Knives in Anchorage. Both were on Quinn's short list of trustworthy people. Ryan wore his hair in a buzz cut and shared his father's easy laugh and religious zeal for all things edged. An expert pistol shot and knife fighter, Ryan carried a straight razor in his belt. Not everyone respected a pistol, he reasoned, but nearly everyone had been cut at least once. It was something they wanted to avoid at all cost—which made a straight razor a formidable psychological weapon. Ray preferred an Arkansas Toothpick. All grins and friendly advice, both father and son gave off a calm but deadly don't-screw-with-me air.

"It looks like you left a kukri and a Japanese short sword in a drawer together and they had offspring," Quinn said.

"We call it the Severance." Ray gave an easy chuckle. "We talked about calling it the Jericho, but I thought you might get pissed. Anyway, when we heard about Yawaraka-Te, Ryan and I wanted you to have something to use."

Quinn turned the knife in the lamplight. It was fourteen inches long and nearly an eighth of an inch thick along the spine. A black parachute-cord strap hung from a hole in the nasty skull-crusher pommel. The olive drab scales felt as natural in Quinn's hand as the throttle of his motorcycle.

He missed Yawaraka-Te, and frankly could not wait until Mrs. Miyagi had her repaired. But for the utilitarian chores he might find in South America, Severance seemed to be the perfect blade. It looked to be the kind of knife that could cut down a small tree or convince an opponent that he should comply in order to keep his head.

"Mind field-testing it for us?" Ray asked, the sparkle in his eyes almost audible on the phone.

"I appreciate this more than you know, Ray." Quinn weighed the blade in his hand, feeling the balance and heft of it. "But the places I go, you might not get it back."

"Good deal," Ray said. "Now about that other matter. Just send her by. I think I know exactly what she needs. . . ."

"Are you really going to buy me a pocketknife?" Mattie Quinn asked ten minutes later when Jericho had her on the phone.

"Everybody needs a knife, sweet pea," he said. "Go ahead and check me right now."

"Okay." Mattie giggled. "Dad, have you got your pocketknife on you?"

"I have my pants on, don't I?" Quinn said, sharing their inside joke. When she was barely old enough to understand, he'd promised her that if was wearing pockets and she caught him without a knife, he would buy her a soda.

"Mom says I might be too young."

"I'll square it with Mom," Quinn said, knowing full well Kim was likely on the other line. "Do you cut up your own steak?"

"Of course, Dad. I'm seven." He could hear her crinkling her nose in that adorable way of hers.

"Well, the way I see it, a steak knife is way bigger than a pocketknife." Quinn practiced the line of reasoning he planned to use on Kim. "I already talked to Ray about which one."

"I like Ray," Mattie said. "He's got the pet piranha."

"All you have to do is get Mom to take you by the store," Quinn said. "Merry Christmas, sweet pea."

"Miss you, Dad," she said.

"Miss you too. Can you put Mom on?"

"Sure," Mattie said. "I'll go get her. But you should know, she's pretty mad about you not coming home for Christmas."

Kim picked up immediately.

"I'm not mad," she said, defending herself. "Just disappointed . . . for Mattie. What's up?"

"Full disclosure," Quinn said, chewing on his bottom lip. "I've talked to Ray about getting Mattie a knife for Christmas." It astounded Quinn that he faced the most ruthless killers in the world without so much as a blink, but shuddered when he talked to his ex-wife.

"A knife?" she said. "Seriously?"

"Seriously," he said, wishing for a terrorist to fight.

The phone went quiet for a long moment. "I guess I'm cool with her getting a pocketknife." Kim changed her tune. "We are talking pocketknife, right, and not some people-killin' cutlass?"

Quinn smiled at how much of him had rubbed off on her over the years. He released a pent-up breath, giving a thumbs-up to his empty living room. "You have my word. I won't buy her a sword."

Kim's voice suddenly took on the playful tone that had snared him in the first place. "I made enchiladas."

"That sounds great." Quinn said. "You know I would be there if I could be."

"Did you know Steve and Connie are getting married at the Academy?" she asked, changing the subject. "I forgot they weren't married already."

"I did. He asked me to be part of the ceremony." Steve Brun had graduated from USAFA the same year as Quinn. They'd both served as Squadron Commanders, Quinn of the 20th Trolls and Brun of the 19th

Wolverines. They'd led the Air Force Sandhurst competition team at West Point and gone through the rigorous pipeline of Air Force Special Operations training. While Quinn had moved to OSI, Brun had remained a combat rescue officer. Quinn had even introduced Steve to Jacques Thibodaux on a previous mission and they'd hit it off immediately. Brun had actually been together with his fiancée, Connie, for over ten years and they had finally decided tie the knot. From the very beginning, the two couples had done everything together. Kim and Connie remained close even after the divorce.

"Are you going?" Quinn asked.

"I don't know," she said. "Connie asked me to."

"Good," he said.

"Listen," she said, her voice suddenly distant. "Gary Lavin has asked if I want to be his date."

"I see," Quinn said, feeling like he'd just been punched in the gut. "That will be interesting. Well, it'll be good to see you anyway."

Captain Gary Lavin was another acquaintance from the Academy, though he'd gone on to fly C-17s and eventually transferred to the 517th at Elmendorf in Anchorage. He'd been sniffing around Kim since they were cadets, so it made sense he'd look her up now that she was divorced.

"Listen, I have to go," Quinn said, suddenly tired of talking.

"I know, I just . . ." Her voice trailed off as it often had when they'd spoken over the last three years.

"You what?" Quinn prodded softly, bracing himself for an avalanche of emotion.

"I just can't help thinking that every time we say good-bye it might be the last. That kills me, you know."

"We won't say it then," Quinn said, consoling her as best he could. "How about Merry Christmas?"

"Okay," she said, her voice hollow. It was obvious he only made her miserable. "Merry Christmas. . . ."

He ended the call and tossed the phone on the coffee table beside the open box.

Over the years of courtship and marriage he'd missed countless holidays because of his job. Kim hadn't liked the idea, but she'd put up with it, more or less. Other spouses missed special events because of deployments. Their loved ones cried a little and sucked it up. The country was fighting two wars.

Kim had left him, trashed him to his face, and even cursed him after he'd saved her life. He still loved her past the point of sanity, but he'd never really understand her. One minute she held him close, the next she wanted to take off his head. Loving Kimberly Quinn was like roasting in an exquisite flame—and getting stabbed a lot with a really big fork.

From the moment they met, he'd made no secret of the fact that he was in love with fast machines, bloody-knuckle brawls, and frequent travel to dark and dangerous parts of the world. She'd climbed aboard his bike and hung on for what he thought would be their grand adventure. Unbeknownst to him, she'd hoped from that very first ride to change him. He, on the other hand, had rolled on the gas and prayed this pretty blonde with her arms wrapped around his waist would stay the same forever.

But now, Jericho couldn't tell her about the bomb. He'd had to tell her he was missing Christmas because he'd entered a motorcycle race.

CHAPTER 26

7:30 PM

Quinn traveled in and out of D.C. enough that he knew virtually every security supervisor at Reagan National. He avoided the larger, more distant Dulles whenever he had the opportunity and now paid for it with a long wait at security. They were already boarding by the time he made it to the gate. Thibodaux was late, likely saying good-bye to his wife for the twentieth time. Good for him. At least he had a wife who missed him.

Quinn found his seat. Out of habit from flying armed it was an exit row with his right arm in the aisle. He took out a couple of motorcycle magazines and some study material, then shoved his carry-on in the overhead compartment. So far, he had the row to himself. He knew such luck would never last, and played a little game guessing the odds that each passenger would be his seatmate as they walked down the aisle toward him.

He dreaded the long flight to Argentina, preferring a poke in the eye to being stuffed into the long tin cans that served as modern-day airliners. He wasn't tall by any standards, but he felt sorry for Jacques, who had to wedge himself into the narrow seats. In truth, he should have paid for a seat and a half because any unsuspecting seatmate ended up with the big Cajun's shoulder and elbow in his or her lap during the entire flight.

More than anything Quinn dreaded the endless hours of flight. He'd never been one to let his guard down enough to sleep on an airplane surrounded by people close enough to smell. He planned to study some Chinese flash cards—they drew fewer looks than Arabic—and read some new motorcycle and gun magazines. But that still left hours with nothing to entertain him but his own thoughts. The flights between Miami and D.C. had given him way too much time to think already—and lately, when he thought, it was about Veronica Garcia.

Still alone in his row, he checked his TAG Aquaracer. Nearly eight in the evening during the Christmas holidays and he was on his way out of the country—again. He couldn't help but wonder what Garcia was doing.

He knew her parents were dead. She had an aunt in Miami, but Miyagi made it sound like the agent trainees would only get a couple of days of break considering the present state of affairs in the country so he doubted she'd traveled far.

Quinn took out his phone to turn it off for the flight and without thinking, pressed Garcia's speed-dial. No one—federal agents or agent trainees—should be completely alone during the holidays.

It rang twice before connecting. A man's voice answered, going a hundred miles an hour.

"Ronnie's phone. She's a busy lady and can't talk right now."

Quinn could hear the rhythmic beat of music and the buzz and crack of people playing pool in the background. A hundred voices seemed to be talking at once.

"I'll call back another time," Quinn said.

"Message?" the man said, shouting over the din.

"No," Quinn said. "I'm good."

"Very well, my friend. You have yourself a happy holiday."

"Yeah, you too," Quinn grunted and hung up. This guy was far too peppy for his taste. Ronnie wasn't alone during the holidays after all. . . .

He looked up just as a heavyset person of ambiguous gender wearing a sleeveless mechanic's shirt and carrying a pastrami sandwich nodded toward the seat beside him.

Quinn stepped into the aisle. Sighing to himself, he turned off his phone for the long flight to Argentina.

Ronnie Garcia walked out of the ladies' room at the Corner Pocket in downtown Williamsburg and pushed through the crowds to rejoin her classmates. Though it was chilly outside, her roommate had persuaded her to dress to party in tight black capris and an off-the-shoulder red silk blouse.

"What'd I miss?" she said, smiling at the youngsters at her table. At twenty-nine, she was in the best shape of her life, but it was still difficult to keep up with the college crowd that made up the bulk of CIA trainees.

Everyone but her had some sort of advanced degree in economics, law, or political science. Some had been interns for powerful senators, others came from rich families, all were incredibly bright. Apart from Garcia and a former Army Special Forces officer, none of her class had ever seen a moment of conflict more violent than a lovers' quarrel. Just hearing their naïve dreams, Garcia couldn't help but think of Jericho Quinn and his maxim: *Everyone thinks they have a plan until they get punched in the nose.*

Sometime it was a fist that gave you that punch, sometimes it was just life.

She scooted back into her seat around the table of eight, showing a tight smile at the thought of another hour with this crew. They were fine in a mock firefight and could interrogate role-players with the best, but she found hanging with them felt like playing Barbie with the twelve-year-olds after she'd already made out with her first guy. It had been a mistake to come, but she just couldn't bear the thought of being stuck alone in the dorms.

Roger, a dark-eyed frat boy of Persian descent, grinned as she sat down, wagging his finger. He made no secret of the fact that he'd had a crush on her from their first day of polygraph class. She'd let him know right away that she was far too much woman for a youngster like him to handle—which only served to inflame his resolve. She'd been annoyed, but not surprised, when he'd showed up that evening and joined their group.

Smacking the finger away, she looked down her nose at him. "Good way to lose a hand, amigo."

"You forgot your OPSEC," he chided, raising his eyebrows as if he had eight-by-ten glossies of her in the shower. There was a cuteness about him, like a Christmas ornament that you could look at for a while but were happy to box up again right after New Years.

OPSEC—operational security—was no laughing matter.

"What?" she said, worried. "What did I do?"

"You could use a man like me watching out for you." Roger held up her phone. "So many of our secrets are stuck in these little devices . . . and now I have access to yours, my dear. They say our brains are in our phones now."

"I don't think your brains are where you think they are." Garcia poured her drink in the kid's lap, snatching the phone away as he worked to catch his breath. "Let me tell you about a man who can handle me, Roger, my dear. When I fall down drunk and naked on the floor in the middle of a party, my man's job is to stand there and fend all the other bastards in the room off of me. If I leave top-secret files in the penthouse of a foreign hotel, he would go all Tom Cruise and climb up the outside windows with those little sticky gloves to get those files back and save my honor. I don't give a shit if I leave ten thousand dollars on the table when I go to pee. His job is to guard it with his life. And, he would never, ever, ever touch my phone. Comprende?"

Roger nodded, blinking quickly.

Ronnie turned to her roommate, who sat next to her. Her name was Bev, an Arabic and Farsi speaker from Maryland.

Bev snickered, rolling her eyes at the hapless Roger.

"You warned him that you were a hard one to handle."
She put a hand on Ronnie's arm. "I almost forgot. You
missed a call."

Ronnie got a jolt to the heart when she saw Jericho's
number. She bumped Roger out of the way with her hip
as she moved quickly out of the booth, punching the
buttons to return the call.

His voice mail answered after the first ring. "Quinn's
phone, leave a message." She rang it again and got the
same response. Turning, she stared back at poor Roger
and tried to talk herself out of killing him.

DAKAR

*Faster, faster, faster, until the thrill of speed
overcomes the fear of death.*

—HUNTER S. THOMPSON

CHAPTER 27

December 31
Mar del Plata, Argentina

The journey to reach the most dangerous race on earth was a race in and of itself. A ten-hour flight from Dulles to Buenos Aires saw Quinn standing in line for over an hour and a half to clear customs. He checked his phone and smiled when he saw two missed calls from Ronnie Garcia. He called her back, but got her voice mail. His phone began to buzz in his pocket again the moment he made it to the front of the line. A female Argentine customs officer waved him forward, her face stern though her gaudy red lipstick was painted into a smile. There was no way he would answer a cell phone call on her watch. Ronnie was back in class by the time the customs officer was through with him.

From the international airport it was another hour and a half through the city skirting crowds of out-of-work thirtysomethings who marched in what the cab-driver grudgingly called *protest del dia*, to Aeroparque Jorge Newbery, where he grabbed a domestic hop to Mar del Plata—the starting line of the Dakar.

A day and half after they'd left D.C., the Quinn brothers and Jacques Thibodaux stood with their orange KTM 450 race bike under the white tent along the breezy beaches of Argentina's third-largest city. Thousands of people had flocked from all over the world to watch the opening ceremonies. The streets were alive with prerace parties and impromptu tangos. Liquor and maté, South America's ubiquitous tea-like drink, flowed in abundance and abandon. The fragrant aromas of baking bread and grilled lamb, seasoned with just a hint of motor oil, settled comfortably over the crowds.

It was late afternoon and the area was a madhouse of prerace activity. Judges and engineers from the Amaury Sport Organisation swarmed over each motorcycle, Mini Cooper, Hummer, four-wheeler, and monster truck that planned to compete in the Dakar. The ASO was the same organization that sponsored the Tour de France and they had their bureaucracy well established. It was a nerve-wracking process known as *scrutineering*. Every item had to be checked, from required safety gear and engine size to the noise level of each vehicle's exhaust.

The contestants had snatched little more than a few minutes of sleep at a stretch over the past days leading up to the race. The additional stress of having their machines scrutinized by the overly discerning eyes of ASO engineers only added to the growing pit in their collective guts.

Quinn trusted Mrs. Miyagi to make certain the KTM conformed to Dakar regulations. The bike was generally stock so there was little chance it would break any rules. Valentine Zamora, on the other hand, was spun into the rafters, spitting and cursing his mechanics in a black soup of Spanish and English.

He stomped back and forth wearing a gaudy Hawaiian shirt and New York Knicks shorts, checking and then double-checking the decibel measurements coming from the muffler of his Yamaha.

"Imbeciles," he shouted at his two sheepish mechanics. They were the same young men he'd had with him at the track in Florida. "I pay you good money to get the motorcycle in perfect order and this is what you do to me? I swear to you." His voice was tight and shrill amid all the buzzing chatter from the crowd of competitors and fans crammed inside the spacious tent.

"Monsieur Zamora," a young Iranian motorcyclist named Navid Azimi tapped him on the shoulder.

Zamora spun, still spitting curses at his staff. "What is it?"

"You needn't fret," Azimi said. He pointed to his own bike, a blue and white Yamaha. "I had the very same issue. Your noise levels are just on the edge—easily remedied with a different muffler. I'm sure your mechanics have several in stock."

Zamora glared at his staff. "Is this true?"

The two mechanics nodded. "Of course, sir."

Zamora threw up his hands. "Then why didn't you say so?" His tirade over for the moment, he looked up and noticed Quinn for the first time. A wide smile spread over his face. "You made it," he said, walking over to grab Quinn's hand between his.

Quinn didn't bother to introduce Bo. Blond-haired and blue eyed, there was little chance he would be thought of as Jericho's brother. Zamora treated his staff as nothing more than a backdrop for the great adventure of his life, so Quinn followed suit.

"If I may be so bold, where is the lovely Ms. Garcia?" The Venezuelan made a show of scanning the crowd behind Jericho.

"She had to check on her friends in New York," Quinn said. "You know, that little bombing they had."

"Of course." Zamora nodded. "I understand the damage was extensive."

"I guess." Quinn shrugged "I stay out of that sort of thing. Too depressing. Anyway, good luck tomorrow."

Zamora canted his head to one side. "I make my own luck."

"Sounds ominous."

"It does, doesn't it? I don't mean it that way. I'm hosting a party at my chalet tonight. You should drop by for some wine and a cigar." Zamora put an arm around Quinn's shoulders. "Because, tomorrow, friendship takes a backseat to the race. Do you understand?"

"I wouldn't have it any other way," Quinn said.

"Monagas will get you the address. Come by anytime after nine. I don't plan on sleeping until tomorrow evening—"

One of the mechanics called for Zamora to ask him a question about the new muffler. Focused again on the bike, the Venezuelan turned and left Quinn without another word.

Bo walked up beside him while Jacques saw to the scrutineering of the KTM. He wore faded jeans and a gray mechanic's shirt with a TEAM QUINN patch over his right pocket.

"See those mean-looking dudes over by the ELF oil booth?" He kept his voice low. Blond hair, mussed as if he'd just gotten out of bed, hung just over the top of his ears. Tan from long hours riding his bike in the Texas sun, he was still lighter than Quinn, fair to his brother's swarthiness, heavily muscled to Jericho's wiry strength. Both looked as if they could grow a beard in a matter of minutes if they concentrated hard enough, but Bo's would have been a sandy red to Jericho's charcoal black.

"Droopy mustaches, look like brothers?"

"They are," Bo said. "Andres and Diego Borregos. Heard of 'em?"

Jericho nodded, looking sideways at Bo. "The Borregos brothers run one of the largest drug cartels in Colombia. Just how is it you happen to know them?"

Bo chuckled. "Relax, big brother. We don't run in the same circles if that's what you mean. I saw their pictures on CNN, that's all. You're not the only one in the fam with a spectacular memory, you know."

"Sorry," Quinn said, still not completely convinced. "I'm not surprised they're here. They may even be sponsoring one of the Colombian riders."

The Dakar was an expensive proposition. The entry fee alone was over twenty thousand and a good rally motorcycle ran well above fifty thousand dollars. Virtually every rider's bike and riding gear were plastered with ads for Red Bull, ELF, Loctite, Gauloises cigarettes, or some other commercial venture. Though Quinn's KTM, entry fee, and operational expenses were completely paid by the American taxpayer, the bike still bore a hodgepodge of sponsor stickers so it wouldn't stand out from the rest.

"Here come the superstars," Bo grunted, nodding to the entourage of crew and paparazzi that surrounded the two race favorites. Both riding for Team KTM and sponsored by the company, Nick Caine and Raynard Geroux could not have been any more different. Caine, the hulking South African, had an easy smile and lumbering gait that belied the grace with which he rode a motorcycle. He was patient with reporters and fans alike, giving interviews and signing autographs while other racers would stalk off to their trailers for a shower and hot meal. Though his brooding accent made him something of a chick magnet, every press conference saw him teary eyed and blowing kisses to his beautiful wife and baby daughter back in Cape Town.

Geroux, on the other hand, looked and acted like a bantam rooster. Famous for the neatly trimmed soul patch beneath a sneering smile, he strode past adoring fans without so much as a glance and had to be prodded into signing autographs by his handlers. The tabloids made a great show of the fact he was rarely seen with the same swimsuit model two times in a row.

Though few Americans had ever even heard of the Dakar Rally, it was third only to the Olympics and the World Cup in global attention. There were plenty of other great riders in the race. Navid Azimi, the promising young Iranian, had stepped outside the confined social restraints of his country to rocket to the top of the leaderboard in rally races around the globe. Exceptional riders from the United States, Europe, all over South America, and even Qatar filled the race board, but everyone knew the real contest was between Caine and Geroux.

"Congratulations," Thibodaux said, wiping his big hands on a shop towel as he walked up. He carried a free emergency kit courtesy of the Loctite booth. "We passed the scrutineers with nary a peep of protest." He threw back his head in a huge yawn that showed his teeth. "Tomorrow's a big day, *l'ami*. We could all use some sleep if we're gonna be alert enough to look for that . . . missing item."

"I've noticed something," Bo said, as they maneuvered back to their bike through the press of onlookers who stood in pockets to watch the scrutineering process. "There is an extremely high percentage of classy women in Argentina. I mean every hot pair of legs I see is sticking out of a pair of designer shorts—hardly a pair of cutoffs among them. I didn't realize it was so European down here."

Thibodaux yawned again, "I just heard some guy say Argentines are a bunch of Italians who speak Spanish but think they're British living in France."

A flash of red by the tent entry caught Quinn's eye as he threw a leg over the lanky KTM. Less than twenty yards away stood Russian FSB agent Aleksandra Kanatova. She met his eye, then froze for a long moment as if trying to figure out which way to run. By the time he'd started the 450's engine, she'd ducked out of the tent and disappeared.

CHAPTER 28

Quinn took the long way home, cruising the bike slowly in and out of the crowds in front of the Mar del Plata Naval Base scanning for any sign of Kanatova. As a competitor, he enjoyed a certain amount of celebrity, and spent a good deal of his ride giving high-fives to children as he rode past.

After twenty minutes he gave up looking for Kanatova and arrived back at the rented flat nearly the same time as Bo and Thibodaux, who'd walked back up the hill. The crickets had already begun to sing and the evening gathered in fast around them.

With all the excitement of the race it was nothing short of a miracle that Winfield Palmer had been able to find them a place in the respectable four-plex on such short notice. Only a mile and a half off the beach, it was perfectly located—far enough from the crowds to sleep, close enough to get where they needed to be with minimal loss of time.

Quinn secured the bike inside the garage and sprinted up the long flight of aged wooden stairs to grab the duffel off the bed in his room. The flight from Dulles, coupled with the stress of the race logistics, left him with a sore back and a knot in his gut.

He'd tried Garcia again, but got her voice mail. Feeling like a stalker for calling so much, he left her a message telling her things were about to get really busy, so he'd check in when he got back. He hoped she understood the subtext of the message—because he sure didn't.

A long run past Zamora's chalet would be just the ticket to work out the kinks and clear his head.

"Dude, you're going for a run?" Bo said, rolling his eyes when Quinn walked back down the stairs dressed in loose running pants and a dark blue T-shirt. "I forgot what an overachiever you are."

"Helps me think," Jericho shrugged. "And I like to get the lay of the backstreets as soon as practical."

"The practical thing is to get some sleep." Bo gave a long, catlike yawn, arching his back so his belly showed under the tail of his wifebeater shirt. "I'm glad it's you on the bike, Jer. And I won't be expected to keep up with you."

"I gotta call my wife," Thibodaux said, still trying to untangle himself from being crammed into business-class seating for so many hours on the plane. He stood blinking at the door, swaying like a huge tree in the breeze. "What time is it back home in Spotsylvania, Virginia?"

Bo looked at his watch, a TAG Heuer identical to Jericho's. "We're two hours later here, so it's about nine-thirty."

"Good," the big Cajun said, moving his head from side to side as he raised his eyebrows. "Kids'll be fed and bathed. Maybe Camille will be up for a game of escaped convict and the warden's wife on the phone. . . ."

By the time Jericho snugged the laces on his Nikes and took a drink from the kitchen tap, Bo and Jacques had already disappeared to their rooms. Jacques's belly laugh rattled the walls.

A long run was second only to a good motorcycle ride for clearing Quinn's mind. Beyond the obvious physical and psychological effects, a run got him outside the false sense of security a rented room gave and allowed him to see if anyone had him under surveillance.

Standing in the moist night air on the cracked concrete driveway of the four-plex, Quinn studied a tourist map of the area under the streetlight. He made a mental note of the streets and alleyways around Zamora's rented chalet less than a mile away.

When he ran at home Quinn usually stuffed the baby Glock 27 in an across-the-chest rig other runners might use to carry a cell phone or energy bars. It was easy to reach in the event of an emergency and snug enough to keep from bouncing around during a sprint. A pretty brunette with a thick Spanish accent had met them with two plain blue Colt Combat Commanders in .45 caliber, one for Quinn and one for Jacques. A proven weapon since 1911, it was still too large to carry on a run, so Jericho left it in his duffel beside Severance.

Unless he happened to be in a war zone, he was often forced by circumstance to be unarmed when overseas. Always happy to have a sidearm or blade, he knew enough not to bank on traditional protection. Weapons were available everywhere if one only knew where to look for them.

Noting the time of 11:40, Jericho turned and trotted into the darkness.

When the Quinn boys were younger, their father had often taken them hunting in areas known for large populations of Alaska brown bear. Rather than letting them hide frightened in the tent cringing at every crack of a twig or crunch in the gravel late at night, the elder Quinn encouraged his boys to step outside and "take a look" at whatever was out there. Likely as not the noise turned out to be a weasel or night bird, but the old man reasoned that if it did happen to be a bear the thin layer of tent fabric was no more than imagined safety anyway. It was always better to see what wanted to eat you. It was a contradiction, but Quinn felt safer in the open than he did holed up in the dark.

A gentle salt breeze jostled the warm night air as Quinn trotted quietly down the dark and deserted streets. Pools of light and raucous laughter poured out from a bar here or a party there. Dakar Village, the ad hoc city within a city three blocks to the east, lit up the night sky. The steady thrum of tango music sulked over the sea wall and coursed between the buildings of Mar del Plata.

Well into his stride, Quinn ran on, jogging uphill to pass two snarling dogs fighting over something in the shadows. A block away from Zamora's, he slowed to a walk, catching his breath and popping his neck from side to side. His plan was to watch, gain information, nothing more. But planning on violent action and being prepared for it were two completely different things.

The houses in the quiet, upscale district sat on a small bluff overlooking the silver ribbon of beach and the blackness of the southern Atlantic. Lofty trees lined the streets and ornamental shrubs and stone sculptures set off the careful landscaping of the larger lots.

Decades old, each was tucked back in the shadows of their own private garden.

It was late and even the most intense of prerace parties had quieting down. Still, Quinn kept to the shadows, keeping up the pretense that he was jogging in case someone happened to look out their window.

He stopped behind a dark blue Volkswagen Passat parked in the street and stooped as if to tie his shoe, watching, straining his ears for signs of more movement.

Zamora's rented stone block chalet sprawled over a large corner lot. An ornate set of wrought iron gates closed off the wide driveway. Thick tree branches brushed the top of a six-foot wall of gray stone that matched the house.

Hearing nothing but chattering music from a dozen different parties, Quinn shot a glance up and down the street, then sprinted across to the far side of the neighboring house. It was set slightly higher on the hill and might give him a better vantage point.

He vaulted to the top of the wall and scrambled up the adjacent patio roof that overlooked Zamora's garden. The thorny boughs of a mesquite tree gave him good cover and by pressing facedown against the ridgeline of clay tile Quinn was able to see the man moving along the inside edge of the wall behind a trellis of flowering fuchsia plants.

Quinn relaxed against the cool tile and watched, taking the opportunity to rest. He didn't have long to wait.

The twin glass doors to the main chalet flung open, exposing the dark garden to a flood of light and sound. Zamora came out, followed by Monagas, who shut the door behind them. Zamora opened his mouth to speak, but the big man raised a small black device Quinn recognized as an RF scanner.

Monagas played the device around the foliage and statuary beside his boss.

In an age where satellites could be tasked with counting the dimples on a golf ball, good guys and bad often grew too dependent on gadgets to keep them safe. Listening devices and long-range weapons were only tools. Entire cities could be carpet-bombed back to the Stone Age, but in the end the powers that be still had to send in a guy with a knife to root out any survivors. All the bug sweepers in the world were worthless if one forgot security measures like drawing the curtains or simply looking up in the trees before speaking.

Satisfied, Monagas returned the RF sweeper to his pocket and nodded at his boss.

"What did you find?" Zamora asked, the coal of his cigar casting an orange glow across his face.

"They have someone in the race," Monagas said.

Quinn's breath caught in his throat.

"Who?" Zamora said, his face falling into a dark frown.

"I do not know yet, *patrón*," Monagas said.

Quinn felt as if he'd been kicked between the shoulder blades. If Zamora found out who he was there was nothing left to do but pick him up and risk losing the bomb.

"We think it's someone on one of the British teams," Monagas continued. "Or maybe even one of the racers themselves. Daudov went to university in the U.K. He has many contacts there who would kill if he paid them well enough."

The doors opened again and one of the gap-toothed twins came out with a glass of wine, begging Zamora to return to his party. The doors shut behind them, throwing the garden into silence again.

Quinn began to breathe easier. So that was it. The Chechen had someone in the race. That certainly added a new wrinkle. It also meant Quinn needed to keep Zamora alive long enough to find out where he had the bomb.

A movement in the shadows closer to the house caught his eye. Behind a plaster statue of a winged angel a woman crept toward the chalet. Dressed in black, she wore her hair in a sensible ponytail. Even in the shadows, Quinn recognized her as the Russian agent, Aleksandra Kanatova—and she was completely unaware of the bearded man moving through the shadows less than twenty feet behind her. Quinn was too far away to get to her in time—with no way to warn her without alerting Zamora's men.

He was over the wall in a matter of seconds, lowering himself silently to the soft grass. Picking up a small stone, he tossed it into the bushes behind Kanatova.

On the ground now and separated by hedges, statuary, and darkness, Quinn heard a muffled thump as Kanatova turned to defend herself. There were two distinct pops of a suppressed weapon, then silence. Quinn caught the unmistakable odor of cordite on the breeze.

The door to a detached garage apartment suddenly swung open, spilling a swath of light and the clatter of voices into the garden. Quinn dropped to the ground beside his unconscious opponent and froze. The door squeaked shut and he heard the snick of metal in the darkness. At first he thought it was the safety of a pistol, but a whiff of burning tobacco told him one of Zamora's men had just stepped out for a smoke. That was good. A smoker would be unlikely to smell the cordite.

Everything seemed fine until the bushes beside the winged angel began to rustle. The movement stopped almost immediately, but the damage was already done.

"*Quién es?*" Zamora's man stepped away from the door and into the garden. Quinn heard the unmistakable rattle of a pistol sliding out of a holster. A flashlight flicked on and the beam began to play back and forth among the trees. It was only a matter of seconds before he would see something he didn't like and call for help.

Quinn pulled a cotton sock from the pocket of his running shorts. It was small, unobtrusive, and easy to carry. Stooping quickly, he scooped up a handful of stones before moving through the shadows. Better than a fist and easy to dump, a sock full of rocks made an excellent and relatively silent weapon.

Zamora's man moved forward, holding his light in one hand and the pistol in the other. The cigarette hung loosely from his lips and he padded through the darkness muttering to himself as if he didn't really expect to find anything. The sock full of rocks hit his temple like a lead sap.

Quinn caught him as he fell, lowering him softly to the grass.

"You again?" a female voice said from the shadows. Alexandra Kanatova stepped out, red hair framing her scowling face. "Why do you follow me?"

Quinn pointed at the guy on the ground. "I'm pretty sure he was about to ruin your evening. Who's the guy with the beard?"

"A Chechen pig."

"I'd like to ask him some questions," Quinn whispered.

"Too late for that." Kanatova's eyes flicked between the back door of the house and the wall. "He is dead. Someone will come to check soon. We should go."

Quinn shot a glance at the door. It wouldn't be long before someone missed the unconscious security man. With any luck they'd chalk it up to an intruder who'd been scared away by the confrontation—so long as they didn't find a dead Chechen in their garden.

"Do you ever take anyone alive?"

"Rarely," she said.

Quinn and Kanatova carried the Chechen out the back gate and half a block away to deposit him unceremoniously in the Dumpster behind a wineshop. He had no identification on him and Quinn reasoned that, with all the international media attention, Argentine police would want to keep such a murder quiet until the race festivities were over.

Three streets away, with the safety of added distance, Quinn turned to look at Kanatova in the darkness. She walked with her head bent, hands in the pockets of her jacket, ponytail bobbing with each step.

Kanatova had very likely guessed he was a government agent by now, but giving up the fact that he even knew who she was would make her certain of it. "At the risk of getting kicked in the nuts again," he said. "I believe we may be after the same thing."

"Is that so?" She walked on without looking up. Her small shoulders were slightly stooped and she bent forward as if she was pulling a heavy load. For the moment they were heading in the general direction of his rented flat.

Quinn stopped. "Hear me out."

"Okay," she said, turning to face him. He stood over her by almost a foot, but she didn't seem the least bit intimidated. Her hands remained in her pockets and it occurred to Quinn that she had the same gun hidden in there she'd just used to kill the Chechen. All she had to do was pull the trigger now that he knew her identity.

Thankfully, she just stood there, staring up at him, blinking in the darkness while New Year's Eve revelers shot fireworks in the background. Her English was excellent, but held the hollow slur of a Russian accent Quinn found pleasant against his ear.

"And what is it you think I am after?" she asked.

"This is the second time we've run into each other near Valentine Zamora." Quinn narrowed his eyes. "I know he's an arms dealer and I also happen to know who you work for."

"Is that so?" Kanatova gave a wary half smile. "You believe we should work together to achieve our goal?"

"The thought had occurred to me," Quinn said. He listened to her rhythmic breathing for a long moment as she considered this.

"I suppose the alternative would be us getting in each other's way at every turn," she said. "Or . . . I kill you, but that might prove messy."

He gave a solemn nod. "It would."

"Work together?" She stared at his face. "To recover the device?"

"That would be the plan," Quinn said. "We're not certain he's even the one who has it."

"I am," Kanatova said without further explanation.

"At first I believed it was the Chechens, but the way Rustam Daudov pesters him, he has to be trying to get the device from Zamora. What I do not yet know is where Zamora has it hidden or what he plans to do with it." She cocked her head to one side. "I find myself at a disadvantage. If we are to be a team, as you Americans say it, I should know who I'm to work with."

He put out his hand. "Captain Jericho Quinn, United States Air Force."

Kanatova raised a wary brow. The corners of her small mouth pricked in the beginnings of a smile as she held on to his hand. "An Air Force captain who fights like *spetsnaz*?"

"It's complicated," Quinn said. "But I've raced the Dakar before, so I was a natural choice for the assignment."

"And I see you have other skills beyond racing motorcycles?"

"I boxed a little in college." Quinn shrugged, working through a plan in his head.

"To play devil's advocate, as they say. If Zamora has such a device—as we believe he does . . ." Aleksandra's voice trailed while she waited for two men wearing red Loctite shirts to stumble past in the darkness, on their way to another party. ". . . why is he going to the trouble to run this stupid race?"

Quinn had been struggling with the same question. A bomb worth over a quarter of a billion dollars on the black market would make anyone change his plans.

"These old Soviet devices would have at least some level of safeguard, right?"

"That is correct," Aleksandra said.

"So, in order to use the bomb, Zamora would have to get past those safeguards."

"And bring the device back into working order." Kanatova nodded. "They are small and portable, but this fact makes them lightly shielded. Radiation is extremely hard on the circuitry."

"Ah." Quinn rubbed his dark whiskers. "It makes perfect sense then. If Zamora values his life, he's going to be as far away from the bomb as possible while his people get it in working order." He looked at her, playing the thought over and over in his head before voicing it. At length, he sighed. "Listen, where are you staying?"

"A tent near Dakar Village where the spectators have a large camp. My government does not pay to put me up in fancy hotels with entertainment, caviar, and endless champagne."

"Mine either anymore," Quinn laughed. "But we'll have plenty of opportunity for staying in tents at the bivouacs on the course. Zamora has already seen us together. It won't be a big stretch for him to assume you came here with our team. We have an extra bed at our place for the night." He raised a wary brow. "Though, considering who you are, my government would consider it a serious breach of etiquette that I'm even talking to you alone right now."

"Breach of etiquette?" Kanatova scoffed, resuming her head-down walk. "I am discussing a missing Soviet nuclear bomb with a foreign operative. My superiors would have me shot."

CHAPTER 29

A hollow pit of exhaustion settled over Aleksandra's stomach by the time she rolled her sleeping bag out on the low bed shoved back under the angled eaves of the second-floor bedroom. It had taken another hour after they'd left Zamora's to gather her gear and make their way back up the hill to Captain Quinn's flat. She'd smiled inside when he'd given her his room and moved his own sleeping bag to the sagging couch downstairs. He was an American white knight—skilled in the brutal arts of violence, but all manners and kindness when it came to women. Her FSB instructors had taught courses about such men—how to manipulate their good intentions and innate trust of womanhood to leverage a proper end to the mission or even turn them as Russian assets.

Still, there was something about this Jericho Quinn's earnest demeanor that gave Aleksandra pause. It reminded her of Mikhail when she'd first met him. The thought made the pit in her stomach worse.

Dead on her feet with abject mental and physical fatigue, she moved to the small window at the foot of the bed. She leaned against the cool glass with her forehead and looked out over the flickering lights from Dakar city a few blocks away. Her breath threw small patches of fog against the window. Chewing on what was left of her sorry fingernails, she repeated the solemn oath she'd made the night she'd heard Mikhail Ivanovich Polzin had been murdered. "Somewhere out there is the man who killed you. I will find him and kill him, Misha. I swear it. And no one, no matter how kind or earnest, will get in my way."

CHAPTER 30

January 1

It was four-thirty in the morning when Boaz Quinn walked to the door with a bowl of cereal. A swarm of moths thumped against the screen, trying to get to the light. He wore only his boxers and a loose white T-shirt. The angry black octopus tattoo contrasted sharply with the tan flesh of his arm. Assorted scars from blade and bullet mapped the rough-and-tumble life Bo Quinn had led since striking out on his own shortly after high school.

Jericho had already finished a protein and carbohydrate shake that would become his pre-breakfast staple over the next two weeks and sat on a bench by the front door snapping the cam-locks on his riding boots. Thibodaux was outside loading extra tires on top of the support truck.

"There's a chickaloon in the shower," Bo said. He slurped placidly on a spoonful of cereal, apparently used to women showing up in surprise places. "She almost cut me when I went in to pee."

"That's Aleksandra. She's working with us now," Jericho said, giving a brief explanation.

"A Rusky?" Bo gave a long, groaning stretch, holding the cereal bowl out in front of him. "You know how I feel about Russians."

"I know," Quinn said. The entire incident—a fight with some drunk Russian nationals talking smack about America during his Air Force Academy parade—had very nearly made it so Jericho wasn't allowed to graduate. It had become the stuff of Academy legend and followed him his entire career. "Behave," he chided. "This particular Russian is after the same thing we are."

Bo held up his spoon and shook it at Jericho to drive home his point. "Did I mention she nearly cut me a minute ago? I thought it was you in the shower. Anyways, I hear Russian women are—"

"Russian women are what?" Aleksandra's husky voice came from the stairs. She was dressed in a pair of white shorts and a blue and white striped tank top. Red hair hung in damp ringlets around her shoulders from the shower.

Bo waved her off, but shot a "save me" glance at Quinn.

"I'm interested too, brother." Jericho grinned. "What is it you hear about Russian women?"

"I prefer American women," Bo grumbled, going back to eating his cereal. "That's all."

Aleksandra let the trill of her accent creep fully into her words. "You spend two minutes with a Russian woman and you will throw rocks at American girls."

Jericho chuckled at that. A woman who could go toe-to-toe with his brother was a rare find indeed.

"Come on," Jericho said, looking at Kanatova. "You can ride with me to ASO headquarters before the start of the first stage. We need to get you a wristband now that you're officially a member of Team Quinn or you won't be able to get into camp every night."

CHAPTER 31

Stage One

The British government wasn't exactly forthcoming about known terror suspects who might happen to be racing under their flag in the Dakar Rally. Palmer had started a process of elimination, and by the time Quinn was at the starting line the first day of actual racing they'd been able to weed down the contestants, leaving them with two possibilities. Both were motorcyclists—Joey Blessington riding a Husaburg and Basil Tuckwood aboard a Honda. Like Quinn, both racers rode as privateers, meaning they had no major sponsor or big team support.

Much of Quinn's cover story had been contrived by populating the Web with phony information and news releases about his investment business and photos of his thrill-seeking adventures.

Quinn was practical enough to know that completely stopping the flow of information to the World Wide Web was impossible. Even from high school he'd tried to keep his presence in the public venue as shadowy as he could. He refused to register new products that asked for his personal information and steered clear of social networking sites.

Palmer's team had done a fair job of scrubbing both Quinn and Thibodaux's online personas, but information invariably popped up. Even pizza delivery companies sold phone numbers and addresses to online people searches. The only way to combat the true information that leaked out was to flood the Web with so much content that the first ten to fifteen pages of any Internet search showed only hits related to the cover identity.

It was the pop-ups that made both Blessington and Tuckwood candidates for the Chechen's British contact and had drawn Zamora's attention.

Five pages into a Google search, a *Daily Mail* article told the story of a Newcastle teen who'd gotten into a fistfight after a rugby match. Since this was his third ASBO—antisocial behavior order—he had been offered the choice of military service or incarceration. Given the secret branches of many governments' propensity for recruiting redeemed social misfits, Basil Tuckwood was a good candidate.

Joey Blessington was an HR executive for a large oil company based in England, but the sheer lack of information online about anything else he'd ever done made Quinn suspicious of him as well.

Now, all Quinn had to do was figure out which one was the agent and get to him before Zamora or his man Monagas did.

A pink orange line ran along the eastern horizon as if a lid over the black ocean had just been cracked open. Dust and gasoline fumes hung with the excitement of race jitters in the chilly predawn air. Riding gear squeaked and heavy boots crunched on gravel between blatting engine noises. Thousands of people lined the streets to cheer on their favorite riders. Some revelers had been up all night from celebrating the New Year and looked as though they might keel over from exhaustion at any moment in the predawn haze.

The motorcycles would start first, battling not only each other but racing to stay well ahead of the other vehicles, especially the monster trucks that threw up huge clouds of dust that choked riders and left them blind and disoriented.

Each day started with the Liaison, the section of the race where riders rode over marked roads and trails, sometimes for hundreds of kilometers, sometimes just a few. During the Liaison, riders were expected to keep to the speed limit and obey all traffic laws. The Liaison route took them to the Special Stage, where they would leave the beaten track and navigate their way through mountains and desert and monstrous, bike-eating dunes to various checkpoints before racing for the finish. Navigation was done without the aid of electronics, using a paper scroll known as a road book that was mounted on each racer's motorcycle. Once a rider made it within two kilometers from any checkpoint their GPS would turn on and help guide him in. Each bike was also fitted with an IriTrak, the tracking system that let race officials keep tabs on everyone—as well as a proximity alarm to warn riders if one of the giant race trucks was looming up in the dust to crush them like a bug.

Helicopters would provide oversight on the route, shoot approved media footage, watch for rule infractions, and ensure rider safety.

Each day while racers battled away on the dunes,

Dakar staff would strike the tents housing medical, catering, and mechanical support, pack them into trucks, and engage in their own race to the next staging area to set everything back up in a new bivouac before the first riders arrived.

It took a very complicated and intricate dance to make it all work.

Beginning life as the Paris Dakar in 1978, the rally beat its way through the deserts of North Africa until terrorist activity in Mauritania stopped the 2008 race. After that, officials moved the rally to the remote stretches of desert in South America and changed the name to simply the Dakar.

Grueling and deadly as it was beautiful, it was a race made for Jericho Quinn.

Prowling on the KTM, Quinn found the number 121 bike next to a row of portable toilets across the parking lot from the Liaison starting line.

Tuckwood, a tall, lanky fellow with a bobbing walk and thinning blond hair, came out of the green plastic toilet nearest to the bike. His face was ghost pale in the predawn light. He glanced up at Quinn with a wan smile.

"Had too much wine and song last night, I did," he said with a deep Yorkshire accent. "I'm lucky to be alive, me."

Quinn sat straddling his KTM, helmet in hand. "I hear you," he said. If Tuckwood was a hired gun, he was a pretty good actor. Goofy didn't even begin to describe him—and at the moment he seemed to be suffering from acute discomfort of the lower intestine.

Quinn rolled on, closer to the starting line.

Joey Blessington was a completely different story. Quinn recognized a dangerous man when he saw one. There was a certain air, a heavy confidence about him that said, "I'm not here to fight, but if you insist, I'd actually enjoy the chance to oblige you."

Quinn shared the sentiment.

Blessington sat on his bike a few yards back from the start, goggles up, ready but relaxed. He periodically scanned the area around him, just enough to stay apprised of possible dangers, but not enough to draw inordinate attention to himself. He kept to himself, but met the other competitors' eyes and didn't appear standoffish.

He had to be the one.

Team Quinn stood behind the barrier tape with other support crews just a little closer than the mass of chanting onlookers in the Spectator Zones. Signs for race favorites Caine and Geroux dominated the group, but local favorites from Argentina, Chile, and Peru had their share of screaming youths and handsome Latin women. Jericho pushed thoughts of Veronica Garcia out of his mind as he rolled by Thibodaux and Bo, giving them each a high-five. Aleksandra, to her credit as a professional, leaned across to touch his shoulder, a tender move a female companion might do when her man went off on a race.

"Number one-sixty-eight." Quinn took off his helmet, holding it in on his lap. He kicked up a foot for the last few moments of rest he'd have for the day. "I think that's the guy to watch."

Aleksandra nodded. "You're right," she said, her face growing dark. "It is obvious."

Monagas stood on the other end of the start on the spectator side of the tape, scanning the crowd. If he'd identified Blessington as the threat, he didn't show it.

Zamora, with the number 159, would be the one hundred fifty-ninth bike to leave on this first day of racing. Blessington would be the hundred sixty-eighth to start and Quinn would follow four bikes later with number 172. Future starts would depend on race results each day, with the fastest times starting first.

"What's your plan, Jer?" Bo stood beside Aleksandra. A little too close, Quinn thought. Bo was a big boy, though, and could, in theory, take care of himself.

"The important thing is to finish near Zamora," Quinn said. "That will put us starting near each other tomorrow and on subsequent days." He shook his head. "The Special Section is a short one today. It'll be crazy out here, but we'll be bunched up most of the day. My biggest worry today is getting mobbed by the spectators."

Bo smacked him on the arm. "Zamora is away," he said. "You best be getting your game face on."

Quinn pulled on his helmet and fastened the chinstrap. Lowering his goggles, he gave one last salute to his team and rolled forward to enter the line of bikes waiting to depart down the cordoned-off streets of Mar del Plata.

"How do you read?" he said, his voice muffled inside the helmet.

"Slurred and stupid," Thibodaux chuckled. "Seriously, bro, you're five by five. You got me?"

"Loud and clear."

The communication gear was completely against the rules, but Quinn didn't plan on trying to win the race. All support teams could track the whereabouts of their racer with smartphones as they made it from checkpoint to checkpoint. With Palmer's help, Team Quinn had been able to hack into the ASO's main tracking system for Zamora's—and now Blessington's—location in real time. It would be Thibodaux's job to keep him in the loop about their respective locations if he happened to lose track.

Quinn took a deep breath and looked down the gauntlet formed by thousands of race fans, volunteers, vendors, ASO officials, security, and Argentine National Police. The sun was just coming up as he made his way to the line along with number 171, a rider from Sweden.

He gunned the KTM's engine, feeling the power between his knees. Thibodaux's thick Cajun drawl buzzed inside his helmet.

"You watch yourself, *l'ami*. There's a gob of lonely spots out there in the desert where a body could find suddenly hisself very dead."

CHAPTER 32

Idaho

Lourdes made it abundantly clear to Marie that the focus of her wrath was baby Simon. Hardly a moment went by that the horrible woman didn't make a threat or voice some horrific plan as to the particular harm she hoped to do to the helpless child. If Marie wasn't standing to work the kinks out of her sore back, she kept herself glued to the lumpy mattress, guarding her little boy as he cooed or played or slept. Even when she went to the bathroom she took Simon with her, unwilling to let him out of her sight even for a moment.

By the second day she realized Jorge, the man with the injured leg, was an ally of sorts. Simon was getting restless from being cooped up without fresh stimulation and was beginning to fuss.

They were alone when Jorge limped in from the kitchen and handed Marie a cup of chocolate milk. He wore a dish towel tucked in his belt that was filthy from his dirty hands and constant kitchen duty, but Marie didn't care.

"Don't tell Lourdes I'm doing this," he said. "My

sister, Irene, she has a son about this age. Heaven knows they can't keep quiet this long. It is not the little one's fault." He stood and watched as Simon drank the bulk of the chocolate milk, then grinned at him with a frothy brown mustache.

Jorge rubbed the little boy's head. "*Pobrecito*," he whispered, sighing. *Poor thing.* He leaned in to Marie as if with a secret. "I will tell you thi—"

Footfalls in the hallway made Jorge snatch up the glass and limp back to the kitchen.

Pete came slouching into the room with his hat on crooked and flopped down in the recliner with his cell phone. Lourdes followed, sliding along on the tile floor in stocking feet as if she was actually happy about something. She held an open laptop in her hand.

Marie's heart jumped at the sight of the computer. She lived for the few moments each day that she could talk to Matt, see his face, and know that he was still alive. The cruel woman hardly let them speak for more than a few seconds, but those were the best seconds in Marie's day. As long as Matt was alive, there was hope—she clung to that single thought more than any other, whispering it to herself as she drifted in and out of her fitful sleeps.

She pulled herself up straighter in anticipation of seeing her husband. Instead, Lourdes walked right up on the mattress beside her, shoving the baby aside with a rough nudge of her foot. Marie recoiled, pulling Simon into her lap as the awful woman flopped down beside them.

"I found a few news articles for us to read together," Lourdes said. "I think you might find them interesting."

Marie clutched the baby to her chest, reading over the top of his head.

RANSOM PAID. COUPLE FOUND MURDERED IN CALIFORNIA CABIN ANYWAY, the headline read.

Lourdes tapped the screen with her finger. "This couple, they have a lot in common with you," she sneered. "Held captive for a week in the woods. . . ." Her voice trailed as she looked over at Marie. She smiled an overly sweet smile that had no kindness in it. "They must have held out hope, don't you think?"

"Stop it!" Marie begged, covering Simon's ears though there was no way he was old enough to understand.

Pete smirked behind the game on his cell phone. Jorge stood stoically at the kitchen door.

Lourdes pressed closer, her head almost on Marie's shoulder. "Everyone has hope," she said. "Just like you. These people sat alone in that cabin and hoped that someone would come and rescue them—as you, no doubt, hope someone will come and rescue you."

"I said stop it!" Marie screamed. She struggled to catch her breath. "Stop talking to me."

Lourdes pressed on. "Certainly they made absurd demands, just as you do now." She snapped her fingers, causing Marie to jump, startling the baby and making him wail as if he'd been pinched. "Quiet the worm," she spat, getting to her feet. "Anyway, I thought you'd like to see this. Very soon you will have much, much more in common." She turned to glare at Jorge, who still watched from the kitchen door. "No matter who brings you chocolate milk. Now, shall we call your sniveling husband and let him know you are still alive . . . for the moment?"

CHAPTER 33

Rio Beni
Bolivian Jungle

Matt Pollard felt like he was in a sauna. Sweat stung his eyes and ran in rivers down his back. Someone had tacked tattered pieces of mosquito netting to the windows and makeshift screen door of the raised wooden hut, but the effort was rude at best. Wind and heat and, Pollard thought, the persistence of the insects themselves left the screens filled with dozens of ways inside. In between bouts of swatting all sorts of biting bugs, he sat on the edge of his cot, chin in his hands, and tried to decide where to start. There were layers of issues he'd have to deal with to make the thing work—if he decided that was what he would do.

Zamora seemed to think that it was all about defeating the locking mechanism, but that was just part of the story. Nuclear devices needed a high-voltage current for detonation. They got this from a series of capacitors, which were charged by a battery. In some units, these capacitors were part of a safety, if not a security mechanism. It was called "Weak Link, Strong Link."

Every other capacitor might be made of a material that melted at low temperatures, or broke under severe shock or trauma, rendering the device inoperable when subjected to unintended stress.

These safety systems, as well as electronic circuitry for signal control and detonation timing, had to be checked and possibly repaired. Wires were generally unmarked and a single color to make bypassing next to impossible for someone without a manual. On newer bombs, all this would be buried deep within the bomb beneath a tamperproof membrane. Even for someone as intelligent as Pollard, it would take a great deal of time to figure this thing out—if it was even possible— and time was a luxury Marie and Simon did not have.

The seventeen-year-old Guarani Indian girl Zamora had left in charge tapped gently at the threshold of the hut. For a guard, she was extremely polite.

"I have come for the computer," she said.

"This is wrong, you know," Pollard said, passing her the laptop. The server, wherever it was, only allowed incoming messages. "Zamora said I could speak to my family every day and make sure they are all right."

The girl looked at him as if she'd been slapped. "I am sorry, señor. I thought that is what you were doing."

Her oval face was smudged with soot from the cook fire and a chicory brown complexion set off the perfect whiteness of her teeth. Just over five feet tall, she was solidly built with a tattered green army uniform hanging from square shoulders that were accustomed to hard, load-bearing work. The military blouse looked three sizes too large, and she kept it unbuttoned to reveal a pink tank top underneath. Pollard guessed it was a reminder to herself as much as anyone else that beyond being a soldier, she was also a young woman.

"That woman hardly allows us two words." Pollard took a deep breath, fighting the desire to smash something. "I don't expect you to understand."

"Lourdes Lopez." The girl gave an understanding nod. "I will ask Señor Zamora if you might not have another moment or two with your wife the next time I speak to him."

"Thank you," Pollard said. He couldn't bring himself to be too nice to someone who was supposed to be his guard. "But why would you care?"

"Because I know Lourdes." The girl shivered. "And . . . other reasons."

Her name was Yesenia and she was surprisingly pleasant for a teenage girl with crossed bandoliers of ammunition and a Kalashnikov slung over her shoulder. The smell of wood smoke and cooked fish clung to her in the muggy heat.

She traded him the computer for a cup of what looked like ropey potato water. Clutching the laptop in one hand and the sling of her rifle with the other, she stood for a moment as if she wanted to say something, but didn't quite know how. He'd seen the look a hundred times from students who wanted to discuss their grades. At length she only smiled and nodded at the cup.

"*Somo*," she said as she left. "Sweet corn drink. It will cool you and keep you healthy."

Pollard took a drink and set the cup on the floor. It was actually pretty good—and he didn't deserve good. Collapsing onto the stiff mattress of his cot, he slouched against the wall. The girl's gun probably wasn't even loaded. Zamora knew all too well he didn't have the stomach for killing teenage girls. He stared at the oblong green case in front of him. He didn't have the stomach for killing thousands of strangers either—but this lunatic had his family. Did the value of a hundred human lives outweigh the worth of one or two?

Pollard rubbed his face with an open hand. It sounded like something he would ask his class—stupid, worthless questions that meant little outside the theoretical world. In theory, theory should mirror reality, he often told his classes.

In reality, he knew that theory was bullshit.

CHAPTER 34

January 5
Stage 5

The oppressive tension and never-ending hours of the Dakar tended to stack up, making mundane tasks like filling up with fuel require intense concentration. Quinn's triple duty of watching Zamora and trying to locate the bomb during the most dangerous race in the world was beginning to take its toll. Mile ran into grueling mile. By the fifth day he wondered if the Chechens would ever make their move.

Staying behind while keeping Zamora in sight proved to be more difficult than simply outracing the Venezuelan. Quinn was an expert rider and still took two tumbles over the first three days while trying to ride aggressively with one eye on the trail and one eye on Zamora—who seemed to ride with the reckless abandon of a teenage boy who thought he could live forever.

The falls had cost Quinn a sprained shoulder and torn a bit of cowling off the bike, but he pushed on anyway. In truth, he hadn't gone more than a couple of consecutive weeks out of the past fifteen years without some sort of tear, sprain, or bone bruise to let him know he was still alive.

The pace of the rally itself was bone numbing.

Quinn rose at 5 A.M. each morning to drink his protein shake, wolf down a quick breakfast, and shrug on more than twenty-five pounds of protective gear. With breakfast still sloshing in his gut, he picked up the KTM from Bo, who'd spent much of the night changing oil, assessing tires, and fixing the inevitable mechanical issues that crept into a highly tuned machine when it was rattled and jumped and run at high speeds over rock and sand and gravel.

After loading the scrolled road book that would give him the day's route, he'd grabbed the Waypoint GPS codes from the boards then raced across the bivouac where he got his time card and prepared for a 6 A.M. start. Battling crowds at gas stations during the Liaison runs, waving at fans, and being manhandled by adoring children at every stop became second nature.

As soon as Quinn started out for the day, Thibodaux, Bo, and Aleksandra struck the tents, packed the support truck, and entered a race of their own to cover as much as eight hundred kilometers over highway and back road—presumably following the speed limit—to reach the next bivouac and set up camp ahead of Jericho. Bo, who had usually worked all night on the bike, slept in the backseat while Thibodaux and Aleksandra took turns driving and keeping tabs on Zamora and Quinn on their smartphones.

Somewhere along the route each day, the Liaison

ended for Quinn and he came to a point known as DSS—Departure Special Stage. Ranging from a just a few to hundreds of kilometers in length, there was no speed limit during the special stages. The fastest time—absent any penalties—was the day's winner. Once the special was over, there was often another section of Liaison back to the bivouac where he would arrive around 6 P.M., make his camp in the blowing dust, grab a quick meal at the catering tent, debrief Bo about the bike's mechanical issues, take a quick shower, study his road book for the following day, eat a quick second dinner to top off on calories, then stagger into bed by eleven. Even then sleep was hard to come by with the constant hubbub, light, and engine noise of the bivouac.

Some racers resorted to sleep aids, but Quinn had to keep an eye on Zamora. He couldn't afford to be groggy if woken in the middle of the night, so he accepted a reduced level of awareness throughout the entire day.

The nights were short and the Liaisons were long, but the remote Special Stages were where the Dakar was won or lost. They were also where Quinn expected the Chechens would make their move.

Now he stood on the pegs of his bike, thirty kilometers into the fifth Special. Zamora was ahead, popping in and out of view along with three other riders as they dipped and climbed the rolling camel-colored dunes. His GPS had easily registered the last Waypoint and the road book showed a fairly straight course to the next. One of the media helicopters hovered overhead, getting official video. Their presence set Quinn's nerves at ease. The Chechens, however desperate, wouldn't do anything with such an eye in the sky. It was midday.

Quinn felt connected with the bike and in the groove of the race. For the first time in five days, he began to enjoy the Dakar.

Without warning, the helicopter banked hard to the left, and flew south, accelerating en route.

Quinn topped the next two dunes with no sign of Zamora. He rolled on more throttle, throwing up a rooster tail of sand, but thought little of the bird's departure until the speaker in his helmet squawked.

"You there, Chair Force?" Thibodaux's voice startled him out of riding nirvana.

Quinn coughed, clearing his throat of dust before answering. "Go ahead."

"Eyes wide, *l'ami*," the Cajun said. "I lost Zamora and Blessington's GPS signals about ten minute ago. It's been fading in and out, so I didn't worry until we drove up on this. We got the mother of all wrecks along the Liaison route. Argentine cops are saying a private truck lost control at a crossing, slammed into a crowd of fans and three riders."

"A private truck?" Quinn dodged a series of hard ruts and worked to get his head wrapped around that kind of an accident. He could hear the sound of car horns blaring in his earphone.

"They're talking multiple fatalities," Thibodaux said. "It's gridlock here and we're stuck behind a mess. I'm betting every emergency vehicle and helicopter is responding this way. Hear what I'm sayin'?"

"I do," Quinn said.

"It's about to get awful lonely out there."

The Liaisons were crowded with onlookers, and even the more remote Special Sections were generally peppered with fans, some huddled under the shade of a single lonely tree, others lined up with coolers and straw hats, braving the sun in order to catch a glimpse of their favorite riders.

Between the three medical helicopters and assorted media birds, not two minutes went by that there wasn't some eye in the sky keeping everyone honest and safe.

Until the accident.

Ahead of Quinn, the dunes gave way to hard-packed dirt and gravel washes. He topped the next ridge in time to see Zamora's bike dart to the right and disappear behind a rock outcrop into a dry riverbed.

The hot dry wind suddenly took on a metallic smell. This was all wrong. He glanced over the handlebars at his road book. As he suspected, the route went straight ahead for another three kilometers.

"Zamora's decided to leave the course," Quinn said.

"Watch yourself," Thibodaux said. "I got your signal on the GPS but still no joy on Zamora. Something's wrong."

Quinn watched the two riders who'd been with Zamora pop over a hill to continue straight on the prescribed course. Wherever Zamora was going, he was going it alone.

Quinn slowed to follow Zamora's tracks at the dry riverbed. There was no sign of the Venezuelan, but he could hear the whine of his bike around the next bend.

Standing in the pegs, Quinn poured on the throttle, wanting to catch up before Zamora lost him altogether. If Thibodaux couldn't track him, Quinn had no choice but to speed up and keep him in sight.

He caught sight of the bike the moment he rounded the next corner. It was close—and something was extremely wrong. Quinn tried to process the new images at the same moment the front tire of his KTM seemed to fold in on itself, throwing him violently over the handlebars. A cloud of fesh fesh blossomed into the air like gray talc, blinding him as he and his bike slammed into the unforgiving ground.

CHAPTER 35

Yazid Nazif held the phone to his ear and listened to the empty line. He'd tried to connect with the Venezuelan for the last four hours only to get nothing but empty ringing and dead air—not even so much as a message. One would think that when a person was paid almost half a billion dollars they would avail themselves of better communication. Nazif wanted to smash the phone against the wall. This stupid race Zamora insisted on running was beginning to be a problem.

The phone buzzed in his hand with an incoming call.

"Yes." He smiled inside, recognizing the number. It was Ibrahim, his youngest brother.

Yazid stretched his back and picked up a small cup of coffee from the table before him, letting the familiar scent of cardamom calm his tattered nerves. Things would be all right, he told himself. All would work out. The stone that was cut from the mountain by the hand of God could not be stopped.

"Peace be unto you, my brother." Ibrahim's voice was familiar, like the comfortable sound of the gate to their garden back home.

"And you," Yazid answered back. "I trust things are going well on your end."

"Very," Ibrahim said. "I am helping out at the church we discussed. There will be quite a large number attending. I believe you would enjoy the performance if you are able to arrive in time. Still, there are alternatives."

"You think we should focus on another event?"

There was a long silence on the phone.

"Perhaps," Ibrahim said at length. "I will text you a photo."

"Watch yourself, brother," Yazid said before hanging up. He ran a hand across his bald head and waited for the ping that signaled an incoming text.

"Not bad," he said to himself, using two fingers to enlarge the photograph of a man with shaggy blond hair standing before a small choir of thirty or so smiling children—all a hodgepodge of race, ranging in age from less than seven to their early teens. They were ripe enough, Yazid's heart raced when he saw the open auditorium behind the children—with seating for thousands. If Ibrahim had a target better than this, it had to be a ripe one indeed.

CHAPTER 36

Quinn awoke on his side, hands pulled unnaturally behind him. His helmet lay in the rocks a few feet away. He'd landed on his left ear after hitting the fesh fesh—superfine particles of dust that blew along the desert floor to fill in any low spots. Fesh fesh looked like regular ground and ate many unsuspecting motorcyclists if those low spots happened to be more than a few inches deep.

The KTM was somewhere close behind him. He couldn't see it but reasoned that he hadn't been unconscious long from the sound of ticking metal as the bike bled heat from the engine.

Quinn tried to push himself to a seated position and realized his hands were tied behind his back. He turned his head slowly and saw Zamora had an even bigger problem.

Ten meters to Quinn's right, Blessington and another man Quinn recognized as the Chechen from the chalet in Mar del Plata stood towering over a bound Zamora. The Venezuelan's riding boots and socks had been stripped off. His bare feet had been strapped to the handlebars of his motorcycle—which lay on its side, apparently another victim of unsuspected fesh fesh.

The Chechen spewed something in rapid-fire Russian, kicking Zamora in the ribs when he didn't answer. The Venezuelan cursed him back, spitting vehemently into the dirt.

Blessington smiled, drawing back a long wooden staff nearly an inch in diameter. He let it hang for a long moment while the Chechen asked another question, then struck cruelly on the sole of Zamora's pink foot before he had time to answer.

Zamora writhed in pain from the blow, thrashing hard enough to yank the handlebars of his bike sideways. Blessington set down the stick to maneuver the bike and his victim's feet back into position as a better target.

Quinn knew both he and Zamora were dead as soon as they got what they wanted. He looked around, shifting his eyes rather than moving his head and drawing attention to himself. Behind him, he could feel the heat radiating off the KTM's muffler. Taking advantage of their preoccupation with Zamora, Quinn inched backward to the bike, pressing the plastic zip ties on his wrist against the exhaust, as close to the engine as he could get. He winced as the heat seared the tender skin inside his wrists, but held them there until the plastic melted, freeing him with a faint pop as they gave way.

Now loose, he kept his hands behind him and took another look at his opponents. The Chechen had a pistol on his hip and Blessington had a knife in addition to his wooden staff. It killed him inside to help a man like Zamora escape. The treatment he was getting was well deserved. But Blessington was enjoying himself too much. It was obvious the Chechens wanted the bomb, but these two were heavy-handed. They were likely to kill Zamora by accident before he told them anything.

Quinn toyed with the idea of giving them a few minutes before he took action, but they could turn on him at any moment. The chance the Chechen would draw his pistol and start shooting was too great.

He moved his feet slightly, wiggling his toes to make sure they weren't asleep. The last thing he needed was to be halfway into his lunge and realize he was working on two dead legs. When he felt reasonably sure his body was in good enough working order after the wreck, he took one final look at the situation and let Blessington have one more whack at Zamora's feet.

The piercing screams provided good cover for his initial movement—and Blessington's feelings of superiority at dispensing punishment to a helpless prisoner made him careless.

Many an advancing army had been beaten when a retreating foe turned and struck them down in the midst of their foolish bravado.

Quinn rolled to his feet at the crescendo of Zamora's tattered cries. He picked up the helmet and threw it underhanded as he moved, catching Blessington center chest. It didn't cause any damage, but surprised him, giving Quinn a precious second to focus on the other man.

A half step out, Quinn pulled up short, stepping sideways as if trying to avoid a confrontation. The Chechen, taking this for weakness, struck out with a powerful right hook. Instead of meeting the punch, Quinn let it sail by, grabbing it across the top, drawing against his center, then reversing directions to turn the wrist back on itself. In Japanese martial arts it was called *kote-gaeshi*.

Quinn kept his own circles tight and powerful as he spun, but extended the man's arm, not only snapping the fragile wrist bones but destroying his elbow and shoulder joints as well. Screaming in pain, the Chechen clutched the damage with his good hand. Quinn grabbed him around the chest, turning to face a maniacal Blessington, the wooden rod raised high over his head like a sword.

Quinn's hand slipped the pistol from the Chechen's belt as he let the man fall. He shot without aiming, putting two slugs in Blessington's belly as he tried to bring the wooden staff down on Quinn's head. The Brit stood blinking for a long moment, slumping against the heavy stick like a cane before toppling forward, his open mouth blowing soft puffs of fesh fesh away as he drew his last breaths.

Quinn used his pocketknife to cut Zamora's hands free, keeping an eye on the wounded Chechen.

"Are you okay?" Quinn said, tossing him the blade so he could cut loose his own feet.

"I'm fine," Zamora said, blinking to clear his head. He tested tender feet before standing. "Thankfully, nothing is broken. . . ." He gave Quinn a long quizzical look before turning toward the glaring Chechen, who lay just ten feet away.

The Chechen peered up at Quinn with brooding eyes. "You think you know this man, but you do not."

Zamora was on him in an instant, striking over and over. Quinn kept the blade of his ZT folder extremely sharp. That, combined with Zamora's white-hot desire for revenge, gave the Chechen no chance for survival.

Zamora's face was covered in blood when he looked up. "We should get out of here," he said, wiping his face with a rag from inside his riding jacket. "Frankly I'm surprised the ASO hasn't sent someone looking for us since our bikes have been stopped so long."

Without the illegal communication Quinn could not have known about the accident or the fact that Zamora's IriTrak was malfunctioning, so he didn't mention it. Instead he nodded at the bodies, feigning shock.

"I'm not in too much of a hurry to get caught out here with these guys. What was that all about anyway?" He shrugged and picked up his bike. He breathed a sigh of relief when it started on the first try.

Zamora was already snapping the camlocks on his riding boots. "Trust me," he said. "You do not want to know."

The IriTrak on Quinn's KTM began to speak, rescuing him.

"Contestant 172, please report your status." The voice was thickly French.

"Good to go," Quinn responded. "Just took a wrong turn. Moving now."

"Acknowledged," the race official said, ending the transmission.

A little more time bought, they dragged the bodies into the deep fesh fesh, making sure they were well covered in the event of a flyover. Quinn made certain the IriTrak on Blessington's bike was disconnected before burying it in fesh fesh as well. The Chechen must have had a vehicle nearby, but it was nowhere to be seen and there was no time to worry about it.

Zamora's Yamaha started with a little coaxing.

"There must be something wrong with my GPS."

The Venezuelan sat on his bike beside Quinn. "I am left to wonder why you followed me if your GPS was functional."

Quinn shrugged. "Sometimes it's easier to follow a pro than it is to lead. Why do you think Geroux and Caine trade wins each day? One does all the work of the leader while the other sits back only to shoot ahead fresh at the end—putting him in the lead for the next day and repeating the cycle."

Zamora nodded. "And you hoped to follow me until the end so you could beat me?"

"It's a tactic."

"Well." Zamora winked, lowering his goggles. "I am fortunate you came along. But sometime in the not too distant future, you may regret your decision to save my life."

Quinn watched as the man raced away, covering him in a rooster-tail shower of sand. He regretted his decision already.

CHAPTER 37

Pollard didn't know if it was the oppressive heat or the fact that he sat three feet away from the remnants of a nuclear bomb, but he had never sweated so much in his life. His plywood hut kept off the daily rain showers but proved more of an oven than shelter. Though sweat ran down his back and stung his eyes, the humidity was so high that none of it evaporated to help cool him. At first he'd shucked off his loose cotton shirt but found he worried too much about malaria-bearing mosquitos without it.

Still on his bunk, he let his head loll sideways to study the device. It occurred to him that the shielding had degraded to the point that he was being irradiated as he sat there, but found that he didn't care. He doubted that he'd come out of this alive anyway. The point was to figure out a way to save his wife and son—and to do that, it looked as though he was going to have to rebuild a bomb that was well past its prime.

The trunk stood on its side with the lid hinged open like a door. The thing Zamora called Baba Yaga was nothing special to look at. A metal cylinder ran diagonally from one end of the box to the other, a length of about four feet. As big around as his leg, the cylinder housed the high-explosive charge as well as the "bullet" and "target," two pieces of plutonium that would be rammed together by the charge to achieve critical mass.

Theoretically, the metal tube was shielded enough to protect someone carrying the device from errant radiation. The rat's nest of wires leading from an ancient battery was white with corrosion. It could have been from the atmosphere or leaking acid, but radiation was highly corrosive to electronics. Without a Geiger counter, there was no way to tell which had caused the decay. So far the capacitors looked intact, though there was something about their array that he still couldn't quite put a finger on.

Pollard sat up to look at the bomb more closely. There was a sinister beauty about the thing—like some kind of poisonous spider. Zamora was insane. There was absolutely no doubt about that. But he was smart enough to pick the right scientist for this job.

Baba Yaga, as the name implied, was an old hag. Built by the Soviets in 1970, she had seen better days. Her battery—last replaced in 1986—was toast, some of the wiring was corroded beyond repair, and she very likely leaked radiation like Chernobyl. Apart from the physical danger posed to Pollard—and anyone else who spent any time near the device—such leakage was also highly corrosive to the fragile electronics. But plutonium had a half-life of roughly eighty million years. That component, at least, was still good to go. If the explosive charge in the initial "gun" portion of the bomb remained viable, there was a slight possibility he might be able to fix the rest.

Old as she was, it was the very age of this device that made her so appealing. In an effort to help ward off the risk of rogue generals with their finger on the launch button, the United States had shared their own Permissive Action Link technology with the Soviets sometime around 1971—two months after Baba Yaga was born.

PALs, as the systems were called, were essentially the detonation codes. In the early days, a PAL was little more than a key and a three-digit combination lock. As devices and technology improved they became more sophisticated, with later generations buried deep within the device, making them impossible to tamper with.

Baba Yaga's lock was analog without the later fail-safe mechanism that would render the bomb unusable after a given number of tries to defeat the code. It would take time to figure out, but first impressions showed a series of wires, covered in some sort of hard resin and suspended in a set of Enigma-like rotors. In order for the bomb to activate, these rotors would have to be turned to the correct location, aligning the wires with the appropriate contact. A simple clock allowed for a prescribed delay in detonation once the device was armed. Pollard thought he could work his way through the puzzle. What he didn't know was what he'd do once he'd finished.

Yesenia's voice saved him from horrible thoughts. He shut the lid to the case, hoping to protect her from what radiation he could.

"I brought you supper." She still carried the Kalashnikov, but kept it pushed behind her back, as if it was more of an afterthought than a weapon of intimidation. At first Pollard wondered why none of the other guards had anything to do with him. A few minutes with the fascinating Guarani girl gave him his answer. Zamora knew he would never hurt someone as articulate and kind as this one. A male guard might bluster and give cause for an outburst. Pollard would only see Yesenia for the fellow victim that she was.

He took the wooden tray of piranha and rice and sat back on the edge of his bunk. The heat and worry over his family pushed a fist against his gut so there was more than he'd ever eat in one sitting. He speared a piece of the flaky white fish with his fork and held it up.

"Would you like some?"

She shook her head, content to stand and smile while he ate.

"I am sorry for you," she said, as he handed her back the tray a few moments later. He'd picked at one of the fish and forced down a few mouthfuls of rice.

"And why is that?" he asked, wiping his hands on his pants.

The Guarani girl squared her shoulders and nodded in thought. "Because you are a good man," she said. "And I see no way out of this for you."

She turned and left without another word. Pollard thought she might have been crying.

He fell back on his cot and looked up at the wooden crossbeams that supported the tin roof. He'd given up on the shredded mosquito netting. None of that mattered anyway. He deserved whatever diseases and misery came his way.

Yesenia was right about one thing. There seemed no good way out of this. But she was dead wrong about the other. Matt Pollard was a lot of things—but he knew a good man was not one of them.

2004
Portland, Oregon

Twitching beetles lay on the pavement under the streetlight in front of Fitzhugh Chevrolet. A black four-door Silverado was parked on the front row next to a gleaming Suburban of the same color. Flanking these like bishops on each side of a black king and queen were two slightly smaller but no more eco-friendly Chevy Tahoes. Row after row of these heavy, earth-killing vehicles covered the four-acre parking lot.

Matthew Pollard hid in the grassy shadows of an overpass, a small set of binoculars pressed to his eyes. A steady flow of traffic thumped on the highway over-head. The lithe coed beside him squirmed with antici-pation. Her name was Audrey, but she went by Care. She wore formfitting unbleached cotton capris that hugged the curve of her hips and a tattered green Che Guevara T-shirt cut high so everyone could see the pair of orange and black koi fish playing yin and yang around her bellybutton.

She pushed a sandy dreadlock out of bright eyes.

"I'm, like, so nervous," she whispered. "Aren't you nervous? I can't believe we're, like, really following through. This is crazy. Don't you think this is so crazy?"

Pollard turned to look at her for a long moment, then shook his head, saying nothing.

A doctorate in nuclear engineering, five years on a nuke sub, mere months away from a second doctorate, and he was hiding in the grass next to a nineteen-year-old dreadlock-wearing trust-fund kid—trustifarians, he called them—who thought wearing underwear and shaving her pits would somehow bind her to the evil elite of the bourgeoisie.

Crazy indeed.

Scanning the Fitzhugh parking lot one last time, he traded the binoculars for a handheld radio that lay in the grass next to his face.

"All clear from station two," he said.

"Looks good from here," a Hispanic voice crackled over the radio. "*Listo?*"

"Ready," Pollard said, holding his breath.

He was sick of his life, embarrassed with the road he'd taken for so much of it. Doing something big seemed the only way to make amends. Sugaring a few bulldozer fuel tanks, attending some sit-ins to stop clear-cutting—all that was well and good, but the damage he'd done required a true penance.

He needed a big bang.

Thanks to a particular B-list movie starlet with enough liquid income to assuage her own guilty conscience, Pollard's little group had the money to up the ante—call in the big dogs, so to speak. She'd put them in touch with a Venezuelan student named Valentine, also at the U of Oregon. He had slick hair, smoked hundred-dollar cigars, and was about to help them take the leap from beginner eco-terrorists using diesel bombs with Ping-Pong-ball and birthday-candle fuses to the big league of military plastic explosives.

Pollard stuffed the binoculars down the front of his shirt and moved in a low crouch toward the car lot. Care, for all her youthful nerves, stayed right beside him. It would be her job to act as lookout while he and Valentine Zamora placed the explosives at each corner of the building. It was one thing to blow up a gas-guzzler or two. They planned to bring down the whole enterprise.

Less than five minutes later, they'd set timers on six two-pound blocks of C-4 explosive. Two under the gas hogs out front and the others under the support columns of the building. Pollard had wanted to use remote detonators, but the good ones, the kind that would ensure they all didn't get blown to hell by some idiot's garage door opener, were out of his price range. Zamora, who seemed to be an expert at such things, had convinced him to use timers, planning the sets so they'd go off at roughly the same time.

All three of them ran across the frontage road to the safety of the overpass, sliding into their hiding spot in the tall grass.

"Put these in." Valentine held a pair of earplugs out to each of the other team members.

Pollard was in the middle of inserting the foam plugs when he felt Care tense beside him.

"Holy shit," she whispered. "There's someone in there."

Pollard snatched up the binoculars.

"Where?"

She pointed with a shaking finger. "Coming out of the service area, just on the other side of that window. It's a girl."

Pollard's breath balled up in his chest as he watched a young woman in a smart gray pantsuit walk from a back office into the showroom. Without thinking, he dropped the binoculars and gathered himself up to run.

"What are you doing?" Valentine yanked him back to the ground. "We have ninety seconds before twelve pounds of explosive and who knows how many gallons of gas blows that place to hell."

Pollard jerked away, staring back at him. "We have to warn her!"

"Be still!" the Venezuelan hissed. "If you tell her about the explosive she'll know you're responsible. I'm not going to prison because some *chica* decided to work late."

Care gave an emphatic shake of her head, eyes wide, body twitching. "Matt's right," she said. "We have to let her know."

She got up to run, but Valentine was on her in an instant. He grabbed a fist full of dreadlocks and heaved, jerking her over backwards. She hit the ground with a groan, but he split her lip with a quick fist to the face to make sure he had her attention.

The fireball from the first explosion reflected off his twisted face as he pulled back to strike her again and again, turning her face into a bloody pulp.

Pollard sat motionless, trapped between the murder of an innocent dealership employee and the vicious assault of one of their own by a member of his group.

The third explosion sent the hood of the black Suburban shrieking overhead to slam into the overpass abutment. The sickening crash snapped Pollard out of his stupor.

"Knock it off!" he said, shoving Valentine off a bewildered Care.

Blood poured from her nose and lips, dripping from her chin and soaking her blond dreadlocks. Her teeth showed pink in the firelight of burning cars. "No one was supposed to get hurt," she moaned.

"Just keep our heads," Valentine said. "If we keep our heads, everything will be fine."

"Oh, you mean like when you were beating the shit

out of me?" Care winced. She clutched at her forehead with both hands. "You bastard, I think you broke my skull."

"You'll be fine," he said, waving her off. "We did what we came to do—send a message. There is often collateral damage in this sort of action."

"Screw that," Care said, stumbling to her feet. "I'm going down there to see if maybe she's alive."

Sirens wailed in the distance.

Pollard froze. He knew Care was right. There was a chance the woman had survived the explosions. Someone should go check on her—but he couldn't bring himself to move. Zamora pulled a pistol from his waistband and made his choice for him.

"You hear that?" he said, pointing the gun at Care. "The cops are on their way."

"Good." She rocked back and forth, clutching her head. "I can talk to them when they get here."

The dealership was fully engulfed in flames now. Every few seconds a fuel tank on one of the gas hogs blew, sending jagged shards of glass and metal whirring into the night sky.

Care swayed, blinking dizzy eyes. She looked at the pistol and smirked, her bloody face backlit by the orange fireball. "Put that away," she said. "You wouldn't shoot me, Valentine."

Pollard felt as if his joints were locked in place. Unable to make himself move, he watched helplessly as Valentine Zamora fired twice. The first shot hit her in the throat, the second in the shoulder.

The gun hung motionless in Zamora's hand. For a terrifying moment, Pollard thought the man might turn it against him.

Instead Zamora shoved it back in his waistband, spitting on the ground in disgust. "Stupid bitch," he said. "I just blew that lady to hell. What made you think I wouldn't shoot you?"

He turned to Pollard, mistaking his fearful inaction for complicity. "Come on," he said, already grabbing the girl's feet. She was still moving, tragic sounds coming from the wound in her throat. "Help me drag her body out of sight." He looked up and grinned. "Like it or not, we're on the same team now, amigo."

CHAPTER 38

Zamora lay naked, facedown on the padded massage table in his motor home with a cell phone pressed to his ear. The soles of his feet were on fire, but luckily there appeared to be nothing broken, no long-term damage.

The shorter of the gap-toothed twins worked on the small of his back and the taller kneaded the knots out of his calves. The familiar buzzing of Lourdes Garcia's angry voice helped to chase away memories of his beating at the hands of the Chechens. He found that he missed her more than he'd imagined and could almost smell the familiar burned-sugar odor she got when she was mad.

"I want to punch this boohooing woman in the face," Lourdes said. "She is so weak . . . and the awful little baby . . . I cannot stand to look at it."

"And you say I get into moods, my darling," Zamora said. His voice shook as the twins began to beat on his back. "Let Jorge and Pete watch them and you relax."

"I cannot relax with the worm squealing his face off every five minutes," Lourdes snapped. "Have you forgotten me completely? The men you assigned here are pathetic. Pete does little but sit in his chair and tell her nasty jokes when he is not playing video games. He is like a stupid teenager—and do not get me started on the whining Jorge. He is useless. I can no longer trust him. He even gave the bawling worm some of *my* chocolate milk. Can you imagine?"

Zamora smiled to himself. Beautiful, crazy Lourdes, she was passionate about so many things. He would have to give her some little something to appease her or risk a mutiny.

"I believe it is time for you to make a statement, my darling."

"What do you mean?" She paused her rant to listen.

"Send Jorge and Pete to buy ten bags of cat litter. When they return, have them dig a grave some distance from the house—large and deep enough to hide the bodies of a mother and child."

"Then I will be alone with the woman and her worm while they work," Lourdes said, sounding almost giddy. "That will probably scare her to death."

"Now, now," Zamora said. "We need them alive for the moment, remember?"

"I know," she said. "I hate it, but I understand."

"I promise you, my love," Zamora said. "When you see what I have in mind, you will find it so very entertaining."

He ended the call and summoned Monagas with a snap of his fingers.

His face pressed against the cool leather bed, he watched through sleepy eyes as his faithful companion ushered in Fabian, one of the mechanics.

"How long have you been with me, my friend?" Zamora's voice was muffled against the table.

"Four years, *patrón*." The man's knees shook.

"Four years . . ."

The gap-toothed twin used her fists to beat the muscles of Zamora's back like a drum.

He groaned as the days of tension began to bleed from him. "You would think that would be long enough to know me. . . ."

The mechanic stood quietly, twisting a ball cap in his hands.

"Have I not treated you well?"

"Very well, *patrón*."

"I think so as well," Zamora said, languidly twisting his neck as the short twin continued with her work down his spine. "That is why I am so distraught at your actions."

"I beg your pardon, *patrón*?" Fabian's teeth chattered as he spoke.

"It had to be you, my friend," Zamora said. "No one else had access to the motorcycle and my road book."

"What?"

Zamora cocked his head. "Monagas, I believe Fabian is having some trouble hearing me."

The mechanic shrieked as Monagas stepped up behind him and sliced off his ear. The gap-toothed twin, numb to such things, continued to knead Zamora's buttocks without so much as a flinch.

Zamora held out his hand, taking the bloody ear and holding it up to his mouth.

"Can you hear me now, my friend?"

"They have my family, *patrón*," the man sobbed. "What was I to do?"

"Well," Zamora said, "certainly not what you did. What else does Rustam Daudov have planned?"

"He says you have a bomb, and he wants it for himself."

"I know what he wants," Zamora hissed into the ear. "I asked you what he has planned."

"I do not know, *patron*," Fabian sobbed. "I swear it. He did not tell me."

Zamora gave a tired sigh, sitting up on the table. The twin felt him moving and scrambled out of the way. "You won't be needing this then." He sniffed the severed ear, then dropped it on the floor, nodding at Monagas.

CHAPTER 39

January 7

It was nothing short of a miracle that Pollard had gotten as far as he had with the austere environment and simple tools Zamora provided. He'd told Yesenia that it would have been easier for the professor on *Gilligan's Island* to build a bomb from scratch than it was for him to try and repair one, but she didn't understand the joke.

On the stifling afternoon of his tenth day in the jungle, he reassembled a section of the PAL and heard a faint click. He grimaced, waiting for whatever came after death, because he knew if the bomb blew, he'd not be conscious to experience the moments in between. There was no detonation, but along with the now living circuitry, Baba Yaga's design clicked in Pollard's brain. As if a veil had been lifted, everything became clear. He understood her.

Peering with a flashlight at the top of the metal tube, deep into the guts of the thing, he took a look at the row of capacitors from a fresh perspective. Dizzy with the new information, he fell back on his cot and rubbed a hand over his face. There was something about her that had bothered him from the beginning—and now he knew what it was.

More dangerous than even Zamora imagined, Baba Yaga was not what she seemed.

Revitalized, Pollard jumped up as quickly as he'd sat down, pacing back and forth, shaking the hut on its piers. Finally, he threw open the flimsy door. Technically, he wasn't even supposed to use the latrine without an escort, but boredom and oppressive heat had made the guards lax over time.

Angelo, the camp's second in command, sat in a folding chair flipping through a magazine about fishing. His rifle leaned against the woodpile beside him. He nearly fell over at Pollard's shrill whistle. Angelo spoke no English and looked terrified whenever Pollard spoke to him.

He held up his hand as if he wanted Pollard to stay in place. "Yesenia," he mumbled, shoving the fishing magazine in his hip pocket and scooping up his weapon. Two other guards, also Guarani Indians, glanced up from the cook fire for a moment, then resumed whatever it was they were doing.

"Yes." Pollard nodded to Angelo. "Yesenia."

The Indian girl came trotting up a moment later, breathless and smiling. Pollard realized he'd never called for her before.

"I need to talk to Zamora immediately," he said, trying to keep his voice calm.

Yesenia sighed, nodding softly before walking away. She seemed to realize that things were about to change.

* * *

"I need assurances," Pollard said, "before I go any further."

Zamora gave a slow sigh on the other end of the phone and was quiet for a long time. Finally, Pollard heard his lips smacking.

"Very well then," the Venezuelan said. "You may be assured that if you play games with me, I will chop your wife and son into fish bait."

"I'm serious, Valentine."

"And I am suddenly playing games? You know what I am capable of, my friend. Do us both a favor and complete your mission."

"So," Pollard said, biting his lip as he spoke. "How does this work when I do figure it out? How can I know that my family will be safe?"

"I do not know," Zamora said. "I have been focused on other endeavors. Present a plan to me and I will consider it. But know this, my customers need your expertise, so you will stay with the device until she is delivered. This is a package deal."

"If one hair on my son's head—"

"I know, you will kill me," Zamora chuckled, cutting him off. "You're making yourself look foolish, Matthew. Call me when you have good news."

Zamora ended the call.

Pollard took a deep breath, clutching the satellite phone in his fist. He looked down at Yesenia.

"Things are about to change," he said.

She smiled, blinking her eyes like a schoolgirl with a crush. "I know."

CHAPTER 40

Zamora set the phone on his chest and smiled. Pollard had done it. It was apparent in the timbre of his voice. He'd figured out a way to arm the device, and though he harbored well-placed concern for his family, the scientist in him couldn't help but brag about his accomplishment. Valentine had known all along that the man could do it, but the fact that plans were moving forward so well was cause for celebration.

The taller of the gap-toothed twins—he could never remember their names—gave a plaintive whine from where she lay beside him. Naked but for an Egyptian cotton sheet pulled up to her waist, she snuggled in close, causing him to sweat despite the chilly desert air coming through the motor home window. The other twin peeked over the point of her sister's shoulder, grinning broadly enough to whistle when she breathed.

"Are you finally done with your calls, Vali?" she asked. He really hated it when she called him that. She and her sister were a pair, though, one never far from the other. He thought of them as bookends, something to admire while he searched for something else but never really study too deeply.

"Almost, my darlings," Zamora said. He stared up at the ceiling, thinking of what to do next. By all rights he should have been exhausted from the long day of riding, but instead of fatigue he felt a sort of wishful anxiety, as if something very wonderful was about to happen and he simply could not wait. There was so much yet to do and Pollard's assistance would be necessary until the end. Still, he could tell from Lourdes's voice she was getting to the very last knot on her rope. He had to figure out a way to placate her somehow. She was like a kiln, a furnace that he needed to feed from time to time.

He picked up the cell phone again and punched in Lourdes's number with his thumb, smiling at his own brilliance.

"Come on, Vali," the shorter twin pouted from behind her sister.

He put a finger to his lips. "Shhh," he said. "If Lourdes suspects you are with me, she'll peel the skin off the soles of your feet and make you dance with her."

Both girls fell silent immediately, taking care not to even breathe too deeply, for they knew he wasn't joking about such a thing. They'd seen her do it.

"Hello, my darling," Zamora said when Lourdes answered. "I need you to do something for me. It will upset the good professor, to be sure, but I believe the time has come to make some changes in our arrangement."

CHAPTER 41

Idaho

Marie's body jerked awake from a fitful sleep when Lourdes stomped into the room wearing her lime-green ski parka and wool tam. Simon, who'd grown even more sensitive to his mother's moods than normal, looked up with a trembling lower lip. Tears brimmed on his tiny lashes and he swelled his lungs, gathering breath for a horrific squeal. He'd already lost so much weight. His little face was sunken and pale. Marie clutched him to her chest and tried to comfort him, but the squeal came anyway. Her teeth ached from constantly clenching her jaw. Stress hormones coursed through her body without a break, wearing her down and eating away at her mind.

"Time for a hike," Lourdes said. She stomped her foot on the tile floor, making a dull thud and rattling the mostly vacant farmhouse.

Pete looked up from his recliner with a sideways eye. "Are you serious?"

"Valentine demands it," Lourdes said, glaring at the bawling baby. "It is not good for me to be cooped up in this house for so long. I become impatient, and when I become impatient, I become violent."

"Well, I haven't been cooped up for that long," Pete said. "I'll just stay here with the prisoners."

"They are coming as well," Lourdes barked. She clapped her hands. "*Apúrate*," she said. *Hurry up.*

"It's freezing out there," Marie argued. "I'm afraid Simon is already getting sick."

Jorge, who'd been making sandwiches in the kitchen, poked his head around the corner. "My leg is bothering me," he said. "I can stay with them."

"Aaahhhhhhh!" Lourdes screeched. "We all go! Put on your coats or not, I do not care. We leave in two minutes."

"Oh, *mi madre*," Jorge whispered, biting his bottom lip. His eyes fell on the crying baby.

Marie scrambled to fit a squalling Simon into his hooded fleece jumper. In between shuddering sobs he looked up at her with accusing eyes, not understanding why she had to be so rough. It killed her inside to force him.

Knowing better than to argue with his crazy boss, Jorge slipped into his ratty Carhartt jacket and limped to the door.

A light coating of snow had covered the yard behind the house, powdering the small utility shed and propane tank. Sagging clotheslines hung in perfect shallow curves against the backdrop of a small orchard of a dozen leafless apple trees. A hundred yards beyond the orchard over a plowed stretch of field, a line of spruce trees marked the entrance to a copse of thick woods that ran up the side of a low hill, one of many islands of trees here and there on the rolling farmland.

Marie stopped at the orchard when she realized Lourdes was leading them toward the dark line of forest. Nothing good could come from walking into such a place with this horrible woman. Still, with Simon in her arms she could not fight, so a moment later she trudged on. Snow kicked up into her Danskos at each shuffling step and melted into her socks.

Ten yards inside the forest, Marie saw the mound of freshly dug earth. Her stomach clenched as she recognized it immediately for what it was. A grave. In the center of a small clearing, it was protected by the canopy of tall spruce trees and frosted with only a hint of snow.

Marie stopped in her tracks twenty feet from the pile of turned earth. She swayed, struggling to stay on her feet. Simon was too big for her to carry far and her legs shook from the effort and fear.

Lourdes raised a sullen brow at Pete and Jorge, who'd been walking single file with Marie in between them, and nodded toward the hole. "It will have to do," she said. Cold pinked her cheeks and the tip of her nose. The tam hung low across her eyes. She retraced her steps so she passed Pete and stood directly in front of Marie.

Simon squirmed and fussed, trying to get down and play in the snow.

Lourdes looked on smugly, studying him.

"We have come to a crossroads," she said with a snarling grin. "Where changes must be made."

Marie's heart told her to run as fast as she could, but she knew there was nowhere to go. Her stomach lurched and the world seemed to spin around her as she felt Jorge's hands on her arm. This couldn't be happening.

She had dreams, Simon had to go to college, have a girlfriend. . . . Her vision blurred with tears and soul-crushing terror. She found it impossible even to swallow.

Pete grabbed her other arm and helped Jorge lead her to stand at the edge of the rectangular hole.

Oddly, once at the edge Marie felt a sudden calm come over her. What made her any more important than the murdered mothers and children she heard about on the news? They surely had dreams as well. She set her jaw and stared straight ahead. If she and Simon were dead, Matt could do what he needed to do. Maybe no one else would be hurt by these awful people. She began to sense everything around her in perfect detail. The toes of her Danskos sent a skittering of loose dirt over the edge with a hollow rattle. Small roots hung snakelike from the sides. The rich earthiness of the forest soil on chilly air tickled her nose. She no longer cared about herself but wanted only to make certain Simon did not suffer.

Beside her, Jorge's hand began to tremble.

"I am sorry, señora," he whispered, a split second before Lourdes shot him in the back of the head.

Jorge convulsed momentarily at her arm, nearly pulling her into the grave before he fell away. His body stiffened and he toppled headlong into the pit.

Every ounce of clarity she'd just felt flew from Marie with the sound of the pistol. Eyes wide in horror, she vomited into the hole. Clutching Simon to her breast, she collapsed to her knees, head bowed, bracing for the next shot.

It never came.

"He was weak," Lourdes snapped. "Weakness is

worse than babies." She looked Marie in the eye. "Besides, I want you to understand what is coming to you . . . in time." She turned on her heels to start for the house, leaving Jorge's body alone in the open earth.

"Move your ass," Pete stammered, clearly shaken that his boss had just shot one of her own.

Marie struggled to stand, scrambling to keep from sliding into the grave with the dead man. Lourdes trudged ahead without looking back. Pete plodded along behind, cursing and giving Marie a shove every few steps to prove there wasn't the tiniest bit of weakness in him.

CHAPTER 42

January 8
Iquique Bivouac
Northern Chile

Quinn sat quietly with a watered-down Gatorade in his hand, staring into the flames of a small campfire. They'd walked a hundred meters outside the bivouac fence and a small sand dune blocked them from the hubbub of scooters, power tools, and foot traffic that went on all night inside the enclosure. There was no suitable wood, but Bo made do by pouring two cups of gasoline on a mound of sand. Orange shadows played off the faces of Thibodaux, Bo, and Aleksandra, who all sat in folding camp chairs watching the same fire.

The KTM's tires and oil had been changed, Quinn had been fed and watered and completed his road book after his shower. All his Dakar duties complete, it was good to sit for a moment and collect his thoughts—and try to figure out Zamora.

"Hey, Jericho," Bo said. One hand held an open bottle of rum, the other was shoved down the pocket of a handwoven cotton hoodie he'd bought from a local street vendor. "Remember what Dad calls a fire like this?"

"Cowboy TV." Quinn laughed, enjoying the memory. "Our old man tells the dumbest jokes."

"I know a joke," Aleksandra said. Flames reflected on her oval face. Both hands rested in the pockets of her fleece vest.

"*A* joke?" Bo said, taking a swig of rum. "Impressive."

She glanced up from the fire to glare hard at him. "Russians are very funny people," she said.

"Yeah," Bo said, rolling his eyes. "That's obvious."

"We do not giggle like maniacs at every little thing." Aleksandra turned back to the fire, her face bordering on a pout. "But Russians have a fine sense of humor."

"I think Mr. Bo should take a little teaspoon full of hush." Thibodaux leaned forward, big arms resting on his knees. "*I* want to hear your joke, *cheri*."

"Me too," Jericho said.

"Okay." Aleksandra sat up a little straighter. The pout left as quickly as it had come. "Sherlock Holmes and Dr. Watson go to camp in the desert," she began. Quinn couldn't help but notice how her green eyes caught the dancing light of the fire. "They have a good meal and go to sleep. In the middle of the night Holmes nudges the doctor awake. 'Look at the sky, Watson, and tell me what you see.' Watson looks up and says: 'I see millions and millions of stars.' 'And what does that tell you?' Sherlock asks. 'Well,' Watson answers, 'astronomically I see there are millions of galaxies and infer that there are billions of planets. Astrologically, I see that Saturn is in Leo. Meteorologically, I deduce from the lack of clouds that we should have pleasant weather in the morning. Theologically, I observe that God is infinite and we are but tiny, insignificant specks. . . . What do you deduce, Holmes?' Sherlock shakes his head and says: 'Watson, you idiot. Someone has stolen our tent!' ' "

Thibodaux's easy belly laugh shook the chill from the night air. Jericho chuckled and even Bo cracked a smile.

Satisfied that her joke had gone over well enough, Aleksandra slid back in the canvas of her chair and closed her eyes. "That was Mikhail's favorite," she whispered.

Jericho looked up at the night sky. Like Dr. Watson, he saw millions of stars splashed across the Milky Way over an infinite desert night. Carina, Alpha and Beta Centauri, and the Southern Cross—they were foreign to the northern sky he'd grown up with.

"You know," he said. "I assume since Russians have a sense of humor, you possess other feelings as well. We've been so busy trying to find this bomb that we've never stopped to check and see how you're doing."

"How do you mean?" Aleksandra looked up at him. "I am fine."

"It's difficult enough to lose a fellow agent." Jericho shrugged. "But I can see you and Mikhail were very close. Losing someone like that is especially painful."

"He was married, you know," Aleksandra said, her voice low and reverent. "He had a lovely wife, Irina, and two beautiful daughters."

An awkward silence fell around the fire, but for the uneasy squeak and shift of camp chairs and the distant sound of engine noise.

"We were not lovers," she went on, now staring a

thousand yards past the fire, into the black desert night. "Though most suspected so, even our superiors. No, my Misha was very much in love with his wife. He was my trainer, my mentor, and oftentimes my surrogate father when I had no one else to trust. But most of all, he was my friend." A tear ran down Aleksandra's cheek. She rubbed her nose with her sleeve. "I have had many lovers—but I have only ever had one friend."

Bo looked around the group with glassy eyes, his chest heaving. Quinn knew his brother could be argumentative, but his emotions ran bright, just below the surface. The younger Quinn sniffed and raised the bottle of rum.

"To Mikhail Ivanovich Polzin, Agent Riley Cooper, and too many other good friends we've all lost to bloody men." He took a drink, then tipped the bottle, letting it run for a moment into the sand. "And to tomorrow, when we find that damned bomb."

CHAPTER 43

"**D**audov has disappeared." Monagas slipped a Walther .22 caliber pistol with a stubby suppressor in the waistband of his pants. Nearly worthless in a true gunfight, the tiny thing was meant for close work where stealth was the key. Within the close and crowded confines of the bivouac, it was perfect.

"No sign at all?" Zamora mused. "My mind is muddled. We've killed so many, maybe we are just running out of Chechens."

"No," Monagas said. "He and anyone we know connected with him have simply vanished."

Zamora threw a hand over his face. He lay alone in his bunk, wearing nothing but an open red dressing gown of rich silk on Egyptian cotton sheets that draped decadently over the edge. He'd grown bored with the gap-toothed twins and sent them to sleep in their own tent. The episode with Blessington and the Chechen had left him fitful and unable to concentrate. Still, in the crowds where he ran, it didn't do to show a shred of weakness, even among friends.

Monagas stood across from him at the door to the motor home, waiting for orders.

Zamora looked up. "I would consider it a personal favor if you were to find Rustam Daudov and cut out his heart."

"I will find him then." Monagas turned to go.

"It is far too probable, my friend, that Daudov has found out our secret and is already en route to Bolivia." Zamora pursed his lips. He was hesitant to voice his thoughts for fear that they would come true. "Far too many know about the camp," he said. "My father's pilots could easily be bought. I know—I bought them. I should have had them killed them long ago."

Monagas put a hand on the doorknob. "The mechanic is still working outside. He will call me if he sees anyone."

"You're certain he had no part in Fabian's betrayal?"

Monagas nodded. "He saw what happened to his partner."

"Very well then. Do your best to find the Chechen dog. But I fear he has already flown." Zamora made a fluttering gesture with his hand. "And that means my dream of finishing the Dakar has flown as well."

"But you have other dreams, *patrón*," Monagas said.

A thin smile perked Zamora's lips.

"Indeed I do," he said.

CHAPTER 44

Quinn and Aleksandra walked back to the bivouac together, keeping up the appearance of a couple. Each carried a folded camp chair over their shoulder. Bo had stayed back a few minutes longer to make sure the fire was out. Jacques hung back as well, using the satellite phone to call his wife in private.

In anticipation of an early start, most riders had already hit the rack, but Jericho's mind raced. Instinct, sixth sense, *haragei*—Japanese art of the belly—however it was described, he'd learned long before to pay attention to such things.

"I am sorry for that display back there," Aleksandra said. "I won't let it happen again."

"It was good," Quinn said. "I don't often see my baby brother get choked up like that."

"You are very different, the two of you," she said.

Jericho shook his head, chuckling. "You have no idea."

"And yet . . ." She stopped to look at him under the light of the tire repair awning. The clank of wrenches and thump of rubber rims went on all night. "And yet you are very much the same."

"I suppose." Quinn walked on. Boaz Quinn was good deep down, but he'd chosen a very different path in his life.

"There's something I need to tell you," Aleksandra said, looking back and forth to make certain no one else was in earshot. "In most—"

She stopped abruptly as Julian Monagas passed. The crooked-nosed thug forced his pockmarked face into a twisted half smile. He raised his hand in a noncommittal wave as he went by.

Beside him, Quinn felt Aleksandra's body go tense, as if all the air around her was suddenly drawn away. She spun, staring daggers at the broad back of a departing thug.

"What is it?" Quinn stared down at her, feeling her hand go hot in his.

She stood stone still, not even breathing until Monagas turned the corner on the other side of the tire shop.

"Are you all right?" Quinn prodded.

"I am fine," she said, shutting down again after all the emotional openness of the evening. She spun toward her tent. "I am very tired," she said. "And you have an early morning."

Inside her tent, Aleksandra knelt on her sleeping mat and rifled through her bag for the long dagger she kept at the bottom. She held her hand out in front of her. Even in the shadows of her tent, she could see it trembling.

The bastard Monagas was wearing Mikhail's double eagle ring. It had been him in the men's room stall at the strip club. He had killed the Chechen pig Akhmad

Umarov. A tear of frustration crossed the freckles of her cheek. He had murdered her friend.

Aleksandra knew she should tell Quinn what she knew. If Monagas had killed Mikhail, then he and Zamora had been present when Baba Yaga was taken. There was no more doubt that they had her. She told herself that it didn't matter. They were watching Zamora anyway. If Quinn started to doubt, then she would tell him. If she told him her plan for Monagas now, he would try and stop her.

"I will make him pay, Misha," she whispered, huge tears dripping from the end of her nose and landing with loud plops on her sleeping bag. Chiding herself for such rampant emotion, she sniffed, wiping her nose with the heel of her hand.

She stuffed the dagger under her belt at the small of her back and press checked her H&K one last time, reassuring herself that there was a round in the chamber. Satisfied that she was ready to wreak havoc on the murderous thug with the flat nose and crooked lip, she listened until she heard the sound of Quinn's rhythmic breathing coming from the tent beside her. She only had to wait a few moments for a scooter to buzz past and used the sound to cover the noise as she unzipped her tent and crept into the night.

CHAPTER 45

Marie woke from a fitful sleep to the sensation of breathing on her neck. Even her nightmares were welcome relief from her actual circumstances, and she clenched her eyes shut, afraid to open them until she heard the familiar sound of Simon's cooing.

Pete sagged in the recliner, snoring loudly with a leg thrown over one arm of the chair. Lourdes was in the back bedroom. The buzz of her voice carried down the hall as she talked to her foul boyfriend on the computer.

Simon cooed again in her ear.

Fully awake now, she wiped the grit out of her eyes and licked dry lips. She needed some water but didn't want to risk waking Pete.

"What have you got there?" she whispered, looking down at Simon's hand. Her heart stopped in her chest when she realized what it was.

He must have wandered over to Pete's chair while they were both asleep and picked up his cell phone.

Marie tugged on the phone, her brain spinning as she tried to figure out what to do. She could call the police but didn't know where she was. Worse, on the outside chance that someone was able to find them, such a thing would surely get Matt killed.

Simon started to whimper. Fearful of waking Pete, she abandoned trying to take the phone for a moment while she thought. Matt might have something planned already. He was smart that way. Whatever she did, it had to involve him. But how?

"Hooray for Simon," Marie whispered, praising him for getting the phone. Pete was no more than fifteen feet away so she kept her voice to a quiet hum. Every move she made seemed as loud as banging a string of metal cans. "Can Mama see?" She held out her hand for the phone. Mercifully, the baby gave it to her. "Hooray for Simon," she whispered again.

Thankfully, Pete had not opted for a screen lock and she was able to access the camera with no problem. She turned the phone around and took a photograph of herself and Simon leaning against the wall.

Lourdes's heavy footfalls pounded down the hall and Marie shoved the phone under her thigh. Pete stirred but didn't wake up. Marie did not breathe until she heard the bathroom door shut, followed by the sound of Lourdes peeing.

Fingers trembling, Marie punched in the number she'd decided on and sent the photograph attached to a text message. As soon as it sent, she deleted the evidence of both text and photograph.

The toilet flushed an instant before Marie slid the phone across the floor below Pete's dangling leg.

Lourdes stomped into the living room just an instant after Marie had tiptoed back across the room and collapsed on her lumpy mattress beside Simon. The horrible woman got herself a glass of water from the kitchen and stood wearing nothing but black panties and a T-shirt. One hand on a thick hip, she glared down at Marie while she downed the water in one long gulping swallow.

Lourdes wiped her mouth with her forearm and sniffed.

"Why are you so happy?" She asked.

Marie bowed her head. She was still shaking. "What do you mean?"

"You have hope. I can smell it," Lourdes sneered. "I thought we talked about that."

"I don't," Marie lied.

Lourdes stood for a long moment, blinking under the stark bangs of her Cleopatra haircut. Without warning she let loose a bone-chilling scream and threw her glass against the kitchen wall.

"Holy shit!" Pete fell out of the chair at the sound of the scream and shattering glass. He scrambled to his feet trying to make sense of what was going on.

Frightened by the sudden noises, Simon let out a screech of his own.

"Enough fun for now," Lourdes said. "Go back to sleep." She shot a hateful look at Marie. "Clean up that mess," she said.

Pete reached to pick up his phone from where it lay on the floor and shoved it in his pocket without a second look. He suspected nothing. Marie had to fight the urge to smile. For the first time in days, she felt a tiny bit in control.

CHAPTER 46

January 9

"**M**onagas is gone," Aleksandra said early the next morning. Her lips were drawn in a tight white line as she set her tray down on the long folding table under the dining tent. "I just heard it from one of his mechanics. Gone!" The sun was just coming up, but the last riders had left the starting line five minutes before.

Thibodaux looked up from his plate of eggs and buttered toast. "Gone?"

"That can't be good," Bo said from across the table.

"No," Thibodaux said. "It's not." He reached for the iPhone in his shirt pocket. "You get Jericho on the horn and I'll check on Zamora."

Thibodaux pulled up his hacked link to the ASO tracking system just in time to see the GPS blip identifying Zamora's bike veer off the designated course and turn east for the Iquique airport. In an unavoidable turn of events, Jericho had come in ahead of him the day before and had to leave the starting line earlier. He was going slow, feigning engine trouble, but was still ahead a half mile.

Thibodaux stood, twirling his hand overhead for the others to abandon their breakfast and follow him.

Bo handed him the phone as they ran toward the support truck.

Jericho tapped the Bluetooth receiver on the side of his helmet. "Go for Quinn," he said. Without a face shield, the wind whirred in his helmet, but the earpiece made it possible to hear well enough.

"Turn around, *l'ami*," Thibodaux said. "Zamora's heading to the airport."

Quinn tapped the brakes, feeling the bike's knobby tires squirm on the cool pavement. If Thibodaux said to turn around, there was no point in second-guessing him.

"Monagas?" he asked.

"He was MIA as of early this morning, beb," Thibodaux said. "Looks like they're making a move. We're on our way to the airport now."

Quinn pulled over long enough to disable the KTM's GPS locator system so the officials—and anyone else who might be watching—wouldn't be able to track him. Race officials would call the IriTrack to check his safety soon enough, but he would tell them he'd had engine trouble. He didn't want to withdraw until later, in case Zamora happened to check in later in the day.

Back aboard the bike, he flipped a quick U-turn and opened up the throttle, no longer fretting about babying the engine through the race. He made it to the tiny civil aviation airpark near Iquique's Diego Aracena Airport less than five minutes later.

The KTM's wheels crunched up on the gravel apron next to a young mechanic in greasy blue overalls wiping his hands on an even greasier rag. A twin-engine Cessna banked northeast over the rolling dunes of the Atacama Desert.

"Have you quit the race too, señor?" the mechanic asked, eyeing Quinn with an empathetic frown.

"I'm afraid so, amigo," Quinn said. He saw Zamora's Yamaha—a fifty-thousand-dollar motorcycle—abandoned, lying on its side next to a neatly painted tin hangar along the edge of the taxiway. "Bad transmission," he lied. He nodded toward the twin-engine Cessna that grew smaller and smaller as it flew into the morning light. "What happened to my friend?"

"It must be in the water." The mechanic smiled. "He too had a bad transmission."

"So he chartered one of your planes?" Quinn asked, still straddling the KTM.

The mechanic shook his head. "No. He bought it. They are going to La Paz." He peered at Quinn. "Do you too wish to buy an airplane to go to La Paz?"

Quinn scanned the tiny airport. Only three other aircraft sat at their tie-downs beyond the building, a Piper Cheyenne twin, a tiny Cessna 150, and a radial-engine plane that looked like some kind of older war bird.

"I'd like to charter one," Quinn said. Thibodaux and the others came rolling up in the support truck, screeching to a stop beside him.

"Very well, amigo," the mechanic said, eyeing the newcomers. "The 150 and the Navy trainer are available for charter. But the Cheyenne is for sale only."

Quinn frowned. Both the 150 and the Navy AT6 were two-place aircraft. They would do no good. "For sale only?" he asked.

"Ah, I am afraid so, amigo. Too many people want to do things outside the law in such a plane. If I was to own it during such an action, I could get into grave trouble." A broad smile crossed his face. "I make you a very good deal at one hundred thousand American dollars."

Quinn tilted his head. "And she's in good condition?"

"Of course, señor," the mechanic said. "And I will fly her for you for an additional fifty thousand dollars."

"That is a steep fee, my friend," Bo Quinn said as he walked up beside his brother.

"It is," the mechanic said. "But I am not the one with a bad transmission needing to go to La Paz."

Five minutes later Enrique Santos had changed his greasy overalls for a pair of faded jeans, a white sweat-shirt, and a ball cap with an Orvis fly-fishing logo on the front—and proclaimed himself a Piper Cheyenne pilot.

"You sure this is safe?" Thibodaux said, as they climbed up the fold-out air stairs at the rear of the air-craft. He ran a thumb around the tattered rubber door seal before ducking his head to walk between the single seats on each side of a narrow aisle.

"He's flying us," Quinn said. "He must think it's safe enough." There were two seats in front for a pilot and co-pilot, then four more with two facing aft and two more in a vis-à-vis configuration. A fifth seat with a re-movable cushion hiding the toilet was at the far aft of the plane behind a sliding curtain. It had space for two more seats, but Quinn guessed they had been removed in order to haul more cargo in the form of coca prod-ucts. Quinn took the forward-facing seat on the right of the airplane so he could keep an eye on Enrique.

"We're in a bit of a hurry, amigo," he said. "I would like to catch up to my friend who left earlier if we could."

Enrique picked up the mike from the console of in-struments and looked over his shoulder. "I could at-tempt to call him on the radio."

Quinn raised his hand. "That won't be necessary.

The young pilot nodded. "I thought not, amigo. You have that look about you."

"What look is that?" Bo asked, sitting across from his brother.

"The look of one who chases bad men."

"And my friend in the Cessna?"

Enrique's face grew dark. "Oh, señor, he has the look of a very bad man. That is why I gave you my sweetheart deal on this airplane."

The Pratt & Whitney turbine engines hurled the Cheyenne off the runway and pulled her up at an angle steep enough that Bo, who sat almost knee to knee across from Quinn, was hanging above him by his shoulder harness. Aleksandra hung similarly over Thibodaux until the plane began to level out at fifteen thousand feet into a shallower climb.

One hand on the yoke, Enrique turned and held up a two-foot length of toilet paper. "We are having a little trouble pressurizing," he said. "I need someone to take this and hold it up to the door." His face was relaxed, as if this sort of thing happened all the time.

"Do what now?" Thibodaux's eyes went wide.

"We're losing air around the door." Enrique held out the toilet paper. "Hold this near the door. When you get to the leak it will suck out of your hand and seal the hole . . . hopefully."

Despite having to use toilet paper to fix the door seal, Enrique proved to be a more than competent pilot. Roughly two hours later he set the Cheyenne down through heavy clouds at Laja Airport a few kilometers outside of El Alto, a suburb of La Paz.

Thibodaux applauded when the wheels touched down in a steady rain. "Damn good aviating, amigo."

"Thank you for flying Air Enrique," the young pilot said as they rolled down the runway. Blue and white lights flashed in by the fog. The prop blast pushed rivulets of water along the windows. "It sounds as if we were the last plane in. The weather has everything grounded. Look, your friend was able to make it in. There is the Cessna he purchased." Enrique pointed to the main operations building looming like a ghost through the fog as they made their way to parking. "I must advise you that if you wish to be legal, you will need to check in with Bolivian customs at the airport in El Alto. You are American so they will charge you a hundred and thirty-five dollars each for a Bolivian visa. That is entirely up to you, however. No one knows we are here. Where do you want me to park your plane?"

"Consider it our gift to you," Quinn said. Both he and Enrique had known all along that he wasn't going to hassle with the aircraft while Zamora got farther away.

"Thank you very much for your generosity," Enrique said, grinning.

Thibodaux looked at him through narrow eyes. "How many times have you sold this same plane?"

Enrique's grin grew even wider as he set the parking brake. "Oh, you would be surprised, señor. I could retire, but the work is good and I get to meet such interesting people."

A thought suddenly occurred to Quinn. "I'm sure you know the pilot who flew my friend here in the Cessna."

"He is my cousin," Enrique said.

"Call and see if the men are still with him. But tell him not to mention us."

Enrique nodded emphatically. "An excellent idea, amigo." He pulled out his cell phone and dialed.

After a quick conversation of rapid-fire Spanish he ended the call and returned the phone to his pocket.

"The men you follow tried to get my cousin to fly them to Rurrenabaque on the other side of the Yungas Mountains. But the weather is too bad. He told them he would wait, but he says they are rude and very impatient."

"Where are they now?" Aleksandra asked.

Enrique shrugged. "They took a cab down to the city."

"Will they come back so he can fly them?" Aleksandra's voice rose in pitch and timbre. "Surely they will come back."

"Not according to my cousin, I'm afraid," Enrique said. "He says they were in too much of a hurry to listen to reason. He pointed them to the Hotel Condeza, but I do not know if they would take his advice."

Enrique paused at the door of the aircraft, his hand on the exit lever. "I must warn you," he said. "The air is very thin here in La Paz. Go slowly, my friends—or you will learn the hard way. And lastly, be wary of unofficial taxis. Some are paid to drive you to certain places where you will be robbed."

Both Bo and Aleksandra smiled at that, taking the pistols out of the duffel and shoving then under their jackets.

"That would prove to be quite a surprise to the robbers," she said.

Oddly, Quinn felt the pressure drop when Enrique twisted the Cheyenne's latch and cracked open the door, as if they'd opened the door in flight. He took a deep breath of what oxygen there was and made his way down the folding stairs to the wet tarmac.

Team Quinn grabbed their duffel bags and stood in the rain to wave good-bye to the young entrepreneur. Jericho had changed out of his riding gear in mid flight and into a pair of nylon 5.11 khakis and a white polo. Prepared for desert nights on the Dakar, he had only a nylon jacket that proved to be lacking against the chilly heights of El Alto at over thirteen thousand feet above sea level.

Enrique called them a cab, and it arrived within minutes. Cramming themselves into the battered Ford

Expedition, they settled in for the looping ride on the Autopista from the high plains of El Alto down, down, down to the great gash in the Andes that cradled the city of Nuestra Señora de La Paz, the Hotel Condeza, and, if they were extremely lucky, Valentine Zamora.

CHAPTER 47

Simon had been crying nonstop for ten minutes. In many ways life had been easier when Marie had given up hope. Now that she harbored even the tiniest notion that she could get her message to Matt and he could use his genius brain to figure out a way to save them—all she wanted to do was scream right along with her baby.

Lourdes seemed bent on giving them just enough food to keep them alive until she could shoot them. A meager diet of nothing but cheese and bread was hard enough on Marie, but it put the baby's stomach in knots. She tried her best to soothe him, rubbing his tummy, bouncing him on her knee, but day after day he got worse, throwing his head back and wailing.

Lourdes kept the laptop computer with her in the back room, where, thankfully, she stayed most of the time. Marie had grown attuned to the faint beep of an incoming video call and could barely contain herself when she heard it. Lourdes's lumbering footfalls as she stomped down the hall confirmed that the call was her daily moment with Matthew.

The evil woman never allowed the calls to last more

than a few seconds, so Marie knew she'd have to be quick if she wanted to get the message across. Often, Matt's face was heavily pixilated and his voice little more than a string of disembodied garble. She prayed the connection would be clear enough this time.

Lourdes stomped to the edge of the mattress and handed her the open laptop. She crossed her arms over her chest and glared. "Say hello and then good-bye," she said.

Marie took the computer and set it in her lap. "He needs to see his son," she said, trying to ignore Lourdes.

Matt's gaunt but smiling face greeted her on the screen.

"Are you all right?" The tension in his face seemed to increase when he saw her, and Marie realized she must look a sight. She pushed her bangs out of her eyes and forced a smile. "I'm fine," she said, pulling Simon onto her lap. Thankfully, he quit crying when he saw his daddy. "We're both fine. I'm worried about Miss Kitty though."

Matt cocked his head to the side. "You're worried about who?"

"Miss Kitty," Marie sniffed. "I left her in the kitchen and we don't have anyone to go check on her."

"Marie, I—"

"That is enough." Lourdes snatched back the computer and closed the screen. Tucking it under her arm, she shook her head in disgust. "You have but seconds to talk to your husband and all you can think of is your silly cat? He will be lucky to be rid of you."

Marie let her head loll back against the wall and closed her eyes. *Oh, Matt*, she thought. *I hope you understood.*

CHAPTER 48

Zamora sat at a tippy wooden table in a coffeehouse off Prado Avenue in downtown La Paz, a cell phone pressed to his ear.

"Don't do anything rash until we speak in person," he said, pressing a thumb and forefinger to his eyes. Surely, someone was digging out his eyes from the inside. "I am on my way there now."

"We feel the need to explore another option," Yazid Nazif said at the other end of the line. "We are after maximum effect, after all."

Zamora pounded his fist on the table, first shouting, then lowering his voice when others in the café looked in his direction. "And that is what you will get! You must stay with the plan!"

"I ask you again, my friend," Nazif said a little too sweetly for Zamora's taste. "Is the device ours or is it not?"

"Of course it's yours," he hissed. "We will speak of this when we get to the location. Tell Borregos to wait in Rio Branco for my call."

Zamora ended the call and rested his head on the

table. "Idiots," he whispered to himself. He should have known better than to trust the Yemenis to follow through.

The quick exit from Chile and the bumpy flight over the storm clouds had left him dizzy and bilious. He had no idea where he was, leaving those particulars to Monagas. The altitude made his temples feel like he'd been hit with a hammer, and his stomach churned. All he wanted was to leave this stinking, airless cesspool and get to his bomb. So far, the weather refused to co-operate.

No flights were leaving the city. They were so high in the sagging clouds that rain hardly seemed to fall, but only rattle around in the mist. It was enough to make someone crazy.

He clicked the touch pad on the laptop computer in front of him, trying to connect to Pollard for the third time. For all he knew, Rustam Daudov and his men were already at the river camp. He almost cried when Pollard's face appeared on the screen.

"Where have you been?" Zamora snapped. He used a telephone earpiece with a small microphone so the handful of other patrons, mostly tourists, couldn't hear the conversation. Pollard stared back at him with sullen eyes, saying nothing.

"Never mind," Zamora said. "Is everything all right there?"

"Valentine, you are insane," Pollard scoffed. "Of course everything isn't all right. You have my family at gunpoint."

"A fact you should keep in mind," Zamora said. "I mean—is the device intact and still in your care?"

"Why wouldn't it be?"

"There is a certain Chechen who wants what is mine. I believe he is on the way to you," Zamora said. "If he gets there before I do, he will kill you without question."

"I doubt that," Pollard laughed. "You've surrounded me with this crack group of guards."

Zamora scoffed, feeling a chill as he thought about Yesenia and the other guards. He'd often employed groups of Guarani and other indigenous youth to guard lesser narcotics labs. He'd thought to hide Baba Yaga in plain sight without making too much of a fuss with a heavily armed encampment. There was always someone with a bigger army. "You know they are just there to keep you honest," he said.

"I know. But anyone familiar with one of these devices knows they will also need an expert to make it work. You said it yourself. Isn't that why I'm here?"

"Believe me, he will kill you and take the device," Zamora said. "Rustam Daudov is a thug."

"And what are you?" Pollard sneered.

Zamora scratched his chin, then ran the tip of his finger along the thin black line of his mustache. "As you say, I am the man who has your family. You would do well to remember that. Now be watchful. I will be there shortly."

He ended the call as Monagas entered the coffee shop.

Zamora motioned for him to sit in the chair across from him. That was the thing about Monagas; he never assumed things. "I hope you have good news."

"I am sorry, *patrón*," Monagas sighed. "They say

this weather will be here for some time. No aircraft are able to fly over the mountains for the Beni." His eyes shifted back and forth around the small coffee shop and he leaned forward across the table. "I do have a way out, *patrón*, but it would be very, very dangerous."

CHAPTER 49

In the valleys of the Andes, La Paz, Bolivia, was a city built upside down. The most desirable real estate was nestled at a more breathable nine thousand feet in the lowlands southwest of the tree-lined central thoroughfare known as the Prado. Much of the city sprawled along a deep trench with middle-class residents occupying condos near the Choqueyapu River. The less well to do clung to the steep mountains surrounding the city in makeshift brick houses. The poorest lived in the thin air of nearly fourteen thousand feet above sea level.

Quinn felt his ears pop for the third time as the rattling Ford radio-taxi turned back southeast on the Autopista and headed down into the city.

The cabdriver, a short Aymara Indian man with a colorful wool hat and tattered homespun coat, pointed to the south with an open hand. "If not for the clouds, you could see the three peaks of Illimani there. The guardian of La Paz."

The man, who said his name was Lupe, never engaged in real conversation, piping up only when they passed a particular landmark or milepost. Quinn suspected he didn't actually speak much English, but had memorized a few lines in order to ingratiate himself to tourists for bigger tips.

Quinn had the taxi drop them off a block above the Hotel Condeza at the bustling intersection of Santa Cruz and Linares. Lupe smiled broadly as Thibodaux paid him fifteen American dollars, twice the agreed-upon fare.

Low clouds sulked in the air, drifting between the red brick buildings. Barrel-chested men and stocky women wearing colorful, handwoven alpaca shawls against the drizzling rain sauntered along the crowded streets. Most wore bowler hats, tied to their heads with pieces of string. The smell of frying meat and roasted corn drifted with the mist and whiff of open sewers.

"I tell you one thing, *cher*," Thibodaux panted as they jostled their way through the crowds of tourists and stall keepers. He clenched his eyes shut. "I am not a mountain man, that's for sure."

Bo, who seemed less affected by the altitude, pointed down the street, less than a hundred meters away. "There's the hotel," he said. "Should we go see if he's there?"

Aleksandra tapped the small duffel slung over her shoulder where she carried her pistol. "Good idea," she said.

"Now hold on a second," Quinn said, pulling up short in the drizzling rain next to a stall selling what looked like dried baby dinosaurs. "Our goal is to follow him to the bomb. Not confront him yet." Passersby spilled around him.

Aleksandra nodded. "That is true," she said, but it was obvious she was trying to convince herself.

A wizened old woman, sitting behind what turned out to be a large pile of desiccated llama fetuses, piped up. "You need good luck." Thinning gray braids hung from a weathered brown derby hat that sat sideways over her broad face, which was wrinkled and dark as a prune. A coca leaf was pressed to her sagging cheek like a piece of jewelry. She chewed on a wad of leaves as she spoke, sweeping a bony hand across the stacks of figurines, amulets, and dried animals that made up her wares. Like traders worldwide, her command of English was remarkable. "Everyone could use some help. I have the llamas to bless new buildings, Ekeko to bring you fortune, Pachamama for protection. . . ." Her rheumy eyes narrowed to look straight at Aleksandra. "You are on a quest, no?"

Thibodaux, who put a little more stock than he should in such notions, raised a surprised brow at the woman's divination.

"Relax, Jacques," Quinn whispered. "A bunch of *turistas* marching along, intent on something down the street. It's not too much of a stretch to guess we're on a quest."

Thibodaux bit his bottom lip. "Take a look up there, beb." He nodded toward a sign on the open front brick building where the old woman's stall was tucked in among others selling similar wares. "*Mercado de las Brujas*," he said as if proving a point. "The witches' market."

"I have the ingredients to capture the heart of a man." The old women grinned at Aleksandra, showing the wad of coca against stained teeth. "But I see you have already captured one." She cackled at Bo, who shot a startled glance at Quinn.

"That's crazy," he said, looking a little too guilty for Jericho's taste.

"How about one of these?" Aleksandra picked up a clay figurine of a little man, apparently anxious to change the subject. The statue wore a traditional wool hat and his arms were laden with packages. It was no more than three inches tall, and a hole in its mouth held a full-size cigarette. "How much?" She shuffled through her pockets for her money.

"Ekeko," the old woman said. "He will bring you good fortune."

Aleksandra pulled her cell phone from her pocket along with her wallet. Quinn, who stood directly beside her, heard a nearly inaudible ping. She handed the woman her money and turned quickly toward the street, staring down at the phone.

"What was that?" Quinn moved closer.

The face of the phone showed a map where a blue dot pulsed on a road leading northeast out of the city.

"Zamora?" Thibodaux said as he and Bo crowded in to look at the phone as well.

"No." Aleksandra shook her head. "Monagas. This signal is from the tracker I placed with Umarov at Zamora's party. It was in a gold money clip. It was Monagas who killed the Chechen back in Miami and must have taken the clip as a trophy." Aleksandra gave the half grin of a hunter. "His foolish habit will be his undoing."

"We've been around Monagas for over a week. Why is the tracker only showing up now?" Thibodaux asked.

"The device is activated by body heat." Aleksandra

shrugged. "Perhaps he had it buried in his luggage and did not have it in his pocket until now."

"It doesn't matter," Quinn held out his hand for the phone. "May I see it?"

Aleksandra gave the phone to him and he showed it to the woman in the bowler hat, who sat smiling behind her stack of dried baby llamas. "Do you know what is in this part of the city?" he asked.

The old woman pulled a pair of cat's-eye reading glasses from behind her table and slipped them on to study the phone.

"Ahhhh," she said under her breath. "Very bad. This is very, very bad."

"What?" Thibodaux's mouth fell open. "Just go on ahead and tell us, will you?"

"This blue spot?" The old woman peered over the top of her bright red glasses. "This is what you seek?"

"It is." Quinn gave her a twenty-dollar bill.

The woman took off her glasses and held them in a clenched fist. "The miners are marching on the new road, making it impassable today. The one you seek goes to El Camino de la Muerte." She pointed to the northeast. "The Road of Death."

CHAPTER 50

Quinn flagged down the first green and white radio cab he found that would hold them all. The driver was a ponytailed Aymara Indian named Leonardo who looked to be in his late teens. He confirmed that the easiest way to get across the Andes to Coroico and on to Rurrenabaque was shut down by a parade of striking indigenous silver miners trying to get the Bolivian government's attention. Until the skies cleared, El Camino de la Muerte, he said, was the only other way. He agreed to take them to Cumbre Pass, beyond the eastern edge of the city, where his cousin Adelmo had a four-wheel-drive van that could make the journey down the Bolivian Road of Death. Quinn wondered if everyone in South America had a cousin who ran a hotel, flew planes, or rented out cars.

Crammed in the middle between Jericho and Bo, Aleksandra kept watch on the pulsing blue dot on her phone. "We have to hurry," she said, her voice breathless from tension and altitude. The heavy mist and lack of oxygen made everyone feel as though they were slowly drowning. "He's still moving away."

"My friend." Thibodaux took a drink from his water

bottle and looked across the front seat at the driver. "We are in a hurry. I will double your fare if you can pick up your speed."

Leonardo grinned broadly and slammed his foot to the floorboard, throwing them all back in their seats. He drove with one hand while he spoke in animated Spanish on his cell phone. The car sped over cobblestone streets, climbing steadily upward thousands of feet, splashing through puddles and drenching pedestrians who trudged too close to the edge of the road. Rain spattered on the foggy windshield but did little to slow the boy down.

"I don't want to be the pantywaist here," Bo said, bracing his knees against the front seat to keep from being thrown completely on top of Aleksandra as the cab made a hard left. "But we don't exactly need a run-in with the local *policia* right now, considering our status in the country."

Leonardo smiled over his shoulder. "Not to worry, amigo," he said, with an apparent understanding of English far greater than that of their last driver. "My cousin Mateo is the captain of the traffic police. His men know my cab."

Leonardo's cousin Adelmo had the van ready to go by the time the cab came screeching to a stop high up on the barren mountainside in front of a terraced yard full of rusted vehicles. Chickens pecked in the mud, oblivious to the rain. A tawny billy goat peered through the mist from the long hood of an old AMC Javelin sitting on concrete blocks.

Not much older than Leonardo, Adelmo was more

somber than his cousin with a curl of black hair hanging over expressive brown eyes. His English was not quite as good, but he was pleasant enough and willing to get them over the Road of Death. His services as a driver, along with a plate of piping-hot meat empanadas and *chunos*, a grayish frost-dried potato, came with the price of the vehicle rental.

"He has stopped," Aleksandra said through clenched teeth, eyes glued to her phone. Her entire body seemed to hum with nervous energy. "If we hurry, we can catch him."

Adelmo's young wife, plump cheeked and pregnant, had given Jacques a small pamphlet on the Yungas Road, as the Camino de la Muerte was more formally known. It was written in Spanish, but the big Cajun's French and Italian helped him pick through the descriptions as they drove.

"Did you know the American tourist books call this place we're going WMDR—the world's most dangerous road—on account of the little factoid that two or three hundred people plummet to their deaths there every year? It says here that we'll be climbing to over fifteen thousand feet at La Cumbre Pass before we drop down to about four thousand feet." He glanced up at Quinn, wagging his head. "But don't you worry because the drop-offs are only eighteen hundred feet or so and we'll have plenty of room since the shittin' road is all of ten feet wide." He turned to stare out the side window. The fog made it impossible to see the sheer cliffs that fell away from the mountain just inches outside the door. "Don't be surprised if I use up a non-Bible curse word or two, *l'ami*."

"We will be fine, señor," Adelmo said, nodding to

the clay statue of a big-breasted Pachamama, the Aymara earth goddess, on his dashboard. It bore a surprising resemblance to his wife.

Traffic grew thicker as they approached the pass, with cargo trucks and brightly painted buses known as *collectivos* inching along in a soggy parade to clog the ever-narrowing road ahead. Within another half mile they were at a complete standstill. Nothing but fog to the left and rivulets of muddy water gurgling down the rock face to their right.

"I don't think anything has passed us from the other direction for quite a while," Bo said, leaning out the window.

"Can we go around?" Quinn asked, pulling a wad of American bills out of his pocket. "It is important that we catch our friend."

Adelmo took a deep breath, reached to touch the statue of Pachamama, then pulled his little van out of line and began to slog forward, past the line of glaring truck and bus drivers, up and over the pass.

Quinn kept an eye out as they drove past every vehicle.

"Do you see him yet?" Adelmo said, eyes glued to what he could see of the narrow road through the fog.

"Not yet," Quinn said.

"He's still ahead of us," Aleksandra said from the back of the van where she got better reception from her satellite.

Well below the pass, Adelmo slowed as a truck driver wearing a North Face fleece jacket and traditional bowler hat ghosted through the fog outside his flatbed. Smoke from his clay pipe curled around his brown face. Adelmo apparently knew him and rolled down his window to shout a greeting. They spoke in a rapid-fire language Quinn guessed was their native Aymara. Adelmo's young face grew grave as he listened to his friend.

"There is a mudslide ahead," he said, pulling his head back inside. He switched off the engine and leaned back in his seat, settling in as if this was something he did all the time. "A road crew is there, but it will take two or three hours to clear."

"I don't like this," Thibodaux said. "I jump out of airplanes and go toe-to-toe with whatever badass you want to shove my way, but you can have this road-of-death shit."

"Oh, señor." Adelmo opened his eyes, chuckling. "We are not yet on El Camino de la Muerte. That does not begin for five more kilometers at the town of Cota-pata."

"Damn to hell!" Aleksandra hissed. She looked up, a dark frown creasing her face. "They made it around the slide. He is moving again!"

CHAPTER 51

Quinn stood beside Thibodaux under a drizzling rain along the edge of the pavement, a satellite phone pressed to his ear. What had been bare, skeletal rock from the Altiplano to Cumbre Pass was now covered by a lush skin of green cloud forest. Towering peaks vanished into the clouds in every direction, blocking the horizon and making it difficult to get a signal. He had to turn every now and again to stay connected.

Bo and Aleksandra had walked ahead a little, passing the line of trucks and buses to see if they could get a feel for how long the road would be blocked. It was eerily quiet but for the gurgle of newly formed streams and waterfalls that tumbled down through the foliage. Drivers and passengers alike dozed in their seats.

Palmer answered on the third try.

Quinn brought him up to speed quickly about Aleksandra's tracker. Few details were as important as the fact that they were about to lose the only link they had to the bomb.

"He's moving north," Quinn said. "We believe he's trying to get to a place called Rurrenabaque."

"Dammit," Palmer said. "It had to be Bolivia."

"Sir?"

"Since Evo Morales shut down cooperation with drug enforcement, we're pretty slim in the way of resources in that part of the world."

Quinn could hear the click of a keyboard in the background and imagined Palmer sitting behind his expansive wooden desk in the study of his Virginia satellite office away from the White House. "I may have somebody," Palmer said. "What kind of a vehicle are they in?"

"Not sure," Quinn said.

"Okay," Palmer sighed. "You realize you're asking me to call a seldom-used asset and ask him to look for two Hispanic men coming into a town of eight thousand or so people who look just like them in a vehicle you can't describe?"

"Bolivian police then?" Quinn offered. "Someone has to stop this guy before he dissolves into the jungle. Maybe regular military."

"That wouldn't go well," Palmer said. "In one scenario they kill Zamora and we are no closer to the bomb. In the other, they find the bomb and Bolivia suddenly becomes a nuclear power."

"We are losing him, sir," Quinn said. "Can you destroy the road? Box him in until we catch up?"

More keyboard clicks.

"The George Washington is off the coast of Brazil with the Fourth Fleet," Palmer said. The line was silent for a long moment. "But that's a no-go. They're too far out to do you any good."

Aleksandra came trotting back up the hill with Bo right behind her. He looked mortified at the thought of being beaten by a girl in a footrace. Their chests heaved under the flimsy clear plastic rain jackets Adelmo had given them.

Bo stopped beside Quinn, bent forward with his hands on his knees. "We found a way around," he said between panting breaths.

"Gotta go," Quinn said into the satellite phone.

"I'll put our Bolivian contact on alert. Call back as soon as practical."

"You have got to be shittin' me," Thibodaux said when Bo explained his plan. He shook the now dog-eared tourist pamphlet at Quinn for emphasis. "We're talkin' about the Road of Death here, beb."

"He'll soon be out of range." Aleksandra looked up from her phone. Rain plastered red hair to her forehead and cheeks in thick locks. "I cannot see another way," she said.

Bo ran back down the hill while Jericho and Aleksandra threw on fleece jackets and shoved their gear into Quinn's daypack. Quinn sighed at the Spartan nature of it all—two pistols, an extra pair of socks for each of them, and the heavy Severance blade.

Bo and Thibodaux had the battered Yamaha 250 dirt bike off the back of a rusted bubble-topped Mercedes truck by the time Quinn and Aleksandra made it down to them. The driver stood at the side of the road, counting his surprise windfall. Adelmo stayed back with his van, unwilling to be a part of such foolishness.

There was only one bike, and since Quinn was the better rider, it was understood he'd go. Aleksandra refused to be left behind, stressing the fact that she was the only one who knew what to do with the bomb once they found it.

Quinn threw a leg over the little blue bike and braced himself for Aleksandra to climb on behind him. An ATGATT man when he was on a motorcycle—*all the gear, all the time*—he felt naked in the flimsy raincoat and 5.11 khaki slacks. Looking ahead at what he could see of the snaking road and steep drop-offs, he consoled himself with the fact that a leather jacket and helmet weren't likely to save him anyway.

Leggy as it was, the Yamaha wasn't made for two riders. Quinn found himself thankful that Aleksandra was built like a forest sprite. Snugging down the pack on her shoulders, she wrapped her arms around his waist and scrunched up tight against his back, her thighs running parallel with his.

Quinn could see the headlines. UNITED STATES AIR FORCE OSI AGENT PLUNGES TO DEATH IN THE ARMS OF BEAUTIFUL RUSSIAN OPERATIVE. . . .

Jacques stood by with a big hand planted flat on top of his head, looking like he might throw up. Rain dripped down Bo's face, curling his shaggy head of blond hair. His lips pursed in a jealous line.

"You be careful with her, Jericho," he muttered.

"Are you kidding me?" Quinn glanced over his shoulder at Aleksandra, then back at his brother, before shaking his head. "That old witch was right about you two."

Aleksandra gave him a rough squeeze around the ribs, planting her doubled fists in his midsection. Her voice was flint hard next to his ear. "Let's go," she said. "Monagas is getting away."

"You mean Zamora," he said.

"Of course," she said over the blatting engine. "That is what I mean."

Quinn toed the bike into first and released the brake, beginning their seventy-kilometer downhill roll. With the angry Russian woman breathing revenge in his ear, the Road of Death was about to grow more deadly.

CHAPTER 52

A thirty-meter chunk of mountain lay in a lumpy tangled heap of roots, tree branches, and ferns across the narrow road. Bits of gravel still tumbled over an abrupt edge that disappeared into a low bank of soupy clouds that filled the valley below.

Crews of men wearing plastic raincoats and wielding shovels had cleared a flattened trail along the edge so they could walk back and forth. A chubby man with a cigarette dangling from his lips maneuvered an orange Kubota backhoe around the slide on metal tracks. It wasn't much larger than a garden tractor and seemed even smaller alongside the gigantic heap of earth.

Rolling past the waiting trucks, buses, and the odd car, Quinn picked his line, aiming for the packed trail just feet from the edge. Quinn felt Aleksandra tense as they neared the mudslide. He assumed she was worried about going over the steep edge, but he was more concerned with one of the workers hitting him with a shovel as they rode past.

Focused on riding, he was vaguely aware of a car door slamming. Aleksandra half turned to look behind them.

"Go, go, go!" she shouted in his ear.

Road workers dove for cover as automatic gunfire cracked in the thin air, splattering the mud. Quinn leaned forward, downshifting and rolling on the throttle. The bike shimmied in the sloppy mud and he dragged the rear brake a hair to help stand it up.

The shooters were close, and judging from the way Aleksandra squeezed him with her thighs, she'd recognized them an instant before they'd opened fire. At this range, Quinn found himself grateful that they used submachine guns and not rifles or even pistols, which they would have been tempted to actually aim.

Quinn could hear the shouts of angry voices behind them. A car door slammed. A car engine revved and the sound of spinning tires on gravel preceded the grind of metal gears as bumpers and fenders crashed together.

Quinn squirted over the mudslide and picked his way through the loose debris on the other side before opening up the throttle again. Another volley of shots cracked past, echoing off the deep canyon walls and splatting into the mud. Aleksandra squirmed behind him.

"They are trying to follow," she said, settling in low against his back.

"You recognize them?" Quinn yelled over the wind and hard patter of rain against his plastic jacket.

"Chechens," she yelled back, tucked in so his body broke the chill of the oncoming wind. He could feel her shivering. "The driver is Salambek. Rustam Daudov's man. A killer."

"He doesn't seem to like you very much," Quinn yelled into the wind.

Only a handful of trucks waited downhill from the mudslide. Beyond them, Quinn and Aleksandra had the Road of Death all to themselves. Waterfalls careened through the dense foliage and down the high mountainside above them, rushing in newly formed ditches across the road to disappear into the cloudy abyss on the other side.

Quinn planted a foot in the soupy gravel to pivot the bike around a sharp turn and still keep it on two wheels.

"His sister, Dagmani, was a leader of the Black Widows," Aleksandra shouted once the Yamaha was stabilized.

Quinn had heard of the female suicide squads in Chechnya, though thankfully he'd never faced one.

"I killed her," Aleksandra said simply, confirming his suspicions.

The snaking road seemed to magically disappear off and on, playing now you see me, now you don't, as banks of fog and cloud drifted down the mountains with the rain.

"Did they make it around?" The little Yamaha had the tendency to dart in whatever direction he looked so he depended on Aleksandra to be his eyes to the rear.

The back wheel shimmied as she turned, but to her credit, she caught herself with her thighs, careful not to upset his balance in the treacherous mud.

"I can't tell," she said, turning just a little farther to get a better look. Her legs tensed again. Her arms squeezed a little tighter.

"I hear them," she said at length, her voice ripped away by the wind.

Quinn rolled on more throttle, counter steering

around a series of deep ruts, then bouncing through a foaming waterfall that sprayed across the entire roadway like a huge bathroom shower. His face stung from the chilly, liquefied air. He'd ridden enough in cold wind to know it would be completely numb in a matter of minutes.

Somewhere ahead was a man they had to catch or risk losing track of a nuclear bomb. Behind was a car full of Chechen terrorists. They were likely after the same bomb, but at this moment were bent on killing Aleksandra—and in a car with the stability of four wheels versus his two, Quinn stood zero chance of outrunning them.

"How many are in the car?" he yelled.

"Three."

Quinn took a series of slow, rhythmic breaths, slowing his heart rate. His eyes scanned the road ahead, noting the angle of drop, the thick tangle of trees and bushes that grew on the cliff side. Rain and the fine spray of dense fog whipped at his unprotected face, popping against his thin plastic raincoat like firecrackers. A cold chill ran down both legs. He fought to keep from shivering so badly he'd upset the bike. In CRO training, he'd endured long soaks with his classmates in ice-filled water in order to induce hypothermia. A lifelong Alaskan, used to the cold more than most, his teeth had chattered so badly he'd thought they might shatter. Though it had been horrific at the time, he'd gone through it, and the training had taught him what to expect—to recognize the promptings of his body before he reached a point of no return. Wind and wet would sap his body of critical warmth and leave him unable to ride, let alone fight.

A hundred meters ahead the narrow road made a sharp bend to the right, putting them out of sight for a period of a few seconds even if the fog happened to thin.

Popping his neck from side to side, he worked to relax his shoulders, drawing on the warmth of Aleksandra's body where she pressed against him. His hands clutched the grips like frozen claws. He made rhythmic fists, trying to work the blood back into them.

"We have to stop around that corner," he yelled over his shoulder.

"Are you crazy?" Her breath buzzed directly into his ear. "They will be on top of us almost at once."

He rolled his palm to give the little Yamaha as much gas as he dared, causing it to give a throaty moan as it dug into the muddy slop.

"We'd better hurry then," he said through chattering teeth, as much to himself as Kanatova.

CHAPTER 53

Yesenia had scored him a more serviceable netting and Pollard lay on his cot and watched the mosquitos try to reach him. Outside the protective barrier, sitting cross-legged on the plywood floor of the metal hooch, the Indian girl looked at him with the adoration of a student with a teacher crush. She'd taken to wearing a green parrot feather in her hair and washing her face before she came to see him. During their conversations he'd let it slip that he held two doctoral degrees and from that moment on, she'd referred to him as Dr. Matt. She said little except when he spoke to her, but spent most days just sitting and watching him like some sort of rifle-wielding disciple.

At first he'd ignored her; then, instead of talking to himself as he worked, he began to bounce his ideas off her. But Zamora would arrive at any time and she did work for him, so he kept his present problem to himself.

What in the world had Marie been talking about? They didn't have a cat. In fact, she knew he didn't care for house pets at all. Still, their time on the video link was always limited, and Marie was smart enough not to waste it on mindless chatter. She had a reason for what she'd said. Miss Kitty was some sort of clue. He just had to get inside that brain of hers and figure out what it meant.

He replayed Marie's exact words over and over in his head. "I left her in the kitchen," she'd said. "And we don't have anyone to check on her. . . ."

Yesenia shook him out of his daydream.

"Dr. Matt," she said, toying with the iridescent green feather over her ear. The beauty of it stood out in stark contrast to the rifle across her lap. "Do you think it possible I could ever attend university?"

He rolled up on his side. The world was somehow softer and less intense when viewed through the mosquito netting. It was easy to imagine he was having a discussion with one of his students.

"Of course," he said. "But you'd have to set new priorities. Leave all this behind."

She hung her head, staring at the floor. "When my debt is paid," she said.

"What debt?" Pollard sat up, parting the net, and moved to the edge of his cot.

Yesenia sighed deeply. "A man came to our village and offered my sister and me work in Cochabamba. Even though my family is very poor and my father wanted me to go, I saw this man for what he was and said no. My sister said yes. He took us both anyway. When we got to the city I saw they were going to take us to Brazil and I . . . how do you say it?"

"Killed him?" Pollard offered.

Yesenia gave a little chuckle and shook her head. "Oh, no, señor. I wish I had, but a man like that is not so easy to kill. I became more trouble than I was worth, stealing things from shops as we walked by, starting fights with tourists . . . you know, to annoy him. The one who runs Señor Zamora's businesses in Bolivia paid my debt, but now I am indebted to him."

"Wait," Pollard said. "I don't understand. What debt?"

"You know, my bus ticket, food and lodging each night. I got an infection the first month so I have the debt for medicine as well. It piles up, you know."

Pollard threw up his hands. "Yesenia, you were kidnapped. There is no debt."

"Someone paid for my food and medicine," she said. "My sister wrote me a letter a few months ago. She says the worst thing about being a prostitute is that you are always sick and your debt grows every week."

Pollard tried to calm his breathing, knowing full well his desire to beat these men to death showed clearly on his face. "May I ask how old your sister is?"

"She is eleven years," Yesenia said, her small hands across the rifle in her lap. "I think that is much too young for such things, don't you, Dr. Matt?"

Pollard shuddered. "Any age is too young for that, Yesenia."

"It makes me feel guilty, but I am saved from . . . that—for the most part." She gave a resigned shrug. "I can shoot and my English is good, so I have other uses—like guarding you. But still, I owe this man for the money he spent to buy my freedom."

"That isn't freedom," Pollard said. Anger churned in his gut like an illness. "Being bought and sold."

"I know," she said. "But it is reality, and sometimes knowing what is real is the closest thing we have to being free, no?"

"I wish you were one of my students," Pollard said.

"Maybe someday," Yesenia said. "I often dream of paying my little sister's debt so we can go to school together." She wiped a tear from her eye with the heel of her hand. Her thumb was bound in grimy white tape to protect some jungle injury. "She is much prettier than me," she sniffed. "Which I suppose is what saved me and got her where she is. I can still see her wearing stupid red lipstick with that stupid Hello Kitty purse, pretending to be a grown woman. . . ."

Pollard's mind was already spinning. He'd figure out a way to help Yesenia and her poor sister in good time. But for now, she'd helped him.

He stood from his cot and strode quickly back and forth in front of the bomb. Yesenia didn't protest when he stopped and kissed her on the top of her head.

CHAPTER 54

A troop of howler monkeys munched in the wet canopy, soft eyes staring down at the spinning back wheel of the blue Yamaha as it teetered over a football-size stone along the abrupt edge. A hummingbird whirred in the shadows, zipping from plant to plant like a bullet, iridescent green against shades of gray.

A steady rain pattered against dense foliage and hanging moss along the winding, mud-choked Road of Death. Brown streams gurgled through delicate orchids and broom-like ferns. Greenery rose up through thick fog on either side, ghosting through the cloud forest on the mountains above and the sheer drops below.

The Chechens' muddy white Jeep Cherokee sloshed to a stop in the center of the road. There was no shoulder, and even the middle provided little clearance for those getting out on the driver's side of the vehicle.

Three feet below the edge, Quinn pressed his chest against the slick shrubs, feeling them soak through his shirt. Being out of the wind had returned a semblance of warmth to his body. His feet braced against one of the saplings that grew in a small stand along the edge.

He clutched another the size of his wrist, bent like a spring under his right arm.

Above him, out of sight, a car door eased shut. Whispered voices barked in guttural Chechen. Footsteps sloshed along the road sending a slurry of mud and gravel skittering over the edge, pelting Quinn's head. His face against the mountain, he waited for the man above to peer over before releasing the sapling he'd pulled with him when he slipped over the edge.

Under tremendous pressure, the arched tree snapped upright, swatting the startled Chechen directly in the face. He staggered backward away from the edge, shouting vehement curses.

Quinn clawed his way through the tangle of slick brush and back onto the road as gunshots cracked to his right.

The man he'd surprised had fallen backwards, landing on the seat of his pants in the mud. Blood poured from his forehead and a nasty gash across the bridge of his beakish nose. A broken branch the size of Quinn's thumb stuck from a wound in his shoulder and a pistol hung loosely in his left hand.

Quinn kicked the weapon from the dazed man's hand, scanning the road for the two others, trusting that Aleksandra was doing the same. A crunch of gravel behind him sent him sprinting again for the mountain edge as the bearded Jeep driver floored the gas and bore down directly on him. The Chechen on the ground screamed as the driver ran over his legs, aimed in on Quinn.

The flat report of two pistol shots cracked the air as Quinn slid over the side, flailing for a handful of branches to keep from tumbling another thousand feet.

Glass shattered and the Jeep's engine revved, gaining speed. Metal groaned as it veered sharply right, glancing off the mountain face to swerve left again. The driver slumped over the wheel, dead from the two well-placed shots to his neck from Aleksandra long before he crashed and rolled through the rocks and trees below.

"Salambek is dead." Aleksandra nodded toward the canyon as she walked toward the injured Chechen who'd been pressed into a muddy rut by his friend's driving. She held the H&K P7 at her side. "Lucky the driver had the window down," she said, "or these little bullets might not have penetrated the door." She spun quickly to shoot the wounded Chechen in the knee. "They do, however go through swine quite easily."

The man howled in pain, forgetting the bleeding gash on his forehead to clutch at his demolished leg. He was pushing fifty, tall and heavily muscled. His face pulled back in a tight grimace showing a mouthful of gold teeth.

Aleksandra smacked him in the back of the head with her open hand. It was odd to Quinn to see such a small woman exercising such control over such an imposing man.

She spoke in clipped Russian that communicated her disdain for the man. Quinn could tell the Chechen would be difficult to break. He'd likely been on the dispensing end of such questioning before. Aleksandra squatted down beside him, just out of reach, her pistol behind her back.

Quinn understood neither Russian nor Chechen, but he had a pretty good idea what the two were saying. They had no time for a lengthy interrogation. Even as they spoke, Valentine Zamora was getting away. Aleksandra was professional enough to know the man would either talk or he wouldn't. In the end, he spit in her face.

Aleksandra stood and wiped her cheek with her forearm. Despite her small stature, she grabbed the wounded man by the collar of his jacket and dragged him to the edge of the road. He was weak from loss of blood, and though he was defiant to the end, it was little problem for the compact woman to shove him over the edge.

"He kills Russian babies," Aleksandra said when she wheeled around to face Quinn, as if he needed an explanation for her actions. "I will not waste another bullet."

"Understood," Quinn said, already moving to pick up the motorcycle. He'd hoped they'd be able to use the Chechens' Jeep to make it down the mountain, but now that wasn't going to happen. "Did he tell you anything?" Quinn climbed aboard the bike and toed it back into gear. He checked the safety on his 1911 before passing it over his shoulder to Aleksandra, who returned it to the daypack.

"They were supposed to catch up to Zamora and kill him," she said, throwing a leg over the back of the bike and settling in around his waist.

"After he led them to the bomb?" Seconds counted now, and Quinn was already rolling.

"No," she said. "He was clear on that. They were to kill Zamora when they caught him, here on the Death Road."

Quinn grabbed a handful of brake and brought the little Yamaha to a slithering stop. A brown slurry of mud and gravel ran around his mud-caked boots.

"Wait a minute," he said, turning to look at Aleksandra whose face was just inches away. "You say these men worked for Rustam Daudov?"

"I am sure of it," she said.

Quinn blinked, letting the words sink in. Turning, he released the brakes, giving the bike as much throttle as the muck would allow.

"That means the Chechens already know where the bomb is," he yelled. "If they get there before Zamora he's a dead man."

"Or the bomb is already gone," Aleksandra said.

CHAPTER 55

The incident with the Chechens had cost valuable time. Periodically, the clouds would thin and Quinn caught a glimpse of another vehicle ahead, winding its way along the steep edge of the twisting road as it snaked back and forth, down toward the Amazon Basin.

The lower they went, the thicker and warmer the air became. Quinn found it easier to think and the suffocating panic of near drowning began to seep away. Feeling crept back to his hands and face. Aleksandra too became more animated, looking around to take in the sights rather than ducking in behind him.

Nestled in the rolling hills, the subtropical village of Coroico was a favorite weekend getaway for more well-to-do La Paz residents when they grew weary of the stark, airless Altiplano. They were, in effect, coming down for air.

The clouds parted, revealing a swath of blue as Quinn pointed the little Yamaha toward the edge of town. Two boys of nine or ten walked barefoot, whacking sticks on the ground at the edge of the lonely road. A low sun hung over the tree-covered hills to the west, drawing clouds of steam from the jungle.

The boys stopped, interested in what the two frozen-looking crazy people were doing on a motorcycle in their town. Quinn rolled up beside them.

"How's it going?" Aleksandra said from the back, her voice trilling in perfect Spanish. The dark skin of his Apache grandmother allowed him to blend in, but for all his language ability, this was one he'd never learned to speak. Aleksandra was close enough to Quinn's ear, though, that she was able to give him the gist of their conversation.

The boys waved politely, ducking their heads.

"We're looking for some friends who came in ahead of us," Aleksandra said. Quinn couldn't help but think of how sweet she could make her voice considering what he'd seen her do just an hour before.

"Which ones?" the smaller of the two boys in a dirty white T-shirt asked.

"Have there been many?"

"Not many," the boy said. "I hear there was a mudslide and the miners are marching."

Alexandra translated in quick whispers.

Word traveled fast in the Andes, a fact that Quinn knew they would have to depend on if they wanted to find Zamora.

"Our two friends are traveling together," Aleksandra said. "One has a tiny mustache like a little mouse." She made her voice go higher as if she was telling a story. "The other has a flat nose like he fell against a wall."

The boys laughed at her impressions. Though Quinn didn't understand all the words, he knew who she was talking about with each description. He couldn't help but think she would have made an excellent schoolteacher if she hadn't gone the professional killer route.

"He stopped at my auntie's store for a coffee," the boy said, smacking his stick against the ground as he spoke. "Then they left for Rurrenabaque."

"How far away?"

The boy consulted with his friend. "All night at least," he said, scratching his nose. His friend nodded his head in agreement.

"Are there any airplanes here?" Aleksandra asked.

Laughing at the thought, the boys suddenly looked up the road. "More friends?" the boy in the white T-shirt said.

Quinn turned to see Jacques Thibodaux's big face looking at him from the passenger window of Adelmo's van. Bo leaned forward from the backseat, a broad grin spreading across his face when he saw Aleksandra.

Valentine Zamora beat on the dashboard with the flat of his hand, cursing at Monagas and ordering him to drive faster. Though not as steep as El Camino de la Muerte, the road from Coroico to Rurrenabaque wound its way deeper and deeper into the jungle, more like a river of thick mud than an actual road. Less than two hundred miles, the trip took nearly ten hours—all night—and Zamora had not slept for a moment.

The sun was just pinking the horizon by the time Monagas rolled the Land Cruiser into the river town of Rurrenabaque, known as simply as Rurren to the locals. It took Monagas less than twenty minutes to rouse a sleeping fisherman and rent his open wooden boat for the river. Zamora rarely used the Beni River camp and had little in the way of staff in the area. He'd thought it better to keep Yesenia and Angelo and a couple of others to guard Pollard and the bomb. Many men would have made it too much of a target.

Once on the boat, he held up his finger to have Monagas wait a moment to start the engine. He took the satellite phone from his pack and punched in the number. Ever the calm adventurer, his hands trembled at being so near his prize.

"*Sí*," Diego Borregos said, answering the phone.

Zamora had expected the Yemeni.

"We are almost there," Zamora said.

"Good," the Colombian said. "I am not so fond of your friends. May I have the location now? I am ready to be rid of them."

"Of course. But there may be a problem," he said, thinking of the Chechens. There had been no sign of them either on the road or in the camp, according to Pollard, but one could never be too careful.

"Don't worry so much, my friend." Borregos laughed. "If you had no problems you wouldn't need my services. I will handle whatever issues I find as long as I can get your friends what they want and be rid of them. Now . . ." The Colombian's voice grew grave. "You pay me for transport along our . . . established routes. Give me the location and I will meet you there."

The Colombians knew nothing of the bomb itself, thinking only that he was selling arms as he usually did and had had a run-in with his tyrannical father.

Zamora held his breath. In the end, he had to trust someone.

CHAPTER 56

January 10

Quinn's eyes slammed open when the van bounced over a downed log half sunken in the middle of the road. He'd been dreaming about a walk with his daughter and the rutted road provided a rude awakening. He rubbed the sleep from his eyes and looked around to get his bearings. The sun was fully up, but it was still early and the relative cool of night still hung in the trees. Roosters crowed behind a line of shanty houses along the road leading into town. Two blue and gold macaws perched like sentinels high in a gnarled branch, looking more like vibrant jungle ornaments than actual birds.

Aleksandra sat in the back of the van beside Bo, and Thibodaux thumbed through a pamphlet in the front seat beside Adelmo.

Quinn sat up in his middle seat, stretching his back, waiting for the old wounded parts of him to wake up. At thirty-five, the life he had led made the years doubly hard on his body. He turned half around in his seat.

"Have you got any kind of signal?" he asked Aleksandra.

She nodded. "He is on the river."

Adelmo negotiated with a fisherman to secure a boat and a sack of provisions including bottled water and several dozen *cunapes*, a sort of bulbous Bolivian cheese bread that, Adelmo explained, got its name because it resembled a woman's breast. Thibodaux ate them like popcorn and took to calling them boob biscuits.

The unflappable Aymara driver had become caught up in the chase and offered to come with them downriver for no extra charge. Quinn wouldn't allow it. Where they were going there was bound to be bloodshed. It was bad enough to have Bo along. They paid him well and said their good-byes while they boarded the slender wooden craft that looked like a sort of canoe made of planks from a wooden privacy fence. It proved to be watertight, though, and the little Nissan motor was sound and had them nosed out into the muddy river in a matter of minutes.

"Where are we now with a signal?" Quinn asked, popping the lid on one of the water bottles. As cold as he'd been the day before, he preferred it to the oppressive heat and humidity of the Amazon Basin. He was an Alaskan at heart and always would be.

"My battery is dying and there was no time to charge it," Aleksandra said. "I have it turned off for the moment, but he was a mile ahead of us when I last checked. Just before we get to that spot, I will check again and so on. Until then we must keep watch."

Thibodaux sat on an overturned plastic bucket at the tiller, steering away from the muddy bank to head downstream through the low green hills toward the Amazon. A youth spent exploring the Louisiana bayou made him the natural choice to drive the boat.

Three miles from town, the boat slid past a group of chunky capybara grunting in the thick reeds along the bank. A giant ceiba tree grew on a heavily buttressed trunk behind the pig-sized rodents. Hanging moss and aerial ferns hung like decorative feathers from the great tree's crown, spread high above the surrounding canopy. Troops of squirrel monkeys scolded from the surrounding trees. The rolling hills gradually flattened. Flocks of birds wheeled above open marshes and grassy pampas that reached back in pockets surrounded by the black green of seemingly impenetrable rainforest. The jungle crowded closer as they motored farther north. Dense branches drooped along muddy banks, skimming the brown water.

Bo dangled his hands in the water with Aleksandra, who crouched beside him on the floor of the boat.

A sudden pop and a whooshing spray caused everyone on the boat to jump. Quinn's hand fell instinctively to his pistol. He smiled when he saw the patches of slick, rubbery skin break the surface of the water beside the boat.

Thibodaux popped another boob biscuit in his mouth. "That's a good sign, *l'ami*," he said. "The little book Adelmo's bride gave me said that when you see pink dolphins you don't have to worry about the crocodile caiman things and can go in swimming. Sort of reminds me of home . . . minus the pink dolphins."

Bo leaned over to take a whiff of his armpits. "I still smell like rosy lilac water." He grimaced at Jericho, the wind blowing a lock of blond hair across his face. "You, however, ought to jump in. You know how you get when you haven't bathed for two days."

"We don't have time," Quinn said. "And besides, just because the caimans are afraid of dolphins doesn't mean the piranhas are."

Bo jerked his hand out of the water. "I hadn't thought about that."

"Or how about those teensy little catfish?" Jacques observed around a mouthful of *cunape*. "The sombitches swim up inside you when you pee underwater and get stuck in there."

Aleksandra crinkled her freckled nose in disgust. "How do you know this revolting thing?"

Jacques took slug of bottled water. "Jungle training."

"I didn't know you'd been to jungle training," Quinn said. "That'll come in handy out here."

"Truth be told"—Thibodaux grinned—"I haven't really. I saw it in that Tom Berenger *Sniper* movie."

"Who knows," Quinn said, looking ahead at the thick foliage along the river. He swatted a mosquito that landed on his forehead. "Maybe that will come in handy too."

CHAPTER 57

Pollard moved like a robot, taking one last look at the bomb before he screwed the false wooden panel on the crate. As per Zamora's plan, a half dozen military-grade Kalashnikov rifles would be stacked in front of the false front in case anyone got nosey. Pollard found it mind numbing what he'd do to keep his family safe for a few days longer.

He was smart enough to know that crazy bitch Lourdes would kill them eventually. He'd seen the black hole in her eyes when she'd first walked in his classroom what now seemed like months before. He'd been away from such things for so long that he hadn't recognized it until it was too late. Marie stood no chance against a woman like her. She was too nice, believing that even people who did bad things were by and large good at heart and would all jump at the chance to mend their ways if only given the right set of circumstances. She gave money to beggars at every street corner and wept at the poverty of people who *had* to send out Internet scams from Nigeria to survive. People are mostly moral, she'd often say, if you give them a chance.

He called such naïve notions the Mermaid and Unicorn Fart Theory, explaining to his classes that though they sounded sweet and fantastical, they were every bit as foul smelling as their normal, everyday counterparts.

Sometimes bad people were just that: bad people. They might pet a puppy because society expected them to, but in their hearts they wanted to kick it across the room and listen to it yelp. Marie just wouldn't be able to get her pretty head wrapped around such a person. Matt was sure of it.

Yesenia startled him out of his inner dialogue when she stepped in the door of his hooch, rifle slung across her chest as always.

"Señor Zamora will be here soon." Her chin quivered ever so slightly as she spoke. "So you are going away."

"It is better for you that I take this thing away from here," he said.

"I wish that I could come with you."

"Me too, Yesenia." He put a hand on her shoulder. "If I can figure a way out of this, I'll make sure you get to school."

"I do not know much, Dr. Matt, but I do know Señor Zamora." She looked down at the toes of her boots. "He will kill you when you've finished—and your wife."

"I know," Pollard said.

She looked up at him. "Then why do you do as he asks?"

"Because every moment that I do, my wife and son stay alive for just a little while longer. And as long as they live, no matter how awful the circumstances, I can cling to the hope that I can figure out a way to save them."

"I like that," Yesenia said. "It makes me think of my sister."

"Me too," Pollard lied. In reality, such futile hope sounded a lot like a unicorn fart.

Yesenia suddenly turned her head to one side so quickly it knocked the parrot feather out of her hair. She lifted the rifle.

"Dr. Matt," she said, looking at the door. "Do you hear that?"

"Something is wrong." Zamora stood in the middle of the wooden boat and watched Borregos's Piper bank in over the jungle from the north. "I don't know what it is, but I can feel it." He toyed with the holster at his side, unsnapping and snapping it absentmindedly while he tried to work out what was going on.

Monagas let the boat drift against the slow current.

"Shall I continue upriver?"

"No," Zamora said, still looking. "Our plan depends on the Yemenis taking possession of the bomb."

Monagas nodded, and aimed the boat for the bank ahead.

A six-foot caiman hung motionless in the shallows, staring at the interlopers to his territory with nothing but the twin bumps of his eyes and the tip of his toothy snout breaking the chocolate surface of the river.

They were roughly four miles up a tributary from the main arm of the Beni, off the beaten path of eco-tourists. Even the local indigenous tribes knew this was a river of no return—a place where piranha, electric eel, and deadly snakes were nowhere near the most dangerous things in the jungle.

Zamora took a deep breath, scanning the shadowed foliage that came right to the water's edge in most places. Angelo stood on the small apron of bank below the boughs of several ceiba trees, hanging heavy with their own weight. Behind him, a barely noticeable trail vanished into the undergrowth, connecting the river to the camp nearly fifty meters away.

Angelo waved with his ball cap, smiling as if he was happy to see his boss.

The roar of the Piper's engines diminished as it touched down on the grassy strip hacked out of the jungle in back of the camp.

Zamora turned back to his companion. "Be watchful."

"As always, *patrón*." Monagas nosed the boat sideways against the muddy bank and killed the engine. He threw the landing line to Angelo, who helped Zamora over the side and up a teetering path of wooden planks he'd placed on the squishy mud.

"All is well?" Zamora asked, still sniffing the air for any sign of the Chechens. "You have not seen any other boats or aircraft?"

Angelo snapped to attention, patting the rifle slung across his chest. "No, *patrón*. I have been on guard. It is only us and Dr. Matt. The aircraft just arrived."

"I see that," Zamora said, still toying with the snap on his holster. He brushed past the stubby Angelo, pushing his way through the thick undergrowth for the camp. They'd purposely left the trail to the camp tangled and choked with vines to discourage visitors from the river.

As he expected, Pollard met him with the hateful gaze of a man with a plan for vengeance. He was so predictable. What Zamora hadn't expected was the same look from Yesenia. He made a mental note to have Monagas kill her after the bomb was loaded and they were safely away from any would-be interference by the Chechens.

Borregos and his camouflaged men were just making it into camp when Zamora emerged from the river trail into the clearing. He wiped the sweat out of his eyes with the arm of his shirt. They were so close now. He would be glad to get out of this place.

A small bird suddenly flew from a branch above him, fluttering away like the sound of a beating drum.

Zamora froze. That was it. That was what had been out of place. He had flown in to this camp no fewer than twenty times over the past five years, and each time, a huge flock of white egrets had exploded from the marshes off the end of the runway at the noise of the aircraft's approach.

There had been no egrets when Borregos's plane had landed. No egrets because someone had already scared them away.

"Daudov is here," he hissed to Monagas an instant before the first bullet rustled through the branches and struck Angelo in the chest.

CHAPTER 58

Quinn saw the boat tied alongside the muddy bank at the same moment he heard the shots.

He ducked instinctively, but kept both hands on the gunnel of the boat, leaving his pistol holstered.

"What you do wanna do, *l'ami*?" Thibodaux said from the tiller.

A steady barrage of automatic gunfire zipped and rattled inside the jungle to their right.

"They're not shooting at us," Quinn said, his head on a swivel as he looked up and down the bank. "This would be a good time to go in and get a feel for things when they have their hands full."

"Agreed," Aleksandra said, pistol already in her hand.

Thibodaux took the boat past the muddy bank at a fast idle, easing around the bend where the river curved back on itself. He pointed the bow around a protruding root that had caught a raft of floating deadfall. It was a natural breakwater where a boat could be hidden from all but the most curious river traveler.

"You can stay here." Quinn nodded at Bo. "I need someone to stand guard."

"Like hell," Bo said. "You don't get to drag me down the Road of Death to have me sit and watch the horses. If the bomb's up there, you're gonna need all the help you can get."

Jericho gave a resigned shrug and stepped of the boat onto springy wet ground. "Okay," he said, drawing his pistol. He gave Severance a tap on the hilt for comfort's sake. "But stay behind me. Mom will kill me if I let anything happen to you."

Quinn led the approach with Thibodaux three paces to his left, each picking their way through dense underbrush and tangled vines. Bo and Aleksandra flanked on either side a few steps back. The shooting grew more intense as the little group made their way through the dripping rainforest. Sporadic shots interspersed with rattling volleys followed angry shouts and periodic cries of the wounded. The vegetation began to thin forty yards in from the river and a series of rusted tin buildings became visible through the trees.

Thibodaux sidestepped alongside Quinn, clearing away a spiderweb with the barrel of his gun. He leaned forward, intent on the gunfire, a half grin crossing his face. Heights and bad juju might scare him, but he melded into a gunfight like he was coming home.

"Just so you know, beb," the big Cajun said without looking up from the undergrowth, "you don't need to fret about my mama if anything happens to me. My child bride would, however, cut your cojones off."

"I'll keep that in mind."

Quinn started to push through the undergrowth, but Thibodaux put a hand on his shoulder.

"So, *l'ami*," he said. "Who are you thinking of right now, this very moment when your life is on the line?"

"Valentine Zamora," Quinn lied. Though focused on stopping the bomb, the face he saw before he pressed it out of his mind as he made his way toward the sound of gunfire was Veronica Garcia.

An unseen hand seemed to grab Aleksandra and pull her forward, toward the sound of gunfire and danger. Some said she had a death wish. A few had accused her of drawing some sort of freakish pleasure at putting herself in harm's way. In truth it was nothing close to either.

She'd had the feeling since she was a small child that her eventual death would be violent. Some boring people died in their sleep or choked on an olive, but by the time Aleks was eleven she'd been certain her own death would be surrounded by a great deal of blood. Where the thought might frighten some or make them live in a sort of plastic bubble of perceived safety, Aleksandra was fascinated by the notion. She reasoned that fate was preordained and, since there was nothing she could do about it anyway, resolved to live moving forward, toward the inevitable, rather than sidestepping through life and hiding from her shadow.

Eyes peeled for the first threat that presented itself, she watched the others in her peripheral vision. The big Cajun plowed his way through the jungle like a bull looking for a lost cow. Bo, the beautiful blond Quinn with the body of a Greek god and the impish smile, moved cavalierly, as if he was eager to impress his older brother, but was a half step out of his natural element.

Jericho, by contrast, seemed more a part of the jungle than someone moving through it. Ducking and turning, stepping and twisting, he made his way around trees and over fallen logs as if there was nothing but the hot humid air between him and his target. She'd known men as cruel as this one, men as intelligent, men as physically capable, and men as driven to do the right thing—but she'd never before known one who possessed all these qualities at once.

Bo had inched his way closer to her as they walked, trying to get out ahead to shield her from danger. It was a sweet gesture and reminded her of Mikhail, but it would not do to allow such a thing. The poor boy would get himself killed. Protecting a fellow combatant was a noble cause, but before one could protect a friend, he had to stay alive.

Frenzied voices shot through the trees with the constant barrage of bullets, directing movement or shouting threats.

Jericho waved his hand in a tight circle above his head, calling the group in close. They lay down on the jungle floor, side by side, shoulders together.

"Count?" Quinn said, looking at Thibodaux.

A greasy centipede-like creature, fully six inches long, slithered over the ground litter between Aleksandra and Quinn. Even if it happened to be poisonous, a bullet would be more permanent, so she ignored it, focusing on Quinn and the more immediate two-legged dangers in the jungle.

"I'm guessing the Chechens only have four or five," the gunny said, still scanning. "Zamora has maybe . . . eight."

Quinn looked at Aleksandra. She nodded, agreeing with Thibodaux's assessment. "That sounds correct," she said.

Bo peered around a clump of ferns. "I'm pretty sure that's one of the Borregos out there," he said.

"Zamora's buyer," Quinn mused.

The gunfire grew more intense, as if someone was preparing to move.

"Whoever they are," Thibodaux said, pressing his face to the ground, "they're well armed and carrying a shitload of ammo."

The angry hiss of a rocket-propelled grenade ripped through the air, confirming Jacques's assessment. Aleksandra hugged the ground out of instinct as the primary explosion shook the buildings at the northern edge of the tiny compound. A moment later, a secondary boom sucked the oxygen from the air. Louder and more powerful than the first, it sent wood and rusty tin whirring through the air, one piece flying like a saw blade over Thibodaux's head.

An orange fireball bloomed over the jungle to the north, followed by a mushroom cloud of greasy black smoke.

Jericho sniffed the air. "Smells like fuel. They must have blown up a plane." He turned and faced her. "What will happen if they hit the bomb?"

"In theory?" She gave a resigned shrug. "Nothing. In practice, it could arm the device. . . ."

The shouting grew louder again after a brief lull following the explosion.

Bo moved closer to Aleksandra, touching her on the shoulder to get her attention. He nodded toward a large woodpile three feet high and a good fifteen feet long.

"Stay with me," he said in a show of bravado that melted Aleksandra's heart.

A sudden movement to her right caught her eye. Through the dense tangle of vines and undergrowth she saw a flash of curly black hair and the unmistakably flat profile of Julian Monagas. An electric current seemed to jolt her body and she raised half up off her belly as if doing a pushup. Locked on, she shook her head. "No, my dear," she said a moment before she sprinted into the jungle. "You go with your brother. I have business with someone."

"Well, I'll be!" Thibodaux whistled under his breath. "Would you look at that?"

Quinn watched as Aleksandra ran amid a hail of bullets to disappear into the undergrowth. In the middle of the compound, a tall man with a coal-black beard sat beside an overturned table of heavy timber. Dressed like someone out of an REI advertisement, he appeared to be unarmed. Instead of using the table for cover, he sat cross-legged in the open, cradling a wounded girl in his lap, stroking her long black hair. She wore woodland camouflage fatigues and was presumably one of Zamora's.

"Why isn't anyone shooting at him?" Thibodaux grunted.

"Let's go ask him." Quinn ran the five paces to the long stack of firewood, crouching behind it. So far, he'd not fired a shot. Bo slid in next to him while Thibodaux, chased by a string of automatic gunfire, dove behind the rusted hulk of a diesel generator ten feet away.

Bullets thwacked against the logs and zinged off the

generator as both Zamora's men and the Chechens focused on this new threat.

Quinn pulled Bo down beside him and assessed the situation. He'd yet to find the bomb, but judging from the fighting, possession of it was still a matter of contention. Less than six feet to his left, the man with the beard sat weeping over the girl, oblivious to all the lead in the air. To his right, Thibodaux engaged one of Daudov's men, who crept through the jungle trying to flank them.

Quinn tossed a piece of wood at the sobbing man.

"Who are you?" he asked.

The man looked up; his reactions were dull, shell-shocked. "Who are *you*?"

Quinn tried a different tack. The guy was sitting in the cross fire. He obviously was beyond succumbing to threats. "Is she still alive?"

"What do you care?"

Quinn took a deep breath. "Listen," he said. "I'm not one of these guys. I can help."

The man blinked his eyes. "She's already dead," he said.

"No, she's not," Quinn said. "Look at her chest. It's still moving. As long as she's breathing there's a chance."

"Not her," the man said. "I mean my wife. Zamora will kill her no matter what I do."

"I told you I can help," Quinn said. "What's your name?"

The man brightened. "Matt Pollard. I'm a professor at Idaho State."

"And the bomb?"

"They have it," the man said, nodding toward Borregos and his men. He hung his head. "Zamora threatened to kill my wife and son if I didn't bypass the locking system."

"Do you know where they're going with it?"

"No idea," the man said, studying Quinn through bloodshot eyes. "Can you really help my wife?"

"I can," Quinn said. "Tell me where she is, and I'll call some people to go check on her. But first we have to stop this bomb—"

Thibodaux loosed three rapid-fire shots, hitting Daudov's man as he came in from the side. The Chechen staggered forward, firing blindly. Bo flinched, as one of the bullets clipped his left arm.

He looked up at Jericho with an embarrassed grin. "Sorry, bro—" A fountain of blood gushed from the wound between his elbow and armpit. Pulsing in time with his heart, it arced into the air, painting the wood behind him.

CHAPTER 59

"I 'll cover," Thibodaux barked from behind the generator. He began to lay down steady fire, a shot at the Borregos crew, then another at the Chechens. "You see to him." He'd run out of ammo in a matter of seconds.

Quinn tucked his 1911 back in the holster and lowered Bo to the ground. He had to stop the bleeding, but he couldn't do that if he got himself killed. With shots cracking and whirring overhead, his training kicked into high gear.

Flat on his back, he grabbed Bo by the shoulders and dragged him backward to the more protected center of the woodpile, scissoring his body in a motion called *shrimping* to help him move but stay low at the same time. Blood pumped from the wound in great spurts with each beat of Bo's heart, and by the time Quinn stopped they were both covered. He kicked a large log loose and slid it under Bo's boots, elevating his legs.

"Jeez, brother," Bo groaned. "I screwed up. Go after the bomb. I'll be fine."

"Shut up, Boaz," Quinn said through clenched teeth. He jammed a fist high under Bo's armpit in an attempt to slow the bleeding while he assessed. "I told you what Mom would do if I let anything happen to you."

It was the nature of war. Some died no matter what. Some lived no matter what. Some would die unless something was done to save them. KIA—killed in action—couldn't be helped. DOW was a different thing entirely. Dying of wounds would not be an option for Bo.

Above all else, Quinn knew he had to stop the bleeding. Two minutes was enough to bleed out completely if the wound was bad enough. The human body was extremely resilient at mending itself, but it needed blood to feed the brain. He had to treat Bo for shock, and the best way to do that was to keep him in the fight—give him a job to do and keep him focused.

Reaching into the channel left by the bullet, Quinn searched behind the bicep and connective tissues to find the bleeder. As he'd suspected, the brachial artery had been clipped. Slick with the warmth of his baby brother's blood, he used his thumb and forefinger to squeeze the offending vessel shut. Just smaller than a soda straw, it was snot slick and wriggled as if it had a mind of its own. His fingers slipped free and a fresh crimson arc sprayed Quinn's face. He used his shoulder to clear his eyes, methodically probing to find the artery again and get a better grip.

"Bo," he said through clenched teeth. "How we doing?"

"I'm good." Bo grimaced. "You done this sort of thing before?"

"A time or two," Quinn said.

"Ever lost anyone?" Bo looked him dead in the eye.

"A couple of the pigs and one goat," Quinn said.

"But they were way worse than you. This is just a flesh wound."

"Pigs," Bo sighed. "That makes me feel better."

Quinn could feel his brother's pulse throbbing quickly beneath his fingertips, working to push the life's blood from his body. The heart pumped faster as it lost blood, working extra hard to get what was left to vital areas like the brain. It was an odd sensation and he found himself thankful he'd experienced it before.

No matter what animal rights activists felt about the practice of "pig lab" training for military corpsmen and combat rescue officers, there was no mannequin or "lifelike" device that came close to working on something that was actually alive. Quivering flesh, the copper scent, and even the slickness of warm blood could be duplicated. But life, that vital essence that made animals different from sugar beets or ears of corn, was inimitable, no matter how sophisticated the tech.

As cruel as it was, cutting a few sedated pigs was a small price to pay for the training that Quinn now used in an attempt to save his kid brother's life.

"Listen to me," he said, ducking a spray of woodchips from a fresh string of gunfire. "We need to get a tourniquet on this A-SAP. You understand?"

"Okay," Bo said, nodding. He was alert and engaged. That was good, Quinn thought. As long as he was engaged, he could fight to live.

"Outstanding," Quinn said. "Now reach in the right thigh pocket of my pants and get my wound kit. I can't let go or you'll start bleeding again."

Bo nodded, breathing deeply. He was no stranger to pain—and Quinn was certain he was causing quite a bit digging around next to torn muscle and chipped bone.

The size of a fat wallet, the Cordura pouch held the basic gear to treat a gunshot wound—windlass tourniquet, coagulant gauze for stuffing the wound, H bandage, chest-seal, and a three-inch needle. He'd seen firsthand how many soldiers died of blood loss while they waited for a medevac. Since his first deployment, he rarely went anywhere without the small kit.

"High or die, brother." Quinn talked him through application of the tourniquet, pulling the nylon strapping tight, then twisting the pencil-size metal windlass to further compress the artery above the wound.

Halfway through the process Bo suddenly looked up. Turning, he grabbed the pistol from his lap and shot over Quinn's shoulder, deafening him in the process.

Quinn glanced back to see one of Borregos's men fall on his way to reach Pollard.

"If I'm going to die," Bo groaned, "might as well take someone with me."

Thibodaux, in a fierce gun battle with two Chechens working their way around the cook shed, hardly had time to look up.

The tourniquet in place, Quinn slowly released his grip on the artery. Blood oozed but didn't spurt.

"Good job," Quinn said, pushing the wound kit into Bo's good hand. "There's a packet of QuikClot gauze in there. Shove as much of it in the wound as you can." He pulled the 1911 from his holster. "I'm going to help Jacques kill the guys who shot you."

CHAPTER 60

Gunfire pinged off the heavy generator as Quinn slid in beside Thibodaux. The big Cajun turned too late as one of the bullets cut a fuel line, spraying him in the face with a slurry of metal shards and diesel fuel.

"Son of a bitch!" he yelled, wiping a forearm across his face.

Quinn felt a wave of dread tighten in his throat. Fighters learned to protect their eyes at all costs. A wound in the arm or leg was preferable to being blind in battle.

"How bad?" Quinn said, throwing a double tap into the sweating face of a man with a red beard and naked upper lip who crept toward them on his belly.

"Bad, *l'ami*," Thibodaux spat. "My right eye is toast."

Another series of shots popped amid the undergrowth. A moment later Daudov staggered out, bleeding from a wound to his throat. A fusillade from Borregos's men finished him off. Quinn was about to fire but caught a glimpse of Aleksandra ghosting through the thick vines.

An eerie silence settled in over the jungle camp immediately after the Chechen leader's body slumped to the ground. Pistol in both hands, Quinn scanned the tree line while he worked to slow his breathing. He looked at Bo, who gave him a weak thumbs-up with his gun hand.

Thibodaux scanned the jungle with his good eye. "Two rounds and one peeper left, *l'ami*," he said. "Afraid I'm not much help to you."

"We want the professor," a voice yelled from the jungle shadows. "We have no fight with you."

Quinn looked at Pollard, who held a small notebook at waist level.

"I'm coming out," Pollard yelled. He dropped the notebook to the dirt at his feet, then looked at Quinn. "They'll kill us all if I don't go with them. Your friend needs a doctor. Please, save my wife. She doesn't deserve this." Raising his hands, he walked like a condemned man to disappear into the jungle with Borregos and his men.

Aleksandra bolted from the trees a moment later and ducked behind the generator. "You should have shot him," she hissed. "They need him to detonate the bomb. I am empty or I would have done it myself." She held up her H & K, slide locked to the rear. Her eyes flew wide when she saw Bo.

"What happened?"

"Chechen bullet," Quinn said, frowning. "Where did you go?"

"I wounded Zamora," she said. "He fell in the river and drifted away. I've been picking off his men one by one."

"And Monagas?" Quinn asked.

"I'm not certain," she said. "He went down, but I could not find the body."

"No time to look now," Quinn said. "We have to get our wounded back to town."

Bo shook his head. "You can't just let the bomb get away from you."

"I know," Quinn said. "I'm working on that."

The Indian girl Pollard had been holding suddenly stirred.

"Please," she said, her voice a rasping whimper. In the aftermath of all the shooting, it was difficult to hear anything.

Still unconvinced Borregos meant to keep his word, Quinn ducked as he sprinted to the girl and dragged her behind the overturned table. He relaxed a hair when no one tried to shoot him.

"I had to pretend to be dead," she whispered, "or I don't think Dr. Matt would have left me."

Quinn found that she wasn't far off from her pretense. Three bullets had torn into her side, shattering ribs and narrowly missing her heart. Her chest rattled as she struggled for breath. Dirt and leaves covered a grisly exit wound that had torn away most of her right shoulder blade. She didn't have long.

"Zamora has another camp," she whispered through cracked lips. "A coca plant with an airstrip." She coughed. "Promise to help Professor Matt and I will tell you where it is. . . ."

Quinn bit his lip.

"Of course," he said, leaning in so he could hear the girl's instructions over the incessant ringing in his ears.

The flat roar of a boat engine carried in from the river. Baba Yaga was already moving.

CHAPTER 61

Marie held her hands over her baby's ears to shield him from the horrible woman's rant. Even Pete's perpetual scowl had fallen into a twitching frown of nervous puzzlement at the latest volcanic eruption.

"This is not like him." Lourdes tromped back and forth in the living room, spinning at each corner to turn and stare accusingly at Marie and Pete in turn. "He always calls me back. It is not like him at all." Tears welled in her black eyes. Her lips quivered like a frightened little girl's. Wheeling, she looked down at Marie, her words gushing out in a fountain of emotion. "He knows what his calls mean to me. Why would he do such a thing? Do you think something has happened to him?"

Marie relaxed her hold on Simon, letting him squirm around to face her. She didn't know what to say. One minute this woman was threatening to kill her and eat her baby, the next she wanted to confide her innermost fears.

Lourdes buried her face in her hands. "Why won't you call me, Valentine?" she sobbed in frustration.

Marie suddenly realized that if something had happened to Zamora, the same thing could have happened to Matt. Her chest tightened and for a moment she thought she might be having a heart attack. She'd heard of women her age whose hearts had just given out under severe stress—and heaven knew what she was going through qualified.

As horrible as the woman was, there was something so genuine about the way Lourdes wept. Sadness was sadness, even in the heart of a madwoman.

"Maybe he's lost his phone," Marie offered, attempting to console her. "Matt sometimes misplaces—"

Lourdes's head snapped up. Her bloodshot eyes seethed with anger. "You dare compare Valentine with your stupid excuse for a man! He cannot even protect his own family." She spat on the floor to show her contempt. "I am surprised he was man enough to father your child—if the boy is even his."

Marie flew off the mattress in a rage.

"You hateful bitch!" she screamed, clawing at Lourdes's face. "Shut your mouth! My husband is twice the man your prissy little Valentine is."

Lourdes put a hand to ward her off, but not before Marie landed a wicked punch that split her bottom lip.

Beyond furious, Marie kept punching and clawing, finally grabbing a handful of black bangs.

All she could think of was killing the awful woman— beating her to death with whatever she could find.

Pete pulled her off before she got another swing in. He gave her a hard backhand across the face to get her attention, then threw her brutally against the wall. She staggered, and then fell backward, landing on the mattress next to a screaming Simon.

"Sit your ass down and stay there," Pete said. He

looked back and forth at the two women as if he didn't know which one was crazier.

Lourdes touched a finger to her split lip, licking away the blood. Her black eyes locked on Marie, who stared right back at her.

A twisted smile crept slowly across the dark woman's bleeding lips. "You surprise me," she said, nodding in approval. "I had thought killing you would be a bore. I am so happy that you will at least fight back." She held up her hand. "Wait, I want to show you something." She disappeared down the hall to return a moment later with a length of stainless-steel chain. On each end was a gleaming steel hook.

"If I do not hear from Valentine very, very soon, I am going to play a game." Lourdes swung the chain in a tight circle in front of her face, causing the hooks to whir in the air. "Maybe I will play the first round with your little worm. . . ."

CHAPTER 62

Quinn estimated the cartel was no more than half an hour ahead of them with the bomb. There was no time to bury the dead, so he left them where they lay surrounded by a dark jungle that hummed and ticked with creatures that would close in and reclaim the bodies in a matter of hours.

Quinn rigged a makeshift stretcher from a nylon tarp he found hanging near the overturned table. With the help of a half-blind Thibodaux, he was able to get Bo back to the riverbank without reopening his wound. There was no time to waste formulating a sophisticated plan, so they boarded the boat without discussion. Aleksandra manned the tiller, pointing the boat downriver toward medical attention—and the bomb.

Moving again, Quinn took the opportunity to pack more QuikClot gauze into Bo's wound and apply an H bandage for direct pressure. He found a pen in Aleksandra's daypack and noted the time on the tourniquet for medical staff.

Thibodaux sat at the bow, keeping his good eye peeled for any sign of Zamora and Monagas, who were still unaccounted for. He'd rinsed his eye with two bottles of fresh water and though it seemed to help, the lid was still badly swollen and inflamed as if he'd rubbed it with sandpaper.

"You're going to have to leave us," Bo said, looking up with sunken eyes. Blond hair matted to his forehead. His normally tan face was pale and drawn. "There's a lot of traffic on the big river. We'll be back in civilization in no time."

"I'll stay with him, *l'ami*," Thibodaux said without turning around. "I'm no good to you as a Cyclops, and you two have to catch up to the bomb."

Jericho shot a glance at Aleksandra, who nodded almost imperceptibly. A soft breeze, caused by the movement of the boat, jostled her hair.

"My phone is dead," she said. "I have no signal with which to track Monagas, even if he is with the bomb. We must rely on what the girl told you and hope for the best."

In a world accustomed to instant communication by radio, cellular, and satellite phone, going off the grid was like a slap in the face. There were few places on the planet where some sort of communication system would not get through. Much of the Himalayas had 3G service and satellite phones worked at least a few hours each day even at the earth's extreme poles but you had to have such a device. Batteries died, electronics broke or fell in the water.

Sometimes all a man had to rely on was himself— Quinn looked up at Thibodaux, Bo, and Aleksandra— and, if he was fortunate, a capable friend.

* * *

A family of fishermen was camped at the confluence and agreed to take Bo and Thibodaux back to Rurren-abaque immediately.

Quinn gave Jacques the notepad with Pollard's instructions about his wife and shook the big man's hand.

"Don't you worry about Boaz," the Cajun said. "I'll look after him."

"I know you will," Quinn said.

Thibodaux shook his head with a squinting half frown.

"I don't get it," he said. "That's Diego Borregos out there. Zamora sold the bomb to the Colombians?"

"Looks that way," Quinn said. "All the money they make with narcotics, they have enough of a bankroll. But I'm still trying to figure out where the Yemenis fit in."

The Cajun put a hand to his damaged eye, wincing. "Wish I was coming with you, Chair Force. I don't trust the Russian to watch your back like I would. She's crazy."

Quinn gave a tense chuckle, still watching his brother. "You say that about every woman we've ever met."

Thibodaux took a deep breath through his nose. "I know I do, and I stand by it. But this one is damaged-crazy. That goes clean to the bone."

"What did you talk about with Jacques?" Aleksandra said, once they were back on the water. Behind her, the little Nissan engine whined in protest as she opened the throttle as wide as it would go. Spray hissed and splashed from the wooden bow.

Quinn smiled. "He told me not to trust you."

"Wise," she said, scanning the river ahead as if her

mind was elsewhere. "The children in my primary school used to tease me when I was very young—*ryzhi krasni chelovek apasni*. It means a redheaded person is dangerous." She shrugged. "My mission is to retrieve Baba Yaga. If I have to sacrifice you, I will do so without pause."

"And if we see Monagas again?" Quinn asked. "Will you chase him without pause—even at the expense of finding the bomb?"

Aleksandra frowned. "There were many people to shoot back there," she said. "Monagas was just as deserving of a bullet as any of them." She stopped, looking down at her boots for a long moment. "Still, I see your point. Such a thing will not happen again."

Quinn settled back against the gunnel, holding the backpack in his lap. He opened a water bottle and took his first drink in over an hour. It was warm, but it revitalized him almost immediately.

He checked the Aquaracer on his wrist. "We're making good time," he said, happy to change the subject. "They're loaded down with at least six men, not to mention the bomb. If we're lucky, we'll catch them before they leave the river."

"And then what?" Aleksandra sat stoically at the tiller, small shoulders hunched forward, red hair blowing in the wind.

"Good question," Quinn said, tapping the curved blade on his belt. "We're a little light on ammo for a gunfight. Your H&K is out. I have two rounds left and Bo's pistol has three." They'd left Jacques with his pistol and two rounds in case Zamora had doubled back. Other than the weapons and scant ammunition, they had the pack, a bottle of water, and three *cunape* that they split between them. Over long periods of exposure, adrenaline and stress ate away at the body's fuel reserves, sapping strength and draining brainpower. The starchy cheese biscuits gave a much-needed boost of energy.

Quinn spotted the bow of the sunken boat two hours after they left Bo and Thibodaux with the fishermen. The point of the bow bobbed just inches above the surface, nearly hidden in the raft of branches and other deadfall caught in a shaded back eddy behind the stump of a fallen tree. Borregos's men had thought to scuttle the vessel and hide their trail, but the river had other ideas.

Quinn nodded downriver, actively ignoring the boat. Aleksandra ran past, slowing the little Nissan only when they were a hundred meters beyond the sunken vessel. Cranking the tiller hard over, she turned in a wide arc, slicing a deep V in the chocolate-brown water. Twenty meters out, Aleksandra killed the engine and let momentum carry them in. A startled caiman greeted them with a splash of his knotted tail as the boat nosed up against the muddy bank, groaning as it rubbed a submerged stone.

Quinn stepped over the gunnel and onto the spongy bank. He carried the pack in his left hand but left the 1911 holstered, reasoning that if someone was going to shoot him, they'd have done it already.

Beyond the sunken boat the bank was a trampled mess. Quinn found a square of mud about a yard long, and counted fifteen separate footprints. Splitting that number in half and rounding up, he estimated Borregos had eight men including himself. Two sets of boots had pressed more deeply into the mud. They would be carrying the weight of the bomb. He didn't waste time trying to age the tracks. Even accounting for the time he'd spent talking to the dying Indian girl and then dropping off Bo and Jacques, the cartel couldn't have been more than a half hour ahead.

Aleksandra stood facing the humming wall of black jungle, her back to Quinn. Sweat darkened her khaki shirt along the spine. "Apologies do not come easy to my lips," she said.

Quinn checked to make certain his pistol was fastened in the holster, then slid Severance from the sheath at his belt. He said nothing.

Aleksandra plowed ahead. "I should not have abandoned you to go after Monagas."

"You are correct there," Quinn said, checking the bowknot connecting the boat to the gnarled root snaking out of the cutbank.

"Perhaps your brother would not have been shot if I would have stayed."

"Or perhaps he would have," Quinn said, knowing such after-action quarterbacking did little good.

"Have you never had a friend you would kill for?"

"I left two of them back there along the river," Quinn said without hesitation. He looked west, shielding his eyes from the low, afternoon sun above an endless ocean of green forest canopy. "Now let's focus on finding the bomb before they make it to the airstrip."

"Very well," Aleksandra said. "If we move quickly we can catch them before nightfall."

"That should be easy enough." Quinn turned, pushing aside a vine the size of his wrist with the tip of his blade. "It's easy to move fast when you're not weighed down with unnecessary things like ammunition."

CHAPTER 63

Yazid Nazif swung his machete as if wielding a baseball bat. He'd never seen so much vegetation in his life and felt as if it was closing in around him. The intensity of the moist heat and droning hum in the surrounding trees caused his heart to pound out of control. He found it difficult to breathe, but consoled himself with the knowledge that he was at last in possession of Baba Yaga. Soon, all of the decadent West would bow to the white-hot power of a new al-Qaeda. He would be the leader of the most feared organization on earth—if Borregos didn't kill him first. With Zamora gone, he realized that was a very distinct possibility.

They walked in a single-file line, each man giving the next room to swing his own blade should he find it necessary to hack a vine or push a troublesome spiderweb out of the way. One of Borregos's men was in front, doing the lion's share of the work, followed by the cartel leader himself. Nazif was next in line with another two Yemenis behind him. The bearded professor stayed with the bomb, which was now carried by two of Borregos's men farther back in the line. He was the only one who seemed unafraid of the thing. Everyone else kept a little distance away from the simple footlocker, as if a few feet would save them when such a bomb went off. A Yemeni and two Colombians brought up the rear.

Strange and colorful birds flitted through the dark canopy of trees overhead, shrieking frightened warnings at the little parade. A troop of monkeys screamed from the shadows, pelting them with bits of wood. Here and there a snake coiled around a low-hanging branch like some sort of prop in an American horror film.

A cloud of mosquitoes buzzed around Nazif's face. Sweat rolled down this back.

"Why do you not take the bomb for yourself?" the Yemeni suddenly asked, preferring to know his fate up front rather than fret over it. If Allah willed his death, there was nothing he could do about it.

Ahead, the Colombian used a long machete to hack his way through a dense stand of bamboo and tresses of hanging vines as thick as his wrist.

He stopped, turning to catch his breath.

"My mother used to read me the Bible when I was a child. I was particularly fond of the Old Testament because it contained wonderful stories of violent men." His eyes gleamed with the memory. "Do you know of David and Saul?"

Nazif nodded. "Of course. The writings of Moses and David were once pure, but corrupted by men."

"Ah, I see," the Colombian said. "Well, they say Saul killed his thousands and David his ten thousands. Unlike Saul, I am happy with my thousands. I find the reputation of a narcotics dealer makes me less of a target for government manhunts than that of a terrorist." He pointed the tip of his machete at the footlocker. A sinister smile crept slowly across his face. "Though I must admit, it does not displease me that you plan to use this to kill your ten thousands. Despair, after all, turns out to be very good for business."

"Oh," Nazif said. "There will be plenty of despair. I can assure you."

Borregos turned and nodded at the lead man, who began to hack away at the wall of jungle before them. The lush rainforest had all but obliterated the vague trail, but thanks to the swinging machetes, they moved quickly, stepping over mossy deadfall and skirting stands of bamboo packed as tight as the bars of a prison.

The leader stopped abruptly by a moss-covered log. Resting on the jungle floor, it was even with the man's waist. He stooped to study something on the ground. Bin Ali, the youngest of Nazif's men at twenty-three, moved up the trail to investigate. His white shirt was stained as if he'd been wearing it for months. His machete hung limply at his side as he stooped in the green gloom to study the five-inch track of a jaguar pressed deep in the jungle floor beside a steaming pile of scat.

"Relax," Borregos roared with a great belly laugh. "Jaguars rarely develop a taste for human flesh. On the other hand, there are dozens of venomous snakes and spiders that will kill you very dead."

Branches snapped and groaned in the gloom behind them, causing the entire group to spin, searching their back trail.

"Probably a tapir," Borregos chuckled. "Fleeing the scent of the cat."

"Maybe." Nazif nodded. Fear was contagious, especially when a bomb worth nearly a half a billion dollars was at stake. "Or perhaps someone is following us. We should pick up our speed."

The Colombian scratched the back of his neck with the dull side of his machete, thinking. "Our load is heavy and the jungle is full of surprises to trip us up if we do not move carefully." He pulled a length of twine from his pocket, then plucked a M67 hand grenade, green and roughly the size of a baseball, from a camouflage pouch on his belt. "We could go faster—or we could leave behind us a nasty surprise."

CHAPTER 64

Quinn's survival instructors had called it "Jungle Eye"—the ability to see the various details of the undergrowth and pick out a safe trail without being overwhelmed by the dense tangle of it all. It was much like the *Magic Eye* books Mattie liked so much. If he stared at it too hard, the way before melted into a glob of shadowed green.

They'd been moving through the gloom of thick undergrowth for over two hours, following fresh tracks and cut vegetation. Any actual hacking with Severance might have alerted Borregos of their presence, so Quinn used the blade for little more than pushing aside vines and limbs. He'd given Aleksandra a broken length of oar from the boat so she could do the same and keep from coming into contact with the many ants and stinging insects that used the jungle plants as a highway.

"I hate snakes," she said from a few paces behind him. "I wish to shoot every one I see in the face."

"We don't have snakes in Alaska," Quinn said.

"I would very much like to visit Alaska," Aleksandra said.

"You would love—"

A gossamer tug along the front of his khakis, just above his ankle, caused Quinn to freeze in his tracks.

Aleksandra sensed his change in mood and stood still as well.

"What?" she said. "A snake?"

Quinn shook his head. Backing up slowly, he used Severance to point at a length of green parachute cord, almost invisible in the gathering darkness. Tied to a gnarled root, it ran directly across the scuffed path to disappear into a cut piece of bamboo the diameter of his forearm. Quinn took a small LED flashlight and shined it into the open end of the bamboo.

"That's what I thought," he said. "A half step more and I'd have pulled this out of its tube right at our feet."

Aleksandra started to move up next to him, but he raised his hand. "See one, think two," he said, scanning the jungle for signs of anything out of the norm. Straight lines in particular were rarely found in nature.

"Ahh," he said at length. He held his hand out behind him. "Can I borrow your oar?"

She handed it forward.

"Think two," he said again before tossing the short piece of wood at a second hidden tripwire.

The foliage to the right of the trail gave a sudden whoosh as a thick piece of bamboo sprang horizontally at chest height directly across the trial. Five sharpened spikes of smaller bamboo had been lashed to it—a whip stick. Quinn had heard his father and uncles talk about such booby traps from Vietnam. He'd never seen one himself, but had long since stopped being surprised at the various methods men could devise to maim and kill other men. In fact, he marveled at the simplicity of both the traps.

"I doubt they took the time to set any more," he said, moving slowly up the trail. "Still, it will be night soon and we can't move safely in the dark. If a booby trap doesn't kill us some venomous spider likely will. . . ."

Aleksandra swatted a mosquito on her forehead, looking uncomfortably at the surrounding jungle. She pointed in disgust at the forest floor that seemed to roil beneath their feet with ants and other roving insects. "I'd rather take my chances than stay out here. We'll be eaten alive if we sit down to rest."

Quinn smiled. "I grew up in the mountains," he said. "But I've watched my share of jungle movies. Can't do anything about the mosquitos, but I think I may have a solution to get us off the ground."

Aleksandra stood on the trail behind Quinn, watching him through a buzzing cloud of mosquitos in the gathering gloom. He'd turned his head to listen, standing motionless amid fronds of elephant ear and giant fern. A dark line of sweat ran down the spine of his shirt, which hung untucked at his waist.

"They're far enough ahead we can't hear them," he said, studying a thick stand of bamboo that stood like a green fence off the path to his right. "That's good, because they won't hear us either."

He picked a fat stalk of bamboo roughly four inches in diameter and well over twelve feet tall. Two quick blows with his curved blade felled it neatly a few inches above the ground. Aleksandra marveled at how fluidly he moved, as if he chopped bamboo as an occupation and the steaming heat of the jungle was his home. He stopped every few seconds to listen. She imagined he had the ability to filter the natural noises of the rain forest, coaxing out any made by man—like the ping of a machete against wood.

"Bring the water bottle," he said, dragging the length of bamboo to rest the cut end in the crook of a low sapling that stood even with his belt. He'd retrieved the piece of wooden oar and, using it as a baton to pound on Severance's hilt, punched a square hole just above the last node ring. He rolled the bamboo and clean water poured from the hollow core.

"Interesting," she said, filling the bottle.

"They don't all have water in them," Quinn said. "But there's a good chance we'll find enough to keep us alive without getting some parasite from the river."

Once they'd drained all the water, he punched another square hole opposite the first. Through this, he shoved a sturdy piece of vine to form a short-topped T. He repeated the process at the other end, wedging the entire length between two trees so it ran parallel to the ground. He wiped the sweat from his face with the sleeve of his shirt and looked up.

"What do you think?"

Before she could answer, a wide grin spread across his face. "I know, it's still a little narrow for the two of us. But just watch."

Using the parachute cord from the two booby traps, he took half a dozen turns around each end of the bamboo trunk. Then, using the oar as a baton again, he drove the point of his blade completely through the trunk so it came out the bottom side. Tapping on the spine of the blade, he split the stem from one end to the other, stopping just before he reached the last reinforced ring and wraps of parachute cord. He repeated the process over and over until he had the entire length of the bamboo split into one-inch shreds down the center but still intact at both ends. He spread the pieces with both hands and, as if by magic, they fanned open to form a sort of hammock.

The last blue hints of light faded and the jungle closed in around them by the time Quinn wedged the ends of the makeshift bed into the crooks of two sturdy trees three feet off the wriggling ground.

Quinn lay down first, testing it slowly with his full weight. Satisfied, he situated himself diagonally, then motioned for Aleksandra to climb in beside him.

"It won't do anything against bloodsucking bats," he said, one arm outstretched, presumably for her to use as a pillow, the other thrown over his forehead. "But it'll keep us off the ground."

Aleksandra settled in next to him, choosing the sticky heat of his closeness over the open vulnerability of rolling away. The smells of La Paz, the Altiplano, and the high mountains of the cloud forest still lingered next to his skin. She marveled at how far they'd come in two days.

Each was silent for a time, moving this way and that, nestling their way into the best sleeping position they could find. Both were completely exhausted, but the urgency of their mission kept them on edge, fighting back against sleep.

"You are in love then?" Aleksandra said at length, seeing no reason not to be forward since she was sharing a bed and would, in all likelihood, die with this dark man. They'd raced, ridden, fought, and killed together. Apart from Mikhail, she would have long since

slept with any other man she'd known under such stress-
ful circumstances. It was the way of things, her method
of forgetting her own mortality. But this one, he had a
wall.

Quinn raised his arm as if to study her.

"I am," he said.

"But for some reason, you struggle with it?"

He shrugged, saying nothing.

She turned slightly, feeling the bamboo slats creak
beneath her. Her face was just inches from his. "You
are in love enough that you have me here, alone, and do
not even make a flirtation."

Quinn chuckled. "Our bed isn't strong enough for
that sort of thing. Anyway, 'making flirtations' is more
Bo's department."

"I'm sorry about him," Aleksandra offered, snug-
gling closer, drawing on the comfort of muscle and
strength of bone.

"He's too tough to die," Quinn said, a catch of worry
in his voice. "If he was here, I'm sure he'd be flirting,
bullet wound or not."

"You are a *b'elaya vorona*, Jericho Quinn," she
whispered.

"What's that?"

"A white crow," she said. "In Russian it would be
like your black sheep—one who stands apart from the
rest. Some say a white crow is bad, but I believe it is a
good thing to stand apart."

For a short moment Aleksandra allowed herself to
be comfortable. The shriek of a monkey somewhere
deep in the blackness of the jungle reminded her that
comfort was a fleeting thing. Baba Yaga, the Bone

Mother, was out there, nearby. She could feel it in her teeth. And they shared a secret she could no longer hold inside.

"I should have told you this before," she said before Quinn had a chance to doze. "Please understand, I could be executed for divulging such information."

"Okay . . ." Quinn's voice was muffled against his arm.

"Do you remember the second North Korean nuclear test in 2009?"

"Of course," he said.

Aleksandra took a deep breath, and then plowed ahead. If she could not trust this man, she could trust no one.

"The arming unit on that device was an older Soviet model. Thought to be much the same as the one used on Baba Yaga." She raised her head, her face close enough to smell the sweet odor of *cunape* on his breath. "The North Korean detonation wasn't a test at all. It was an accident."

"You're saying the bomb detonated on its own?" Quinn was now wide awake.

"Not quite," she said. "The Korean bomb was indeed armed, as part of a testing procedure, but there was no delay with this particular detonation. We believe the Bone Mother will malfunction the same way. There will be no final countdown, no last-second clipping of the red wire to save the world. The moment the arming sequence is entered into the Permissive Access Lock, the Baba Yaga will detonate with immediate effect. . . ."

DETONATION

A zest for living must include a willingness to die.

—ROBERT A. HEINLEIN

CHAPTER 65

Quinn lay flat on his belly in the shadowy haze of a jungle morning. He ignored a beetle half the size of his hand that scuttled through the dead leaves in front of him. They'd risen well before dawn, braving possible booby traps and venomous creatures, knowing Borregos would want a pickup as close to daybreak as possible. Clouds of steamy fog hung here and there among the various layers of canopy. Two troops of monkeys, apparently angry at the intruding airplane, screamed from opposite ends of a grass runway. Night birds gave their last few shrieks before sunup. Egrets and other early birds squawked and flitted in the branches.

Aleksandra lay beside him, green eyes burning a hole in the foliage. Dense cover had allowed them to get within a few meters of a wooden supply shack off the side of the dirt runway hacked out of the jungle.

His initial assessment of eight men looked correct. Borregos stood at the aft of a Cessna Caravan supervising two younger men as they struggled to get a long green footlocker into the swinging cargo door. An older man, bald and much thinner than the drug lord, stood at the tail of the plane.

"The Bone Mother," Aleksandra whispered. "We cannot let them leave."

"I don't intend to," Quinn said, eyes darting around the narrow clearing.

The professor's face was visible leaning against a forward window in the aircraft. Apart from the four at the aircraft, four more of Borregos's men stood guard, each taking a corner and facing outbound into the jungle. The one nearest Quinn was less than thirty meters away, to his right. A Kalashnikov clutched in his hand, he looked capable enough, peering into the wall of foliage in front of him. He wore sunglasses, so it was difficult to see which way he was looking. On his belt was a Glock pistol with a set of extra magazines, much like a police officer would wear on duty. A rectangular pouch on his left hip, opposite his pistol, held extra magazines for the rifle. The long sleeves of his camouflage uniform blouse were rolled neatly over muscled forearms.

Quinn took a quick moment to study the other three. All were similarly armed; two looked much younger and one had a full beard with black hair that stuck out from under a green Castro-style cap. None were as squared-away as the professional soldier to Quinn's right. This one was the type to clean his weapon every night and practice weekly because he enjoyed the smell of gunfire.

Quinn didn't want a man like this shooting at him while he worked and the only way to see that didn't happen was to take him out at the beginning.

He cocked his head toward Aleksandra, keeping his eye on the soldier. "Five rounds against a squad of eight well-armed men," he said. "I'll need two for what I have in mind. You take the other three along with this." He gingerly slid the grenade from the booby trap out of the length of bamboo, keeping his hand around the compressed spoon. "We need to get this under the plane. I'll get into place and cover you. You count to sixty and start shoot—"

The Caravan's single Pratt & Whitney engine began to whine to life, the prop slowly catching up to the spinning turbine until whirred contentedly.

"Better make that twenty," Quinn said, already scuttling backwards.

Her mouth hung open. "You only have two bullets."

"And I hope that's one more than I need."

Quinn moved quickly through the brush, thankful now for the rising whine of the aircraft engine. The three other guards looked back and forth at each other in the orange light, eager to give up their posts and make a run for the plane. But the professional soldier stood fast, manning his station until properly relieved.

In order for this to work Quinn needed the soldier DRT—dead right there. He'd seen too many fighters on both sides of a battle absorb a great deal of lead only to keep fighting long past the time they should go down. He needed a target that would ensure that didn't happen.

The moment Aleksandra fired her first shot Quinn rose up from the vines and bushes, approaching from the side, moving obliquely. The soldier spun toward the racket, bringing his rifle to bear and firing as Quinn moved up behind him less than five yards away.

Intent on firing his weapon at the threat to the aircraft, the soldier never heard the real danger padding up behind him. Ten feet out, Quinn let the front sight of his pistol float over a spot at the base of the man's skull. He squeezed the trigger twice, using both rounds.

Borregos's soldier fell in the peculiar corkscrew motion of someone shot in the brainstem, one leg folding before the other did. Quinn dropped the empty 1911 and was on him before he hit the ground. He scooped up the rifle and let the soldier fall away, leaving himself clear to engage the other guards. He was relieved to see one of Aleksandra's shots drop the guard with the beard and Fidel Castro hat.

A man on the plane leaned out to pull up the boarding door. Quinn sent him tumbling onto the ground with two quick rounds to the chest. Incoming fire from one of the other sentries sent Quinn diving for cover as the pilot spun the Caravan and threw on the power, causing it to gain speed quickly since it was five people lighter than expected.

Quinn returned fire carefully, counting his shots and expecting the weapon to run dry at any moment. For all his professional demeanor, the dead soldier had used up much of his magazine in the first full-auto burst to protect the Caravan.

Scanning over the top of the rifle sights, Quinn tried to figure out what Aleksandra was doing with the grenade. A booming concussion answered his question. Shrapnel screamed through the air, rattling through the jungle leaves. For a split second a blossom of black smoke and falling debris obscured the Caravan's tail.

To Quinn's horror the plane kept rolling unaffected by the blast or the rounds. Aleksandra continued to engage the two surviving sentries while Quinn focused on the rapidly departing Caravan. With the engine pointed away he aimed for the thin walls of the fuselage, hoping to throw enough rounds into the avionics to stop them. If he was lucky he'd hit the pilot. Two rounds later, he was empty.

The plane continued to roll, picking up speed with every yard down the grass strip. It was airborne in a matter of moments, banking hard right to get beyond the trees. Quinn ran for the downed soldier, ignoring the bullets that thwacked the dirt at his feet as he grabbed for a fresh magazine on the dead man's belt.

Aleksandra silenced the last sentry with a commandeered rifle at the same moment the Caravan disappeared over the treetops.

Quinn stood in the middle of the clearing wrapped in stunned silence. He held the freshly loaded Kalashnikov to his shoulder, though there was nothing to shoot at but air. By degree, the shrieks and chatter of the jungle crept back to normal as if the gunfight had never happened and Borregos's plane had not just flown away carrying a five-kiloton atomic bomb.

CHAPTER 66

Movement along the edge of the grass strip caught Quinn's eye. When he went to investigate, he found the man who'd fallen out of the plane was still alive.

Quinn's first round had hit him in the chest, but the second had gone low, entering the back of the knee as he tumbled down the boarding stairs. He lay in the grass with his leg turned unnaturally underneath his body. Dark eyes had sunken into deep sockets as if the life was seeping out from behind them. His chest heaved in ragged breaths.

He didn't have long.

Quinn turned to Aleksandra. "Ask where they're taking the bomb."

She did, prodding his wounded leg with her toe to get his attention.

"Laa! Laa!" he cried. *No, no.*

Quinn looked down, shocked. He was speaking Arabic.

"Who are you?" he asked in Arabic.

The wounded man looked up, blinking his sunken eyes.

"*Allahu Akbar*," he sighed with his last breath, the sound of air seeping out of flattening tire. *God is great.*

"Damn you stupidly shit!" Aleksandra attempted to curse in English, kicking the man again in frustration.

Quinn touched her arm.

"Let's think," he said. "This guy is an Arab and there were Yemeni AQAP reps at the party where you and I met. Borregos was there as well, but I'm betting this guy's people picked the target. Borregos is a narcotics smuggler . . . probably moving the bomb for a share in the profits."

Quinn stooped to search the dead Arab's pockets and found a satellite phone. He pressed the power switch and held his breath as it cycled. As he suspected, they'd been in the jungle long enough the battery was completely spent.

"Dead," he said, holding up the phone so Aleksandra could see it.

"There is a small generator beside that building," she said.

None of the other guards had a satellite phone or a charging cord, but there were a handful of tools and a few spare aircraft parts in the shed. It took over four hours of scrounging wire and other materials to jury-rig a charging cord that would attach to the satellite phone's battery—and another two to get the generator chugging long enough to give the phone enough juice to make a call.

It was nearly noon by the time Quinn was finally able to connect with Win Palmer. He had no idea how long the battery would last and uncharacteristically told the boss to shut up and listen as soon as he answered. He gave Palmer a CliffsNotes version of the past few hours' events.

"I'll take some photos of these guys with my phone and text them to you as soon as we get a signal," Quinn said. "We could use an extraction for two ASAP. In the meantime, I suggest you get Diego Borregos's photo out to every law enforcement agency within two hundred miles of the border."

"I'll get someone to you right away," Palmer said, pausing. The sound of clicking computer keys dominated the line. "Bo is stable, by the way," he said while he typed. "And Thibodaux is too damned stubborn to take it easy until we know for sure about his eye."

"Thanks for the update," Quinn said, relieved. "I wonder—"

"How long is the strip there?" Palmer spoke before Quinn could ask any more about Bo.

Quinn looked from one end of the grass field to the other. "Maybe twenty-five hundred feet," he said. "But I got forty feet of jungle canopy rising up right off both ends of the runway."

"Twenty-five," Palmer inhaled sharply. "That's awfully tight for anything fast enough to get to you anytime soon and big enough to carry you both. . . ." His voice trailed off giving way to more clicks of the keyboard. "Okay, I think I have something," he said at length. There was a long silence, followed by a resigned sigh. "Hope you don't get airsick."

CHAPTER 67

2:00 PM Bolivian time

Quinn recognized the high-pitched whine of the Cessna A-37B before it screamed over the tree-tops, rolling slightly so the pilot could get a better look at the cramped jungle runway. The twin GE turbofan engines gave rise to the aircraft's nickname of the Tweety Bird or Super Tweet—but Quinn had always agreed with those who called it a six-thousand-pound dog whistle. All but mandatory in just about every South American coup since the 1970s, the A37 had a slender tail and broad, tandem cockpit that gave it a toady look. Bulbous tip-tanks hung at the end of each Hershey Bar wing. A seven-round rocket pod was attached to the pylons on either side, midway between a second set of fuel tanks and the fuselage. This one was painted olive and brown and bore the red and white flag of the Peruvian Air Force.

"We are supposed to leave on this flying tadpole?" Kanatova scoffed as the little jet made another low-altitude pass. It skimmed the trees, low enough Quinn could clearly make out the pilot as he turned his head back and forth, planning his landing—and his eventual takeoff—in such cramped quarters.

Two minutes later saw the squat aircraft banking over the treetops, minus the external fuel tanks that had been under each wing. Engine whining, airbrake deployed, it settled in over the grassy strip and rolled to a stop with a nearly two hundred feet to spare. Both Quinn and Kanatova plugged their ears as the twin turbofans—little more than kerosene-burning sirens—pushed the little jet to the end of the field and finally spooled down.

A short, bantam rooster of a man with broad shoulders and stubby legs to match his airplane flipped up the bubble cockpit cover and climbed out. He wore a green Nomex flight suit and a flight helmet with a dark face-shield.

He peeled off a Nomex glove and extended his hand.

"J. C. Fuentes," he said with only the slightest of Latin accents. Black hair hung across his forehead in a Superman curl. "Fighter Squadron 711 of the Peruvian Air Force. Are you Señor Jericho Quinn?"

"I am."

"Very well then," Fuentes said. "Climb aboard and we'll get under way. My orders are to fly you to Talara at once."

Aleksandra looked at the cockpit, then turned to the pilot. "There are only two seats."

Fuentes shrugged. "I am lighter on fuel now. It will be tight, but you are small enough we can fit you in on Señor Quinn's lap. Unfortunately, neither of you will be able to wear a parachute."

"Then do not crash," Kanatova said, giving the jet a sullen frown.

"As you wish." The pilot smiled. "I will remove crashing from my list of things to do today."

Aleksandra wrinkled her freckled nose, not amused.

Quinn worked his way into the Super Tweet's right-hand seat, one leg on either side of a control stick matching the pilot's. He was surprised to find the low sidewalls made him feel as though he was sitting on rather than in the plane.

"It's interesting to see the Peruvian Air Force here in the middle of Bolivia," he said, buckling in.

"Your friend Señor Palmer is our friend Señor Palmer." Fuentes held Kanatova's hand as she stepped gingerly into the aircraft. "He made a call to my commanding officer and my commander made a call to me. It is simple really."

"But Peru?"

"Bolivia is landlocked." The pilot shrugged. "My government has an agreement to give her access to our seaports. In return, she is friendly to us at times such as this when we need a little favor."

Quinn put his arms around Kanatova, resting them on her thighs to keep them out of the pilot's way. Though spacious for two pilots, shoehorning three into the cockpit wasn't anywhere in Cessna's specs. Quinn found himself hyperaware of the rudder pedals at his feet and the array of controls just asking to be bumped or flipped in the close confines of the cockpit.

"I used the extra tanks to get here from my base in Arequipa." Fuentes nodded toward the wings once he was seated. "I have enough fuel to get you to Talara in time for your connecting flight."

"What sort of connecting flight?" Quinn asked. Oppressive heat and humidity closed in around them and he was anxious to get into the air.

"I honestly do not know, señor." Fuentes buckled his seat belt and turned before putting on his helmet. "I only know Señor Palmer wants you back in the United States as soon as possible. I am left to assume that, whatever it is, it will be extremely fast. Now, if you will excuse me, I must figure out how to make this airplane jump off the ground like a helicopter." He pulled on the helmet, then pushed a button in the console to bring the Plexiglas bubble down over the cockpit.

Fuentes had plenty of swagger. He'd been able to set the plane down in the narrow jungle gash without a problem, but taking off with the added weight of two more people would prove much more difficult. He'd need every bit of his swagger—plus a healthy dose of skill and luck.

Quinn pulled Aleksandra closer in an effort to make them both as small as possible during the dicey takeoff. The smoky odor of the jungle clung to her hair.

Fuentes brought the turbofan engines to whining life, standing on the brakes as the entire plane began to shake and tremble, trying to move. When he appeared to be satisfied that all the instruments on the console were reading correctly, he released the brakes and let the plane jump forward, hurtling down the narrow strip. The jungle loomed ahead, dark trees growing quickly as the end of the bumpy runway screamed up to meet them. Three fourths of the way down, with less than five hundred feet to spare, he tugged back gently on the stick.

The little jet leaped into the air, engines screaming.

Without warning, Fuentes fired two missiles at the trees in front of him. Each left its respective wing-pod with a hissing shriek. The little jet flew straight through the rolling ball of flames and black smoke.

"Did you do that to clear the trees?" Quinn said, surprised at the tactic.

Fuentes flipped up his dark visor, chuckling. He appeared relaxed now that they were safely in the air. "No, señor." He grinned. "Far too much peace lately. I do not often have the opportunity to fire missiles." He banked the airplane hard, coming around again over the little strip. "I think I will shoot a few more and give the drug lords a little surprise the next time they try to land."

CHAPTER 68

Idaho

Marie held the baby tight to her chest. She kept her back to the corner, her knees drawn up defensively. Lourdes stood across the room beside the doorway to the kitchen, swinging the hook and chain in front of her like a hypnotist's watch. Bright red lipstick formed a wicked smirk across the darkness of her face.

Pete perched at the edge of his recliner. The lustful stare in his eyes said he was about to profit from something bad.

"It's time to play our little game," Lourdes said, speeding up the chain to make it whir through the air.

Marie shuddered. She was past the point of being sick. There was nothing left to throw up, nothing but worry and despair. Pressing her back against the wall, she pushed to her feet. "I'm not going to make this easy," she said, amazed at the calm in her own voice.

Lourdes's eyebrow twitched, rising to disappear beneath the stark black line of her bangs.

"Funny enough," she said. "Pete and I had a wager that you would wet yourself when the time came."

Pete stood up from the recliner, folding his arms across his chest. "And it just so happens that I win," he said, leering at Marie. "You are braver than she thought you'd be. And that means you and me get to spend a little quality time together before . . ." He chuckled. "Well, you know."

Lourdes leaned against the wall, yawning as if she was bored.

Pete shot her an annoyed glance.

"What? Are you gonna stay and watch?"

Lourdes threw up her hands, wagging her head. "Very well, I will take the worm for his walk in the woods and come back for Mommy after I am finished with him. . . ."

Jacques Thibodaux sat on the frozen ground with his back to the toolshed, a scant fifty feet from the back door of the red brick farmhouse. A stubby MP5 hung around his bull neck on a single-point sling. His Kimber rested comfortably on his right thigh so he'd have easy access while wearing his ballistic vest. A heavy patch, matching the rest of his black clothing, covered his right eye.

Palmer had wanted him to sit this one out, but he'd argued that a one-eyed Marine was worth two and a half mortal men and sitting out a mission was not in his skill set.

Palmer grudgingly agreed, assigning Emiko Miyagi and Ronnie Garcia to round out the team because of their experience working together.

Though she was rarely his fan, Miyagi had been the consummate professional from the start. Since Thibodaux had tactical command of the operation, she took direction as though he'd been her boss for years. Each had spent the last ninety minutes creeping up on the house, wearing white parka smocks and pants over their tactical gear so they would blend in to the snow. Kneeling just to the right of the back door, Miyagi had already placed two small charges of C-4 in the jamb and now knelt just to the right, MP5 around her neck, her finger on the detonator.

Ronnie lay belly-down in the snow beside Thibodaux, her eye pressed to the night-vision scope on an M4 assault rifle. Her razor-sharp intellect and tactical savvy made her a perfect third person for the team.

Thibodaux held an iPhone his hand, tilting it back and forth to maneuver a tiny, unmanned aerial vehicle next to the dusty living room window. Known as a Dragonfly, the UAV was not much larger than its namesake. It was intuitive to operate, using the phone's gyro technology to control pitch, roll, and yaw and sliding a thumb up or down to climb or descend. A micro camera and laser microphone relayed video and sound back to the Bluetooth headsets of all three operators.

None of them liked what they were hearing.

"I won the bet fair and square," Pete said. "You have to give me some time with her."

"You will have plenty of time to do what you need to do," Lourdes scoffed. "Make certain you are finished with her before I return—"

"Stop it!" Marie hissed. "No one will touch my baby while I'm alive."

Pete smirked, unbuckling his belt. Lourdes laughed

softly. She let the hook and chain slither from her hand to the floor, then took a black revolver from behind her back. Her face fell into a pinched frown.

"Make no mistake, my dear. We will touch whatever, whenever we please," she said. "Shall I explain to you how this will go? First, I will shoot you in one knee. While you flop around in pain, thinking it cannot possibly get any worse, I will shoot you in the other knee for good measure. I will then allow you to experience that pain for a few moments before I very gently and against your hopeless sobs, peel the little worm from your pitiful grasp."

Marie breathed in short pants. She and Simon were dead, that was a given—but how they died was not yet written. She'd do what this evil woman didn't expect. She'd take the fight to her, force her hand, and take away the fun of torment.

The crash of breaking glass took a moment to register. Out of habit, Marie shielded Simon from the sudden noise. Lourdes turned toward the sound. Pete held up his pants with one hand, reaching toward the recliner for his pistol with the other.

A half second later the room exploded in a brilliant flash of light. A sudden woofing bang shook the paint off the ceiling and rattled the dishes in the kitchen. A series of muffled pops filled the smoky room. Blinded by the intense flash, Marie was vaguely aware of someone standing in front of her, shielding her from the events unfolding only a few feet away. As her vision began to clear, one of the biggest men she'd ever seen came into focus.

A black patch covered one eye.

* * *

Emiko Miyagi blew the door an instant after she tossed the weighted flash grenade through the living room window. Thibodaux rolled through the opening, peeling left to cover the woman and her baby while Garcia and Miyagi engaged the two bad guys. The idea was to take them alive if possible. Peter De Campo had gone for his weapon, forcing Garcia's hand. A string of nine-millimeter rounds to his chest from her MP5 dropped him instantly. He was thought to be a minor gun thug hired by Zamora strictly for this part of the operation, so was likely to be of little help regarding Baba Yaga.

Lourdes Lopez was a different story. Her name popped up in government databases almost as often as Zamora's. Though she hadn't been with him in Florida, the two appeared to be a team. Miyagi saw to it that she was taken alive—barely.

Her first two shots had taken out the sullen woman's knees. Two follow-up bursts destroyed each elbow.

"We are in America!" Lourdes screeched writhing on her back in a pool of blood. "You cannot just let me die."

Miyagi stood over her for a long moment, her smooth face emotionless. At length, she knelt to apply four windless-style tourniquets, one over each bicep and another above each knee.

Thibodaux gathered a trembling Marie and her baby in his big arms, attempting to shield them from all the bloodshed. The sight of little Simon made him think of his own boys.

Marie pushed him away so she could see.

"I need a hospital," Lourdes moaned, looking fearfully at the tourniquets. "If you leave these on me without attention I will lose my limbs. I will be helpless!"

Miyagi nodded, a tender smile on her lips.

"As a matter of fact, you will," she said. "But in this life one must often depend on the kindness of strangers."

Marie reached up to touch Thibodaux's arm.

"Matt?" she asked.

The Cajun shook his head. "We're still looking for him. I need you to think hard and tell us anything you might have heard that could help us find your husband and the men who have him."

Marie nodded toward the hallway. "We talked on the computer every day until . . . a few days ago. I'm not sure how many. They all run together."

"You're one smart lady," Ronnie said. She cleared the chamber of Pete's pistol before slipping it in her waistband. "The photo you texted to your cell phone gave us the GPS coordinates that led us here."

Marie brightened. "So Matt figured it out." She kissed Simon on top of his head, tears flowing in earnest now. "Daddy figured it out," she said. "Did you hear that, buddy? Daddy saved us."

"Your pathetic husband," Lourdes coughed. Her low groan carried across the room like a bad smell. "He was not the kind man you thought him to be. . . ." she gasped, vindictive even in defeat.

Miyagi grabbed the hateful woman by her collar and propped her roughly against the wall. Her useless arms flopped to her side, starting a fresh flow of blood and bringing a bloodcurdling wail.

"How's that cruelty thing working out for you now?" Thibodaux shook his head in disdain. "Karma's only a bitch when you are one your own self."

CHAPTER 69

Talara, Peru

Landing gear squawked on the tarmac an hour and ten minutes from the moment the little green jet jumped from the dense Bolivian jungle.

As small as Aleksandra was, her hips dug into Quinn, cutting off his circulation and jamming him against the Spartan cockpit. Thankfully his legs had fallen asleep halfway into the flight.

Fuentes flipped open the cover during the back-taxi, allowing in a warm but welcome ocean breeze. A squad of six crewmen in green coveralls swarmed the aircraft as the screaming engines wound down.

On the tarmac, Quinn checked his phone and found he had six missed calls from Palmer. Kanatova took out her own phone, but Quinn shook his head.

"I'm not sure it would be a good idea for you to call your people on this," he said, bracing himself for the onslaught of nails and knees he'd received at Zamora's party.

"The battery is dead." She shrugged, handing the

phone to him. "Take it if you wish, but you needn't worry."

Quinn believed her sincerity, but took the phone anyway. He checked the battery, then gave it back to her.

She took it, smiling. "All we have been through and still you do not trust me."

Quinn shrugged. "You would do the same if this was unfolding in Russia."

There were dozens of spy apps available to turn almost any smartphone into a bug. But it was much easier than that. Turning on the auto-answer, then deactivating the ringer and vibrate functions transformed an ordinary cell phone into an inconspicuous listening device. Any operative would know better.

Aleksandra slipped the useless phone in her pocket and sighed. "I would never call my people on this. They would take a week to get a plan together and another to receive the levels of approval needed to implement the plan—and that's if they wished to become involved."

Quinn gave her an understanding smile and pressed the speed dial for Win Palmer.

The national security advisor began talking the instant he picked up. "The photo you sent came through a half hour ago. Quantico's already got a hit through facial recognition. Tamir Mukhtar, a soldier they believe is attached to al-Qaeda on the Arabian Peninsula under Yazid Nazif."

"Nazif," Quinn mused. "That makes sense."

"And here's the most interesting part," Palmer said. "Nazif has a cousin who drives a cab in Houston."

"I'm assuming FBI has eyes on that cousin?"

"In the next hour Houston, Texas, will have more feds than oilmen," Palmer said.

"Targets?" Quinn asked, then mouthed, *Houston, Texas,* to Aleksandra in an effort to mend fences from his earlier showing of mistrust.

"The Martin Luther King Jr. parade is less than four days out," Palmer said. "It's on par with the Rose Bowl parade in size—a juicy target. Listen, a Bone left Abilene two hours ago. I spoke to the pilot personally and told him to put a boot in his bird's ass. Expect him on the ground in . . ." He paused, doing the math. "Less than ninety minutes. I want you and the Russian in Houston helping out on the search as soon as possible."

"Roger that," Quinn said. "We'll be ready."

Officially known as the Lancer, the B-1, or B-One, was often called the Bone. Officially, it could reach speeds of Mach 1.25—over nine hundred miles an hour. At that rate they would make the trip from northern Peru to Houston in three hours and change.

"Call me back when you're in the air," Palmer said and ended the call without another word.

Quinn turned to Aleksandra, who tapped her toe on the tarmac beside Fuentes, the A37 pilot.

"May I offer you a place to wash up and something to eat?" Fuentes looked back and forth between the two of them. "We have excellent facilities here on base."

"That would be welcome." Quinn nodded. "I wouldn't mind a glass of water that didn't come out of a length of bamboo."

Aleksandra smiled, her freckled nose crinkling in a

way that belied her ruthlessness. "I could use a quick shower, even if I have to put these dirty clothes back on."

"I am sure we can find something for both of you," Fuentes said.

Quinn glanced at the Aquaracer on his wrist. "Lead the way, sir," he said. "But we'll have to hurry. Our ride will be here before we know it."

CHAPTER 70

Texas
Noon

Yazid Nazif, his surviving two men, and Matthew
Pollard poked their heads out of a two-mile tunnel
under the Rio Grande River and into the outskirts of
Laredo at approximately the same time the United
States attempted to slam the door on the border. Luckily for Nazif, the United States had miles of border to
patrol and only so many resources. The problem was
they seemed to have brought all of these resources to
bear at once. Green and white patrol vehicles threw
clouds of dust on every back road. Military jets streaked
overhead as if an air show was in town. Helicopters and
specialized Predator drones with sophisticated camera
pods loitered along a corridor formed by the river and
an imaginary line thirty-five miles to the north.

Diego Borregos had remained in Mexico, reasoning
that the U.S. Marshals held several warrants for him
and his presence would only add to the likelihood of
their capture. He sent his nephew, Carlos, to negotiate
the crossing. Though Carlos was only in his twenties,

Borregos assured Nazif that the young man was extremely loyal and could be trusted above anyone else to always "do the right thing."

A Suburban with a Halliburton oil company logo was waiting outside the self-storage unit where the tunnel emerged to carry them and the bomb north, along the Interstate 35 frontage road toward San Antonio. Twenty-seven miles northeast of Laredo, the Suburban slowed and turned off the pavement, bouncing down a dirt track. Pump jacks rose and fell on either side of the road like giant, bigheaded ants.

"There is a CBP check station two miles up the Interstate," Carlos said, punching a number into his cell phone.

Border Patrol aircraft still roared back and forth overhead.

"And you have a plan to get us around it?" Nazif asked, his voice tight in his throat.

"Of course." The boy put the cell phone to his ear. "It is time," he said. "Very well. 'Sta bueno." Ending the call, he turned to look back, smiling broadly.

A minute later and the skies were quiet.

"What happened?" Nazif whispered, craning his head to look out the window.

Carlos snapped his fingers. "The United States government is not the only organization with drone aircraft. You would be surprised at the rapid response when such a thing speeds across the border at low altitude from Mexico. The trip wires and radar alarms near the checkpoint on State Highway 83 ten miles west of us just went crazy. We should have a few minutes of freedom from their increased oversight before they return. If the normal balloons see us, we will just look like oil field workers coming and going about our daily chores."

Carlos ushered them into a concrete pump house partially hidden by feathery green mesquite trees. Under a piece of greasy plywood on the floor they found a ladder leading down into a second tunnel. The boy waved his hand in a flourish of pride.

"My uncle's men posed as oil field workers for over a year to dig their way around it." He smiled. "Our services are well worth any price, no?"

Nazif gave a curt nod. He supposed that being a relative of a drug lord as powerful as Diego Borregos made the boy feel free to act so flippant. He glanced at the Omega on his wrist. It was almost seven. "You will stay with us until we reach my brother?"

"Of course, señor," Carlos said. "I will accompany you as far as Austin."

"We won't be going to Austin," Yazid said, thinking better of it the moment he did.

Carlos cocked his head to one side. "Perhaps my uncle was mistaken," he said. "I was told you were going to Austin."

"Plans change," Yazid said. "But you will still transport us to San Antonio?"

"We will be there before midnight." Carlos nodded. "Did not my uncle tell you? I may always be counted on to do the right thing."

The tunnel, complete with lighting and an electric handcart, emerged inside another well house a mile past the Border Patrol checkpoint. A second Halliburton vehicle, this one a battered white Suburban, idled in the sparse trees. Yazid's men loaded the footlocker in back and threw a blue tarp over it before piling inside.

Carlos took the front passenger seat.

An F16 fighter screamed overhead, flying west as the dusty Suburban merged into traffic on Interstate 35. A helicopter crossed a quarter mile behind them, skimming the treetops. Two Border Patrol sedans raced south in the oncoming lane, headed for the checkpoint.

"We were lucky," Nazif whispered, repenting his lack of faith even as he uttered the words. He mouthed a prayer of thanksgiving. "There is no God but Allah. . . ."

Carlos looked over his shoulder, grinning at all the noise.

He waggled his eyebrows up and down, Groucho Marx style. "My uncle makes his own luck."

Yazid's heart leaped when he saw Ibrahim waiting at the wheel of a rented Penske van beyond a row of idling semi trucks. They were so close now. The event held by Sacred Peace Church would have been a decent target with ten thousand spectators, but the blast would be partially contained. Ibrahim's research showed the parade in Houston would provide for at least double the immediate casualties and an untold number of those exposed to radiation. If Allah willed it, and Baba Yaga was as powerful as they had been told, the death toll could reach a hundred thousand as paradegoers packed along the route.

Yazid climbed out of the Suburban with a full heart at the blessings that had gotten them this far. He'd only gone a step when he realized something was incredibly wrong. Ibrahim stared straight ahead, unmoving. A hiss from the shadows behind a nearby tractor trailer caused Yazid to turn. His mouth fell open when he saw the two men standing there.

He shot an angry glare at Carlos, who'd hung back to wait beside the Suburban. "What is the meaning of this?"

"I am very sorry, señor." The boy shrugged. "But as it turns out, the 'right thing' was to tell him where you planned to meet."

CHAPTER 71

The B1 Lancer did a turn and burn, stopping only long enough to pick up its two passengers.

Quinn was surprised to find Major Brett Moore in command of the aircraft. Moore had been an assistant physics instructor at the Academy when he was a brand-new captain and Quinn was a cadet. A tall man, dressed in the green flame retardant flight suit pilots called a "bag," his dark hair was beginning to gray at the temples. He'd been quite a boxer during his days at USAFA and followed Quinn's success throughout his Academy career.

The two shook hands and the pilot showed them on-board, anxious to get underway.

"You've dropped off the radar, son," Moore said, helping Quinn and Aleksandra get settled in the two weapons systems officer seats in a compartment the size of a phone booth, six feet behind and slightly above the cockpit.

Quinn smiled. "You warned me how OSI types

were. 'Got their hands in all sort of secretive mojo,' isn't that what you said?"

"And here you are proving me right," Moore scoffed. "This bird burns sixty thousand dollar bills every hour her fans are turning. By my estimation that means I'm giving you two a four-hundred-thousand-dollar taxi ride home from whatever you've been doing down here. Not to mention the fact that the president's national security advisor called me personally and ordered me not to spare the horses. I'd say that qualifies as secretive mojo."

Moore handed each of them a helmet and headset. He pointed to the array of instrumentation on the console in front of the weapons system officers' seats. "You can make encrypted calls with this." He pointed to a touch-screen keypad. "Just put us on mute if you need to discuss your secret-agent shit. But don't touch anything else."

A consummate pro, Moore asked no questions about Aleksandra, assuming that whoever she was, it was Quinn's business. He turned to duck down the center hatch toward the cockpit, then looked back.

"You hear Steve Brun is finally tying the knot?"

"I did," Quinn said, pushing away thoughts of his last conversation with Kim. "He's invited me to be in the saber arch if I survive this mission."

"Roger that," Moore said, turning to go. "You'll be there then. I've seen you fight. You're too mean to die."

With the wings swept forward, Major Moore had the Bone off the runway in a matter of seconds after he started his takeoff roll. Climbing at nearly six thousand

feet a minute pushed Quinn's stomach down like someone was standing on it. Moore leveled off three miles
above sea level and kicked the plane into gear.

Quinn took a deep breath, letting his stomach settle.
He shot a glance at Aleksandra. Her face hidden by the
shaded face shield of her helmet, she gave him a
thumbs-up and settled back in her seat. He was unsure
what the gesture meant in Russia—"it's all good" or
"up yours"—but felt he knew Aleksandra well enough
now that if it had been the latter she would have followed it up with a knee to his groin.

Taking a long hit on the oxygen, he put the cockpit
on mute and dialed his boss.

For all Winfield Palmer knew, Quinn was dangling
off a parachute over the Pacific Ocean, but he started
talking the moment he recognized Quinn's voice. There
was, after all, a nuclear device headed toward an unknown target on American soil.

"Bexar County sheriff's deputies just found Yazid
Nazif's body along with that of his brother Ibrahim and
two unidentified males dumped in a Penske moving
van outside San Antonio. We'd sent out Nazif's photograph in a BOLO just two hours before, so they were
able to identify him right away."

Quinn nudged Aleksandra awake, flipping the radio
bug so she could hear his conversation as well.

"I've got Kanatova on the air with us," he warned.
"We can use all the help we can get here."

"Very well," Palmer said, sounding a little annoyed.

"What of Baba Yaga?" she asked.

"Still missing," Palmer said. "Do you think Borregos double-crossed him?"

Quinn shook his head, though only Aleksandra could

see him. "Makes no sense. He didn't need AQAP to get the device into the U.S. Why drag him all the way across the border just to kill him?"

Quinn thought for a moment. "You said Nazif has a cousin in Houston."

"The FBI's swarming every known place associated with him," Palmer said. "But he's still at large."

"How about changing the parade route?" Aleksandra chimed in. "Or canceling it entirely?"

"We've discussed that," Palmer sighed. "But the moment we deviate from a normal schedule, we show our hand—and they pick another target."

Quinn drummed his fingers on the desktop in front of him, thinking. Something wasn't right. He thought for a full minute, the time it took the B-1 to travel nearly fifteen miles.

"Did they take any crime scene photos?" he asked.

"As a matter of fact, they did," Palmer said. I can send them to your phone if you can get a signal."

Quinn checked with Major Moore and found that though there was no cellular signal, the plane had its own version of satellite Wi-Fi to aid in communications when loitering for hours at a time over targets.

By the time he'd switched the radio dial back to Palmer, the supersonic bomber had already transited Guatemala and sped over the Gulf of Mexico.

"Go ahead and send 'em," he said. "We have a signal."

"Already done," Palmer said. "Listen, while you're waiting—Thibodaux led the raid on a farmhouse outside Moscow, Idaho. The professor's wife and baby are safe."

"Are the kidnappers giving you anything useful?" Quinn asked, watching his phone for the incoming photos.

"Only a woman survived," Palmer said. "And she's giving us zero. Looks like they killed one of their own and dumped him in a hole they dug for Marie Pollard and her kid. Garcia took care of the only other guy. According to Jacques, it's lucky they got there when they did. Sounds like Lourdes Lopez was Zamora's main squeeze and she had just given up hope on him coming back alive."

"And Boaz?" Aleksandra asked.

A twinge of guilt cut Quinn's heart at the thought of dragging his baby brother into all this.

"He's still in intensive care," Palmer said. "President Clark assigned his personal physician to see to him. He's not out of the woods, but things look positive. Your mom is already down from Alaska sitting with him night and day."

Quinn nodded, smiling to himself. That figured. A woman who'd raised two boys like Jericho and Boaz Quinn had to be tough as a boot, but no matter what they did for a living, they were still her babies.

His phone lit up with an incoming message.

The crime scene photos were small but clear until he tried to zoom in. Quinn raised his visor to get a better look, then flipped the switch so he could talk to the cockpit.

"Major," he said. "You there?"

Moore came back at once, voice crackling over the intercom. "Sure hope so."

"I need to ask a personal question. . . ."

"Relief tube is at your feet," the pilot answered. "Looks like a little horn."

"I'm fine that way," Quinn said. "I'm wondering though, an old codger like you is probably wearing cheaters to read the fine print, right?"

"Don't you have anything better to do than pick on your elders?"

"Seriously, Brett," Quinn said. "I need something to magnify a photo."

"Well, shit," Moore said. "Why didn't you tell me my failing eyesight was a matter of national security? Heads up and I'll toss them back."

A moment later a pair of cheap drugstore reading glasses sailed through the small hatch from the cockpit. Quinn played them across the face of his phone like a magnifying glass. What he saw made him catch his breath.

He looked again to make certain, then passed the phone and glasses to Kanatova.

"Look at Nazif's left wrist," he said, tapping the face of the phone with his index finger.

"I don't . . ." Her voice trailed. "I see it!" she exclaimed. "He has a tan line indicating a missing watch, but there are still two gold rings on his hand."

"I'm betting he still had money in his pocket," Quinn said.

"I'm looking at the police report now," Palmer said, still on the line. "You're right. Bexar County said this wasn't a robbery—more like an assassination. Initial shots to the chest, then a coup de grâce in the back of the head."

"And who do we know who assassinates people and takes something from them as a memento of the act?"

"Julian Monagas," Aleksandra whispered. "And if he went after the bomb . . ."

"Then Zamora is still alive." Quinn finished her thought.

"But why would Zamora kill the guy he sold the bomb to?" Palmer mused.

Quinn continued to scroll through the photos. "There are no photos of Matthew Pollard here. His body wasn't found?"

"Nope," Palmer said. "He's MIA along with the bomb."

"Maybe Zamora wanted a different target than Nazif did," Quinn mused. "Anything else going on in Texas in the next couple of days?"

He heard the click of computer keys as Palmer searched the Internet.

"Son of a bitch," the national security officer gasped. "The governor of Texas will attend an interfaith youth choir concert in the Frank Erwin Center at the University of Texas. Press release says the event will consist of children representing all faiths from around the world. It will be televised live before a sold-out crowd of over sixteen thousand. . . ."

"And Zamora was kicked out of the University of Texas on suspicion of rape," Quinn said. "The events drove a real wedge between him and his father. From what I've seen of Valentine, he's the type to carry a grudge."

"Think you can get the Bureau to send a couple of guys to talk to the people putting on this show? Maybe have them postpone it?"

"Everyone is so invested in the target being Houston, it will take me hours to get ahead of the investigative inertia. It's too late for that anyway," Palmer said. "Curtain goes up in less than three hours."

"Hang on, sir." Quinn flipped the radio and spoke briefly to Moore before switching back to Palmer. "I'm just informed we can be there in two."

CHAPTER 72

Austin

Valentine Zamora limped slightly from the bullet wound to his thigh. Nothing vital had been hit and some antibiotic under a few wraps of tape had made him as good as new. The wound had given him the perfect opportunity to slip away—and he would have stayed away but for the fickle Yazid Nazif. If he'd only kept with their original plan, he and his brother would still be alive to carry on with their jihad. But they hadn't, so there they were, dead on the grimy asphalt, along with their dreams.

Pastor Mike Olson stood grinning like a fool at the delivery entrance on the south end of the huge, drum-shaped building. He vouched for them with the overweight security guard at the loading dock.

"You have already given us so much, Mr. Valentine," the pastor said, shaking his head in disbelief. "May I ask what is in the box? It looks heavy."

Monagas wheeled the green footlocker containing Baba Yaga up the ramp, a forced smile on his crooked lips. Pollard slumped along behind, looking as if he'd been whipped.

"Merely some little gifts for the children," Zamora said, flipping his hand.

"That is a large case," Olson said. "But there are over three hundred in the chorus. Not to seem ungrateful, but I'd hate for any child to be left out."

"Not to worry, my friend." Zamora put up his hand. "College savings bonds take up very little space. There will be plenty for everyone."

"I need to check it." The security man walked toward them. Monagas's hand drifted toward the pistol under the tail of his sport coat. Zamora gave an imperceptible shake of his head.

"And you, Officer . . . ?" Zamora looked at him sweetly.

"Potts," the security guard said.

"How about you, Officer Potts? Do you have children?"

The man shook his head. "I got a nephew."

"Is he in the choir?"

"No."

"No matter." Zamora gave a flip of his hand. "I'm sure a thousand-dollar savings bond would come in handy. Stop by and pick one up for him after the performance."

The corners of the man's mouth perked with a hint of guile. "Well, okay," he said. "I'll see you after the show." He walked away whistling to himself, no doubt already making plans on how to spend the new windfall.

"My goodness," Pastor Olson sighed after Potts had

gone. "I don't understand you, Mr. Valentine. What have we all done to deserve this kindness?"

Zamora pointed to a series of thick concrete columns under the auditorium, motioning for Monagas to put the case there. He shot a glance at Pollard, who stared back with glassy eyes. "In my experience, Pastor"—Zamora clasped his hands together and held them to his lips—"at some point, we all get exactly what we deserve."

CHAPTER 73

6:15 PM

Austin-Bergstrom International Airport's tower gave Major Moore clearance for an unscheduled landing after received a direct order from FAA brass. A maroon Ford Crown Victoria bristling with antennas waited on the tarmac, just off the taxiway.

Quinn thanked the pilots for the ride and climbed out of the bomber with Aleksandra to a Texas winter evening. The western horizon still glowed with a faint orange line and a crisp twilight had settled in.

A tall man in a tan golf jacket and a gray felt Stetson stood beside the sedan. Razor-sharp creases ran up the front of heavily starched blue jeans.

"Detective Lonnie Fulton, Austin PD." He shook Quinn's, then Kanatova's hand in turn. "I'm assigned to the regional intelligence unit. We just got the call an hour ago that you were coming in." Fulton spoke with a thick Texas accent, friendly and earnest.

"How far to the Erwin Center?" Quinn asked.

"Eight or ten miles," Fulton said. "You wanta tell me what's going on?"

Quinn nodded toward the sedan. "You drive. I'll explain on the way."

Detective Fulton was wide-eyed and quiet by the time he turned off I-35 frontage road and into the University of Texas campus. On Quinn's direction, he drove past the event center, watching and getting a lay of the land. Crowds of people milled around the entrances, chatting like good Southern folk as they worked their way in. The governor's motorcade had been delayed with a call from Palmer but had not been given a reason why.

"He's in there," Aleksandra said from the backseat. "I can feel it."

Quinn wondered if she meant Zamora or Monagas.

"Let's park in there." He pointed toward a secluded lot across Red River Street, behind the nursing school. He looked at his watch—6:45.

A white Crown Vic pulled in next to them, followed by two marked sedans and two more motor officers on BMW RTs. A muscular man in a tight black T-shirt and 511 Tactical khaki slacks got out of the white unmarked and stood beside the door, arms crossed and sneering at the new arrivals. Quinn had seen the type before and was amazed the man wasn't already pissing at each corner of his vehicle to mark the territory.

Detective Fulton leaned in as they approached from their parking spot fifty feet away. Every other officer present had gathered around the frowning man as if the white sedan was a mother ship.

"That's Tony Hawker, lieutenant over SWAT. He's sort of an asshole, but his heart's in the right place."

"We'll see," Quinn said. He looked at Fulton's shirt pocket. "Is that a Sharpie?"

"Yep. I was marking case files when your boss called." The detective took out the permanent marker and handed it to Quinn.

"Listen, Detective," Quinn said when they were twenty feet out. "Good or bad, this is going to go fast." He took out his phone and punched Palmer's number as he walked.

He looked at his watch again—6:47, and wondered if he'd feel the wind from the blast before it turned him to ash.

Palmer answered immediately. "Are you in place?"

"I have someone I need you to convince," Quinn said, handing the phone to Lieutenant Hawker. The man took it and stepped away, clenching his square jaw as he listened. Palmer wasn't above putting the president on the line.

"Okay, gentlemen." Quinn took charge immediately, gesturing with an open hand toward the Erwin Center. "Who's ever been below decks in there?"

A blond motor officer who reminded Quinn of a short-haired Bo raised his hand, looking sheepishly at his cohorts. "I've answered a couple of prowler calls," he said.

Quinn handed him the permanent marker and nodded at the trunk of Hawker's white sedan. "I need you to draw me a diagram."

The motor officer looked from the permanent marker to the lieutenant, then back again. His face went as pale as the clean white trunk. "I don't know. . . ."

Quinn pointed again to the car. "I need you to show me where you'd put a nuclear bomb if you were a terrorist." He looked at his watch again—6:48. "And I need you to do it right now."

"A nuclear bomb?" The motor officer bent over the trunk and began to draw.

"Listen up," Hawker said, handing the phone to Quinn. "As far as I know, this guy's full of shit and his friend called me pretending to be the president." He looked at Quinn, jaw muscles tensing; veins—which made inviting targets—pulsed on the side of his beefy neck.

"I thought you might say that." Quinn shrugged. "Your phone will ring again in a second or two."

Hawker's mouth fell open when he saw the black lines on the trunk of his otherwise spotless sedan. "What the hell, Reinhart?"

"He said there is a bomb, LT."

"Give me that!" He snatched the marker and threw it against the curb, turning to point his finger at Quinn. "I don't know who you think you are—"

"If you touch him I will cut off your balls," Aleksandra hissed, her voice thickly Russian.

Quinn shrugged again praying the phone would ring soon. "Frankly, I'm surprised she hasn't already clawed your eyes out."

"I'm hauling you both to jail," Hawker said. "We can sort this out there." He reached to handcuff Quinn, but his phone rang. "Watch him," he snapped at Fulton, taking the call.

"Yessir," Hawker said into the phone, his entire body wilting. "No, I do not, sir. . . . Absolutely. . . . Mine? Right away, sir. . . . I will—" He hung up.

Fuming, Hawker pulled the Sig Sauer .45 from his holster and passed it to Quinn. "Reinhart, the chief says to give the Russian your sidearm."

Quinn thanked him and tucked the weapon in his

belt. Identical to OSI's issue sidearm but for the caliber, the Sig felt at home in his hand.

"Now," he said. "I need you to pull everyone back as far as you can get."

"How far is that exactly, smartass?" Hawker folded his arms again.

"Start driving now and keep going until you run out of gas," Quinn said. "If he's in there, this guy is apt to arm the bomb any second so he'll have time to get away."

"He does not know it," Aleksandra chimed in. "But when this device is armed, it will go boom immediately." She clapped her hands for effect, causing the young motor officer to jump. She leaned in to Hawker, blowing him a little kiss. "Too bad your chief called. You were about to touch my friend and I would have enjoyed keeping my word."

Quinn looked at his watch for the last time.

It was 6:51.

Quinn used his OSI credentials to get past a pudgy security guard named Potts at the loading dock.

"Dammit! I knew it was too good to be true," the guard said when Quinn described Zamora and Monagas. He hooked a thumb over his shoulder. "They put some sort of box in the boiler room. It's locked though so you can't get in."

"How'd they get in?" Quinn said, eyeing the fat ring of keys hiding under the guy's muffin top.

"Well, shit, I'm sorry," Potts said, embarrassed. "I can let you in."

"Just give me the key," Quinn said. "Then you get

out of here. He's liable to shoot it out with us." There was no way Quinn was going to tell this man about a bomb. He'd run upstairs and start a stampede.

Twenty seconds later Quinn and Aleksandra stood on either side of the metal door of the hall leading to the boiler room. The three hundred kids and at least fifteen thousand guests sat in the stadium only a few yards above them. The sound of thunderous applause echoed through the ventilation system.

"We need to stay quieter than the boilers," he whispered, pulling Severance's curved blade from the scabbard under his jacket. "There won't be a second chance." He left the pistol in his waistband. Aleksandra covered the door with her sidearm. She took a deep breath and nodded when she was ready.

Quinn used the tip of his blade to give the door a metallic clank, like someone knocking softly. The hollow sound of footsteps answered the knock almost immediately. A short moment later, the door cracked a hair, paused briefly as if the person on the other side was listening, then began to yawn open.

Aleksandra gasped when a hand holding a black pistol appeared in the darkness. The fat third finger wrapped around the grip of the gun bore Mikhail Polzin's double eagle ring.

Quinn brought Severance down in a lighting fast arc, separating the gun and gun hand from its owner. Monagas staggered forward, arm reaching as if his hand was still attached. Quinn grabbed the startled thug by his collar and yanked him out, throwing him to the floor.

"The devil take you!" Aleksandra spat and shot him three times in the face.

Quinn looked up at her, gun in his hand now. "What about us being quiet?"

He did a quick peek inside the open door and found Matt Pollard standing fifteen feet away, hidden but for his shoulders and one arm. A green footlocker sat before him, its lid opened like a closet door revealing the shining guts of Baba Yaga.

The top of Zamora's head was barely visible behind a portion of the boiler. There was not enough of a target to get a shot at either man.

"Come on out, Valentine," Quinn shouted above the hum of machinery. "It's over."

Zamora threw two wild rounds toward the door. They clanked harmlessly into the heavy concrete wall.

"You?" Zamora cried, giggling. "How funny is that? How is Monagas? Well, I hope. He is quite devoted."

"He was a serial killer with a sponsor," Quinn said. "But he's done."

"You can kill me if you wish, Jericho, but Professor Pollard has already entered three of the five numbers for the code. Once the bomb is armed, there is no disarming it. Thousands will die even if you begin an evacuation now."

"You're right about that," Quinn yelled. He tried to edge sideways, cutting the pie for a better shot. The Venezuelan forced him back with another volley of gunfire. "Listen to me, Valentine," he yelled above the ringing in his ears. "Once that thing is armed, it'll go off right away."

Aleksandra leaned in, the side of her forehead touching Quinn's. "Do you see the row of small silver tubes?" She nodded at the bomb.

"I do."

"Shoot them," she said, keeping her own gun trained on the section of pipe where Zamora hid.

Quinn's head snapped around to look at her.

Pollard's arm moved as he entered the fourth digit of the PAL.

"Shoot them now!"

Quinn let the front sight of his borrowed Glock float over the array of metallic tubes near the center of the bomb. Bracing for an immediate explosion—though he knew it was pointless—he fired three shots.

The rounds slapped into the soft metal, destroying a section about the size of a pack of cards—but nothing happened.

Quinn stared at Aleksandra, but said nothing.

"Trust me," she said.

"Matt," Quinn shouted. "Marie and Simon are fine. My friends got them out without a scratch."

"Lourdes?" Zamora shrieked.

"I hear she's not doing too well," Quinn yelled. "Now come out. I told you, it's over."

Pollard stepped into the open and let his fingers slide along the damage caused by Quinn's shooting.

"I can't believe I even considered killing thousands to save my family. . . ." His hand hovered over the numbered wheel.

"Matt," Quinn shouted. "Come on out."

"I don't think so," Pollard said. "I've done a lot of thinking about this. Valentine, you're messed up. But I'm little better than you. Some people are just too evil to be allowed to live."

"Matthew!" Zamora shrieked.

"Tell Marie I love her," Pollard yelled to Quinn, keeping his eyes on a cowering Zamora. His voice went quiet, barely audible. "You cruel bastard. Didn't figure on this, did you?"

Pollard's finger fell on the button as the Venezuelan fired. Baba Yaga gave an audible click. Quinn felt a tremendous pressure wave slam into his chest. Unable to breathe, he was vaguely aware of heat and screaming metal and the smell of singed hair . . . then blackness.

CHAPTER 74

Quinn woke to Aleksandra touching his face. He'd never seen her do anything so gently. Coughing, he rose up on one elbow, testing each limb and joint for broken bones. A persistent whine assaulted his ears, providing background music to the drumbeat of pain in the front of his head.

The door to the boiler room hung half off its hinges. A layer of greasy smoke curled through the room.

"I don't know what we've been worried about all these years." He coughed again, nodding at the door. "Looks to me like you Russians build some pretty poor nuclear bombs."

Tears dripped from the tip of Aleksandra's freckled nose as she looked down at him. "I thought . . ."

"So did I." Quinn touched a large knot on his forehead, wincing. "Seriously, why aren't we a speck of ash in crater right now?"

"Both our countries build weak links into such devices—a row of capacitors or something similar that will fail and render the bomb useless in the event of a fire or unintended plane crash."

Quinn nodded. "And that's what you had me shoot."

"Correct. The initial explosive went off but was not able to trigger a nuclear detonation." She sniffed. "The blast was localized to the boiler room . . . and your forehead. We will need to be decontaminated since some of the nuclear material was surely released—like a dirty bomb—but everyone upstairs is safe."

"You know, we've been through a lot over the last couple of weeks," Quinn moaned, falling back on the floor with his eyes shut. "And this is only the second time I've seen you cry."

Aleksandra gently smoothed his hair. "I have only ever had two friends."

Epilogue

United States Air Force Academy
Colorado Springs

Two weeks after what was reported as a horrific boiler explosion that shut down the Frank Erwin Center for extensive cleanup, Jericho Quinn stood holding a shining saber with five other Air Force officers on the steps to the Academy chapel. He had the honor of standing to the right of the bride at the front of the line, nearest the audience.

Mattie waved at him from the bottom of the steps. But for her dark hair, she was a miniature Kim in a robin's-egg dress with a yellow bow. Gary Lavin stood farther back in the arch. To Quinn's surprise, he had no urge to hack the man to death like he'd thought he might. Kim waited for him below, mouth tight as if she was sucking on a lemon drop.

Thibodaux stood in Marine mess dress blues with Camille tucked in tight beside him. Their youngest looked tiny sleeping across his huge arm. Each of his other six boys wore a black eye patch with their suits in support of the new addition to their dad's uniform.

Standing at attention, Quinn shifted his eyes to see Veronica Garcia standing next to the big Marine. Sensing his gaze, she smiled brightly, the sunshine yellow of her cap-sleeved dress accenting the richness of her skin—and bringing to mind the swimsuit she'd worn in Miami.

The Bruns appeared at the top of the stairs. Connie had never looked so beautiful. Colorado's Front Range weather had cooperated for the wedding, giving her the perfect bluebird day.

On command, Jericho and the five other officers raised their sabers, edges to the sky so they formed an arched tunnel. The bride and groom walked ceremoniously under the blades until they got to Quinn and Major Moore, who lowered their sabers to block them and ordered them to kiss.

"You can do better than that," Moore chided, forcing them to kiss again.

At that point, the sabers were slowly raised until the bride passed. By tradition, Quinn reached out to swat Connie on the bottom with the flat of his blade.

"Welcome to the Air Force, ma'am," he said, grinning.

Ronnie Garcia kept to the side at the end of the ceremony. She knew few of the guests but was perfectly content to watch Jericho chat with his friends in the bright sunshine. He was as happy as she'd ever seen him, grinning and cracking jokes that actually made people laugh. Who knew Jericho Quinn had such a great sense of humor?

Kim came up beside her, breathing heavily as if

something was on her mind. She was a head shorter than Garcia, more finely boned, but fit and certainly very beautiful.

"I like your date," Ronnie said, to break the ice and obliquely point out that Quinn wasn't the only one to show up with someone on his arm.

Kim brushed the comment aside, focused on Jericho. "You should know," she said through clenched teeth. "I intend to fight you for him."

Garcia sighed, shaking her head slowly.

"I am sad for you," she said, as Quinn turned to grin at her. "All those years and you just figured out he's worth fighting for. I knew from the moment I met him."

Across Academy Drive, a thousand meters to the west, in the shadowed stands of pine and cedar, a lone figure pressed a dark eye to a powerful Leupold scope, playing mil-spec crosshairs from guest to guest. Killing Jericho Quinn would end things much too quickly. No, she would take one of his friends. That would draw things out, make the game more enjoyable, test the temper of his metal.

Too disciplined to laugh out loud and disturb her sight picture, the sniper's lips perked into the slightest of smiles.

ACKNOWLEDGMENTS

As always, I owe a tremendous debt to those who assisted me with this story.

First things first: Many thanks to my agent, Robin Rue—what a patient lady to stick with me—and Gary Goldstein at Kensington—an editor and a friend.

Thanks to my pilot and motorcycle buds who've let me pick their brains: Sonny Caudill, Scott Ireton, Steve Arlow, and others who want to remain anonymous.

My friend Rod Robinson provided valuable color commentary on living in Bolivia and driving the Death Road as a young missionary.

Jujitsu master and dear friend Professor Ty Cunningham continues to provide invaluable instruction on the way of strategy and the philosophy of violent conflict.

Ray and Ryan Thibault of Northern Knives in Anchorage talk to me for hours about all things bladed and allowed me to field-test their Severance design in all kinds of ways—though none quite as interesting as what Jericho did.

Talking to Professor Matt Wappett via Facebook was entertaining and enlightening, but I wish I could travel to Idaho and attend one of his ethics classes in person. It would be great fun to discuss evil. Thank you, sir, for allowing me a peek into your curriculum.

I've never run the Dakar, but sometimes I pretend when I'm riding my GS on the back roads of Alaska. The timing of the race is perfect to get a motorcycle fix during our long winters. Third only to the Olympics and the World Cup, the Dakar is followed by millions of fans around the globe, but most Americans have never heard of it. ADVrider.com has numerous threads on the event, with a particularly great one that gushes like a fire hose giving minute-by-minute updates contemporaneous to each stage. A special thanks to Ted Johnson for sharing an advance copy of his wonderful book, *Tales from the Bivouac*, that is just chock full of great photos and details of his experience on a Dakar team.

To my gun-toting friends: many, many thanks for all the lessons—about tactics and life in general. You will, I hope, find little bits and pieces of yourselves within these pages. To quote Robert Louis Stevenson: "Of what shall a man be proud, if he is not proud of his friends?" You give me much to be proud of.

And finally, for my wife, Victoria—an icon of patience—thank you for helping me plot and plan and connive.